About

Susan Stephens is passionate about writing in fabulous locations where... comes to grips with a cool, feisty ... an's hobbies include travel, reading, theat..., ...g walks, playing the piano and she loves hearing from readers at her website susanstephens.com

Sharon Kendrick started story-telling at the age of eleven and has never stopped. She likes to write fast-paced, feel-good romances with heroes who are so sexy they'll make your toes curl! She lives in the beautiful city of Winchester – where she can see the cathedral from her window (when standing on tip-toe!). She has two children, Celia and Patrick and her passions include music, books, cooking and eating – and drifting into daydreams while working out new plots.

Lynne Graham lives in Northern Ireland and has been a keen romance reader since her teens. Happily married, Lynne has five children. Her eldest is her only natural child. Her other children, who are every bit as dear to her heart, are adopted. The family has a variety of pets, and Lynne loves gardening, cooking, collecting all sorts and is crazy about every aspect of Christmas.

European Escapes:

An Italian Christmas

SUSAN STEPHENS

SHARON KENDRICK

LYNNE GRAHAM

MILLS & BOON

First Published in Great Britain 2024
by Mills & Boon, an imprint of HarperCollins*Publishers* Ltd,
1 London Bridge Street, London, SE1 9GF

www.harpercollins.co.uk

HarperCollins*Publishers*
Macken House, 39/40 Mayor Street Upper,
Dublin 1, D01 C9W8, Ireland

European Escapes: An Italian Christmas © 2024 Harlequin Enterprises ULC.

Bound to the Tuscan Billionaire © 2016 Susan Stephens
The Italian's Christmas Secret © 2017 Sharon Kendrick
The Italian's Christmas Child © 2016 Lynne Graham

ISBN: 978-0-263-39669-0

BOUND TO THE TUSCAN BILLIONAIRE

SUSAN STEPHENS

For my Tuscan teammates, Linda, Ann, and
the inimitable Sharon

CHAPTER ONE

PLUNGING HER SPADE into the rich moist earth of Tuscany, Cass smiled as she reflected on her good luck in landing the job in Italy. She loved nothing more than being outdoors, using her body to the full. And where better than here, to an accompaniment of birdsong and the gurgle of a crystal-clear river. Her job was to help out at a grand estate over the planting season.

The staff had a day off on Wednesdays to break up the week, so she had the place to herself, making it all too easy to imagine that she was the chatelaine in charge of the glorious grounds—though perhaps not kitted out in mud-caked boots, braless in a skimpy vest she'd ripped on some barbed wire, topped off with a baseball cap that was as frayed and faded as her shorts!

The estate was miles from anywhere and the solitude was bliss, especially after the clamour of the supermarket where she worked back home, and being on her own was better than facing the owner of the estate. Marco di Fivizzano, an Italian industrialist, hadn't been near the place since she'd arrived. She was in no hurry to meet a man who, according to the press, was as bloodless and cold as the Cararra marble he mined.

She didn't need to worry about him, Cass mused as she stabbed her spade into the ground. She couldn't imagine a man like Marco di Fivizzano taking time out of his busy schedule to drive down from Rome to his country estate in the middle of the week. When she'd asked Maria and Giuseppe—housekeeper and handyman, respectively—if and when she was likely to meet her boss, they'd just looked at each other and shrugged.

Which was probably as well, Cass reflected as she returned to vigorously prepping the ground for the seedlings she was planting. She had no problem with hard work. Tugging her forelock was something else.

She'd always been a rebel, though a quiet one, all the rebellion being in her head. Dumb insolence, her headmistress had called it, when Cass, at seven, had refused to cry on the day she'd been made to stand on the school stage as all the pupils had trooped past. That had been the headmistress's idea to shame her on the day Cass's parents' had been arrested for drug offences. Young as she had been, she had determined never to be bullied again.

One thing still perplexed her. If her parents hadn't been the type of people the headmistress had wanted to encourage, why had the school been so keen to take their money?

She couldn't stand snobbery either. Her late father, better known as the infamous rock star Jackson Rich, could easily afford the school's extortionate fees, but that hadn't stopped the staff resenting him, his beautiful wife and Cass, his quiet, plain daughter.

Leave the past in the past where it belongs, and enjoy the Tuscan sunshine...

It was easy to do that, Cass reflected happily. Dappled sunlight sifting through the trees warmed her skin, and the scent of wild oregano was intoxicating. It was unseasonably warm for springtime in Italy, and how much better was this than her old job, squashed up in a stall, bashing the life out of a till at the local supermarket?

Closing her eyes, she smiled as she weighed up her choices: a nylon uniform that gave her static and stifled her; or the comfortable outfit she was wearing today?

No contest.

She loved working with plants, and had begged the store manager to allow her to work in the garden section, promising him that his plants would never droop again if she were in charge. He'd given her this weird look and said he liked his women clean and free from mud. She'd handed in her notice the same day.

Wiping the back of her arm across her face, she turned full circle with her arms outstretched as if sunlight were something she could touch. Birds were singing, bees were buzzing, and she could already see the fruits of her labours in fresh green shoots. On an impulse she reached for her phone to take a selfie to send to the godmother she adored and had lived with since her parents' death. When she'd taken this job she'd had it in mind to save money to buy a plane ticket for her godmother to visit her son in Australia. It would have been nice to be able buy it in time for his birthday, but that was a dream too far.

After emailing the shot, she received a reply from her godmother almost at once:

You look as if you're having a good time! Suggest a wash before anyone sees you. xoxo

With a happy laugh Cass reached up to brush away a bee, only to realise that the sound she could hear wasn't an insect but something much larger...something coming steadily closer, casting a pall over the flawless Tuscan day. Her heart rate doubled as a black helicopter swooped over the trees and hovered overhead. It blotted out the sun and obliterated the calm with noise and dust. Shielding

her eyes, she tried to see who was inside, but as 'Fivizzano Inc.' was emblazoned on the side, she didn't have to
test her imagination too far. Her best guess was that 'the
Master', as Giovanni and Maria referred to *He who must
be obeyed*, had arrived. He couldn't have told anyone he
was coming or Giovanni and Maria would never have
taken the day off.

She could handle it, Cass determined. She was hardly
a stranger to awkward situations. She would simply stay
out of his way.

Her heart beat wildly as the helicopter descended slowly
like a sinister black bird, flattening the grass and driving
the songbirds from the trees in a panic-stricken flock. She
hadn't met anyone who travelled by helicopter since she'd
been a little girl in her parents' exotic world. Thrusting
her spade into the ground, she realised her hands were
shaking.

Wiping her hands on her shorts, she stood rooted to the
spot as the rotors slowed to a petulant whine. The passenger door opened and a tall, commanding figure, dressed
immaculately for the city, sprang to the ground. Marco di
Fivizzano was infinitely better looking than the press suggested, and for a moment she stood trapped in his stare.

What had got into her? She'd done nothing wrong.

Who the hell...? Marco's frown deepened. Then he
remembered vaguely that his PA had mentioned something about temporary staff for the summer. He was in
no mood for dealing with that now. Surely Giovanni and
Maria would have laid out the ground rules—that no one
approached him when he was here on his Tuscan estate.

Swearing softly under his breath, he remembered that
today was Maria and Giuseppe's day off. He had been in
such a hurry to leave the city for the country that his only
thought had been how fast he could get here. Now he had

some scruffy youth to deal with. He would have expected a new member of his gardening team to be an older and more experienced man, not some beardless boy. Coming closer, he stopped dead in his tracks as *she* turned to face him.

A grubby urchin? No make-up? Ragged clothes? Hair hidden beneath a faded baseball cap?

Legs like a colt...body like a ripe fruit, bra-free nipples pressing imperatively against her fine cotton top, her young face work-flushed and appealing...

His body responded violently and with approval. Beneath the mud, sweat, and rosy cheeks stood a very attractive young woman. The cap was crammed down hard on her head, with the brim pulled low to shade her eyes from the sun, as if she cared nothing for vanity—and that in itself was a novelty. Her clothes consisted of a ripped and mud-daubed singlet that clung lovingly to her full, pert breasts, while the frayed shorts emphasised the length of her slender legs. Striding up to her, he saw that she wasn't as young as he'd first thought, and neither was she intimidated by him—far from it. This girl wasn't afraid of anything, he sensed as she held his stare.

'And you are?' he prompted shortly.

In contrast to his irritable mood, she appeared to be relaxed and slightly bemused.

'Cassandra Rich. Your new gardener?'

Something about the surname chimed in his head, but he pushed that aside for now. Evaluating staff was his strength. The success of his business had been founded on that skill.

He stared deep into a frank, cornflower-blue gaze and ran a quick assessment. She was fresh, bright and intelligent. Inner strength, combined with the summing up *she* was giving *him*, was so novel and unexpected that he almost broke into a smile—something he did so rarely that his body took the cue and responded more insistently.

'I'm here for the summer,' she volunteered, glancing around.

Good. That gave him time to work with, he reasoned dryly.

Was he in lust with this woman?

Possibly. She was so unlike the sophisticated types he was used to she required further study—and a category all her own.

'Where's the rest of the gardening team?' he demanded, frowning.

'They're taking staggered holidays,' she explained with a shrug, drawing his attention to her bright blue eyes as she pushed a lock of her honey-gold hair away from them. 'That's why I'm here,' she added, 'to plug the gap.'

He had moved on from assessing her unusually forward manner to wondering about the rest of her hair, hidden beneath the ugly cap. He could so easily imagine freeing it and seeing it cascade down her back, just before he fisted a hank of it to pull her head back to kiss her throat.

'You can handle this entire estate on your own?' he demanded sceptically, bringing himself back with difficulty to the business side of this encounter.

'I'll have to, won't I?' she said. 'At least until the others return.'

'Yes, you will,' he confirmed sharply, still trying to work out whether her manner was impudent or overly straightforward. Meanwhile, she was staring at him inquisitively, as she might study an unusual exhibit in a gallery. They were polar opposites, curious about each other—the billionaire, hard and driven, and the mystery girl who gave casual a new edge.

His groin tightened when she smiled. He liked the way

her full lips curved and her ski-slope nose wrinkled attractively.

'I'm not as helpless as I look,' she assured him. 'And I promise I won't let you down.'

Her promise pleased him. 'If you were helpless you wouldn't be employed here.'

He turned away, knowing he should feel exhausted, but he was suddenly wide-awake.

He hadn't slept for the past twenty-four hours as he'd wrestled a trade agreement to the table that would benefit not just his own group of companies but his country. Word of his success had spread like wildfire in the power halls of Rome, attracting lean, predatory women with crippling shoes and sprayed-on clothes—another reason he had been pleased to leave the city. He could have called any one of them to accompany him to Tuscany. They were decorative and efficient and they knew the score, but none of them had appealed. He didn't know what he wanted, but it wasn't that.

'If there's anything I can do for you?' the girl called after him, stopping him in his tracks.

Was she referring to a cup of coffee or something more?

'No. Thank you.' He didn't want company, he reminded himself. At least not yet.

Success in business rode him. It also turned him on. He'd been cramped up in the city for too long. He was a physical man, bound by convention in a custom-made suit, who was forced to spend most of his working life in air-conditioned offices when what he longed for was his wild land in Tuscany. Tucked between majestic granite mountains, his country estate was an indulgence he chose not to share with anyone—certainly not with some member of his part-time staff.

'Anything at all?' she pressed.

Did she have any idea how provocative she was? As he had turned to face her she had opened her arms wide, putting her impressive breasts on show.

'Nothing. Thank you,' he repeated irritably. 'Get back to your gardening.'

He needed relief in the form of a woman, but this woman was too young and too inexperienced for him to waste his time on.

He ground his jaw with impatience when she started to follow him, and made a gesture to indicate that she should go back. The only conversation he was interested in was with real people like Maria and Giuseppe, and he resented her intrusion. She had changed the dynamics completely. She was an outsider, an interloper, and though she might hold appeal, was that smile as innocent as it looked?

If there was one thing he understood, it was the needs of a woman's body and the workings of her mind, but this girl was so different it frustrated him that he had yet to make a judgement about her.

Cass shivered involuntarily. What was wrong with her? After deciding the safest thing was to steer clear of Marco di Fivizzano, she was doing the absolute opposite. It was as if her feet had a mind of their own and had decided to follow him to the house. She should know better, when he came from the same shallow, glitzy world as her parents—

'Watch out!' he snapped.

'Sorry.' She jumped back with alarm, realising he'd stopped, and she'd almost cannoned into him.

'Have you nothing better to do than follow me to the house?' he demanded in a tone that spoke of deals hard won and nights without sleep.

'I've finished for the day,' she explained, 'and I just thought—'

'I might need help?' he queried. He stared down at her

from his great height as if she were an irritation he didn't yet have an answer to. 'If you're going to be here for the summer, you'd better tell me something about yourself.'

Her brain had stalled beneath the blazing stare. What could she tell him?

How much did she want to tell him?

'Come on—keep up,' he insisted, striding ahead. 'Let's start with where you come from.'

'England—the UK.' She had to jog to keep up with him. 'It's a region called the Lake District. I don't expect you—'

'I know the area. Family?'

The word 'family' was enough to spear her with ugly memories. That was what she didn't want to talk about, let alone take her thoughts back to the day a small bewildered child had stood at the side of the family swimming pool looking down at her parents floating, drowned after a drug-fuelled fight. She settled for the heavily censored version.

'I live with my godmother,' she explained.

'No parents?'

'Both dead.'

'My condolences.'

'It was a long time ago.'

Almost eighteen years, Cass realised with shock. She'd been so young she'd hardly known how to grieve for them. She hadn't really known them. She'd had one carer after another while they'd been on the road with her father's band. Her emotions had died along with her parents, until her godmother had arrived to sweep Cass up in a hug. She'd taken Cass home to her modest cottage in the Lake District where the only drug was the scenery and her godmother's beautiful garden. Cass had lived there ever since, confident in her godmother's love and safe in a well-ordered life.

Maybe part of her had hidden in this security, she reflected now. That would account for a personality as compelling as Marco di Fivizzano giving her such a jolt. After her turbulent childhood, she had welcomed her godmother's cocoon of love, but increasingly had come to realise that something was missing from her life. Challenge. That was why she was here in Tuscany. This job was out of her comfort zone, and never more so than now.

'You are lucky to have a godmother to live with,' Marco di Fivizzano observed as he strode ahead of her.

'Yes. I am,' she agreed, chasing after him.

The warmth and strength of her godmother's love had never wavered, and when the day had come when Cass had been ready to fly the nest, she had helped her to get the job here in Tuscany.

She stood back when they arrived at the front door.

'Come into the house,' Fivizzano instructed when she hesitated.

She'd never been beyond the kitchen. She'd never entered the house through the front door. Her room was in an annex across the courtyard. The house was grand. She was not. She was covered in mud and she knew how hard Maria worked to keep the place spotless.

But the real reason for her hesitation was that she didn't want to be alone in the house with *him*.

'It's Giuseppe and Maria's day off,' she explained, still hovering outside the door.

'And?' he demanded impatiently.

'I'm sure if they had expected you—'

'I don't pay my staff to *expect*.'

She flinched when he added, 'Do you have a problem with that?'

Yes. She had a problem. She had never met a man so rude or so insensitive. Giuseppe and Maria would do *any-*

thing for him. Did he know that? And she was definitely
not going inside the house. 'I'm sure Maria must have left
something in the fridge for you to eat—'

His expression blackened. 'I beg your pardon?'

She had to remind herself that she loved this job, and
that it would help to pay for her godmother's trip to Australia, and therefore she should say nothing and just get
on with it.

'As Maria isn't here, you'll have to do,' he said, giving
her a scathing appraisal. 'Clean yourself up and fix lunch.'

Her face blazed red beneath the arrogant stare. She had
to remind herself that she had dealt with plenty of difficult customers at the supermarket. Sucking in a steady-
ing breath, she told herself that for all his immense wealth
Marco di Fivizzano was just another man.

Just another man?

She would have to remind herself of that several times
a day, Cass guessed wryly, but she couldn't deny that if
there was one thing she loved it was a challenge.

'My cooking isn't up to much,' she admitted, kicking
off her boots.

'Do what you can.'

Senna pods in his omelette sprang to mind.

Stepping inside the beautiful old house, she was silenced for a moment. Overwhelmed by its beauty, she
stared around in awe. This had to be the most beautiful
hallway outside a palace. It was square and elegant...beau-
tifully proportioned, with a high, vaulted ceiling. It was
decorated with burnished antiques, as well as the most exquisite rugs—rugs Marco di Fivizzano was simply striding over in his outdoor shoes on his way to the foot of an
impressive mahogany staircase.

'You can clean yourself up in the back kitchen,' he instructed, as if she were a latter-day Cinderella. 'An omelette shouldn't be beyond you.'

'I'll pick some fresh herbs—'

Her suggestion was wasted. He was already halfway up the stairs.

So much for that challenge she'd been looking forward to!

Her first assessment of Marco di Fivizzano had been correct. He was insufferably rude and incredibly insensitive. She didn't even register on his radar. He was hungry and he expected to be fed.

Then she remembered with a little pulse of interest that Marco di Fivizzano was always hungry, according to the scandal sheets—and she doubted they were talking about food. He was also a spectacular lover, according to the same magazines…

She definitely needed that wash down in cold water before she saw him again.

Having cleaned herself up, she went back into the garden and, selecting a clump of herbs, she slashed them with her knife.

No supressed emotions to deal with at all, Cass concluded with amusement.

As she walked back to the house she glanced at the upstairs windows. She could just imagine all that brute force naked beneath the shower. She'd always had a down-to-earth attitude when it came to men and sex, though living in the remote beauty of the Lake District with her godmother had hardly provided her with a wide pool of men to choose from. And when she had chosen, she'd got it wrong. She'd had one or two unsuccessful attempts to make a go of a relationship, but the men had disappointed her in a way she couldn't really explain. There had been nothing wrong with them. They just hadn't fired her imagination, and she had always dreamed of being swept away.

One thing was sure, nothing could have prepared her poor frustrated body for the arrival of a force of nature like Marco di Fivizzano.

Sheathing her knife, she wiped a hand across the back of her neck. Would he need a cold shower after meeting her? Somehow she doubted it. She guessed she was more of a wasp he'd like to swat than a beautiful butterfly he'd like to do other things with. Sex radiated from him. Even clothed in what had to be the most expensive tailoring known to man, there was something primal about him—something dark and hidden at his core—an animal energy that suggested he would consider any woman fair game.

But not this woman.

Because she had more sense?

It was time to stop daydreaming and get on with making his meal.

He took an ice-cold shower. His senses had received an unexpected jolt thanks to a most unlikely woman. He smiled grimly as he soaped himself down, imagining the type of chaos she would be creating in Maria's pristine kitchen round about now. He could only hope she'd washed her hands. He didn't care for soil in his food.

He shook his head and sent water droplets flying. Stepping out of the shower, he grabbed a towel. He felt refreshed—reinvigorated. Food followed by a few hours of vigorous sex would suit him perfectly, but it would take more than an untried girl to tempt his jaded palate. Pausing by the window, he stared out. His eyes narrowed with interest. Maybe he'd written her off too soon. She was sheathing a knife like a female Indiana Jones, and her capable, no-nonsense manner fired his senses.

* * *

She beat the living daylight out of the eggs. She had to do something to calm herself down before Genghis Khan arrived. It didn't help that all sorts of wicked thoughts were parading through her head—some including a spatula and a pair of iron-hard buttocks.

What was wrong with her?

She cleaned off the egg spatter from the wall, only for her thoughts to wander off in a new direction—to the day when she had made her first omelette. She'd been six years old and hungry. She knew now that the eggs needed watching or they'd catch and become bitter and inedible. Her first omelette had been black but she'd eaten it. She'd been hungry enough to eat the pan as well. She'd seen enough domestic disruption to last her a lifetime, and had her godmother to thank for knowing her way around a kitchen now. Anyone as sensible and good-humoured as Cass could learn to cook, her godmother had insisted when Cass had expressed doubts.

Cass had lost confidence when her parents' lives had descended into drug-fuelled chaos, but her godmother had rebuilt her brick by brick; cooking and gardening, nurturing and caring, providing the cure. These activities that were at the root of everything good, her godmother had explained, and the rewards were not only plentiful but you could eat them as well.

That had been the start of Cass finding pleasure in watching things grow. And that was why she knew she could deal with Marco di Fivizzano. Nothing he could throw at her could compare with Cass's life before she'd lived with her godmother. There were no whirlwinds in her life now, only well-ordered certainty, and that was how it was going to stay.

Tipping out a perfectly cooked omelette, she put the plate on a tray with a bowl of freshly picked salad, timing her delivery to perfection as he walked through the door.

CHAPTER TWO

IN SPITE OF his determination to treat her like any other member of staff, the sight of Cassandra Rich leaning over the kitchen sink as she scrubbed a pan thrust his basest of needs into overdrive. The swell of her hips was so perfectly displayed, though, disappointingly, she had changed her clothes—the ripped and mud-smeared singlet having been replaced by a neatly pressed T-shirt. Though a streak of mud on the side of her neck was just begging to be licked off.

'I hope you enjoy the omelette,' she said with apparent sincerity.

He dragged his attention away from one potential feast to glance at the surprisingly appetising meal she had laid out on the table. 'It looks good,' he said approvingly, 'but, where's the bread?'

He noted the flash of fire in her eyes, more typical of the way she had behaved in the garden, but then she said meekly, 'I'll get it for you, sir.'

For some reason her unusually compliant manner annoyed him too.

'For goodness' sake, call me Marco.'

He couldn't be sure if she was mocking him or not, he realised, though his best guess was yes, and blood pounded through his veins as he accepted the challenge.

'It's only a simple meal,' she explained as he grunted his thanks and sat down.

Her attempt to take out her frustration on the eggs had failed completely, Cass concluded. On second viewing, Marco di Fivizzano was even more improbably attractive than the first time she had seen him. Glancing down to make sure her top wasn't clinging to her breasts, she found her nipples were practically saluting him. In a tailor-made suit, garnished with a crisp white shirt and grey silk tie, her boss had been staggeringly attractive, but in snug-fitting jeans—she had unavoidably scanned his outline beneath them—together with a tight-fitting black top that revealed his banded muscle in more than enough detail he was an incredible sight—

'Bread?' he reminded her sharply.

He was also the rudest man she'd ever met.

She hacked at the bread with a vicious stab. The large, country kitchen seemed to be closing around her—no wonder with his arrogant animal magnetism taking up all the space.

'Have you eaten yet, Cassandra?'

She was surprised by the question but had no intention of sitting down to eat with him.

'I'm not hungry.' She was always hungry after working in the open air. 'I'll have something later.'

'See that you do,' he said, laying down his cutlery. 'You're far too thin.'

Apart from the fact that she had never once been called thin—she loved her food, and wasn't prepared to sacrifice a tasty meal for the sake of wearing jeans a size smaller—he was completely out of order, making personal comments like that.

You love this job—remember?

Heaving a calming breath, she held her tongue.

The girl kept his attention, and though she wasn't pristine, as he expected his women in Rome to be—even after cleaning herself up she had mud on her neck and more smears on her arms—at least she wasn't a simpering fool. Neither could she be grouped with the career women with whom he sometimes had a mutually satisfactory arrangement. Cassandra was unique—and not everything on his Tuscan estate was pristine, he reminded himself. He had always thought his estate better for its quirkiness.

'You're enjoying the omelette?' she guessed as he forked up the last mouthful.

'Very much,' he admitted.

He hadn't realised how hungry he was until he'd sat down to eat—or how different this kitchen was from his sleek, steel and black granite, largely untouched kitchen in Rome.

And he wouldn't change a thing, he mused as he stared around. His critical stare returned to Cassandra. 'How did you get this job?'

'A friend of my godmother's recommended me—she's another keen gardener.'

'Who employed you?' he asked, frowning.

'You did— I mean your...' Cass was stumped. Her knowledge of office hierarchy was non-existent.

'My PA?' he offered. 'She's the only one with the authority to hire my personal staff.'

'Must have been,' Cass agreed. She didn't have a clue what she was talking about. One piercing stare from those compelling eyes and her mind had been wiped clean.

'I haven't seen your CV yet,' he pressed, holding her pinned in his stare. 'What are your qualifications for this job?'

She had none, other than her passion for the plants she nurtured and the earth she turned. 'I'm self-taught,' she admitted. Her knowledge came largely from gardening books and, of course, her favourite book, *The Secret Garden*.

'And your previous job?'

She watched Marco—as she must somehow learn to think of him—push his plate away before she spoke. 'I worked the tills in my local supermarket—when I wasn't stacking shelves.'

'Education?' he prompted, the furrows on his brow deepening.

The derision directed at her by the teachers at her very expensive school had led Cass to contribute little in class, and even less when she'd sat down to take an examination. She didn't have a clutch of brilliant exam results to crow about.

'I have no formal qualifications,' she admitted, upping the tempo on her dish-clearing technique in the hope of avoiding more uncomfortable questions.

She assumed that he hadn't made the connection between the scandal of her parents' death and her surname—not yet. And why should she tell him anything more, when he revealed nothing about himself? She could understand that having his idyll trespassed on by a stranger must be an irritation for him, but a powerful, wealthy man like Marco di Fivizzano only had to make a phone call to find out everything about her. Let him do that, if he was so interested.

Calm down, she cautioned herself.

It was all very well telling herself to calm down, but she could just imagine what a man like Marco di Fivizzano would make of her past. The media had gone to town on the story of a small child wandering about in a house full of drug paraphernalia while her parents had floated dead in the swimming pool. If he knew that, then, just like everyone else, he'd make the assumption that she was tainted, when nothing could be further from the truth. She only wished she could reach back into the past as an adult to help her parents.

She sprang to attention when he got up from the table. Having him prowl around made her feel vulnerable, but he left the kitchen without a backward glance or a word of thanks.

'Rude man.' Staring out of the window, she watched him cross the yard. But he was beautiful. That easy stride… that incredible body.

Her summer had changed irrevocably now Marco di Fivizzano had arrived and only one thing was certain: her fantasies had moved on from *The Secret Garden*.

He'd had a lousy night's sleep.

He'd had no sleep. Why try to dress it up?

Dragging on his jeans, he scowled as he prowled the room. He should have had the house to himself but now *she* was in a room across the courtyard.

Lust surged in his veins at the thought that Cassandra's window was directly opposite his. He'd surfed the internet and had found out everything about her. He'd been right to recognise the name. Cassandra was the only child of the notorious rock legend Jackson Rich and his broken doll of a wife, Alexa Monroe.

So why was she working as a gardener? What had happened to all the money? Jackson Rich had been phenomenally successful. Was it possible he'd spent it all? Cassandra didn't seem to have a penny to scratch her backside with. He could only concluded that Rich's hangers-on and numerous drug-pushers had spent it for him. He had no sympathy. He'd been forced to fight every step of the way, and had had no one to rely on but himself. Rich must have been swept up in ego and success, making him an easy target. He had probably been happy to put up with the hangers-on if it had meant scoring his next fix.

For now he would give Cassandra the benefit of the doubt. It didn't follow that she had inherited her parents' weakness. If she was a yet another gold-digger, she was destined for disappointment. He didn't have a vacancy for a mud-daubed mistress in Rome. The women in Rome knew how to dress, how to talk, and how to behave—both in bed and out of it. He doubted Cassandra would be interested in acquiring any of those skills—with the possible exception of the last of them, he reflected dryly.

It was time to remind himself that he avoided complications like the plague. His childhood had proved that women couldn't be trusted, and he'd had no reason to change his mind. Cassandra Rich might be quirky and appealing, but she was no more than that.

She'd overslept! Catapulting out of bed, Cass gazed around blankly, trying to get her bearings. The simple courtyard room was the same…the house was the same…the scent of blossom coming in through the open window was the same…even the birds carolling in the crisp morning air was reassuringly the same. But everything had changed, because of Marco.

Forget the boss! She should be up and out, and working in the garden by now.

Forget him?

She would forget him, Cass determined—until she threw off the bedclothes, leapt out of bed, and rushed across to the widow, looking for *him*. Nothing like this had ever happened to her before. Tall, dark strangers with bodies made for sin had never once flown into her life in a sinister black helicopter, demanding that she feed them.

He'd demanded and *she'd* fed him. Would she handle that situation any better today?

Could anyone handle Marco di Fivizzano?

Opening the shutters, she was just in time to see him stride across the courtyard. He looked better each time she saw him—dangerous and more ruthless, more stand-well-back-unless-you-want-your-fingers-burned, in a really serious way. Especially this morning when, like last night, he'd consigned his city look to history. The men in her fantasies were always rugged and tough, but Marco made her imaginary men seem pathetic. His well-packed jeans and heavy-duty belt added fuel to her already over-heated fantasies. There wasn't a spare inch of flesh on him. In jeans and a chequered shirt with the sleeves rolled back to reveal his powerful forearms, he appeared to be made entirely of hard muscle. And she would have to be made of wood not to wonder what it would be like to be in his bed.

She didn't have time for this!

Just as well, Cass thought, ducking back behind the window as Marco stared up.

Could he feel her looking at him? Were his animal instincts switched to super-alert this morning? She would have to be more discreet if she stood a chance of keeping this job.

Once she was out of the shower and wrapped in towels, she considered her vast selection of clothes. These amounted to one summer dress, 'just in case', a couple of pairs of shorts and half a dozen tops. She'd packed two pairs of jeans and a fleece in case the evenings turned cold...

And why was she taking such trouble over the selection of clothes to garden in?

Any other day and she would have grabbed the first thing to hand—shorts and a clean top. She was working with the soil, not auditioning for the role of the next notch on Marco di Fivizzano's bedpost.

So what underwear should she choose?

She scanned the unpromising heap.

Something comfortable, obviously! Did it matter, so long as she could work all day and not feel as if she was in danger of splitting her difference?

She chose her biggest knickers and a sports bra that supported her full breasts properly.

Maria and Giuseppe were back, so she dropped in a few casual questions over breakfast. They knew about as much as she did about their boss's plans for the next few days. Giuseppe mentioned something about a visit to the Fivizzano vineyards to choose some wines for an important party in Rome, but that was the only nugget she managed to glean before she went back to work.

A few days passed and then a few days more, and she barely caught a glimpse of The Boss. She kept telling herself that this was great—no pressure—but she was always on the lookout for him. She couldn't help herself. Marco di Fivizzano was a once-in-a-lifetime attraction. She gathered from Maria that he spent a lot of time inspecting his estate. It certainly felt as if she was very much 'below stairs', while he was the master of the house, whose daily life was none of her business. There was no common ground between them, no reason for them to meet—but she could dream, Cass consoled herself ruefully as she collected up her tools to go to work.

Dreams were free, and dreams were safe—or they were until Marco emerged from the house. He only had to glance her way for her heart to go crazy. He was formally dressed and had brought up the Lamborghini.

Was he going out on a date?

And why should she care?

Because smart chinos and an ice-blue shirt pointed up his pirate tan?

Lame.

But he'd teamed them with a casual, beautifully tailored taupe coloured linen jacket, and if she could just see his face…

Nope. He had lowered his sunglasses and his expression was hidden from her.

Good. Did she want him to think she was interested?

She returned to digging the trench she had started to protect her seedlings if the rains came. And those rains would come. Straightening up, she tested the air like a hound on point.

Maria had told her that although the house and estate seemed ageless and indestructible to Cass, it was, in fact, as vulnerable to the elements as any other ancient structure. The path of the river had changed over the centuries and it now presented a danger to the house. Maria had also said that in the fierce storm of 2014 trees had been uprooted and the river had flooded its banks. It was unusually still today…ominously so. Even the birds had stopped singing. She noticed Marco was also glancing at a sky tinged with acid yellow and streaked with angry clouds. She wondered briefly if he'd remembered an umbrella, and then accepted with a grin that men like Marco di Fivizzano never got wet because divine alchemy would ensure that rainclouds blew away from him.

So it fell on poor saps like me, Cass reflected wryly as she thrust her spade vigorously into the moistly yielding earth.

She was doing it again—driving him crazy with that ripe, mud-streaked body. No other woman had ever come close to affecting him the way she did. He doubted any of them had ever held a spade. They certainly didn't possess Cassandra's nonchalance when it came to using her body to the fullest. She was a very physical woman...and complex. How could she be otherwise with her past? He'd read every newspaper article he could find detailing the horrific tragedy. He knew how badly she'd been neglected until her godmother had adopted her. The media had speculated, as he was bound to, on how her parents' debauched lifestyle might have affected a young girl. His need for caution when it came to women was heading for overdrive where his new young gardener was concerned.

But since when had he been a cautious man?

Gunning the engine of his Lamborghini, he glanced across the garden to where Cassandra was swinging her spade. Her top looked as if it had shrunk in the wash and revealed inches of taut, tanned belly. He imagined dropping kisses on that smooth, silky skin and then working his way down—or up. Either way would be a pleasure for him.

He powered out of the gates, trying to distract himself from thoughts of Cassandra by thinking about all the other women he could have—maybe should have—brought along to entertain him while he was in Tuscany. Women were always eager to share his Tuscan bed, because they knew it was his private retreat, which gave it added mystery. He could think of several cute women who made him laugh—until he tired of their endless quips. There were clever women who challenged him—and gave him earache, he remembered, and beautiful women who could capture his attention and hold it for a night, but no longer. They all wanted the same thing—that his power would rub off on them, and, after that, money and sex. He had even identified a few women who would make ideal wives, but he doubted they could dig a trench, let alone turn that horticultural activity into a pornographic work of art.

Casandra's bare limbs gleamed with effort as they would after sex, and his groin tightened at he watched her thrusting her spade into the soil. She was giving it everything she'd got, as he imagined she would in bed.

Why was Marco staring at her? Cass wondered as he sped away in a storm of dust and gravel.

Why was she staring at him?

He was probably just checking she was doing her work, she reasoned sensibly. And she wouldn't look at him ever again.

That was what you said the last time.

But she meant it this time.

Did she? Marco only had to look at her for lust to stab clean through her.

That was her imagination working overtime—hopefully— she concluded as Marco's bright red Lamborghini powered away down the road. Lots of perfectly decent women lusted after the most inappropriate men, and in most cases nothing came of it—and if it did in this case, she'd run a mile. Marco di Fivizzano was one fantasy too far, she told herself sternly as his car roared away to the accompaniment of a low roll of thunder.

CHAPTER THREE

MYSTERY SOLVED. MARCO HAD gone to have lunch with the mayor. Should she feel quite so relieved when Maria told her this? Was she *jealous*?

Crazy girl! Get back out in the garden where things made sense!

Brushing her hair out of her eyes, she rammed on her cap after offering to clear up, so Maria and Giuseppe could get straight off to the fiesta in town.

'Don't get caught in the rain.' She glanced up at the darkening sky.

She waved off her friends and then contemplated the happy state of having the whole afternoon to work uninterrupted in the garden. The happy state didn't last very long. She should have listened to her own advice, Cass concluded as a flash of lightning stabbed the ground just a few feet away from her. It wasn't safe to be outdoors, but there was plenty she could do to help Maria in the kitchen.

It had quickly turned dark, and the air was as heavy as if nature was stuck in a cupboard with a headache. As the first fat spots of rain hit her in the face she collected up her tools and beat a hasty retreat. Making a dash for the kitchen door, she launched herself through it, already soaked through. There would just be time to check the windows were closed before the storm hit full force.

She raced up stairs, by which time the storm had arrived. It was like all the fiends of hell roaring around the house, testing its defences. Slapping her hands over her ears as a thunderclap shocked her out of her skin, she shrieked with alarm as lightning flashed repeatedly, and did a little dance on the spot to reassure herself that the house was still standing.

Pull yourself together! Things need to be done.

She switched on the lights and felt better immediately, but on her way downstairs they all went out again. Now the power was down. She huddled against a door in the dark, and then told herself to get over it. Finding a light switch, she flicked it on and off, more in hope than expectation. It was dead. She reached for her phone. The line was dead too. There was a house phone on the landing—

Dead.

Feeling her way carefully down the stairs, she screamed as she stepped into icy-cold water. Leaping back onto the stairs, she clung to the banister like a limpet, trying to think what to do. She told herself calmly that the house had stood for centuries, and Marco had renovated it to the nth degree, so even if the river had changed its course, the house was hardly likely to leave its foundations and float away. She was safe, and she was confident that any damage could be dealt with. If there had been similar storms in the past, Marco would have prepared for bad weather. And if the river had flooded its banks and the road from the village was closed, she was cut off, so it was up to her to sort it out.

As day turned into night in the middle of the afternoon, everyone knew that a really bad storm was coming. Making his excuses, Marco left the mayoral reception early, and as he jogged down the steps he noticed that even the stall-holders were packing up. They had all sensed the drama in the skies, and the bad weather was sweeping in much faster than expected. Some said it might be as bad as the explosive weather conditions of 2014, and with that in mind he'd called Maria and Giuseppe to warn them to stay in town. It was then they told him that Signorina Rich had never had any intention of joining them at the fiesta.

She was still at the house. And in who knew what sort of danger?

Cassandra Rich was an irritation he didn't need. Was anything straightforward where that woman was concerned? Any other woman he knew would have been drawn like a magpie to the stalls on the market, but not Cassandra. Oh, no. She had to be the one member of his staff left unaccounted for as the storm of the century approached. If the river flooded, the authorities would close the bridge and then he wouldn't get home. There were sandbags lined up outside the kitchen door, if she had the wit to use them, and an emergency generator in case the power went off.

The power would go off, he predicted, glancing again at the sky. Ribbons of lightning were slicing the boiling clouds into ugly black fragments, to a soundscape of earth-shattering thunderclaps. Then, quite suddenly, the noise subsided and it went ominously still.

Just as suddenly, rain started falling in vicious, freezing rods. Jumping into his car, he knew there wasn't a moment to lose if he was going to get across the bridge before the emergency services closed the road.

His was the last car through. Men in uniform warned him to turn back. He thanked them and then ignored them. How he longed for his rugged pick-up. He grimaced at the sound of metal crunching as he rode a bank to avoid a fallen tree. He'd almost certainly wreck the engine and the brakes. Water was rising up the wheels, and the wipers couldn't work fast enough to clear the windscreen.

He pressed on with one thought driving him. Cassandra was alone in the dark, stranded on his estate, and whether or not that was thanks to her own stubbornness, she was a member of his staff and he had a duty of care towards her. He could only imagine her relief when he arrived to save the day.

He had never been so pleased to see the house. He was less pleased to discover that floodwater was lapping around the front step. Parking up, he waded to the front door. Inserting his key, he pushed, but the door wouldn't open. He put his shoulder to it, but that made no difference. The house was in darkness. He glanced across the courtyard and called out. There was no sign of life. Where was she?

'Cassandra!'

Framing his face with his hands, he peered into one of the windows, but all he could see was blackness beyond. Turning up his collar, he retraced his steps. It brought him a moment's humour to see the ground might be flooded but Cassandra's trench was doing its job in directing the water safely away from her seedlings. He skidded to a halt at the back door. It was wide open. His heart jumped at the thought she might have run out into the night; people had died in similar weather conditions.

'Are you just going to stand there, or are you going to help me?'

He spun around at the sound of her voice. Moonlight framed her. She was at the far end of the kitchen soaked to the skin, with her hair hanging in straggles down her back as she dragged a sandbag across the floor.

'Those candles have gone out again,' she shouted as she backed into the hall. 'Can you close the door and light them for me?'

'Leave that!' He swore viciously as he tore off his jacket. He was at her side in an instant. 'You light the candles. I'll take the sandbag.'

She shook him off. The brief contact between them was electrifying.

'If you want to help me, grab another bag!' she yelled. 'The river must have burst its banks—'

'Clearly,' he said dryly, wrestling the sandbag from her grasp. He laid it down on top of the others. That was why he'd been unable to get in—and now she was rolling up his Persian carpets.

'Help me,' she insisted impatiently. 'It will be faster if the two of us do it.'

'Have you lit those candles yet?' he pressed, frowning.

'Have you got any manners?' she fired back with a scowl twice as deep as his.

He straightened up with surprise. No one had ever talked to him this way before.

'Thank you would be a start,' she told him sharply.

An almighty thunder crash brought an end to their discussion. As lightning flashed repeatedly he could see the wide-eyed shock on her face.

'You're safe,' he insisted, when nature paused to take a breath.

'If it doesn't stop raining soon, we'll be sunk—quite literally,' she said. 'Here—catch this.'

She tossed him a towel to mop up the water leaking through her barricade. Far from cowering in a corner, waiting for her white knight to arrive, Signorina Rich was firmly in control. He surprised himself by liking that.

But, then, he liked her. He couldn't help himself. He admired her grit.

'Well? Are you going to help me to roll up these rugs or not?' she demanded, glancing back at him as she lit the candles on the hall table.

There were plenty of things he would like to help Signorina Rich with, and rolling rugs wasn't at the top of his list.

It was all going well for her until she crossed the room in the half-light and caught her foot under a rug. As she stumbled he caught her close. It only took an instant to absorb how good she felt beneath his hands. Candlelight mapped the changes in her eyes from blue to black. She held her breath, almost as if she thought he was going to kiss her. Would she fight him? Would she yield hungrily? It was irrelevant to him. He might want to kiss her, he might even ache to kiss her, but he would never be so self-indulgent.

Delay was the servant of pleasure, he mused dryly as he steadied her.

'Be careful you don't trip up again.'

The look she gave him suggested that tripping up over a rug, or anything else for that matter, was the last thing on her mind.

'Shall we carry on?' she suggested. 'The rugs?' she added pointedly.

She got more brownie points for effort, and his senses got a second jolt when she brushed past him. She'd keep, he reassured his aching flesh. She wasn't going anywhere.

Having been forced to work together, Cass was surprised to discover how well they could read each other's intentions—to her surprise, they made a great team. It was certainly a pleasure watching Marco wielding his immense physical strength.

'I'll move things out of the way so you can take that rug

into the dining room,' she told him, holding her breath as Marco shouldered the weight of the wool rug as if it were a bag of feathers. Opening the door wide, she cleared a space for him, only to find him breathing down her neck. Their hands brushed. Their bodies touched. Their breath mingled as he turned around. They were just too dangerously close—

'Great job,' she said, stepping back. Now she realised that in her hurry to get away from him she had made it sound as if their positions in life had been reversed and Marco was her assistant. Oh, well. There was nothing she could do about that now. Ducking beneath his arm, she slipped away.

'Where are you going?' he demanded.

'To my bed.' She turned and shrugged. 'We've done all we can tonight. I'm going to have a bath first—try to warm up. The power may be off but the water should still be warm in the reserve tank—and I promise I won't use it all.'

'A bath in the dark?' he queried.

'I'll manage—I'll take some candles.' She glanced at his fist on the door. Was he going to try and stop her leaving? The tension between them had suddenly roared off the scale.

'You're in a hurry to get away.'

His murmur hit her straight between the shoulder blades in a deliciously dangerous quiver of awareness. 'I'm cold,' she excused herself, hugging her body and acting fragile. She doubted he was convinced, but at least he lifted his hand from the door.

'You've done well tonight,' he said as he stood back.

'And now I'm freezing,' she reminded him in a stronger voice. That wasn't so far from the truth. She was soaking wet. 'If you could get the power back on...' she suggested hopefully.

Marco narrowed his eyes and looked at her. 'You'd better take that bath,' he said, to her relief. 'And don't forget to reassure your godmother that you're safe. A storm like this will have made the international news. And anyone else, of course, who might be interested,' he added as an apparent afterthought.

He didn't fool her. 'There is no one else.' She guessed that was his real question. 'And I will speak to my godmother as soon as the phone line comes back.'

'You obviously think a lot of her.'

Passion and gratitude swept over her. 'My godmother is the most wonderful woman on earth. She took me in—'

'When your parents were killed,' Marco supplied thoughtfully.

'Yes.' She firmed her lips, reluctant to say anything more. How much did he know?

'Why did you leave her to come here to work in Tuscany?'

'It's a great job,' she said frankly. 'And I can't just live off her. She found this opportunity for me when I left my last job. She found it through one of her friends, another keen gardener. It would have been churlish of me to turn it down.'

Though maybe she should have done, Cass reflected as Marco continued to stare at her. He was beginning to make her nervous. She decided to give him a little more. 'I can easily get a job at another supermarket when I go home, and in the meantime this job is perfect for me.'

'Perfect,' Marco echoed without comment or expression.

He might want to know more, but she wasn't going to discuss her personal life with someone who was practically a stranger.

'Don't catch cold,' he reminded her.

She didn't need another prompt. She left him and ran across the courtyard without a backward glance. Racing up the steps to her room, she felt as if the devil was on her back.

He stood in silence when Cassandra left him. She had handled the crisis with impressive calm and now she intrigued him more than ever. Apparently uncomplicated and open, she was, in fact, as much a closed book as he was. He would like to find out more about her. She was hopeless at taking orders, but she was a breath of fresh air. Having worked closely with her, he now felt the lack of her, like a caged lion, penned in with a woman he wanted in his bed. He would be ill-advised to seduce her, he reminded himself firmly. He never slept with his employees.

He eased the physical ache with practicalities, starting up the generator and checking the garden to assess the damage. He huffed dryly to see her seedlings had survived when trees that had stood for centuries were lying broken on the ground. He should give her a long-term contract just to build drainage channels for him.

Having checked the sandbags were doing their job, he marvelled that she could lift them at all. He was trying to exhaust himself, he realised, in an attempt to put Cassandra out of his mind. That didn't stop his body craving her, or his mind from examining every tiny detail he knew about her. Cassandra Rich was the most unsettling woman he'd ever met. She was everything he would usually avoid. She was too young, too naïve, and she had no inkling of their relative positions in life—which was something else he liked about her, he now discovered. There were far too many toadies in his world. Cassandra Rich was real, he concluded with a shrug. If he were stranded in another storm, would he want Cassandra at his side or one of those fragrant types he usually went for? He'd choose Cassandra every time.

He laughed as he jogged up the stairs. There were so few surprises left in life, he almost welcomed her arrival into his remote, complex world.

So few surprises?

He was about to get the surprise of his life. He stopped dead on the threshold of his room. His window was closed, but his shutters were open and Cassandra's light was on.

She would never know what made her do it, other than to say she had seen pictures in magazines and films, as well as images in her head, of the type of sophisticated temptress a man like Marco would most likely be attracted to. That woman would be a minx, a siren, a temptress—all the things that capable Cass, as they had called her at the supermarket, most certainly wasn't. But there was nothing to stop her playing out her fantasy.

Perhaps it was the warmth of the evening and having a man like Marco close by and yet at a safe distance that had made exploring her own sexuality not just irresistible but an imperative. She'd missed having fun, but Tuscany seemed to have released something in her.

Working side by side with Marco had certainly released something in her, Cass reflected mischievously—and that was her excuse for dancing around the room while she waited for her bath to fill. In her dreams, she was dancing for him—and Marco was drooling, of course.

In reality, he wouldn't want his gardener, but what fun were bare facts? Her job here would end soon and he would be out of her life, but for now…let the dream continue!

Taking a breather, she went to peer out of the window. Marco's lights were safely off and his room was empty. Thank goodness! For a moment she had felt a rush of concern, wondering if he was watching her from the shadows. But no. It was just her and the moonlight, and she was safe to continue with part two of the show, dancing on her imaginary stage, beneath the moon, her imaginary spotlight...

He stood transfixed as Cassandra started to undress. She had her back to him, and was performing a slow and rather skilful striptease. When the top came over her head and he caught a glimpse of the ripe swell of her breasts, he was disappointed that the angle at which she was standing prevented him from seeing more. His imagination lost no time supplying the detail, and he groaned at the prospect of another night without sleep.

Allowing her top to drop to the floor, she removed the band from her ponytail and let her hair flow free in a shimmering cascade down her back. Running her fingers through it, she shivered a little as it fell around her shoulders, as if the touch of her hair on her naked skin aroused her. Still moving with a tantalising lack of haste, she freed the fastening at the waistband of her jeans, and reaching her hands behind her back she slipped her fingers beneath the denim, pushing it down over the swell of her hips. When she arched her back, it was almost as if she was presenting her buttocks for his approval. He did approve.

He went still as she stepped out of the jeans. Many women had tried to seduce him, and a good few had succeeded, but no one had made him feel as hungry as this. He was transfixed by the sight of Cassandra running her fingertips lightly over her breasts, her hands lingering, as if she appreciated the pertness of her nipples as much as he did. His senses roared as she pinched them. She appeared to cry out softly at the pain. Rolling her head back, she cupped her breasts and drew them forward as if inviting him to suckle. He would go mad if this went on for much longer.

He tensed as her hands travelled down over the swell of her belly. She had reached another place he would like to take his time exploring. She traced the swell lightly with her fingertips before delving deeper, and when she withdrew her hand he sucked in a noisy breath, only to realise that for the past few seconds he hadn't breathed at all. Cassandra had seemed so innocent, and yet these were the actions of a very sensual woman, who knew exactly how to torment a man. For all her physical strength and forthright manner, Cassandra was as lush and womanly as he could wish for. And, in the biggest surprise of the night, she had turned out to be the most erotically provoc-ative female he'd ever met. He wondered if her pleasure was always self-administered. Her right arm was undu-lating lazily. Was she touching herself intimately? He had never been so aroused by the sight of a woman doing that. He was in agony.

What was she doing? Cass asked herself in shock, bring-ing a sudden halt to her performance.

She should be curled up safely in bed. She could only put her behaviour down to a release of tension now the storm had passed, and the old house she was coming to love had survived, because this was way over the top, and she had to stop doing it right now.

Had she lost her mind completely? She hadn't even closed the windows—

Grabbing the towel she'd laid ready for her bath, she se-cured it around her body, and then turned around to check that she hadn't been seen.

Marco's shutters were firmly closed, thank goodness. Closed? Had they been closed before?

She couldn't remember. She could only remember thinking that his room had been in darkness. Maybe they had been closed. They must have been closed, she reassured herself sensibly.

CHAPTER FOUR

HE WAS TENSE at breakfast for obvious reasons. Cassandra, on the other hand, appeared to be totally relaxed, and was her customary rosy-cheeked self. After her assertiveness during the storm, and her astonishing striptease performance afterwards, she appeared to be as cool, calm and collected as ever.

'Sorry—didn't you want eggs again?' she asked him as he groaned out loud, thinking back to her dance in the moonlight.

'Eggs are good—eggs are fine. Thank you.' He sat back in his chair and tried to not to think about Cassandra and her night-time activities.

'My cooking skills are pretty basic,' she added, as she busied herself at the business end of the kitchen. 'Maria should get back today, so tomorrow you'll have better food.'

And then she bent down to put a pan away and her faded denim shorts clung tightly to the outline of her bottom. The urge to join her—to stand behind her and press his body into hers—to map her buttocks with one hand holding her in place, while he pleasured her with the other—

'More bread? Eggs? Coffee?' she called out.

'No. Thank you.'

When she turned to face him, his thoughts were not of

breakfast but of slowly sinking into her welcoming body and sheathing himself to the hilt. Her long, slender legs would wrap around his waist, and she would move with him. Her soft cries of need would urge him on, as he worked steadily to bring her release—multiple releases, he amended. He sat up as she put a hand to her forehead. 'Something wrong?'

'Dishwasher tablets!'

He blinked. 'I beg your pardon?'

'We're out of them,' she explained, frowning.

So much for his fatal charm! Though, far from being discouraged, her quirky ways had only fuelled his hunger for her.

Marco di Fivizzano was driving her crazy. He was about to start clearing the garden after the storm as she set out to go shopping, and he was stripped to the waist with an axe in his hand, looking like every one of her fantasies come true. But who was he, really? Her boss was so wealthy and powerful he could keep his backstory under wraps. That didn't stop her wondering about him. He made her curious. Everyone had an interesting backstory, once she had scraped the surface, but Marco didn't allow anyone to get close enough to tickle his back, let alone scrape his surface.

She wouldn't mind tickling his back... She wouldn't mind digging her fingers into those impressive shoulder muscles—

The spell broke abruptly as Maria came bustling out of the house. There had obviously been a call for Marco. Burying the axe in the tree stump, he led the way back into the house.

Sometimes life was so unfair, Cass mused wryly as

Marco and his delightful body disappeared inside the house. But there was always a next time…

She spent the afternoon in the village, where it was tranquil and cool after the storm. She still had some work to do in the garden to make sure everything was straight again, so she set off back to the house as soon as she could, and was surprised to find Marco pacing the kitchen, waiting for her.

'Leave that now,' he said, as she started to put away the shopping.

'What's wrong?' She frowned as she straightened up.

'We need to talk.'

She felt a frisson of alarm, and couldn't help wondering if she was about to lose her job. She couldn't bear to lose this job. It was perfect for her. It was her first step out of the shadows without having to confront a complex world. She had shunned the spotlight since escaping the tarnished glitter of her childhood, and here in Tuscany she was taking her first step back into the light.

'Come into my study,' Marco instructed.

His tone was stern, adding to her apprehension. She glanced around, thinking to learn something of him from this inner sanctum, but there was no clutter or ornament… no softening touches anywhere, as far as she could tell. There were no plants sunning on the windowsill, or papers left lying casually about. The room was still, and preternaturally tidy. It was also very expensively fitted out. He didn't invite her to sit down. She wouldn't have felt comfortable if he had.

He launched straight in. 'I've got a problem.'

'A problem?' For a moment her brain refused to compute the idea that Marco di Fivizzano could have any problem he couldn't solve, let alone a problem he was about to share with her.

'I need your help, Cassandra,' he elaborated, spearing her with one of his hard looks.

'What can I do for you?' Unless he was seeking advice on root propagation, or wanted to discuss soil management in a country that was basically a long piece of rock with almost unworkable clay loam soil, she couldn't think how she could help him. And she somehow doubted he'd brought her in here to talk about gardening.

'I've been let down.'

'Oh. I'm sorry.' Had she let him down? Was her dream job here about to shatter into a shower of tiny pieces?

'Not you,' he snapped impatiently.

Coming around to the front of his desk, he leaned back against it and folded his arms.

Narrowing his eyes, he looked down at her as if she were a cup cake amongst many in a cake shop window and he was trying to decide if she would do.

She didn't like that look in his eyes one bit, so she decided to seize the initiative. 'What can I do for you?'

Marco took his time replying, which gave her the chance to study him. Did he ever shave while he was in Tuscany? He really relaxed here. As she did.

She quivered with awareness, realising that his stare had dropped to her lips. She now realised that she had pursed them in an unintentionally sexy way. Quickly chewing the pout out of them, she straightened up and adopted a more businesslike manner.

'I need you in Rome.'

'In Rome?' She was jolted out of her trance in an instant. Rome—bustling, glittering, sophisticated. She couldn't go to Rome! But then another, far more calming thought came to her. 'You have a garden there?' Her heart soared at the thought of tending a city garden. It would be very different from here. She could imagine it would be enclosed and quiet, and an entirely different challenge from Tuscany. But a garden...that was something she could handle for him.

'It's nothing to do with gardens,' he rapped impatiently. 'I have a charity event I host each year.'

'I see,' she murmured, frowning. She didn't see at all. In fact, her mind was a blank canvas on which he could paint pretty much anything.

'It's a dinner,' he explained, as if she should know all about it. 'And I need a plus one, or there will be an empty space next to me.'

And that would be unthinkable, she silently supplied.

'The organiser of the charity was supposed to be my dinner partner,' he elaborated with an impatient gesture, 'but a family emergency has prevented that.'

'So, you'll have an empty seat next to you,' she said, frowning as if such things were a mystery to her.

'No. I won't,' Marco assured her, 'because you will be sitting in it.'

'Me?' Horror filled her. This was everything she had spent her adult life avoiding, and she had no intention of going to some glitzy party.

'I don't know why you sound so shocked,' Marco countered. 'I'm only inviting you to join me at a party.'

What the hell was wrong with her? Other women would be falling over themselves to accept this invitation, but not Cassandra. Oh, no. She was looking at him as if he had suggested some extreme and arcane form of torture—that, or a Roman orgy.

'A charity event in Rome? A dinner?' she confirmed, paling as she continued to frown.

'I don't know what's so hard for you to understand. Just say yes. I'll provide the clothes, the hairdresser, the manicurist. You'll have beauticians and stylists on tap—whatever you need.'

Her eyes widened, and then, to his astonishment, she said, 'You are joking?'

'I'm being perfectly serious.' Her reaction baffled him. 'I have just invited you to join me at the event of the year.'

'Well, I can't,' she insisted. 'I just couldn't do it. I couldn't pull it off,' she insisted, when he stared at her with incredulity. 'I'd be falling over the hem of my gown, knocking into people—'

'Hopefully not,' he said wearily.

'You are serious,' she added quietly, as if he had been speaking in a foreign language and she had only just worked it out. 'You want me at your side, at the top table at a charity event in Rome?'

'Yes. I do,' he confirmed. How many more times did he have to say it?

She shook her head. 'I'm really sorry, Marco, but the idea of me all tricked out in a gown and on my best behaviour is about as likely as you getting down and dirty in the garden.'

'But I do get down and dirty in the garden,' he reminded her, all out of patience now. 'Of course, if you're not up to this…'

Her heart was hammering in her chest. Marco had to be crazy—or desperate, asking her to do this. 'Thing is, I function best in a garden,' she explained firmly. 'I don't function at all at a…function.'

'I'd pay you for your trouble.'

That stopped her. 'You'd pay me? How much?' she said faintly, thinking of her godmother now.

Marco named a sum that drained the blood from her cheeks.

As he had expected, the mention of a large sum of

money turned the tide. Every woman had her price. But then Cassandra started stuttering something that sounded dangerously like no—and no was not an answer he could accept.

He turned up the pressure to put her back on track.

'What are you going to do when you leave here and go back to England? Will you work at the supermarket, stacking shelves?'

'Why not?' she demanded, showing no reaction to his scorn. 'It's honest work, and I've made some very good friends at the supermarket.'

'And you can make some very good friends in Rome,' he said, seething with frustration. 'Friends with fabulous gardens that need a lot of care and attention. You can network at the party, if nothing else.'

She blinked and appeared to reconsider. 'You'd introduce me round?'

He balked at that. 'Well, my people would. You'd get your money, and you'd get the chance to network. I don't see much wrong with that.'

And neither did she, from the look on Cassandra's face. His senses sharpened as she bit down on the full swell of her bottom lip while she considered his suggestion.

'I suppose—'

'You'll do it,' he said.

'I suppose if it will help—'

'It will help.'

'But I've only brought one dress with me—'

'I've told you,' he said, forcing patience into his tone. 'I will provide a dress for you to wear.'

'I'll pay you back.'

'The dress and all the other expenses will form part of your payment. You may keep the dress afterwards,' he added as a generous afterthought.

She hummed and frowned.

'You'll have everything you need,' he promised. 'I'll see to that.'

'And you're quite serious about this?'

'Cassandra, I never say anything I don't mean.'

He sat back, confident that this time she'd say yes.

'I need more time to think about it.'

'No,' he said flatly. 'You give me your answer now. Yes? Or no?'

She couldn't pretend she wasn't anxious at the thought of making a return to a shallow world of sophistication that had proved so damaging in her youth, but when she weighed that against the fact that the money Marco had offered would help to pay for her godmother's ticket to Australia. She knew it was a golden opportunity, and one that might never come around again.

She had to remind herself of this as she walked self-consciously into one of the most exclusive hotels in Rome. At the back of her mind she still had this nagging suspicion that Marco had bought her. But at least she could comfort herself with the thought that he had got the raw end of the deal. She was a gardener, not a socialite, and no number of designer gowns would change that.

But it was too late to worry about it now. She was here, with one of Marco's *people* shepherding her through the lobby.

She tensed as the hotel manager approached. The memories of her childhood had faded, but she was sure she had stayed in a place like this when she'd been a little girl. She couldn't remember her mother being around, but there had always been women. Her father had used women like commodities, and according to the press had possessed an animal magnetism that had made him irresistible. *Much*

like Marco. In her father's case, this had led to serial in-
fidelities that had broken her mother's heart.

She had vowed to stay away from this world, and yet
here she was.

Cass swallowed convulsively as the manager bowed
over her hand and smiled. She had to remind herself that
this was all in a good cause, and that it would enable her
to buy the ticket to Australia for her godmother.

'I hope you will be very happy here, *signorina,*' the
hotel manager said with practised charm.

'I'm sure I will be,' she lied, for his sake. This was his
hotel, and it was very beautiful. Located on one of the
main streets in Rome, it was as discreetly labelled as the
dress size of a couture gown. She knew quite a lot about
couture gowns now, since her first stop of the day had been
to the *atelier* of a designer who specialised in 'the style of
gown Signor di Fivizzano favoured', according to Marco's
people, who had arrived in a squad to take her in hand.

Atelier was a posh word for a workshop with a rather
uncomfortable sitting room attached, she had discovered,
as the designer measured every inch of her so he could
prepare a toile, or pattern, from which any number of *visions,* as he called a frock, could be created.

Signor di Fivizzano might favour a particular style of
gown, but she had made it clear from the off that if she
didn't feel comfortable she wouldn't play the game. Plunging necklines and sausage skins were out. She didn't care
how exclusive the fabric might be, the shape had to be right
for her. The designer had shuddered at her mention of sau-
sages, but he had promised to supply her with a rail full
of his *visions* to choose from. That had taken up a great
deal of time and the event was closing in. There was no
time to lose, and so she made the best of things, pinning
a smile to her face as the hotel manager led her forward.

'I'll leave you now,' Marco's man said briskly, according her a small bow. 'You'll have half an hour to settle in, and then your assistants will arrive.'

'My assistants?'

Too late! Having nodded briskly to the manager, Marco's man was on his way.

The manager's face was now a professional mask, devoid of all expression, but she had to wonder what he made of her in her one shabby dress—a sale rail number that had seemed a good idea at the time but which now, she realised, having just caught sight of herself in one of the mirrors in the lobby, made her look like a galleon in full sail. And as for the hideous pattern—

'*Signorina?*' he prompted with an almost balletic gesture. 'No expense has been spared,' he added approvingly as they waited for the elevator. 'Three hairdressers will attend you in our best suite—on the top floor.'

Three hairdressers? Was she a three-headed hydra?

Snake charmers this way, she thought dryly as the steel doors slid open.

They exited the elevator into a lobby discreetly decorated in tones of cream, taupe and ivory, with just a hint of Caligula in the crumbling Roman busts that lined the walls on marble plinths. She didn't need any more encouragement to shudder with a sense of impending doom.

'Your people will be with you shortly,' the manager announced, opening the door onto the suite with a flourish.

The suite was at least twice as big as her godmother's house. Picture windows overlooked Rome—towering antiquity existing happily alongside modernity—and it was a stunning view, but her mind was full of Marco. She only had to look at herself in the mirror to know how out of place she would be at his function, and how quickly he would realise his mistake. It would take more than a team of beauticians to put this right—she'd need a miracle.

And there was another thing—what man would spend this sort of money on a woman without expecting more than small talk? Fantasies were fine, but reality was something else with a man so potent and virile he made Genghis Khan look like a drooping weed. And she had far more sense than to get hot and heavy with her boss. She wanted to keep this job—

She jumped at a knock on the door. Swinging it wide, she stood back as her *team* filed in.

'Where is she?' a man with a lavender quiff demanded, staring about.

She pressed back against the door, quailing beneath his scrutiny. She could only imagine the many faults he would find with her.

Narrowing his mascaraed eyes, lavender quiff stared at her. 'Are *you* Signorina Rich?' He couldn't have sounded more horrified.

'I'm afraid so.' She smiled and jumped to attention.

Lavender quiff did not smile. Finely plucked brows rose at an improbable angle as he leaned in to examine her more closely. He almost, but not quite, managed not to groan.

'Well. We'd better get started,' he said, pursing his lips. 'I can see that I've got a lot to do.'

'What exactly are your instructions?' she asked, glancing around nervously as beauty professionals laid out what might be instruments of torture, for all she knew, along with an improbable quantity of make-up and scent.

Lavender quiff consulted his phone. 'Do what you can with her,' he intoned.

Marco clearly didn't expect too much of her. No pressure, then, Cass concluded wryly as she resigned herself to her fate.

CHAPTER FIVE

'AND THE GRAND REVEAL! Come on, sweetie, do try and put a good face on it,' lavender quiff, whom Cass now knew was called Quentin, pleaded as he heaved a theatrical sigh. 'The livelihoods of all these people depend upon you making a good impression at the party. And, believe me, they have definitely earned their money tonight.'

Cass laughed as Quentin took hold of her hands. He had relaxed her—and he had surprised her by turning out to be the best fun. Every time she had worried that she couldn't pull this off, Quentin had shaken her out of it. He was just the best at bolstering her confidence. With a purse of his lips, or a tweak of her hair, he'd made everything seem that it might be all right. This was one occasion when first impressions were most definitely wrong. Quentin had turned out to be a real fairy godmother.

'You look beautiful,' he said.

'Why don't I believe you?' She pulled a face.

'I have no idea,' he protested. 'Nigel? Mirror, please...'

The room felt silent and she was stunned.

'Well? Say something, sweetie,' Quentin prompted.

She couldn't. She was too full of emotion. She was normally so down to earth, and yet after years of trying to blank out the past she was seeing not herself, looking spruced up and almost passable in the mirror, but her mother instead. Had her mother felt like this—like a chicken being prepared for the feast? She could remember enough to know that her mother had tried so desperately hard to keep the interest of Cass's father, and that to do that she had been forced to compete with much younger groupies. How helpless she must have felt…

'Sweetie?' Quentin prompted anxiously. 'Are you okay?'

'I'm fine,' she said, lifting her chin and adding a smile. Quentin and his team had worked so hard that she owed it to them to put a good face on this. 'I can't thank you enough,' she said to him and to everyone else.

To her embarrassment and amazement people started clapping, until the whole room was ringing with applause.

'Well, I can't pretend it's been easy,' Quentin admitted with a sigh. 'But I suppose it's a mark of my genius that you've turned out as well as you have.'

Where the hell was she? He had waited long enough. He glanced at his watch and then at the door. The event was being catered at his penthouse in the centre of Rome. One hundred carefully selected sponsors were attending. They would be raising a lot of money for the charity tonight, and everything had to be perfect. Cassandra could not be late. They'd be sitting down to dinner soon, and it was unthinkable that he would have an empty place next to him.

His internal rant ended abruptly when Cassandra entered the room. Everyone stopped talking and turned to look at her. His mind blanked completely. She looked stunning. Where had that poise come from—that enchanting smile that lit up the room? He was more used to seeing her up to her elbows in mud, leaning on a pitchfork handle.

She saw him at once and smiled, but her eyes were wary as she darted a glance around the room. This was not her comfort zone, though she was a good actress and stepped forward with apparent confidence. Only he had seen the momentary falter in her step; everyone else was riveted by the sight of her. But why was she alone? Where were his people?

He felt protective suddenly, and held his breath as she walked towards him. It was then he realised that Cassandra didn't need anyone to escort her, and that she could hold everyone's attention without any effort at all.

'So you got here eventually,' he said curtly as she halted in front of him.

'Good evening to you too,' she murmured, extending her hand. 'I wasn't in a position to speed things up.' Lifting her chin, she held his stare steadily. 'I think I presented the beauticians with more problems than they had anticipated.'

He ground his jaw, admiring her even more for her honesty. 'I doubt that.'

'I'm sorry if I've kept you waiting,' she added. 'This sort of transformation takes a lot of time. Do you approve?'

Her concern on this point at least was genuine. Did he approve? So much he wanted to tell everyone to leave.

'You'll do,' he offered coolly. She looked magnificent. She looked like a queen—like a goddess, a fact that hadn't been lost on any man in the room.

'Do I look good enough?' she prompted, with real concern in her voice.

'Of course you do,' he said shortly. 'Can you really imagine Quentin setting you free unless he was completely satisfied?'

At last she laughed. 'I suppose not,' she confessed, smoothing her hands down her dress.

The gown was composed of some floating sky-blue fabric, cunningly cut to mould her ripe figure. He would give the designer a bonus on top of his extortionate fee for designing a dress so perfect for Cassandra. The shade of blue brought out the colour in her eyes, and while the neckline was higher than he would have preferred, maybe he was wrong in thinking it should be lower. As it was now, it hinted at the treasures underneath without revealing them. He found this more provocative than putting everything she had in such lush abundance on show.

The gown was sculpted so precisely it made him wonder if she had room for underwear beneath. His best guess was no.

And her hair— *Dio!* Her hair! Flowing free to her waist, it shimmered like a golden cape as it flowed in thick, glossy waves down her back—a back that was naked, he noticed as she turned around. The gown had been cut high at the front, yet it dipped practically to the swell of her buttocks at the back.

'Shall we sit down?' he suggested, feeling the need to get out of range of all the hungry male glances.

'Why not?'

Why not? Because he wanted to take her straight to bed.

Tonight was shaping up to be the most extreme form of torture he'd ever known. He led her to the table and pulled out her chair. He was determined to make her feel at ease, relaxation being a prerequisite for seduction.

He employed the best chefs in Rome and the food was delicious. Cassandra ate little at first, but he tempted her until she met his gaze and grinned. After that she relaxed enough to steal titbits from his plate. And she was charming to his guests. He'd never had a dining companion like her before. They usually took their lead from him—waiting for him to initiate a conversation or to introduce them to one of the other guests. Cassandra simply spread her natural charm about, and everyone, from the starchiest diplomat to the snootiest aristocrat, soon fell under her spell.

'You've hardly eaten anything,' she pointed out towards the end of the meal.

'I've been too busy watching you,' he admitted.

Her cheeks flushed red, and then she turned to answer a question from the guest on her other side.

Marco was looking at her in a way that made her body yearn for more than a bath and a good night's sleep. His eyes were so wicked and confident that it was becoming hard to remember why she was here, which was to be a seat-filler and not his companion. From mud to magnificent, she mused wryly as she surveyed the glittering throng. It still seemed incredible that one minute she had been in the garden and the next she was here—

'Would you like to dance?'

'What?' She stared at him stupidly.

'I said would you like to dance?' Marco repeated. 'More specifically, would you like to dance with me?'

Dance with Marco di Fivizzano? Was he mad? She had two left feet and a sense of rhythm to rival a rhino's. She had to quickly change her expression when she realised that she was staring at him open-mouthed as if he had suggested they have sex on the table.

'You do dance?' he pressed.

'I have been known to.' But on her own—most likely jigging along to the latest hit tune. This kind of dancing, though—the up close and very personal variety—she wasn't very good at that at all.

'We're the only people left at the table,' Marco pointed out, glancing around.

'And you're worried that people will talk if you don't dance with me?'

His lips slanted as he raised a brow.

Okay, so Marco wasn't worried what people thought, but maybe she was. She was happy to help out by chatting to his interesting guests, but anything more than that... She glanced down a table lit by legions of candles that cast a warm glow over the glittering crystal and silver. What was she doing here in Marco di Fivizzano's fabulous penthouse in the best part of Rome?

What would her mother think about it?

That she was holding a candle to the devil?

She felt a stab of pain, realising that she'd been too young when her mother had died to have a clue what she'd say.

'Just say yes,' Marco advised, standing up.

As he broke into her thoughts, she looked up blankly. If she remained seated, people would notice, and this event was for charity. So she stood and walked as if in a dream as Marco led her towards the dance floor. Anticipating his touch was stealing the breath from her lungs. When he actually touched her, she knew she might faint.

Don't be so ridiculous, she told herself firmly as he drew her into his arms. *It was the most amazing feeling...* But she had to look on this as a job with perks, and nothing more.

'Relax.' He laughed softly in her ear, making a tingle race down her spine as he added, 'I can't dance with a board.'

'And I can't dance with you at all. I did warn you.' She definitely couldn't—shouldn't be dancing with a man who made her feel like this. She was bound to trip over her dress or step on his feet—

'I'll lead,' he murmured, as if there was any doubt.

The next moment her body was moulded to his—her body had a mind of its own, as she'd noticed since arriving in Tuscany, but it wasn't long before the music wooed her. Marco wooed her. Pressing her close against his iron-hard frame, he seduced her into dancing with him, while the melody soothed her, reminding her of so many happy days in Tuscany. It wasn't hard to dance with him at all. The Italian music was just so beguiling. It had a charm all its own...

'You're a good dancer,' he said.

No one was more surprised than she was by that comment, but when he added, 'You should dance more,' he sent tremors of excitement racing through her.

But then she reasoned, who was she going to dance with—and where? Marco surely didn't mean she could dance with him—on what occasion? But what could possibly compare with this? She would never dance with another man again, because it could only be a disappointment after Marco.

This was turning into a magical night, and a magical occasion, and she was going to make the most of it, because she knew deep down that it would never happen again.

And then one of the sponsors asked if he could cut in. Marco stopped dancing and smiled. 'It would be ungracious of me to keep you all to myself,' he explained. 'Do you mind if I allow the ambassador to dance with you?'

'You? Allow?' she queried softly, out of the ambassador's hearing, she thought, but the ambassador had overheard, and he laughed.

'It appears that this young woman knows you, Marco. And quite right, my dear. It's up to you to choose your partner,' he added, smiling at her warmly.

'Then I would love to dance with you,' she said as she slipped out of Marco's arms.

When she started dancing with the ambassador, she

noticed Marco watching her. It might not be sensible, but she liked that he was watching her.

He had grudgingly—very grudgingly—given way to the ambassador. He missed having Cassandra in his arms. He missed the warmth of her soft body pressed up close to his.

He was paying the woman to be here, he reminded himself. He should not mistake this for anything more—though there was nothing to stop him enjoying her company while they were in Rome.

He could tolerate the older man dancing with her, but when one of the younger sponsors tried to cut in, he returned to the dance floor and reclaimed her.

'Excuse us, Ambassador. I'm sure you'll understand.' He didn't care if the man understood or not. Cassandra was coming with him. 'The auction is about to start soon. Cassandra?' he prompted.

She looked daggers at him, though she was charm personified to the ambassador, who was a courtly old man and hadn't deserved his rough treatment. 'I apologise for denying you the company of this young woman,' he felt bound to add, brought to book by the piercing stare of his assistant gardener. He had to do some serious thinking on that front, but as the auction was about to start...

'I quite understand,' the ambassador told him, with a look that said he did—absolutely. 'I'll see you again someday, my dear, I hope.'

'I hope so too,' she said, with what even he had to admit was a lovely smile.

'There are some wonderful things in the auction,' Cassandra told him with enthusiasm as soon as they were seated back at the table.

Of course, he thought. All the items on sale were unique

and extremely valuable, in order to raise as much money as possible for the charity.

'Have you seen something you like?' Placing a bid was the least he could do when she had worked so hard to charm his guests.

'As a matter of fact, I have,' she said.

'Tell me,' he prompted indulgently.

'It's that lovely sketch of a dachshund puppy—the Hockney? In my fantasies, I imagine taking it home for my godmother as a gift. Don't worry,' she said before he had chance to say a word. 'I know they fetch tens of thousands, hundreds, probably—maybe millions by now—but it doesn't cost to dream.'

They both knew that works by the artist David Hockney could go for a fortune. All the auction lots would go for fabulous amounts of money, their value further increased by the fact that they were being sold for charity. Part of him wanted Cassandra to bid—he'd cover any amount she went to. But what would that say to the watching world?

Surprising himself, he covered her hand with his, as if to reassure her. Tender gestures were not his thing, but there was something about Cassandra...

CHAPTER SIX

THE BIDDING WAS over and everyone had left the table. Most of the charming older people had left, Cass discovered when she scanned the glamorous main salon. The networking she'd planned to do wasn't so easy when the people who were left behind didn't want to talk to her, and those who had gone were too nice to touch up for a job. She had just wanted to talk to them and enjoy their company.

Spotting Marco across the room, she thought now might be a good time to ask him to introduce her round. But, contrary to his earlier, sympathetic manner, when she had lusted after the Hockney sketch, his back was like a wall against her when she turned up, as if he regretted his brief display of almost being human, and was once again the aloof billionaire, untouchable and cold.

She hovered for a little while, uncertain. People moved around her as if she weren't there... She wished she wasn't there. This was a world she had avoided and had no desire to become part of again—a world where people said one thing and did another.

She moved into the shadows of a corner where she could observe, without being observed, and that was how, in a brief lull in the general conversation, she heard Marco say, 'That girl in the blue dress, sitting next to me at dinner? She's no one.'

Shock chilled her, but what he'd said was true. She wasn't anyone—not compared to all these rich and influential people. She was an amateur gardener—an enthusiast who had taken a summer vacation job on Marco di Fivizzano's country estate. When she returned home, she would be back stacking shelves at another supermarket.

Hearing Marco say what he had was actually a welcome wake-up call. She had nothing in common with anyone here. She must have been mad to think she could network.

But then her fiery nature kicked in. What he'd said was true, but he shouldn't have said it to another guest. How would Marco like it if she had dismissed him like that?

Working her anger out, she kept on moving around his guests without stopping to talk to anyone. She'd lost her confidence to speak to anyone, thanks to him. Finally, locking herself in the bathroom, she stared at the face of a stranger in the mirror—a woman with false eyelashes and rouged cheeks…an actress playing a part.

Exactly. She was playing a part. And therefore she could do this. Even if she was no one, on a scale of ambassador to prince, she could still hold her head high and go back to the party to do exactly what she'd been paid for.

And that was what she did. She guessed that the same driver who had brought her here would take her back to the hotel, and meanwhile, as the last guests began to think about leaving, she set about doing what she could to tidy up. She had always felt compelled to tidy up, maybe because the last time she had seen her mother alive, her mother had been stumbling about amidst the squalor of spilled ashtrays, discarded needles and upended champagne bottles. Since then Cass could never leave the debris of the night before until the next morning.

'What the hell are you doing?'

She froze as Marco roared at her. And then she fired

up. His manner was insufferable. Why had he paid her to come here at all? She was a member of his staff, and she saw no reason why she couldn't make a start on tidying up.

'Leave it!' he insisted. He was at her side in a couple of strides. 'I have staff to do this.'

'Are you going to make them work through the night?' she demanded, shaking his hand from her arm.

'Of course not,' he exploded.

The last thing he had expected was for her to answer back, Cass suspected as they glared at each other.

'My staff will be here in the morning,' Marco informed her brusquely.

And meanwhile they were alone…the last guest had left. And so far there was no sign of Marco's driver.

'What are you so angry about, Cassandra?'

She wasn't angry. She had just realised the compromising position she had put herself in. 'You think you can insult me and I won't feel anything?'

'Insult you? What on earth are you talking about?'

'You,' she fired back. 'You talk about your staff as if they're robots programmed to obey. You promised to introduce me round. You said it would be a great opportunity for me to network, and I thought so too, but you ignored me all night. I'm not sure why I'm here at all.'

'There were plenty of opportunities for you to network. It was up to you to take them. Everyone was here.'

'Everyone in your world,' she pointed out, 'and though I'm usually quite good at chatting to people and introducing myself, they just didn't want to know. An introduction from you would have broken the ice…' She paused. 'Or was it that you didn't want anyone to know you had brought your lowly gardener to the party?'

'Don't be so ridiculous. What about the ambassador?

You were talking to him. The embassy has beautiful gardens. There was an opportunity for you right there.'

'I was chatting to the ambassador because I wanted to talk to him. He was a really interesting man. Should I have taken advantage of that? Was I supposed to ingratiate myself with him for no better reason than to persuade him to give me a job?'

'Why not?' Marco demanded with a dismissive gesture. 'That's what networking is all about.'

'In that instance, it would have been calculating, and not very nice.'

'That's your opinion.'

'Yes, it is.'

'It's possible to be too nice, Cassandra.'

'Is it? Is it really? I had no idea there was such a thing as being *too* nice. I liked the ambassador. We got on well together, and I had no thought of using him for networking, as you suggest.'

'He could have given you a glimpse into another world—'

'As you can?' she flashed. 'Maybe I don't want to see what's in that other world—maybe I already know. You've got no idea, have you, Marco? You live such a privileged life you don't have a clue what it's like to be on the outside, looking in.'

'You couldn't be further from the truth,' he assured her tensely. 'I know exactly how that feels.'

'Do you?' she exclaimed angrily. 'Do you also know how it feels to be described as a nobody?'

Marco's expression blackened 'Who said that?'

'You did!' she flung back at him. 'Is that how you think of everyone who works for you? Are we all nobodies?'

'I have no idea what you're talking about.'

'I heard you say it.' And when Marco looked at her

blankly, she spelled it out for him. 'When one of your guests asked you about me, you said I was no one.'

'Ah...' Marco nodded his head. 'Let me explain. The man I was talking to was a major fundraiser for my charity. He's always on the lookout for new sponsors, as he should be—'

'And, of course, I'm no use to him. I couldn't do anything practical to help your charity, could I, Marco? And what can you do? Write another cheque?'

She had a point, he conceded. 'I'm sure you could do a lot for my charity, and if my shorthand way of telling a fundraiser that he was wasting his time asking you for money has offended you, I apologise. Maybe you shouldn't be so touchy.'

She shrugged. Her face was burning. Maybe she had overreacted.

'I agree that I'm no one where the funding side of your charity is concerned, but I could do other things apart from giving money. I could give my time, for instance.'

'I have no doubt of it,' Marco said, and then he surprised her with the hint of a smile.

It was the fact that they came from two such different worlds that was at the heart of her anger, Cass realised. Marco's world frightened her because she'd had experience of it, and, however many years ago it had been, there were some memories that never faded.

And Marco? Sometimes, when he relaxed like this and showed her a warmer, more caring side, she knew that his pain cut as deep as hers—he was just better at hiding it. They had never really talked, so she didn't know what lay behind Marco's armour. Why would they talk? She was paid to do a job. She was his gardener, briefly on an outing to help him. She was a place-filler, a puppet. 'You must think I'm stupid, overreacting like that...'

'Not at all,' he said firmly.

'But I am naïve enough to allow you to dress me up like a doll, and then expect you to be interested enough to spend all evening with me.'

'You are an extremely forthright woman,' he remarked with amusement in his eyes.

'Yes, I am,' she agreed.

'You did well tonight.'

'Are you mocking me now?' she asked suspiciously.

'No,' Marco murmured, the faint smile still in place. 'I'm very grateful to you. I can't think of anyone who could have pulled this off with such style and grace at such short notice. I'm only sorry I didn't make more effort to…break the ice for you, as you put it. I do know that society here can be very hard to break into.'

Cass slanted a rueful smile. 'And, I suppose, in fairness, your guests hadn't come here tonight to interview staff for their gardens.'

'I should have thought of that,' Marco admitted.

'And so should I.'

'Then we both got carried away.'

His eyes were deeply unsettling as they stared steadily into hers.

'Yes, we did,' she said.

'Truce?' he said.

'Truce,' she agreed, shaking hands with him.

Oh, how good that felt. She was almost disappointed when he let go and moved away.

'I've got something for you,' he said, turning back to her with a smile.

'Something for me?' She couldn't have been more surprised. 'You've paid me more than enough.' But she couldn't pretend she wasn't thrilled at the idea of a small gift—something personal from Marco. She'd keep it always, and long after this night was a memory she would find it and look at it, and think, *He gave it to me...*

'Oh, my word!' She couldn't have been more shocked. 'What have you done?'

'Please allow me, just this once, to fulfil someone's fantasy.'

She stared at the Hockney sketch in amazement. 'But this must have cost you a fortune.'

'In spite of what you think of me, I do value things in more than just monetary terms. You said you wanted this for your godmother. Well, now you can give it to her.'

'I can't possibly accept,' she protested.

'It's not for you, it's for her. You must accept,' Marco said.

'I don't know what to say.'

'Well, I do. She must be a very special woman.'

'She is.'

Marco was still staring at her with eyes turned thoughtful, while her head was muddied with feelings—too many feelings. A few more tense seconds passed, and then, just when she had found the words to form a polite refusal, she saw something flare in his eyes, and the next moment she was in his arms, and Marco was kissing her.

Her world had telescoped into this. Her world was this. Shocked, she resisted him for barely a moment before her body overruled her mind. This explosion of feeling and super-awareness was the very best way to end an argument, though seeing Marco every day and weaving fantasies around him had no bearing on the wealth of sensation flooding her now. He smelled—tasted—felt so good. She had never experienced anything like it. Being pressed up hard against his muscular frame, and having his arms tighten around her, was impossible to describe...not in words; only her body could respond with a burning desire to have not one fragment of space between them.

Breaking free, she was focused and breathless as she stood on tiptoe, pushing his jacket from his shoulders. She had to feel more of him—all of him. The sound of fabric ripping told her that her exquisite blue dress was a *vision* no more.

And now Marco's mouth was on her shoulder, claiming her, kissing her, licking and biting as he drew a cry from her throat by turning to rasp his sharp stubble across her neck. She was crying and laughing at the same time, while her hands worked with real purpose to tug off his clothes. Having managed to open his shirt, she gasped to see the power in his chest, the muscles flexing. He was so hard and tanned, and he was hers to explore.

Passion was running high between them as she ran the palm of one hand over his hot, smooth flesh. He dragged a cry from her throat, taking advantage of this brief distraction to cup her breasts. And he wasn't done with her yet. Taking hold of what was left of the fabric, he ripped her dress from neck to hem.

She was reduced to the flimsiest of underwear. This consisted of little more than flesh-coloured net that revealed every contour of her body in absolute detail. Looking down, she saw her rose-tinted nipples extended impertinently for his appreciation, and the soft mound between her legs, swollen and moist. If she had drawn this scene in one of her fantasies, she might have imagined feeling uncertain, standing practically naked in front of such a sophisticated lover, but the heat in Marco's eyes and the touch of his hands gave her confidence.

'I'm going to pleasure you,' he growled, angling his chin to stare into her eyes. 'I'm going to make you beg for more.'

'Okay.'

Throwing his head back, he laughed at her forthright acceptance of his offer.

Let him laugh. She had no intention of being a docile partner. She had needs too.

Smoothing the palms of her hands across the width of his shoulders, she removed his shirt and let it drop to the floor. Then she turned her attention to the buckle on his belt, and after that his zipper. She held his stare as she pushed his black silk boxers down over his taut, hard, muscular buttocks. Cupping them briefly, she indulged herself for a moment, before studying his erection. Thick and smooth, it was standing almost perpendicular, and her body ached to have him deep inside her. But Marco was the master of delay. Capturing her wrists, he pinned them behind her back, holding her still for him, while his other hand conducted a lazy exploration. Still staring her in the eyes, he protected them both, ripping the foil with his teeth. Anticipation was part of his foreplay, she gathered—and it was working, she would be the first to admit.

Cupping her breasts, he stroked them and weighed them appreciatively. He teased her nipples until she thought she'd go mad. Every part of her was responding eagerly to his touch, allowing her to sink into a rich velvet pool of sensation.

Frustratingly, Marco kept a space between them, although he did allow her to feel the brush of his erection. And then he touched her. But too lightly. And his hand never lingered long enough to satisfy her needs. And all this time he was smiling down at her, as if he knew exactly how frustrated he was making her.

She'd had enough and broke free.

Their tussle went up a notch. They were both determined to have the upper hand, and of course she couldn't fight him, but wrestling Marco was so much fun, and only added to her arousal. She rubbed her body against his—she rubbed every part of her against him. He seemed amused by her strength but she'd been working outdoors for weeks and had never been a weakling, but she would never be strong enough to dominate Marco.

That made it more fun. One minute he would let her think she was strong enough, and the next he would master her. Right now he had her in a firm hold and was tormenting her at his leisure. She tried calling him names, but it only made him laugh.

'You love it,' he said.

She would never admit to that, but he was right. Marco's expression, his wicked smile, and even the blinding flash of his strong white teeth—she loved everything about him.

'Do you think you can fight me?' he said.

'I know I can,' she hissed back.

She shivered, exultant when he slipped his hand beneath her flimsy bra. She thought for a moment that he was going to rip it off, but still he kept her waiting. The master of arousal had her in the firmest of grips, and he allowed her no choice other than to accept the pleasure he was dealing her. He stroked her breasts with the lightest of touches, and then had the nerve to smile when she whimpered with frustration. When she was least expecting it, he slipped his fingers beneath the delicate join holding the fragile cups of her bra together and ripped them apart. His eyes flashed with triumph when she cried out with surprise. Disposing of the ruined bra, he tossed the remnants aside, before turning his full attention to her breasts.

Now she could only breathe and exist as Marco touched her. He had robbed her of the power to do more. It wasn't just that he was holding her so she couldn't move while he pleasured her—it was more that she didn't want to move. Why fight pleasure? Wasn't it better to relax into sensation such as this, and enjoy?

She exclaimed with delighted shock when he pinched her nipples, and the sensation travelled rapidly around her body. She rested in Marco's arms, a willing victim to his skill—so much so that when he finally took hold of the waistband of her thong, she exclaimed with relief. She should have known he was still teasing her. Tracing the tiny scrap of lace around her waist, he slipped his fingers down between her buttocks, before returning to trail them across the swollen mound that was aching for his attention.

'More?' he suggested, angling his chin to shoot her a look with those wicked eyes.

She garbled something, which was all she could do. In answer, Marco cupped her with his hand, though with a touch so light it was even more frustrating than not being touched at all. With a growl of frustration she arched her back and thrust herself firmly against his hand, and then she worked her body shamelessly against it in the hunt for more contact, more pleasure...

'You have to tell me what you want, Cassandra.'

Marco's tone was deliciously stern. 'You.' She blazed a frank and fiery stare into his eyes. 'I want you.'

'And where do you want me?' he said calmly.

'Deep inside me.'

Before the words were out of her mouth Marco had lifted her arms above her head. Ramming her back against the wall, he held her in place with the weight of his body. Catching hold of her buttocks, he encouraged her to lift her legs and wrap them around his body as tightly as she could. She was happy to do so. She was claiming him. He wasn't going anywhere.

Lacing her fingers through his strong black hair, she

kept him close with their mouths just a fraction apart. His fierce stare burned into hers, but he refused to kiss her.

She thought she knew why. Marco didn't want her to close her eyes. He wanted to see everything she was feeling reflected in their depths. He wanted that degree of control over her, and that level of contact between them, when he took her for the first time. She wanted that too. She wanted to see Marco's responses just as hungrily as he wanted to see hers.

CHAPTER SEVEN

'Now?' Marco suggested softly, his mouth tugging a little at one corner as if he were mocking her need. Before she had a chance to answer, he tested her, and parting her with the tip of his erection he slid slowly and steadily into her until he was lodged deep, to the hilt.

'You're so tight...so wet...' he murmured appreciatively over her grateful moans.

And he was so big. She gasped with delighted shock, and then Marco worked some magic with his hand, and she was reduced to wordless sounds of need and pleasure. She was just building to an exciting climax when he withdrew completely. She had no sooner voiced her complaint with a cry and with fingers digging cruelly into his shoulders than he drew his hips back and thrust deep. Holding on was impossible. She fell gratefully into a series of violent pleasure waves. He didn't wait for her to quieten. Lifting her, he walked with her across the room where he lowered her down on the sofa. Standing over her, he spread her legs wide over his shoulders. 'Well?' he said with the faintest of smiles.

'Hard and fast?' she suggested.

Breath shot out of her in a noisy rush. Marco had taken her at her word, but nothing could have prepared her for this.

They made love all night in every part of the penthouse. They had hungry sex, fierce sex, and even playful sex, and there wasn't a surface they didn't sample. Their appetite for each other proved inexhaustible, and when she finally fell asleep in Marco's bed, it was with a happy smile on her lips and more contentment in her heart than she could ever remember feeling.

He woke at dawn and his first thoughts as always were centred around his work. He rolled out of bed and glanced at Cassandra. She was sound asleep. She had proved to be every bit as enthusiastic about sex as he had imagined. But that was all it had been, he told himself.

His mother had lived a lie for the sake of hooking up with a wealthy man. He would not be making that sort of mistake any time soon. The man he thought of as his father was a man his mother had tricked into marrying her, in order to provide her with an income stream and a father for her unborn child. Cassandra had briefly made him question his belief that women couldn't be trusted, but when he recalled the damage a woman could do, it was easy to shut down his emotions.

After his shower, he went into his dressing room and emerged ready for the day. Cassandra was just waking... stretching her limbs like an indolent cat. The image she presented—naked and lush, and so obviously sated—was quite different from her common-sense self in Tuscany.

'Marco...' She reached out a hand as if the effort was almost too much for her. 'Come back to bed...'

He frowned, and then realised that some words were necessary if he wasn't to appear wholly inconsiderate, but the affection and reassurance that Cassandra seemed to be asking for was beyond him.

'That was great, *cara*...' Walking over to the bed, he

dipped down to brush a kiss against her cheek. 'But I have to go now.' Leaving her side, he paused at the door. 'I left your money on the table in the hall…'

Her money?

For a moment Cass couldn't understand what Marco had said, and then she remembered that she was to be paid for filling a seat at his party, and that it was the money she could use to send her godmother on the dream trip.

That didn't make her feel any better. Sitting up in bed, she hugged herself, wishing that Marco's arms were around her, and that he was cuddling and reassuring her. She had wanted to tell him how much last night had meant to her. But now…

Scrambling out of bed, she dragged a sheet with her to wrap around her naked body. Crossing to the window, she waited until Marco had left the building, and then she watched him step into his car. She felt empty inside. As with everything else in his charmed life, Marco's trip to the office would be seamless. He wanted sex. He had sex. He wanted the car. The valet brought it to the door for him. No interruptions were allowed to the busy billionaire's schedule. Tenderness or a few moments of humour were beyond him—unless he was in seduction mode.

Blinded by tears, she turned around, furious with herself for being so stupid. Last night had been special for her, and she had thought it had meant something to him.

She took a long, hot shower in the hope that it would stop her shaking. She felt cold to the bone, and sick at the thought that Marco hadn't treated her much better than a prostitute. After paying for her services, he had all but ignored her at the charity function—but he hadn't ignored her when everyone had left. Then he'd been different, then he'd been interested—very interested indeed. And she was the fool who had allowed it to happen.

Ignoring her scattered clothes, the ripped reminders of an explosive passion that hadn't lasted the night, she pulled on the same frock she'd arrived in. Thank goodness Marco or his staff had had the foresight to have her things sent on from the hotel to Marco's penthouse. Scraping her hair back, she didn't bother with make-up. Why would she? Who would notice? Picking up the phone, she checked on flights home to England and then booked a cab to the airport. She'd got enough money to fly home, and there was no point in staying—not on Marco's terms.

Just thinking about it made her so angry she had to blink back tears. She had never been a victim, and she wasn't about to start now. When things went wrong, she did something about it.

When the cab driver called to say he was outside, she checked around one last time to make sure she'd got everything—and then stopped, frozen to the spot, at the sight of Marco's cheque on the hall table. She picked it up and studied the amount. She studied the bold script of Marco's signature. She couldn't imagine what he'd been thinking when he'd come up with such a ridiculous amount, let alone what she had been thinking when she'd accepted it. There was enough money here to send her godmother around the world first class with money to spare. A second call from the cab driver distracted her.

'Coming now,' she answered.

'Cassandra…Cassandra?'

He stared around the empty penthouse. Where the hell was she? He had expected a welcome, a smile, and a whole lot more. Was she still in bed? He felt a buzz of anticipation as he went to find out.

The buzz didn't last long. His room was empty, the bed neatly made. He knocked on the bathroom door…

Nothing.

He checked inside to be sure.

He searched the whole place, but it was silent and empty. There was no sign of her—no clothes on the floor, nothing out of place, not even a scribbled note to indicate where she had gone. And he'd distinctly told her to expect him later. He went back to the hallway where he'd left her cheque beneath a plant pot on the console table. *Where she couldn't have missed it.*

His cheque was still there.

He thought about calling her on his phone and then changed his mind. She must have gone back to the hotel. He dialled the number and reeled at the information that the receptionist gave him. Signorina Rich had called by to pick up her passport and suitcase *on her way to the airport*.

She'd left him?

He huffed a humourless laugh. Maybe it was for the best that she'd gone. The strength of his desire for Cassandra was warning enough to end it now. He would have done, if she hadn't gone.

But she'd gone.

Dio! He was her employer. She couldn't just walk out on him.

Striding across the room, he snatched up the cheque. Gripping it in his fist, he rang his PA. 'Find her.'

'Yes, sir.'

He slammed down the phone, refusing to accept that a small part of him couldn't let Cassandra go—not completely.

Cass made sure she wasn't easy to find. Her experience in Tuscany had bruised her. Bought and paid for like her mother, she was determined that she would not suffer the same fate. No one knew better than she did that a clean break with the past was the only chance anyone had to move forward. The person she had been in Rome wasn't her. Or, rather, it wasn't the person she wanted to be. She was Cass, plain and simple—not some glittering socialite with a rampant sex life, who stayed the night with the boss in order to keep him sweet.

Not everything was doom and gloom. Her godmother had flown to Australia to join her son, explaining that he had sent the fare for her, and, on Cass's recommendation, she had rented out her house to bring in some extra cash while she was away.

This was just the opportunity Cass had needed to quit the address Marco's people held on file for her and start over. She got a job at another supermarket, which paid just enough money to rent a small house in a nearby village. Her new home was tiny, but she loved it. She had put up a notice in the local post office, offering her services as a gardener, and to her surprise she was soon fully booked. With that and her work on the tills she was almost too busy for regret—until the day she fainted on the job, and an elderly lady she was serving asked her if she was pregnant…

'No. Of course not,' she protested, laughing at the absurdity of the question. 'What makes you think that?' But even as she spoke, a spear of alarm stabbed deep.

'A strong, healthy girl like you has no reason to feel faint—unless you're ill, which I doubt. I've had six children myself,' the old lady confided, 'so I know the signs.'

'I'm sure you're wrong…'

Cass tried to laugh it off, while all she wanted to do was to leave the store and rush to the pharmacy to pick up a pregnancy test, but she had to wait until she finished work.

It was the longest working day of her life. Back home, she stared at the test in shock. The thin blue line didn't lie, according to the instructions. But Marco had used protection, so how could this happen?

Quite easily, those same instructions informed her as she scanned the printed sheet.

No protection is foolproof.

Well, they'd got that right, and she was the fool.

'A call from Signorina Rich?'

Marco sat back in his leather seat, staring out across the majestic skyline of Rome. His secretary knew never to interrupt him unless it was to announce his next appointment, or unless it was a matter of vital importance, so Cassandra must be kicking up a fuss. The lack of her pained him, but the fact that she had walked out on him without a word had ended it as far as he was concerned. How long had it been now? Almost three months? What was so important she had to call him at the office? Had she changed her mind about the cheque?

'I have a ten o'clock meeting,' he snapped, frowning.

He drew breath to give himself a chance to weigh up the facts. Cassandra was back in his life, asking to speak to him. He needed to think about this for a few moments.

Calm reason triumphed. They hadn't expected to hear from each other. When something was over it was over, as far as he was concerned.

'Tell Ms Rich I'm too busy to take her call, but I'm happy to send her cheque on.'

Thoughts of Cassandra plagued him for the rest of the day, and flashbacks kept him from his work. These were not just of Cassandra, but of the past. Maybe because their pasts were quite similar he was thinking back to that frozen Christmas Eve when the man he had called *Papa* had thrown him and his mother out on the street, cutting them off without a penny or a word of farewell.

His mother must leave with nothing, the man he had thought was his father had instructed. That was the price of betrayal. More disillusionment followed when his mother had explained that *Papa* wasn't his father, and that the man who had fathered him had been an odd job man around the house, and now that man was gone too.

Even though their circumstances had been much changed, to begin with the two of them had rubbed along well enough. His mother hadn't been a fool, but the unrelenting hardship of their new life had eventually ground her down, and she'd begun to drink to blot it out.

Cassandra's mother had been a drunk too, so Cassandra knew how it felt when a mother chose to lose herself in a bottle of liquor, rather than care for her child.

When his mother had died he had found ways to make himself useful—carrying trash for restaurants in return for a good feed and carting logs for the rich folk who could afford them. He had vowed that one day *he* would go to school, and one day *he* would be rich.

And Cassandra?

She had been cast adrift in just the same way, and she was a survivor too.

With a frown of impatience he got back to his work and vowed not to allow thoughts of Cassandra to distract him. He relied on no one. He shared his past with no one. He never had. He couldn't afford this sort of disturbance to his working day. There must be no more calls from Cassandra.

'Your ten o' clock appointment is here, sir…'

'Thank you. Send him in.'

Closing the book on Cassandra Rich, he turned his attention back where it belonged, to the business that had never let him down.

* * *

Precious time was passing and Marco was still refusing to take her calls. Soon it would become obvious that she was pregnant, and he had to know. She had called her godmother in Australia and, typically, her godmother had shared Cass's delight. She had asked who the father was, and when Cass had enthusiastically said she'd be doing this alone, her godmother had immediately offered to come home. Cass had had to insist that this wasn't necessary, and had pointed out that her godmother's time with her son was precious. Cass had friends around, as well as the best of medical care, and she promised to get in touch with regular updates.

Marco's refusal to speak to her was one difficulty she had no intention of burdening her godmother with, Cass thought as she placed yet another call to Fivizzano Inc. She was tired of speaking to the same PA and receiving the same firm, but polite answer: 'I am sorry, *signorina*, but Signor di Fivizzano cannot take your call. He's too busy today.'

She would have to be back at the supermarket for her lunchtime shift in ten minutes, Cass realised, glancing at her phone. She had called Marco every day at different times of day, hoping that eventually she'd be put straight through to him. She still couldn't believe that she'd slept with such a cold-hearted man—or that she had never asked for his private number, but there was no point in regretting that now.

The same PA picked up, and Cass received the same stock answer, but this time she interrupted before the PA had a chance to hang up. 'I'm sorry…did you say Signor di Fivizzano is too busy to speak to me?'

'That is correct, *signorina*. I do apologise—'

'He wasn't too busy to sleep with me.' She paused—

not that she needed to as the silence was crushing. 'He wasn't too busy to make me pregnant. Could you tell him that, please? Thank you,' she added politely before she cut the line.

Sitting back, she firmed her chin. The die had been cast. She'd done her part. She wanted nothing from Marco in the material sense, but it was her duty to let him know. What he did next was up to him. What she did next would be all about her baby's future.

He didn't say a word when his red-faced PA recited Cassandra's call back to him, but his mind was racing.

'Thank you.' His curt nod of the head revealed nothing of the turmoil inside him.

A child?

He had given life to a child?

How could that have happened when he was always so careful?

Had he been so careful that night? Hadn't he been out of control for the first time in his adult life...because of Cassandra, and the way she had made him feel?

He was never out of control. He was confident on that point. But had he been as meticulous as he usually was when it came to using protection? They had indulged so many times it was hard to be certain. He had been consumed by a fever of lust and so had she. He'd never known anything like it, which made her behaviour afterwards— leaving him without a word of explanation—all the harder to understand. Until he brought up the past and put what he'd learned from it into the equation.

This ruse had been used before, he remembered, getting up to pace the floor—false pregnancies, floods of tears, women trying to tell him that it was better without using protection, and *of course they were on the Pill*. Not one of those women had been telling the truth. He'd had them all investigated. There were no babies, just dishonest women looking for an easy ride.

Did that sound like Cassandra?

He didn't want children. Why would he, with his history?

Could he find feelings? Could he buy them? Since learning that he'd been unwanted, he had learned not to care. He'd been doing that for too long now to change, and a child needed more. A child needed everything.

He struggled with the thought that Cassandra had done this on purpose to secure a meal ticket, like other women, like his mother. But was he the father of her child? Cass hadn't been a virgin when he'd met her. How could he be sure?

He couldn't go on like this. Thoughts of Cassandra were interfering with his life. He'd have to ring and have it out with her.

In a trick that only fate could play on him, he discovered she had changed her number.

Don't you trust your own judgement? Cassandra is different from all those other women. Have you forgotten that so easily?

The past vied uncomfortably with what he knew about Cassandra. She wasn't weak. She wasn't greedy. She had never asked him for anything. It was he who had pressed things on her—the dress, the makeover, the sketch, and then the cheque.

He called the team that handled his business investigations. 'I want protection for her around the clock,' he told the head of the investigative team. The man he was talking to was an expert in surveillance, and Marco was confident that from day one he would know as much about Cassandra as if he were standing next to her.

CHAPTER EIGHT

SHE HAD GIVEN up trying to contact Marco. If they did meet again, it would be on her terms. She may not have his power and money, but she was not going to take this insulting behaviour from a man who apparently refused to believe she was carrying his child.

Being a prospective single mother with no money wasn't easy, but it taught her a lot of things—things she had never imagined learning—things about her mother, for example. If she had one complaint, it was that she felt isolated sometimes in the tiny house she was renting. She realised now that her mother must have felt just the same in the grand mansion where Cass had been born. She only wished she had been old enough to understand her mother's loneliness, and that she could cross time and space now to put things right. Her father would still have slept with all his groupies—she doubted anyone could have changed him—but she hoped she could have helped her mother. No wonder her mother had wandered around in a drug-fuelled stupor. She must have been desperate to work out how to compete for the attention of a man who'd no longer wanted her.

She had learned these lessons from the past and could look after herself, Cass reassured herself, as she closed her hand tightly round the scan of her baby. She would shut her heart to Marco di Fivizzano, if it meant bringing up their child free from guilt and heartache. And if Marco was an example of how the rich and famous lived, she was glad to be poor and no one.

Not so glad to be sick again, though...

Leaning her hand against the wall, she retched on an empty stomach. *Hyperemesis gravidarum*, the doctor had called it, telling her that her morning sickness should ease soon.

Soon couldn't come soon enough for Cass. She was usually so healthy and full of pep, but these days she felt tired from the moment she woke up to when she fell exhausted into bed, and she was feeling particularly nauseous today. She was pale and grey, with an unattractive green tinge, she acknowledged ruefully as she stared at her reflection in the bathroom mirror. Bloodshot eyes didn't do much for her either. She wasn't blooming, as pregnant women were supposed to do, according to the magazines—she felt wretched and too ill to work. Thankfully, she had an understanding manager, but his compassion would only stretch so far, Cass suspected. The upside of her situation was the news from the midwife that her baby was thriving. So she'd keep on keeping on—what else could she do? And she would try to eat healthily—when she could bear to eat at all.

It was all in a good cause, she told herself firmly as she picked up a nourishing snack on her way back to bed in the vainest of hopes that she could keep it down. She took the phone with her to call her manager to ask if she could change shifts, and then she crawled back under the duvet with relief to wait for her twitchy stomach to calm down.

He had called his pilot, who was having the jet made ready before his PA had a chance to ask him if there was anything more she could do for him. His investigators hadn't disappointed him, though their latest report had thrown him. If Cassandra was sick it changed everything. As a past member of his staff, he had a certain responsibility towards her, whether or not the baby was his.

A baby that might be his...

And he missed her. *Dio!* Just admitting those words made him frown. Had he grown soft?

No. He was merely doing what had to be done, and it was a job that couldn't be delegated. After she'd called the office, he wouldn't put anything past her, so he had to see for himself exactly what was going on. The fact that, according to his sources, Cassandra had been living an exemplary life didn't really surprise him, but it was welcome news. He wanted her to look after herself. His experience of women before Cass was hardly reassuring, and it was in his nature to be suspicious and think the worst. When the baby was born there would be a DNA test. He would have to be sure before committing himself further. With a shake of his head he cursed at being the cause of history repeating itself. Because of him another child would come into this world subject to scrutiny, subject to suspicion, and then maybe that child would be discarded...*and by him.*

He stopped outside the modest door and checked the address. Lifting the serviceable knocker, he rapped sharply three times. He waited and knocked again.

The door opened and there she stood. His whole body tensed as she stared at him in amazement. 'Marco?'

Her voice was faint with surprise, but it was the fact that Cassandra was so diminished in both body and spirit that shocked him. He had expected to be greeted by the robust woman who had taken him on and fought back, but this frail-looking girl seemed incapable of doing anything.

She was like a wraith, a mere shadow of her healthy, sun-kissed, capable self. To say he was concerned would be an understatement. 'May I come in?'

Wordlessly, she stood back.

The interior of the small terraced house was as neat as the exterior. It was compact but functional, with a tiny kitchen at the street end of the room. At the other end there was a solid fuel burner with a couple of battered sofas either side of it, and a fireguard already in place.

The fireguard looked new, as if she was planning ahead and buying things bit by bit. A narrow staircase led up to what he suspected would be a maximum of two small bedrooms and a simple bathroom. Her front door opened directly onto the street, and he guessed there was no garden. There was certainly no display outside the front door to say that this was the home of an avid gardener, though he noticed that the pot plants on her windowsill were drooping. Seeing that almost jolted him more than anything else.

Emotion got the better of him, and he launched straight in. 'Why didn't you tell me you were pregnant as soon as you knew?'

'I did—I tried to get in touch with you, but you wouldn't take my calls.'

'You should have come to Rome.'

She laughed. 'That's easy for you to say with a private jet at your disposal.'

'You shouldn't have left Rome in the first place,' he argued. 'But you could have texted me, written to me.'

'How cold do you think I am, Marco? I'm not like you. I had to see you face to face and hear your voice before I could tell you about the baby. I couldn't just type out the news that we were having a child like an invoice and submit it to you.'

He ground his jaw, knowing she was right. 'How are

you getting on?' He could see for himself, but for once he couldn't find the right words to say.

She shrugged.

'You don't look well. You look exhausted.' She'd lost far too much weight.

'I'm pregnant, Marco. Would you like to sit down?' She remained standing stiffly and as far away from him as she could.

'Thank you, but I'll stand. I've been sitting down long enough in the jet coming over, and again in the car that brought me from the airport.'

'I'm sorry if I've interrupted your busy schedule.'

'Stop it,' he warned softly.

'Why are you here, Marco? What do you want?'

'To see you. To see how you are.'

'You won't speak to me on the phone and now you're here?' She shook her head. 'What you do never makes any sense to me. How did you find me?'

'The village you live in isn't exactly a big place.'

'And you had me watched,' she guessed. 'How dare you?'

'You walked out without a word. Is that acceptable behaviour?'

'You paid me off. You only wanted me for sex.'

'I did not,' he said quietly. This wasn't the time to examine his motives, but he had not wanted her just for sex. Cassandra had made him laugh. She had made him relax. She had made him feel young again when he couldn't ever remember feeling young.

'What, then?' she demanded, rallying herself to stand up to him. 'Take that occasion at your charity function in Rome when you barely spoke to me. And then, as soon as everyone left—'

'You leapt on me,' he remembered, finding it hard to suppress a grin as he thought back.

'I did not leap on you.'

'You did,' he argued with a shrug. 'We leapt on each other.'

She tightened her mouth and her face went red, but she didn't deny it.

'Can I get you something to drink?' she asked, avoiding his gaze.

'Why don't I get you a glass of water while you sit down?'

'I should get you a drink,' she insisted. 'Your journey—' She stopped when she saw the expression on his face.

'Sit.'

Reluctantly, she did so. She had no option. She was swaying and looked on the point of collapse. This was so much worse than he had imagined. Turning to the sink, he ran the tap and filled a glass with cold water. 'This isn't a social call, Cassandra. I've come to take you home with me, back to Rome.'

'I beg your pardon?' she demanded.

'You can't stay here.' He glanced around, and by the time his assessing stare had returned to her face it was to see her cheeks flaming with the knowledge that he was right. She wasn't finding this pregnancy easy. She was sick and weak, and he doubted she could work in her current condition. How was she supposed to support herself, let alone a baby? *A baby that might be his child.* If there was even the smallest chance of that he couldn't leave her here— *Dio!* He couldn't leave her here anyway. With her godmother away, Cassandra had no one else but him to turn to.

'Pack a small case,' he said. 'We can buy anything else you need in Rome. We'll leave as soon as you're ready.'

'I haven't agreed to go with you yet,' she pointed out, raising her chin to stare at him with defiance.

'But you will,' he said. 'If you care for your baby at all, you will.'

She followed Marco's glance to her wilting plants and wondered if he could be right. She felt just like them, but it wasn't in her to give up without a fight. She was carrying his child—a child he didn't want—but she had to give her baby every chance. Should she go with Marco for the sake of their child, as he suggested? Was she being selfish, staying here?

'Do you need some help packing your case?'

'No, thank you.' She frowned. She refused to be rushed into this. She had always dreamed of having a family—but a family very different from her own. She supposed now that this perfect dream was yet another example of her naivety. Life wasn't simple, and there was no such thing as an ideal family. The only thing she did know was that she would fight like a lioness for her child. And if living in the lap of luxury in Italy turned out not to be the best thing for her baby, she'd come home.

'Where were you planning to take me?' she asked Marco, blaming pregnancy hormones for the vision of his home in Tuscany swimming in front of her eyes. She even allowed the daydream to progress… That wouldn't be so bad, would it? Tending that beautiful garden as she waited for her baby to arrive? The sunshine would do both of them good—

'To Rome, as I said,' he repeated briskly. Her illusion was instantly shattered as he added, 'That's where the best doctors are, so that's where you'll be going. You'll live in my penthouse, of course. What?' he asked seeing her expression change from frowning to downright refusal. 'Where did you think I would take you?'

'Rome,' she murmured distractedly. He'd said Rome, and she knew that to many people Rome would seem to be a dream destination, but Marco was so different in Rome, and he expected her to act differently too. What sort of life would she lead in Rome? Would he even be there when she had the baby? And how would she occupy herself until the child was born? And what would happen afterwards?

Questions crowded in on her. She was weak. She had been sick for days now, and though her doctor had promised the nausea would pass, she just couldn't face dressing up and living Marco's social life in Rome. But then it came to her that, far from parading her in front of his friends and business associates, he was probably thinking more about hiding her away. He wouldn't want to flout his pregnant mistress in front of everyone. Not when she was his gardener, his part-time holiday staff, a young nobody with whom he'd had an ill-judged fling. His peers in Rome would expect a man like Marco di Fivizzano to settle down with an heiress, a princess or a celebrity at the very least. No. Marco wanted her under his nose so he could keep an eye on her—hide her away from the press, from everyone, so she couldn't talk about her affair. He wanted to imprison her in his penthouse in Rome.

'Cassandra?'

She stared up at him in shock.

'Call me when you want your case carried downstairs.'

'Wait,' she called as he turned away. 'I'm not coming with you. I'd have to give this a lot of thought first.'

He raked his hair with frustration. 'What's there to think about?'

'My life—my child's life.'

'What kind of life are you going to give a child here?' Marco countered.

'What kind of life am I going to have shut away in

your penthouse in Rome? Just because you can't imagine bringing up a child in anything but palatial surroundings, it doesn't make it right.'

Blinded by tears, she turned away. She knew her pregnancy hormones were racing out of control, making everything harder to work out than it should have been. Maybe it would be better to go with him, at least until she had regained her strength.

'Please, *cara*…please, try to be sensible and come with me. I'm not going to imprison you. I'm going to treat you as my guest.'

'Your guest?' As if that didn't hurt. 'Your life is so different from mine.'

'Yes, it is,' Marco conceded, 'but I can't change it—not even for you.'

'You can't go anywhere without the paparazzi following you, and I don't want that.'

'You'll learn to ignore them.'

'Will I? I've got enough to do, learning how to be a mother.'

'It's not like you to avoid a challenge, Cassandra.'

'I've never been pregnant before.'

Her feelings were so strong, so confused. Marco was inviting her into his world, which was everything she had always told herself she must avoid. He was the father of her child, and there wasn't a part of her that didn't yearn for them to take that journey together. How often had she longed for a real home and a real family? But that wasn't what Marco was offering her. He was offering a part-time solution, which would make the inevitable break-up that much harder when it came.

'You need help, Cassandra, and you know it. What's most important to you? Are you thinking of yourself or your baby?'

'The baby, of course. You don't need to ask.'

'Then you don't need to debate any longer. Come with me and your baby will thrive. I promise you that.'

'Give me until tomorrow morning. I'll give you my answer then.'

On this occasion he couldn't refuse a pregnant woman the chance to think things through and so he booked into a local hotel. His frustration was mounting, likewise his impatience with Cassandra, who refused to give ground. He had made several fortunes and had found that process a whole lot easier than this. He had raised himself out of the gutter without half so much soul-searching.

When it came to it he found he couldn't wait until the morning, so he called her up on the phone.

'I've given you my answer, Marco. I need more time.'

'Nonsense. You know what you want. You're not an indecisive woman, so let me hear your decision.'

There was a long silence and then she said, 'All right. I agree I probably do need a rest, but the sickness will pass, and then I want to work for as long as I can until the baby is born. I can't just come to Rome and do nothing. If I agree to come back with you, you have to allow me to choose a job, and you can't interfere with that. I don't want your influence helping me, and I don't want your money supporting me, but I am prepared to accept that my baby needs its mother in better health. So, if your offer's still on, you can pick me up in the morning, but only on those terms.'

She was setting terms for him? He had never, in all his years in business, been in a position where he was on the receiving end of terms.

'This is what I want, Marco. You're right in saying I'm not an indecisive woman, and what I've suggested seems fair to both of us from my perspective. I won't be a drain on you, and you'll have a guest staying for a while who promises not to get under your feet.'

It wasn't his feet he was worried about.

'Are you still there, Marco?'

'I'm riveted.'

She ignored his sarcasm. 'Do you agree to my terms?'

Her place was small but homely, and Cassandra was not a helpless woman. He knew that to have her agree to his suggestion was a measure of how sick she felt.

As for her terms, terms were negotiable. Cassandra's health was not.

CHAPTER NINE

SHE WAS SO sure she had thought things through properly before leaving for Rome, but this was so much worse than she had imagined. Exchanging her tiny, cosy home for Marco's vast, impersonal penthouse was like being stranded on a desert island. The impressive door had barely swung open on the all-too-familiar hallway with its Caligula overtones when Marco turned to go.

He gave her no explanation. Why would he? He'd been working on the flight, and when they'd disembarked he had been on the phone in the limousine. Some important business deal, she'd gathered, judging from his decisive speech and stern expression. They hadn't spoken once during the trip, and were as distant now as if they were once again the billionaire and his part-time gardener.

She cringed with embarrassment when his driver put her shabby suitcase down in the hall before following Marco out. Her case looked like a boil on the pristine marble floor, and when she went to pick it up, a maid as starchy as her uniform whisked it away before Cass had the chance to touch it.

'Your room is ready for you, *signorina*.'

'Thank you.' She felt the hallway was spinning. Everything was happening too fast. She followed the maid to the suite of rooms that would be her home for the next few months.

How had she agreed to this? Cass wondered as she stroked her stomach protectively. She knew that her health had made it necessary, but even so her heart sank as she looked around. She knew how ungrateful she must seem, but she didn't need all this. She would happily swop these gracious surroundings for a few calm words with Marco.

'If you need anything else, *signorina*...'

The maid was hovering by the door.

'I won't, but thank you.' All Cass wanted was to be left alone.

'If you change your mind, please call me on the house phone.'

'Thank you,' she said again, wondering what Marco's staff made of her.

Nothing, she guessed. They probably saw lots of women arrive and leave without ever exchanging a friendly greeting with them.

When the door closed she turned full circle slowly. Everywhere was beautiful and light, and very spacious, but though it was all incredibly impressive, Marco's magnificent penthouse had more of an air of an exclusive hotel than a home. People slept here, and occasionally ate here, but they never left a personal mark. There were no photographs, no trophies, no memorabilia at all. There was absolutely nothing to give a hint of the type of man who lived here. Maybe that was Marco's intention. He had the reputation of being a cold, aloof man.

But not in bed.

That was all over now, she told herself sensibly. She was pregnant. He was suspicious. They were at an impasse. And for now there was nothing to be done about it.

The maid brought her a light supper of delicious salad and freshly baked bread. When the phone had rung earlier she had nearly jumped out of her skin, and had rushed to answer it, only to hear the dispassionate tones of Marco's chef, enquiring what she would like to eat and where she would like to eat it. She had said that she would prefer to remain in her suite. She couldn't face rattling around the opulence of the grand salon on her own, or the even grander dining room.

She had picked at the food and now she pushed it away. Crossing the room, she opened the door. It was all still and quiet on the corridor leading to the kitchen. Guessing the staff must have gone home, she took her tray back, only to find the chef and the maid eating supper there.

'Oh, I'm sorry— I didn't mean—'

They stared at her as she backed her way out again. The kitchen was their preserve, not hers, their hostile stares clearly told her. This was a very different set-up from Marco's country estate, where Maria had always welcomed Cass into the kitchen for a friendly chat.

Marco's kitchen in Rome might have every sort of appliance known to man, but it lacked the one thing Maria's kitchen could boast, which was heart, Cass concluded. If only she could have gone to Tuscany to wait for her baby. It wasn't nearly as formal there, and Maria and Giuseppe had always treated her like a member of their family.

It wouldn't be so easy for Marco to keep an eye on her in Tuscany, Cass suspected.

Hugging herself, she returned to her room. She felt cold and lost. And she was stuck here. Until the sickness lessened she couldn't look for a job.

The vista beyond the floor-to-ceiling windows seemed to echo her feelings. The sky was uniformly grey, and the giant panes of glass were flecked with rain. A stubborn mist had descended over Rome, obscuring the stunning view. Pressing her hands flat against the cold, unyielding surface, she stared out, knowing Marco was out there somewhere...but where? She didn't know who he was with, or even if he'd be home tonight.

And it was none of her business.

With nothing else to do, she ran a bath in a tub big enough for two. The tub took ten minutes to fill, and it took her two minutes to take a bath. Climbing out, she grabbed a towel and headed off to bed. Drawing the covers up to her chin, she stared around what had to be the most luxurious bedroom she had ever spent the night in. It felt like a prison cell.

He spent a couple of nights away from the apartment, knowing Cassandra would be well looked after. His staff were under strict instructions not to let anyone in.

And no one out?

Cassandra needed to rest. He'd been quite firm about that. She'd been overdoing it and she still didn't look well. He had arranged a check-up for her with one of Rome's top doctors, a man known to be discreet. She would remain in the apartment until then. He had sent her a text with the man's contact number should she need to call him, together with his own emergency number, which was manned by his staff twenty-four seven.

Thx. That was her response.

He couldn't blame her for being abrupt. He was hardly a wordsmith himself. The less said the better, he concluded, remembering his mother's drunken confessions once she had accepted that the man he had called *Papa* would never take them back. He had always thought the embarrassing confidences she had shared with an eight-year-old boy had damaged him for life. He had certainly never shared his

feelings with anyone since. He would never impose that
type of situation on anyone else.

His life had changed overnight at the age of eight. From
having two loving, if distant parents he had become the
sole carer for his alcoholic mother and estranged from his
fathers—both of them—not that there had been any sign
of the handyman who'd spawned him once the gravy train
had crashed and burned.

He glanced at his phone and was tempted to call Cassandra, but he killed that idea. It was better that he stayed
away from her.

And how long was he going to do that?

He smiled as he stretched out naked on the bed. The reaction of his body when he thought about Cassandra said
it wouldn't be too long.

She heard the latch slip on the front door at about the
same time she heard the maid and chef leave—her prison
guards, as she'd come to think of them. In fairness, she had
enjoyed the rest. She'd needed it. Once she'd slowed down
the sickness had gone, just as the doctor had predicted. She
tensed, hearing footsteps approaching. Who else had the
key to the door? It had to be Marco. Her heart was thundering. This was the first time she'd seen him since she'd
settled into his apartment. Feeling self-conscious, having
allowed herself to relax, she quickly finger-combed her
hair and bit some colour into her lips, and was then angry
with herself for being so obvious. She was supposed to
be resting after all.

'Can I come in?'

Why ask when he was already inside the room?

Her heart was hammering so hard she couldn't trust
herself to speak. She wanted to be angry with him for giving her no word of when he'd be back—or *if* he'd be back.

But she was hungry for company—Marco's company—and her heart turned over at the sight of him, though he looked more dark and menacing than ever in his immaculately tailored suit.

And more remote, she thought as he stared at her. They really did come from two different worlds.

'It's not too late, is it?' he enquired crisply.

Much too late, she thought, pressing back against the pillows as he walked deeper into the room. He took her breath away. He was so handsome, so swarthy, so compelling, and yet there was danger in those cold, remote eyes. She was determined not to let him see how forcefully he affected her.

'I think I can stay awake long enough to say hello.' She shrugged, as if having a man like Marco walk into her bedroom didn't put her at a huge disadvantage. She was rumpled, and practically naked in bed, while he looked as if he had just stepped from the pages of a society magazine. Catching the pillow close, she hugged it like a shield. 'I wasn't expecting you tonight.'

'I didn't say when I was coming back,' he conceded.

'Did you have a good trip?'

'Yes, dear,' he said dryly, reminding her that where he went and what he did was nothing to do with her.

She held her breath as he prowled closer. There could be no running away or backing off. And that wasn't in her nature. She had come here of her own free will, with the intention of recovering her health. That was why Marco had brought her here... Or was it? she wondered, seeing the look in his eyes. It was a look she knew she should ignore, but her body thought otherwise. And it wasn't just her body calling out to him. It was her soul, her being, her essence doing that too. Because Marco was the father of her child. He was her mate. And she wanted him. She wanted to be in his arms again. She wanted to be lost with him—one with him.

Her world tilted on its axis as he sat down on the bed. He didn't speak. He didn't need to. He just drew her into his arms.

'Tell me if you don't want this and I'll stop,' he whispered huskily.

She might have pressed her hands against his chest in some sort of weak protest, but there was no force behind it because she did not want to push him away. Whether or not it was pregnancy hormones driving her, the way Marco made her feel couldn't be ignored. It wasn't just the sex or the pleasure he gave her, it was being with him—just being with him and being close to him. There was no one on this earth who could make her feel the way he did.

She helped him to shrug off his jacket and watched as he loosened his tie. Breath shot out of her when he yanked her against his body, and she groaned when his hand slipped through the buttons on her pyjama jacket on its way to cupping her breast. His touch was so familiar, and so long missed. She grabbed a noisy breath, wondering if she would ever breathe normally again.

He set about teasing her senses, his thumbnail lightly abrading her puckered nipples. 'Your breasts are bigger,' he commented with approval as he stripped off the rest of his clothes. 'I like that.'

And he was magnificent. Naked and fully erect, Marco di Fivizzano was a big, rugged man, with none of the city sheen people generally associated with him. This was the man who hefted sandbags and hewed logs. This was the father of her child. And she wanted him—no questions, no criticisms, no complaints—she wanted him in the most primal way possible. She wanted to be one with her mate.

She was not expecting him to hunker down at her side,

let alone that he would place the palm of one hand very gently on her belly. Dipping his head, he replaced his hand with a lingering kiss. She held her breath, but by the time he pulled back he was once again the brooding lover. Still, for that one moment he had been someone else— someone caring. Someone she would want to be the father of her child.

Marco soon distracted her. Burying his face in her breasts, he took her wrists in one big fist and pinned them above her head, and then he used his hands and mouth to drive her to distraction, forcing her to arch her hips towards him in an attempt to catch more contact from him.

'Is this what you want?' he demanded softly as he trailed his fingertips over her body.

'Yes,' she confirmed, shivering with excitement, knowing just how long Marco might be prepared to withhold her pleasure if she didn't answer him.

He eased her pyjama bottoms down and tossed them away, by which time she was going crazy for more and nearly screamed the first time he touched her. He knew exactly what to do. There was no teasing now, just gentle pressure in the right place, and a dependable, stroking rhythm. She had no option but to let go.

'That was so good!' she exclaimed, gasping out the words when the starburst of sensation had dimmed enough for her to speak.

'It seems to me that your healthy approach to life and sex is fully restored,' Marco observed dryly.

'Seems it is,' she agreed.

'Better now?'

'Not yet,' she said quickly.

He smiled. 'More?'

'Please...'

As Marco eased one powerful thigh between her legs

she exclaimed softly in anticipation of more pleasure. She felt so abandoned and exposed, and so deliciously excited. She loved the way he liked to watch. It always increased the level of her arousal. She didn't hold back— she couldn't. She had no reason to, and was still exclaiming in the grip of pleasure when Marco moved over her.

'I'll be gentle,' he promised.

He kept his word, and she discovered how extraordinary this new, gentle sex could be. Marco used it to his advantage as he extended her pleasure for the longest time. She heard him laughing softly when, surprised by her inability to hold on, she wailed with shock and bucked vigorously beneath him. She writhed contentedly, beyond caring now—beyond anything but basking in sensation.

When she finally quieted, he slid slowly into her again and lodging himself deep he rolled his hips so that she lost it again, and then again. Withdrawing with a deliberate lack of haste, he paused, looming over her to stare down. His face was masterful and brooding as he watched her grip his arms and work her body hungrily on his. The last time before she fell asleep was so violent she might as well have been unconscious afterwards, and she only woke when Marco swung off the bed.

'Where are you going?' She reached out a hand to bring him back. She was sated for now, but it was lonely in the big bed without him.

'You need to sleep.' Dipping down to kiss her cheek, he added, 'I do too. I have a lot on tomorrow. But don't worry,' he added dryly, 'I'll be back in the morning to see if you need anything more before I leave.' His sexy mouth curved in a smile as he strolled naked out of the room.

He was so beautiful, and so totally un-self-conscious— and yet so quick to close himself off. Tonight had been wonderful for her, because her emotions had been fully engaged, but what about Marco? Was she just offering him sex on tap?

She suddenly felt shaky and vulnerable, wondering if she had just unwittingly volunteered for the position of Marco di Fivizzano's short-term mistress. What else would his part-time gardener be qualified to do in this billionaire's fast-moving world?

The more she thought about it, the more it seemed that her body's needs had ruled her head. She was living in Marco's apartment of her own free will. She was under his protection. She only had the reverence with which he had kissed her swollen belly to hang on to, but even that had started to worry her. A man like Marco di Fivizzano needed an heir. Was she just his convenient womb?

CHAPTER TEN

THE NEXT MORNING Marco left early, as he'd said he would, and he didn't stop by her room as he had promised.

And why did she want him to? Wasn't it better to try to keep him at a distance as he was keeping her? She didn't know any more...

Pregnancy had turned her brain to mush, Cass concluded. She had never been reliant on anyone but her godmother when she was very young—and had certainly never hung around to see if a man wanted sex before she got out of bed. If she had lost her self-respect to this extent, it was time to turn herself back into someone with a pre-pregnancy brain.

In the short time that she'd been living in Marco's penthouse she had become far too complacent. She'd be cleaning his shoes and running his bath next. She didn't even have morning sickness to use as an excuse any more—so what was she doing letting the days drift by?

Things had to change.

She carried her tray back to the kitchen. Who cared what the unfriendly maid and chef thought of her doing things for herself? She had strong arms and a pair of perfectly capable hands, and she didn't need people to run after her. She thanked the chef for breakfast, and apologised for not finishing it, with the excuse that she had eaten too much at supper the night before.

'But it was delicious,' she said, thanking him.

'Do you need anything else, *signorina*?' the maid asked her.

'Nothing. Thank you.'

She closed the door and then cursed her acute hearing.

'Is there something wrong with my food?' the chef complained.

'She's pregnant,' the maid whispered. 'That's why she can't face food.'

'He's made one pregnant?'

Cass froze, then tensed as they both started to laugh.

'About time too,' the chef declared, forgetting Cass might overhear him, or perhaps not caring if she did. 'A man like that needs an heir.'

Hearing her own thoughts echoed sent a chill down Cass's spine. She stilled as the maid hummed in disapproval.

'I don't know why he picked this one when there are plenty of society women who would oblige him with an heir.'

There was a silence, and then the maid added, 'News like this is worth money.'

Cass had heard enough. It wasn't her business to berate Marco's staff, so she bit her tongue and walked away. She had to believe the chef and the maid would remain loyal to their employer and keep what they knew to themselves. Loyalty in any household was an unspoken rule, surely?

The news about his staff's disloyalty broke while he was in a meeting. His PA texted him so he couldn't be caught out by the reports already appearing online. He remained outwardly impassive, but inwardly he was furious. He was a private man, and he didn't care for his private life to be on anyone's lips. He hadn't wanted that for Cassandra, which was why he'd kept her presence in his penthouse quiet. He had wanted her to have these last few months of pregnancy calmly, and in private. No one should be talking about her, let alone his trusted staff—

Trusted staff?

'My PA selects a short list of potential staff members, and you are supposed to vet them,' he railed at his team of investigators. 'You're supposed to be the best. That's why you get my work. You're fired.' He cut the line when they launched into an excuse that the chef and the maid at the penthouse had been thoroughly checked out but there was no accounting for human nature.

Everyone has a price, he conceded angrily, showing nothing of his mounting fury as he cancelled his next appointment. Why was business so straightforward, and everything to do with Cassandra so complex?

Was he really worried about people talking? Or had he finally been forced to face the fact that life was changing for him? It would never be the same again now there was a child in the equation—a child that was probably his.

Possibly his, he amended.

Now he had to wonder why he could never trust his feelings. Why couldn't he believe Cassandra? Would the past always haunt him?

The staff at the penthouse had been fired by the time he got there, but there was no sign of Cassandra. His heart rate soared as he hunted for her. He checked everywhere, knowing it didn't make sense for her to leave him. Where would she go? She had been recovering her health in Rome, and already looked so much better. He called the cab company—he called every cab company in the city—but no one had taken a young, pregnant, English woman to the airport—or anywhere else, for that matter.

So where was she?

Absentmindedly, he turned on the TV to scan the news as he paced the apartment. The news item shocked him— angered him. It focused on him and Cassandra, picking over the history between them. The shot they used of him made him look like a demon out of hell, unshaven and riding a Harley—God knew where they'd found it. The picture of Cassandra showed an angel, fair of face and sweet of temperament—like a martyr he'd pinned to the stake. The press wasn't just milking the story, they were making a production number out of it. He had to find her before the paparazzi swarmed all over her—

Too late!

The news had moved on from stock photographs to live shots. He didn't hang around to switch off the set. Cassandra was in the park across the road, and the paparazzi were already swarming.

She understood now, Cass thought, shoving her hands in the pockets of her maternity jeans as she marched along with her head down, looking neither to the left nor to the right. This must be how her parents had felt *all* the time, not just some of the time. She had never understood the pressures they'd been under before today. She had only tasted fame briefly—or should that be infamy, she mused, chewing her lip.

The papers had been full of the small child playing amongst discarded syringes and empty bottles, and the internet had a long memory, which the bullies at school had taken full advantage of. Even her godmother hadn't been able to shield her from everything. In her turbulent teenage years, when her hormones had been racing, she had thought differently about her parents' notoriety, imagining it must have been glamorous and wonderful to be surrounded by so much attention all the time.

She could see now that those had been the misguided musings of a hormonal only child, looking back at her mixed-up childhood through a veil of resentment. Her parents had thrown their lives away on drugs and alcohol, but they must have been running scared in a doomed attempt to keep up with failing celebrity. And then that stupid fight that ended with them both dead in the swimming pool. It still bemused her to think that it had been over nothing more important than which of them got the last bottle of beer!

But they must have been under incredible pressure if they'd had to contend with this on a daily basis, she reflected as she glanced back over her shoulder at the following pack. She wasn't easily intimidated, but this frightened her. It was relentless, and if the reporters would chase her in her maternity clothes, looking a fright with her hair bundled up in a knot, they'd have no mercy on anyone. They weren't interested in pretty shots—there was no money in them, she supposed. They were like hyenas, feeding on trouble and misery—hyenas with cameras, shoving them in her face. Microphones, mobile phones, television cameras—even members of the public were joining in with anything they could lay their hands on, and all to have a better look at the pregnant mistress of Marco di Fivizzano—to scrutinise her, to examine every blemish and weakness, so they could expose them to the world. Especially her belly. She almost laughed out loud when one man knelt in front of her to get a shot of it, and then darted around to the side to capture another view.

'This is ridiculous!' she exclaimed, only to be hit by a barrage of questions:

'Do you have a statement?'

'Do you know the sex of the baby?'

'Will you live with Marco when it's born?'

And then, like a miracle, he was there at her side—shielding and protecting her, his strength and power, and sheer presence alone enough to scatter the following pack.

'What the hell are you doing?' he demanded, directing his fury at the paparazzi as he tucked her firmly beneath the protection of his arm.

For once she didn't try to resist him as he marched her away. 'What does it look as if I'm doing? I wanted some fresh air.'

'I can understand that, but why didn't you call me?'

'I didn't want to trouble you,' she admitted. 'And I couldn't stay in the penthouse a moment longer with people who were laughing at me.'

'The staff? They've been fired. That was a misjudgement on my part—I should have checked their references myself.'

'And I shouldn't be so pathetic, but this pregnancy is making me emotional all the time.' She turned around, and was glad to see the reporters falling back. She guessed they weren't too keen to take on Marco in his present mood.

'Do you think your staff at the penthouse did this?' she asked.

'Who else do you think would alert the press?' he said as he flashed his security card at the controls on the private entry system. He held the door for her and then let it slam in the hyenas' faces.

'They said there was money to be made,' she remembered.

'A short-term gain,' Marco rapped crisply, standing back as the elevator doors slid open. 'Neither of them will work in this city again. They'll never be trusted after this.'

'So their blood money will prove a double-edged sword?'

'It will,' he confirmed. 'But I'm only interested in you. Are you okay?'

She glanced up at him, and saw only genuine concern in his eyes. 'The staff reinforced my thoughts on you using me for sex—for a child, for an heir.' Marco's frown deepened. 'I had to get out of the penthouse to clear my head—and it did help, though not in the way I expected. It helped me to understand how my parents must have felt when they were chased everywhere by the paparazzi.'

'This is the first time you have spoken about them.'

'Yes. Like you, I suspect, I've pushed the past behind me for so long it isn't easy to speak about it to anyone. But even all these years after their deaths, I feel guilty.'

'You too,' he murmured.

'I was so unforgiving when I was a teenager. All I could see was that my parents had abandoned me when I was small…' She stopped, noticing how tense Marco had become. 'Did I say something to upset you?'

He didn't speak, but a muscle worked in his jaw. She guessed he felt as she did, that years of practised silence couldn't be undone in one night.

'There's something else,' she said as the elevator doors swung open.

'What?' Marco said.

'I can help you.'

'You can help me?' He stared at her incredulously as the elevator headed for the penthouse floor.

'You don't have time to handle everything, which is how you ended up with those people working in your home—'

'And your suggestion is?' he demanded.

Marco wasn't used to people challenging him. Too bad.

She had something to say and he wasn't going to stop her. It was crucial that he could trust people who worked in his home. 'You must try to hire more people like Maria and Giuseppe. If you'll let me, I'll help you find them.'

When Marco shook his head with amusement, she added, 'Just think how much more effective you'd be if you could delegate more. Maybe you wouldn't be so distant—you could make a start with your staff, and then try the same with me.'

She should take the look he gave her as a warning to back off, but instead, she stared straight back at him.

He had to admire her cheek. After her experience in the park he might have expected Cassandra to be shaken and thinking about no one but herself, but she was always thinking about other people—not that he would allow his feelings to run away with him where she was concerned. 'Are we going to stand outside the door all day?'

'You haven't answered my question,' she reminded him. 'Do you want my help with recruiting staff?'

'There's no need. I will be vetting staff personally in future.'

She cocked her head to one side to stare up at him. 'Would I have made it through your selection process?'

Her question silenced him. He stared at her, realising the answer was probably no.

Was that what made him make one small concession?

'It must be boring for you, sitting around the penthouse all day. You needed to rest, but now you're well enough I can see that you need something to do. I'll ring round tomorrow—make some enquiries about part-time work for you.'

She shook her head. 'That's very kind of you Marco, but there's no need.'

'What do you mean?'

'I rang the embassy. To be more accurate, I rang the ambassador's private number. He gave it to me at the party. I thought about what you said, and I realised that I wouldn't be using him, and that I actually had something to offer him—I'd be giving, not taking. I'd be doing a fair day's work, and I would be prepared to work in the embassy gardens for nothing, though he wouldn't hear of that. He said I would make a very welcome addition to the embassy's gardening team.'

'You've got a job?'

'Yes, Marco. I have.'

His protective instinct flared into life. 'After today's experience, you're happy to go to work each day with the paparazzi shadowing your every move?'

'I thought you were going to ring around to try to get me a job?' Before he could answer, she added, 'And it won't be every day. The work at the embassy is part time.'

'If I had found you a job it would have been different.'

'In what way would it be different?' she challenged.

'I would have made sure of the security first.'

'You know as well as I do that the gardens at the embassy have security so tight I couldn't slip a worm in there unnoticed, let alone a pack of hyenas. This is the perfect solution, Marco. No one will get within a mile of me,' she added confidently.

'You might have told me what you had planned.'

'As you always tell me what you've got planned?'

There was a long silence, and then he said tensely, 'That's not the point.'

'Isn't it? I thought we were equal—or is one of us more equal than the other? I don't have to ask your permission before I do something. Or do I? I really appreciate what you've done for me. I know I wasn't well when I came here, and I know I was too stubborn to admit it back in England, but now I'm well enough to go back to work.'

'You will still need to rest.'

'I don't need to rest. I'm fine. I'll be even better when I'm working outside in a garden again.'

She refused to back down. He loved her fire, but it irked the hell out of him.

'What are you doing, Marco?'

Reaching out, he removed the single clip holding up her hair so that it tumbled in unruly waves around her shoulders.

Gathering it up again, she pinned it firmly back in place.

'Am I supposed to take that a sign?' Marco demanded.

'Yes. A sign that I need fresh air,' she said, staring levelly at him until he stood down.

'What about the roof garden?'

'What about the roof garden? You've never mentioned a roof garden to me. Are you telling me there's a garden here?'

'Let me show you.'

He led the way through the door that took them up via some steps to one of the most magnificent views in Rome.

'Oh, my,' she breathed, so taken aback that for a moment she didn't even notice the carefully laid-out garden and just soaked up the view. 'To think I didn't even know this was here.'

'I should have mentioned it to you,' Marco admitted, 'but I so rarely come up here—'

'And you couldn't wait to get away as soon as we arrived,' she suggested, careful to keep her expression neutral.

'Maybe,' he admitted. 'But now you know it's here, couldn't you keep yourself busy up here?'

'Fill my empty hours, do you mean?' She shrugged.

'This is beautiful, Marco, really beautiful, but it's all planned out—down to the last, carefully manicured square inch. There's nothing here for me to do, except admire—which I do. But I need more than this. I need a proper job.'

'Isn't the baby enough for you?'

'My question is this: will I be enough for the baby if I just sit here idle and wait for our child to arrive?'

Marco flinched a little at her mention of *our* child, and then he turned away to lean his hands on the wall as he stared out across Rome.

'You're never going to accept that I could make life easy for you, are you, Cassandra?'

'I don't want easy. I just want a chance to do the job I love.'

He seemed to understand that. Turning, he reached out his hand to capture a stray lock of hair to tuck behind her ear.

'I could admire you if you weren't so damned annoying,' he admitted.

She huffed wryly and relaxed a little. Perhaps they were both guilty of taking themselves too seriously at times.

'I'll try to be worthy of your admiration, and slightly less annoying,' she promised. And then, for the first time, they shared a smile.

They left the beautiful roof garden, and went down to the main part of the penthouse, where she hovered as Marco prowled the room. Tension grew between them, and threatened to engulf her when Marco came to stand in front of her.

'Come to bed with me, Cassandra.'

Breath hitched in her throat as he stared down at her. She knew that smouldering look in his eyes, and her body was desperate to respond to him. This had nothing to do with pregnancy hormones. She wanted Marco, and not just physically but with every yearning, aching part of her soul.

Leaning forward, he brushed her lips with his.

Several seconds passed. It was as if time stood still in those potent, charged moments. Resting her hands on Marco's arms, she allowed him to back her towards his bedroom.

Putting his arm around her shoulders, he shut the door behind them, and then he worked on the buttons of her shirt and let it fall. Cupping her breasts, he dipped his head to suckle through the fine lace of her bra, and then he unhooked it and disposed of that too. Lowering her unflattering maternity jeans carefully over the swell of her belly and her hips, he helped her step out of them. Taking hold of her hand, he led her towards the bed, and pushing the bedclothes out of the way he lowered her gently onto the pillows.

'Turn on your side,' he instructed, 'and wait for me.'

She watched him undress and felt her arousal grow. Marco's back rippled with muscle as he moved. His entire body was a work of brutal masculine art. She could hardly breathe for excitement by the time he joined her on the bed.

Stretching out his length behind her, he rested his hand in the small of her back. She responded immediately, and arching her back she waited in tingling anticipation for his first touch.

Having arranged her to his satisfaction, Marco took hold of her and gently parting her legs he slipped the tip of his erection inside her until he was sure she was relaxed. Then he sank deep. He hardly needed to move at all as her hunger took over. Working with ever-increasing intent, she used him shamelessly.

'Nice?' he enquired softly when, after the longest time, she was quiet again.

'Very nice,' she confirmed groggily, smiling into the pillow.

'Again?'

'Oh, I think so, don't you?'

They made love so many times she lost count, and each time was better than the last. She drifted off to sleep, safe in Marco's arms, and woke to find him making love to her again.

'How do you do that?' she muttered, still half-asleep.

He hushed her and continued to move steadily back and forth.

She remained quiescent and silent, the grateful recipient of pleasure, with no effort required from her at all. She had no argument with that, not when this was turning out to be the most incredible experience of her life. Just the thought of Marco doing what he was doing, and so skilfully, was enough to make her lose control. As sensation claimed her, she cried out his name, and clutching the pillow in a vice-like grip she gave her body over to violent convulsions of pleasure. And when she was quiet, Marco started all over again.

Sex wasn't an end in itself, she knew that as well as anyone. But until a solution could be found to their situation, it was the one thing that brought them as close as this.

CHAPTER ELEVEN

CASS'S WORK AT the embassy gardens was turning out even better than she had hoped. She was smiling when she returned to the penthouse at the thought that she loved everyone she worked with, and was even picking up the language. Working with the plants she loved, with her hands in soil and her head in a better place, she could even start to think of the penthouse as home—at least, for now—and then without dwelling too much on what would happen in the future.

One thing was sure. She loved her baby already, and she would do everything in her power to give her child the best life possible. Two things were sure, Cass amended as she caught sight of her passport in her bag. She had made up her mind to return to England for the birth. She couldn't risk the uncertainty of staying in Italy, if only because Marco seemed to be working harder than ever. He was either trying to avoid getting in too deep, in an emotional sense, or maybe he was trying to exorcise his own demons. Either way, their child would be born soon, and she was determined that her baby's future would be stable, unlike her own as a child.

Marco had been away on business for the past few days, and was due back tonight. The thought thrilled her, even as it made her more determined than ever to pin him down and explain what her plans were. Time was running out on her pregnancy, and he had to face the future. It was a future she hoped they would share with their child, even if Marco and she lived in different countries.

She hadn't been idle while he'd been away. As well as her job at the embassy, she had interviewed new staff for the penthouse. She wanted to earn her keep. She wanted Marco to know that she wasn't waiting for him to do everything.

She also had to tell him that she was well enough to go home, and though she was grateful to him for allowing her to recover here in Rome, her mind was made up to return to England.

Tears pricked the back of her eyes at the thought of leaving him. She was falling in love with him, Cass realised as she brushed her hair.

There were no if, buts or maybes. She had fallen in love, and with a very complex man who was coming home tonight, so she would leave her hair loose…for him.

Marco looked exhausted when he walked through the door. He also looked gloriously striking in a navy suit so dark it was almost as black as his eyes. His crisp white shirt was open at the neck and his stylish silk tie was hanging loose. She didn't need him to tell her that it had been a hard trip. His hair was ruffled, his stubble was thick, and his frown was so deep she knew he'd had a difficult time, though his face lit up at the sight of her.

'*Cara mia*, you look beautiful.'

It was the first time that Marco had called her *his*. Instead of resenting this, she found she liked it, and perhaps more than she should have done, bearing in mind what she had to say to him. She was an independent woman, but she liked the sense of belonging, as well as the feeling that she wasn't alone. The 'beautiful' she'd take with a pinch of salt. She knew she wasn't beautiful. The mirror told her that every day. She was bloated and heavy, and—

She turned her attention back to Marco. 'You look wiped out. Can I get you a drink?'

He smiled and shrugged. 'I should be looking after you, *cara*.'

'Okay, then.' She grinned. 'We can take turns.'

He prowled towards her until she was backed up against the wall.

'Does this bring back memories?' he asked, staring down at her with the faintest of smiles on his dark, brooding face.

'A few,' she admitted. She longed for him to kiss her. She wanted to feel his hard body pressed against hers...

'What about this?' he murmured, scraping her sensitive skin with his stubble as he scorched a trail of almost kisses down her neck.

'A few more memories seem to be returning,' she conceded wryly.

'How about this?'

She closed her eyes and exhaled shakily as Marco's big hands captured her breasts.

'You have the most magnificent breasts, Cassandra.'

'And you haven't closed the front door.'

He put his foot to it. 'Better now?'

As he was cupping her between the legs as he asked the question, her answer could only be a shaky 'Not quite yet...'

She looked up and knew Marco could see the heat in her eyes.

'Is there anything I can do to improve the situation for you?' he asked.

'There might be,' she conceded.

Moving his hands to cup her face, he dipped his head and kissed her…very gently. It was a tender kiss of a type they'd never shared before, and it fired every nerve ending in her body.

'The bedroom?' he suggested with a shrug, pulling back.

'If you think that's best,' she whispered.

'In your condition, banging you against the wall probably isn't advisable,' he pointed out. 'Try not to look quite so disappointed. I promise to make up for it with something you'll like just as much.'

'Are you sure?' she challenged in a whisper.

'I'm certain of it.'

She gasped as he swung her into his arms.

'You'll have to wait while I take a shower,' he said with reluctance as he lowered her down at the side of the bed.

'That long?' she complained.

Marco's eyes were full of wicked promise, and she was breathless with excitement by the time he sauntered back. Drying his thick, wavy black hair on one towel, he had another looped around his waist. His torso was staggering. Bronzed and muscular, she wondered if she would ever get enough of looking at it.

Marco only had to catch her glance to be instantly aroused, and as he prowled towards her all she could think about was pleasure. He knew just what she needed, and his appetite matched hers. Her glance dropped to his mouth. She had never experienced anything like this all-consuming hunger. She was quivering with excitement as he came to stand in front of her. His thick hair was still curling damply and catching on his stubble. She smiled a little to see he hadn't shaved.

Drawing her into his arms, he kissed her neck. And then, putting his arms around her, he moved with her to some silent music. Then he turned her so she had her back to him, and looping his arms around what was left of her waist he whispered into her ear, 'I love this position with your back to me—it's perfect for making love when you're pregnant.'

'Perfect when I'm not pregnant too,' she replied.

She could feel his hard need pressing into her. It only made her hungrier for him than ever. Arching her back, she invited him to take full advantage of her pregnancy-fuelled, wild-for-sex body, and then she rolled her hips against him.

Marco brought her down on the bed beside him. 'I need this,' he groaned, sinking into her.

'Me too,' she gasped out, holding onto him as her breathing quickened.

Marco braced himself on his forearms to keep his weight off her as he stared down. That look in his eyes was enough to break her apart.

'I guessed you needed that too,' he teased her as her violent release shattered her thought processes into a starburst of light.

'More?' he asked as she writhed beneath him.

He turned her on her side the way she liked, and whispered, 'You're going to bend your knees while I sink slowly into you, and I'm going to touch you at the same time.'

His hand had barely found its destination before she greedily claimed her next release.

'I think you like that,' he murmured. Resting his chin on her back, he waited as she dragged in some noisy breaths.

'Definitely,' she confirmed.

'Are you ready for more?'

Marco only had to rest his hand in the small of her back for her to lift her buttocks so he could cup them and slowly take her again. Moving to a steady and dependable beat, he worked her with his hand at the same time, steering her unerringly into her fiercest climax yet.

Cassandra was sleeping so heavily he decided to make her breakfast in bed. She should rest—wasn't he always telling her that? He should tell himself that—he'd kept her up half the night. He couldn't get enough of her. He'd never felt like this before—had never made love to a woman all night and woken her up in the morning by making love to her. Hell, he'd never cooked a woman breakfast before— not since he had tried to coax his mother to eat in the latter stages of her alcoholism, a thought that shattered his current idyll.

The priest who had buried his mother had seen to it that he had a roof over his head and had gone to school with enough food in his belly to keep him going for the day. The orphanage had been a chilling experience, but he'd survived that too. There was nothing in this world he couldn't overcome—with the exception of his feelings for Cassandra.

But he couldn't offer her anything more than this, he mused as he backed his way into the bedroom. He'd been dead inside for far too long to make any form of commitment, and he would never lead Cassandra on.

She woke slowly and smiled with her face still pressed against the pillow as he carried her breakfast tray into the room.

'You made me breakfast!' she exclaimed with pleasure.

Pressing his lips down, he shrugged. 'It's in my best interests to keep your strength up.'

'Stop acting tough, Marco. Even if you're joking, I know you're kinder than you make out. You've got a whole bank of feelings inside you, but you're like a miser afraid to dip into them.'

'Afraid?' he queried, already tensing in preparation for retreating into himself as he put the tray down.

'I know. You're not afraid of anything…except what's inside you,' she said, losing her smile. 'And we all have demons in the past to fight.'

'I don't know what you mean.'

She stared at him for a moment, and then she held out her hand. 'Come here…'

'I have to go to work…'

'Please,' she insisted. 'Give me your hand.'

He frowned, but he did as she asked.

Taking it, she guided it beneath the bedclothes. 'Can you feel him? Your son is saying hello.'

'My—' He recoiled, but she caught hold of his hand, and with more strength than he had guessed she possessed she brought his hand back again and made him rest it on her swollen belly.

'Don't be frightened,' she whispered. 'We're both new at this. Babies don't come with a manual, and I don't want you to miss out on a single thing.'

He'd weakened once before and kissed her belly. He had survived that. The miracle of life was something even he couldn't resist. He calmed his breathing and stilled, and then he felt it…he felt the little pulse of life, trying to kick his hand away.

'*Dio!* I can feel him.' His eyes were full of wonder as he turned to look at her. 'That's your baby!'

Cassandra looked at him steadily for a good few moments and then she said, 'That's our child.'

There was so much she wanted to say to Marco. She wanted to reach out to him in a way that would break through all his issues, but before she could do that he had to trust her...trust her enough to tell her what had made him this way.

'Marco?'

He was heading at speed for the door, and looked stricken. Yet she knew he'd had that same moment of wonder and bliss that she had experienced when she had felt their child kicking her for the first time. What was it about this baby that frightened Marco? What had rocked the foundations of his world? If his only concern was that her baby was his, he could resolve that with a test. She suspected it was something more than that—something so devastating that it had shaped Marco's life. She wanted to know what that was, so she could help him.

These thoughts plagued her, though she went on to have a productive day. She had been allowed to redesign a tiny portion of the embassy garden, and hadn't realised how late it was when she finally finished up. Marco's driver, an elderly man called Paolo, was waiting for her. Paolo was full of courtly charm and he insisted on seeing her to the door of the penthouse. It was while they were travelling up in the elevator that he offered her a small insight into Marco's past.

'He's a good man,' Paolo said, turning to face her. 'I used to work for his father, you know? Bad business, that.'

'His father?' She was instantly alert, but Paolo had already tensed, as if he knew he'd said too much. 'You used to work for Marco's father?' she repeated. She had to try and prompt more out of him.

'Yes,' Paolo offered, saying no more.

'So, how did you come to work for Marco?' she pressed.

Paolo thought about this for a moment, as if he were weighing his loyalty to both men.

'I drove Marco to his father's funeral,' Paolo revealed at last. 'He wanted to show his respect to a man who had never shown him any, especially when Marco was a child and had needed it most. I have worked for Marco ever since.'

'Thank you. Thank you for telling me that.'

Before she could stop herself she had leaned into a hug. Paolo was surprised, but he was Italian so he understood big emotions.

'I'm sorry I can't tell you more,' he added with a shrug. 'I don't think I'm breaking any confidences if I tell you that Marco's father was a difficult man. We were never close, as I am with Marco. But I am a loyal man, and I've already said too much.'

'I understand, and I shouldn't have asked you.' But she was glad she had.

'You should have some rest now,' Paolo advised as the elevator doors slid open on the penthouse floor. 'You must be careful not to overdo things at this stage of pregnancy.'

Paolo saw her safely inside, and when she had closed the door behind her she leaned back against it and cradled her growing bump. There was so much more she wanted to know about Marco, but at least Paolo had helped her to take the first step. She could only hope that one day Marco might trust her enough to tell her the rest.

She decided to stay up until he came home, and try, for Marco's sake, to coax him into telling her more.

CHAPTER TWELVE

HE ARRIVED BACK at the penthouse after midnight, having stayed out deliberately in an attempt to analyse his feelings. Cassandra would be asleep when he got back. He didn't want to talk to her, brain-weary after work, having felt the baby kick back at him. It had shaken him too much for that. Feeling that little life beneath his hands had made it all too real. In a few months' time Cassandra would be a mother, and he...

He couldn't be sure of anything yet. Denied the certainty of parenthood, he was condemned to wait in limbo. And he wasn't sure he wanted to be a father, much less sure that he was equal to the task. He didn't have time for a child. He wasn't programmed to enjoy a traditional family life. What sort of example could he draw on? And what made him think he could do any better than the man who had disowned him, or the blood father who had never wanted to know him in the first place? He wasn't such an egotist that he imagined he'd got everything covered, including parenthood. And he couldn't treat Cassandra as if she were just another business deal to be dealt with and then a line drawn under her. He needed more time.

'Marco?'

'You're still up?'

'I waited up for you.'

She was propped up on the bed, where she had been dozing with her head on a cushion. She looked very young, very pregnant and very vulnerable. He crossed the room and dropped a kiss on her cheek. 'You should have gone to sleep, *carissima*.'

'I couldn't sleep. I had to talk to you.'

'What about?' He frowned and straightened up.

'Your past,' she said frankly. 'I want to understand you, and I can't do that unless you open up.'

Standing up, he put distance between them. All the warmth that had been so briefly between them had evaporated, as far as he was concerned. No one intruded into his past.

'The baby,' she said quietly. 'Our child gives me the right to know more about you.' She paused when he huffed. 'If you'd explain why feelings frighten you—'

He spun around on his heel to pierce her with a stare. 'I have no fear.'

'Believe me Marco, I understand—'

'You understand nothing.'

She remained silent for a moment and then, completely undaunted by his harsh tone, she said, 'Tell me about your father.'

'Which one?' he flashed, incapable of caring if he hurt her now. She had found his wound and had twisted a knife in it.

The expression on his face must have frightened her, as she pressed back on her seat, but he couldn't stop now. 'The man I called father disowned me, along with my mother. He threw us both out on the street when he discovered that I wasn't his child. He did that on Christmas Eve,' he added bitterly.

Cassandra had turned ashen and looked horrified.

He should have known she wouldn't leave it there.

'And your mother?' she pressed. 'What happened to her?'

The look he gave her would have warned anyone else to back off, but not Cassandra.

'You mother, Marco,' she pressed him again.

'She died when I was a boy,' he said quickly, wanting to gloss over it. His mother's death in poverty and squalor was something he preferred not to dwell on. He could never think back without feeling guilty, as if an eight-year-old boy could have somehow saved the situation.

'And you?' Cassandra queried. 'What happened to you when your mother died?'

His lips felt wooden as he thought back. 'I went to live in an orphanage.'

She was silent and then she said, 'What about your real father?'

He laughed bitterly. 'My *real* father? He had no interest in me. When the money tree shrivelled and died, he was gone.'

Cass was shocked into silence. What Marco had told her made her heart ache for a small child who had grown up thinking that he could never hold onto love. But she knew there was more, and even a tiny seed of bitter memory could grow if she didn't root it out.

'Why did the man you called father disown you? Didn't he love you?'

'Who knows?' Marco's keen stare grew unfocused as he stared blindly into the middle distance. 'Maybe he did love me at one time. I thought he did, but once he knew the truth of my parentage he changed towards me. The child went with the mother, he said, and that's all I know. That was how he insisted it must be. Paolo told me that he never forgave himself, that he was a changed man after that, and that it was the shock of my mother's adultery that

had unbalanced him that night—that and the way she had
tried all those years to pass me off as his child. He regretted what he'd done to the day he died, Paolo said, but he
was too proud to go back on his word.'

'Oh, Marco.' There were no words to console him; only
love over a long period of time could do that, and now they
had to talk about the future, and Marco's child with her.

For the first time she put her hands flat against his chest
when he tried to sweep her into his arms. 'No, Marco. We
have to talk.'

'Talk?' He frowned. 'What about?'

'About the future, of course.'

'What future, *cara*?'

His words cut her to the heart, but she carried on. 'I
can't stay in Rome for ever.'

'For another three months?' Marco shrugged. 'I thought
you were happy.'

'I am happy, and I love my job at the embassy, but I
have to look forward to when the baby's born.'

Marco's lips pressed down as he shook his head, as if
he couldn't understand her concern. 'You've got nothing
to worry about,' he said as he shrugged out of his shirt.
'Not tonight, at least,' he insisted when she shifted position fretfully on the bed. 'You're tired. I'm tired—'

'But we can't just let things continue,' she said. Sitting
up, she searched his eyes for some flicker of reaction to
this, but all she could see was heat.

'Why can't we?' Marco demanded, smiling darkly as
he move to drop kisses on her lips. 'Everything's perfect,
Cassandra.'

'Perfect?' she said.

'Sleep now,' he soothed. 'I'm going to take a shower
and then I'll join you in bed.'

He closed the bathroom door with relief. He didn't want

this conversation about the future until the baby was born and he could be sure he was the father. Talking about the past had brought everything back to him, and he would never subject a child to the experience he'd had. Yes, he had brought Cass to Rome to keep an eye on what might well turn out to be his unborn heir. He would claim the child if it was his, and he would provide for it financially. But emotionally? That was a step too far for him.

He came back after his shower to find Cassandra still propped up on the pillows, still waiting to talk to him. He might have known she wouldn't give up, but while he admired her perseverance, his answer hadn't changed.

'After what you told me tonight, Marco, I know how hard this must be for you.'

'You don't know anything,' he said, tossing his towel on a chair.

He hadn't meant to shout at her, but the past was his alone to deal with. It was a wound he showed no one, and he'd been careless tonight.

He felt guiltier than ever as Cassandra, pregnancy-heavy and clumsy, struggled off the bed. 'No,' she said, shaking her head at him. 'You can't avoid the past, Marco. It's made us both what we are, and you and I have to face up to that. I can't even imagine how terrible it must have been for you to be thrown out by the man you thought was your father. To be rejected like that on top of everything else must have been terrible for you, but if you keep on pushing people away because you're worried they might do the same to you you'll barely live…you'll only exist. You'll never know the pleasure of true friendship, let alone love. We're in this together, Marco, whether you like it or not.' She drew his glance down as she cradled her stomach. 'This is your baby as much as mine, and I have to know what I'm getting into—what the future holds for all three of us. This isn't all about you,' she said angrily, when he shook his head and turned away.

'I never thought it was all about me,' he said as he turned back to face her. 'I just can't see how my past affects you, or any of this—'

'Then you're blind,' she flashed. 'This is a baby, Marco, a precious life, so don't you ever refer to our child again in such a dismissive way. Your past has *everything* to do with the way you're reacting. Your past is the reason you can't trust me—it's the reason you keep backing away from believing that I'm carrying your child. You're horrified by the prospect of a rerun of your own childhood. Even when the child is proved to be yours, you're still going to wonder if you can be any better than the man you called father—the man who deserted you, and your blood father who never cared about you.

'Well, here's some news for you—I don't know what kind of mother I'm going to be. I didn't exactly have the best of starts, but unlike you I'm not running away from my feelings. I'm going to do the best I can for my child— and if that's not up to your high standards, tough! If it's not good enough for my child, I'll up my game—and I won't stop upping my game until I get it right.'

'You don't understand—'

'Oh, yes I do,' she argued firmly. 'I know you care. I know that, however hard you try to hide it, you care for me, and for our baby, and I know you'll do anything you can to protect our child from the type of rejection that you experienced. I know you're a good man—'

'Don't make me out to be some sort of saint, because I'm not. Even if the baby is mine, I don't have the capacity to love a child.'

'The capacity?' she queried incredulously. 'This is the first time I've ever heard of love having limits, or a heart having boundaries. Your heart will expand to include the new baby, and your love will grow.'

Angry and frustrated at a situation he had no control over, he thumped his chest. 'How can I do any of those things when I feel nothing?' Cassandra had asked him for reassurance he was unable to give her.

'I do know this,' she insisted fiercely. 'We can't go on as we are.'

'Why? What's so bad about it?' he demanded. 'You've got a great job that you love, and you live in one of the most beautiful apartments in Rome—'

'My prison cell, with a man who feels nothing?'

Her sad laugh chilled him. He was suddenly conscious of how close he'd come to destroying the vigorous, spirited girl.

'My life here isn't real,' she said in a quiet voice that disturbed him more than Cassandra's anger ever could. 'It's play-acting.'

'It seems real to me.'

'That's because nothing's changed for you, Marco.'

He forced out a short laugh, but Cassandra had distanced herself from emotion and was calmly evaluating things as she saw them. 'Yes, I live here in your fabulous penthouse, and I challenge you with difficult questions you don't want to answer, but we're not close—not really. It takes two people to be close, Marco, and I am more of a convenience for you than anything else. You have sex on tap,' she explained with a small grimace.

'I haven't noticed you complaining. What's your point, Cassandra?'

'That I'm in a holding pattern here until the baby's born.'

'Like every other woman who's expecting a baby,' he pointed out.

'Every other pregnant woman can make plans for when

her baby's born, but I can't,' she explained. 'This isn't real life and I'm not living in a real home. I'm living in someone else's home—your home, your penthouse, which is more like a luxury hotel.' She glanced around. 'You keep nothing personal here. There's no clutter, no mess. What happens when I bring the baby home? Where will you hold your grand receptions then?'

'That should be the least of your worries.'

She wasn't listening. 'Or will I come back here at all?' she said frowning. 'Where *will* I go when I've had the baby?' Her troubled gaze met his. 'What's going to happen, Marco? If I don't take control I'll never know. We haven't even talked about it. You've just blanked out the future, as if it will never come.'

'Stop,' he murmured, drawing her into his arms. 'You're upsetting yourself and the baby...'

'Yes. You're right,' she agreed, moving out of his embrace. 'I should rest—for the baby, not for you.'

Swinging out of bed the next morning, Cass threw back the curtains on another glorious Roman day...the day when she finally came to her senses. However much she wanted to be with Marco, it was time to face the truth: their affair was going nowhere. The light bulb hadn't just gone on in her head, it had dazzled her. There was no more time left to waste on daydreams. She had to make firm plans. If Marco didn't want to be part of them, so be it. If she wanted change, she had to change things. If Marco wouldn't make time to talk to her about the future when they were together at the penthouse, then she would just have to chase him down and make him have that face-to-face talk.

Picking up the phone, she called him at the office. Predictably, he was in a meeting. She left a message, asking for him to call her back, but when she heard nothing in the next hour she firmed up her plans to make her next move.

It wasn't easy to make this decision. She had never pretended to be the bravest person on earth, but Marco had to listen to her.

Dressing discreetly, she called Paolo to ask him for a lift to Marco's office. She wasn't setting out to deliberately embarrass Marco in front of his staff, but as their affair was hardly a secret, her appearance surely wouldn't cause much of a stir.

She lost a little bit of her confidence when the car drew up and she gazed at Marco's gleaming white office building. Her mouth dried when she saw the discreet sign for Fivizzano Industries. It didn't have to be a big sign when Marco's impressive building took up half the block.

CHAPTER THIRTEEN

HE COULDN'T HAVE been more surprised when his secretary told him who was waiting to see him in the outer office. Cursing softly beneath his breath, he wondered what the hell Cassandra thought she was doing. What was so urgent she couldn't have spoken to him at home?

He stood as she entered the room.

Marco looked so menacing, framed against the window with the light behind him.

She refused to be intimidated, though his svelte, blonde secretary had made a point of reminding him that he had another appointment in ten minutes. Was that the usual drill for females who turned up unexpectedly, or was she getting special treatment for being pregnant?

'Cassandra.'

'Marco.'

'Why are you here?'

'May I sit down?'

'Of course.'

Immediately, he was thrown, she noticed, but his good manners came into play. She could only pray they would last.

They didn't.

'What do you want?' he asked sharply, all the veneer of

the gracious Italian lover gone now he was over the shock of seeing her there.

'It's important that I speak to you, Marco.'

'You had to come to the office to speak to me?' he demanded with no warmth in his voice at all. 'We live in the same apartment,' he pointed out in the same cold tone.

'Where you avoid speaking to me every chance you get.'

'I spend more time with you than anyone else.'

Yes. In bed. Her cheeks flamed red as Marco's impassive stare levelled on her face.

'True. But we still haven't talked about the future.'

'That again?'

'Yes, Marco. That again.' She stood to confront him.

This wasn't the young girl he had first met in Tuscany but a lioness defending her cub, he reflected as Cassandra folded slender hands across her stomach. She was so different from any woman he'd ever known that he was thrown for a moment, and when his secretary knocked discreetly on the door to remind him about his 'fictional' next appointment, he was quite curt with her. 'No more interruptions, please. Hold all calls until further notice.'

'Yes, sir.'

His secretary closed the door behind her with exaggerated care—in response to the tension in the room, he guessed.

'Well?' he prompted, fixing his gaze on Cassandra.

'It's time I went home.'

He turned to look out of the window, knowing that if any other woman had said that to him he would be feeling relieved round about now. He felt anything but relieved.

'Why?' he demanded softly.

'Your attitude towards the future tells me that I must plan for the long term,' Cassandra insisted, trying for calm and ending up impassioned—those pregnancy hormones raging again, he suspected. 'And while you seem to think that my living at your apartment as a guest is fine, I want to have a proper home to bring my baby back to—and that means going back to England. This isn't an impulsive decision, or something you can put down to my hormones racing.' He said nothing. 'It's the sensible thing to do. I have to go soon, or I won't be allowed to fly—plus I need to get things ready for the baby while I can still get around.'

'You seem to have it all worked out.' He felt stung, insulted, discarded, superfluous to requirements. He was the one who made decisions. Other people carried them out. Not the other way around.

'I can't just mark time here until the birth,' she insisted, 'or face a blank, uncertain future. I have to get organised.'

He placed a call. 'Signorina Rich is ready to leave, Paolo. Front entrance? Yes. Thank you.'

Replacing the phone in its holder, he met Cassandra's shocked gaze. 'I have only ever wanted what's right for you, Cassandra.'

Cold, unfeeling bastard. She was right to leave. And the sooner the better!

She was in a state of shock as she followed Marco's ice-cool secretary to the bank of elevators. More so when the woman remained at her side until Cass stepped in and the doors slid to. Was she checking that she'd gone? Was she going to report back to her stone-hearted master that the mission had been accomplished, and another woman who hadn't taken the hint soon enough had finally departed?

She was overreacting, Cass accepted as she pressed her back against the cold steel wall. This was what she had wanted. It was what she'd come here to tell him—that she was going home and he couldn't stop her. Stop her? Marco had practically kicked her out!

She was overreacting again, Cass told herself firmly. It was those pregnancy hormones at work again. That was why she was biting back tears. She had expected more of him—she had expected some real emotion, when she should have remembered that Marco di Fivizzano could feel none. She was beginning to wonder if it would be better to cut all ties. Marco was such a frightening contradiction, and she couldn't be certain that he would ever be anything else. He was so tender and loving one moment and so completely detached and unfeeling the next.

The drive back to the penthouse was swift. The traffic was unusually light. She was feeling better, more composed and ready for the next stage in her life, unaware that a second shock was waiting for her. The first thing she noticed when she walked through the door was her battered old suitcase standing in the hallway. Waves of ice lapped over her as she walked up to it and tested the weight. Someone had packed it for her. The maid, she supposed. Marco must have rung from the office. He had wanted her gone before he returned home.

For some reason, her gaze flashed to the hall table, where once he'd left her a cheque. Her heart gripped tight when she saw the message waiting for her. It wasn't in Marco's hand. He must have dictated it to the maid. It was certainly brief and to the point:

'Call me at the office when you're ready to leave. My jet's fuelled up ready to take you home. Marco.'

She leaned back against the wall and slowly slid to the floor. She should have known how easily Marco could detach himself. It was too late to think about all the things she had wanted to say to him—there wouldn't be a chance for that now.

Why had she wasted the opportunity at his office to tell him that she would never shut him out, and that when the baby was born he could visit them at any time? She glanced at the suitcase, knowing that she would still call him when the birth was imminent, and even before that, to reassure him that she had enough money saved to support both herself and her baby until she could get a job. She had wanted to tell him about the wonderful crèche and primary school in her village. More than anything, she had wanted to tell Marco that she loved him. Regardless of what he thought of her, or what he was capable of feeling for her, she had wanted to tell him that.

Resting her face on her knees, she folded her arms over her head, as if that could shut out the world. Deep down, she knew it was too late. Marco had released his cold, empty side, and there would be no going back for him. She should have known that for a man who had achieved so much in life, Marco was hardly likely to allow any situation to stagnate, and that once he understood that she wanted more than he could give her, he had moved remorselessly forward, leaving her behind in his turbulent wake. That didn't stop her loving him, or recollecting every single time he'd been warm, or funny, or sexy, or tender towards her. Love really did have no boundaries, she reflected as she clambered awkwardly to her feet.

She had a shower and found some clean clothes in the case. She called his office, but the same icy secretary took her call and assured her that she would pass a message on.

Cutting the call, she told herself that her leaving was the right decision for both of them. Marco belonged in Rome and she couldn't stay with him, like a brood mare waiting to foal.

But if this were the right decision, why did she feel so empty?

Because there were no certainties in life, and because Marco had consistently refused to discuss the future. Of course she felt empty. She had no idea if she would ever see him again, but she was starting over and that was a good thing. The past had taken a bite out of them both, making it impossible to have a future going forward together. When their baby was born they would come to an agreement, but where their personal relationship was concerned...

There was no personal relationship, except in her head. She had been trying to get Marco to commit to a future he wanted no part of. It wasn't like her to admit defeat, but this time she might have to. She doubted Marco would want any sort of life with her away from the privacy of his penthouse. He was probably glad she was going home. He could get on with his life now. She would call the head of the gardening team she had so much enjoyed being part of at the embassy in Rome on her way to the airport, and she would write to Maria and Giuseppe.

She froze as the front door swung open, but, as she should have known, it wasn't Marco but his driver, Paolo.

'Are you ready?' Paolo asked with his usual warmth as he reached for her case.

'Yes. Thank you.' She took one last look around the echoing penthouse and wondered if she had ever felt so empty in her life, though Marco had done everything she'd asked for. He'd set her free so she could cut all ties with him for good.

He stood and watched the jet take off. He watched it until it had disappeared behind a cloud. He never stood watching people fly away. He had neither the time for it nor the inclination. But flying home was the right thing for Cassandra to do. It was right for both of them.

So why did it feel so wrong?

It was a swipe against his male pride? No woman had ever left him before, but Cassandra had made it quite clear that she wasn't happy living with him in Rome.

Cassandra was different. She was pregnant, maybe with his child. That thought haunted him as he cut a path through the bustling terminal building. She would need consistent health care leading up to the birth, he reasoned, and she was right about getting on with her plans for the future.

Plans from which he was excluded.

Plans that he wanted no part of—not until he was sure. In the meantime, his people would watch her.

Was a second-hand report good enough for him?

It would have to be.

'No comment!' he snarled as the clustering paparazzi hounded him to the door.

Anticipating the fuss he'd create, Paolo had the car waiting for him with the engine running. He jumped in and they roared away. He glanced at the sky in the direction Cassandra's jet had taken. He had never felt so conflicted. When she gave birth a simple DNA test would tell him everything he needed to know. No one, not even Cassandra, could bounce him into making a commitment, and even a positive DNA test didn't point to a future where he committed his emotions to Cass and the baby. Financially, yes. She would have every support. But emotionally...

He wouldn't have long to wait for the answer, and he would be fully occupied in the meantime with his work. His people would inform him if a problem occurred. This was the end of his personal involvement with Cassandra Rich.

He tossed this reasoning back and forth, trying to convince himself that he believed it, until he walked into an empty apartment, and for the first time in his life he experienced loneliness. The penthouse was too big for him. It was empty and impersonal. Why hadn't he noticed this before? He found himself wandering from room to room, searching for something of Cassandra's to hold, to keep... and, yes, to cherish. He should have remembered how meticulous she was. For a healthy, vigorous and very physical woman, she had the organised mind of a scholar. But she was quirky too, he remembered, slanting a smile as he walked to the window to stare up at the sky, and there were moments when she could be adorably messy. Basically, she was down-to-earth and natural. She was also unpredictable, cheeky and confrontational. She was a strong woman. She had wanted to go, and she had left him. She was Cassandra.

He turned full circle slowly in the hope of spotting something she'd left. Had he found a scarf that she'd worn wrapped around her neck, he would have brought it to his face and inhaled deeply in the hope of catching a hint of her scent...

But there was nothing, and he finally gave up. The penthouse unsettled him. It was far too quiet. He turned on his music. He loved music, and this particular piece of low-key jazz usually soothed him, but today it irritated him, because it reminded him of the dance he'd enjoyed with Cassandra. Switching it off, he flopped down on the sofa and reached for that day's untouched newspaper. Leafing through the pages, he barely glanced at them, and was about to toss it aside when he saw a picture that stopped him. A chain of popular low-cost fashion stores had copied the dress Cassandra had worn for the charity event. Just to rub salt in the wound, it appeared under the heading 'Cheap and Cheerful', next to a shot of Cassandra entering the building looking absolutely stunning.

The heading over Cassandra's picture read: 'The Billion-Dollar Babe Version'. There was a snarky piece beneath about the heights that could be achieved by an ambitious woman, who, if she had only known it, could have looked just as good in the chain-store version of the dress without compromising her principles.

Tossing the paper aside, he closed his eyes, and for the first time he was glad that Cassandra had left Rome, so she could escape the vitriol that went with being with him.

He could still remember the shock he'd felt when he had first seen her in that dress. Her transformation had been complete—from no-nonsense girl into a unique and very beautiful woman. From there it had been inevitable that he would remember the sex—the furious sex—the sex she had enjoyed as much as he had. He'd never known anything like it, and doubted she had. It was quite possible that a child had been conceived that night. They had certainly given it their best shot. He had never been so reckless...

With a sound of self-disgust, he sprang up and headed off to bed. Much good that did him. Everything reminded him of Cassandra—his bedroom, the bed, the shower. Was there anywhere in the penthouse they hadn't made love?

Would he ever be rid of her ghost?

Did he want to be?

He didn't sleep. He paced for half the night and dozed fitfully for the rest of the time, and all of it with his mind full of Cassandra. At first light he rang his people to make sure she had arrived safely. They reassured him that she had. He cut the call and looked around, knowing that this was his life now. This was his lonely, bitter life.

CHAPTER FOURTEEN

ONE THING FOLLOWED ANOTHER. It was as if fate was conspiring against him. His workload had never been heavier, and when it became necessary for him to visit the UK to get an overview of some properties he was considering buying, he was conflicted. He had been trying to keep his distance from Cassandra. They didn't have a future together, and it was kinder to them both if he avoided relighting old flames. That she took second billing to his work seemed cold and contrived, even to him, but as things stood, it was the best he could manage.

Cassandra, meanwhile, seemed to be doing very well without him. She was as doggedly independent as always, and to his frustration she made no call on him at all. She was designing gardens, rather than digging them, his people had told him, adding that, in their opinion, there was no reason for concern, as she was taking good care of herself and doing very well. *Without him.*

Each time he sat down at the computer he read these emails again, as if they could somehow bring her closer. Perhaps a relationship at a distance was the best his stony heart could manage, he reflected grimly as he returned to the mountain of work on his desk. While the past had its hold on him, distance from him was the best thing for Cassandra, and though he had no difficulty accepting responsibility if the test proved he was the baby's father, it would almost certainly mean discharging his duty from a distance—which was probably just as well. What did he have to offer a child, apart from his money?

Sitting back, he pushed all thoughts of work away. He received daily reports on Cassandra's progress, and that should be enough for him.

It wasn't nearly enough. He felt as if something precious was in danger of slipping away from him. Was there a chance for change? Or would he relive his father's mistakes, and all because of his pride?

She missed Marco more than words could say. It was as if she had been complete and now she had a vital part of her missing. Marco was damaged and she couldn't help him until he was ready to help himself. She hated to admit it but she was about ready to admit defeat.

Never. Defeat wasn't in her nature. She smiled ruefully and chomped on her lip as she pictured him lounging back in his warm, state-of-the-art office, while she was here, freezing her butt off in a neighbour's overgrown orchard that she was trying to rescue.

Marco could make her life so much easier than this.

Maybe he could—if she was prepared to sell out, which she wasn't. And that was even supposing Marco would want to stick around after their baby was born. She had no idea what he wanted to do. There might be a custody battle once it had been had proved to his satisfaction that he was the father of her child. He should know that there was no one else. He had enough investigators on the case. She'd 'made' his man on her first day back in England. There couldn't be many burly men who would reach for packets of hair dye and scrunchies when caught staring at her in the supermarket.

Leaning back against the tree trunk, she stared up through its contorted branches. Birds wheeled overhead in a hostile, grey sky, which made her think back to the warmth and sunshine in Tuscany. She was as wary of commitment as Marco, and it was going to be a long, lonely Christmas with just the bump—the very active bump—for company. She hoped that she would see Marco again, but it wouldn't be until some time in the New Year when she gave birth.

He scanned the latest report from his people in the UK again. There were no new developments, and nothing for him to worry about, they said. That wasn't good enough for him. Today he felt the need to hear that reassurance from Cassandra's lips. As an ex-member of staff she was still his responsibility.

He called her up, but there was no reply. Was she was ignoring his calls?

Was he going to hang around to find out?

With his pilot on leave for the holidays he flew the jet to London himself. He felt better just being in charge—until he landed and tried to cross the airport concourse, when all hell broke loose. The paparazzi were waiting for him and the one question they all wanted an answer to was whether he would be going straight to the hospital. He scanned his phone. He'd missed *how* many calls? There were seven from Cassandra and three from his staff. He knew what this meant. The one thing he could not control was the birth of this child. Nature would determine the time, not him, and that was a humbling realisation for a man who controlled every aspect of his life without exception.

This wasn't the end of his journey of discovery when it came to the birth of a child but just the start. He was about to learn that giving birth didn't come neatly packaged or with a reliable timetable to suit him. Neither did it come with the automatic 'all areas' pass he was accustomed to being granted. Not one of the nurses in the Christmassy, glitzed-up hospital where, he was reliably informed, Cassandra was about to give birth would tell him when or where this would take place. His best guess was to take the elevator up to the maternity suite and take it from there.

All these practical things he could look at logically, but the feelings inside him could not be neatly organised or even accounted for. He was in turmoil. He was frightened for her. He was so far out of his comfort zone he had no answers, only questions, and producing his passport as proof of identity meant nothing here. He was made to stand back, stand aside, and he began to feel increasingly unsettled as his power was stripped away. He wanted to see Cassandra. He *had* to see her. She was expecting him. How was he supposed to help her if they wouldn't let him see her?

'From what I've seen, Ms Rich is quite capable of helping herself,' a fierce-looking midwife wearing flashing antlers in honour of the holiday season told him when he was his usual assertive self. 'She doesn't need any additional stress now,' she added, planting herself staunchly between him and the labour room door.

'I'm not here to give Cassandra stress,' he insisted, nearly going crazy with the delay as his mind tried to penetrate beyond the firmly closed door to find out what was happening.

The hospital had numerous ways to hold him in check, he now discovered. His passport had to be taken away and verified, and even then he was made to wait until his relationship to Ms Rich could be established with certainty. From the donning of a mask, gown and over-shoes to his entry into a temperature-controlled room where Cassandra was working towards the moment of birth with a stoicism that everyone but him found remarkable, he was out of his comfort zone, tossed headlong into a situation that was completely new—and, he admitted silently, alarming to him. He pushed that aside now he was with Cassandra. His heart gripped tight with all sorts of emotion, concern for her being uppermost amongst them. She looked so young—too young to be going through this—but when she saw him *she* reached out to him.

'Marco…you came.' Her eyes lit up as she held out her hand.

It was that look that stopped him. It held love, trust and gratitude, none of which he deserved, and he couldn't— mustn't—encourage it. Love deeply, and it was always stripped away and denied. Hadn't he learned that by now?

'Marco?'

She sounded concerned, but then a nurse hustled him out of the way. 'You can sit over here,' the nurse told him. 'Or stand, unless you think you might faint.'

He glared at the nurse. Cassandra defused the situation.

'Could he hold my hand?' she asked in that way she had that made everyone warm to her and want to do things for her.

'Would you like to?' one of the nurses asked him dubiously, as if this could be in doubt.

He noticed the glances exchanged by the staff. They knew his press. They didn't think much of him. Why would they when they only had his lurid backstory as depicted by the world's paparazzi to go on? They thought even less of him now a woman of his acquaintance was in labour.

'Of course I'd like to—I must,' he insisted.

He was at Cassandra's side in a stride. Pain he understood. The need for reassurance he understood. He could also comprehend that a new and frightening experience was better shared. It was the look in Cassandra's eyes that baffled him. How could she still feel this way about him when he could give her nothing back?

'What can I do of a practical nature?' he asked the same fierce-looking midwife, now masked and gowned like him. He felt useless, just standing by the bed.

'Be there for her. That's all you have to do. If she asks you to leave, you go. If we ask you to leave, you go faster. Understood?'

He ground his jaw and agreed.

The quiet efficiency of the staff impressed him. An aura of purposeful calm prevailed, and it was not allowed to be disturbed. Cassandra was the centre of everyone's attention, as she should be, and she was everything he might have expected of her. She made barely a sound as she clung to his hand, then his wrist, and finally his arm with a ferocity of which he would not have believed her capable. He was drawn in. She drew him in so that he was part of her experience—a very small part, admittedly, but a necessary one, her unflinching stare told him.

And then a baby cried.

Lustily, he noted with relief.

'Your son,' the midwife said, bypassing him to put the child in Cassandra's arms.

Cassandra had a son.

Her face was spellbound as she stared down at the tiny, wrinkled bundle in her arms.

'Oh, Marco...'

She couldn't bear to rip her enraptured gaze away from her baby's face. She was mapping every feature in the way that only a mother could, he guessed from his scant knowledge of what a mother might do. His brain was still frantically trying to patch together all the new information. The expression on Cassandra's face was new to him.

This situation was new to him. Love, raw and new, confronted him. There was no escaping it. He was consumed by it. He had no response ready, and he doubted that one could be prepared in advance.

'What do you think of him?' Cassandra asked him, her gaze still fixed on her baby.

'He seems healthy,' he observed, trying not to look too closely. 'Sturdy,' he amended as one tiny arm flailed as if the child would like to catch him with a blow.

'Isn't he beautiful?' Cass exclaimed softly. 'I bet you looked exactly like this when you were born, Marco.' Glancing up at him, Cass smiled and her expression warmed him. 'Don't you want to hold him?'

'I'm not sure I should,' he said, suddenly nervous when confronted by such a tiny life.

'Of course you should,' the midwife told him. Taking the infant from Cassandra's arms, she placed him in his.

As his brutish arms closed around the small warm bundle, he sucked in a shocked breath. The tiny child was somehow familiar, as if he were seeing someone he knew well after a really long absence. It was a defining moment, a shock, a wake-up call, and also a dilemma he had never expected to confront. He hadn't expected to feel anything, let alone this detonation of emotion inside his heart. His heart didn't just beat faster, it took off—it swelled, it exploded.

He cried.

'Marco?'

Cassandra's voice was concerned—for him.

Rigid control allowed him to pull himself together and hand the child back.

'Thank you,' he bit out awkwardly. No words could explain.

'He's your son, Marco,' she said, staring again into the tiny face. 'There's no mistaking it, is there?'

'No mistaking it,' the same midwife agreed in his place, beaming fondly as she stared down at the baby.

'We don't know that yet.' He was reeling from reality, from his son—gut instinct told him this tiny, vulnerable child was his son, and that made him fearful. Could he protect the child as he had failed to protect his mother? Could he love his son, as the man he had called father had failed to love him? Overwhelmed by love, he was in danger of being destroyed by the fear of losing it again.

It was as if the air had frozen solid when he spoke. Everyone in the room remained motionless, as if they couldn't compute what he'd said, let alone his reason for saying it now, at what had to be the most inappropriate moment possible. He felt as if time and space had slowed to take full account of his crass remark as everyone turned around to stare at him.

'We can't be sure that he's mine,' he said, reverting to the emotion-free tone he always used in business. He added a shrug for good measure. 'Only science can do that.'

It was as if, having dug the hole, he had to go on digging. The midwife looked as if she'd like to push him into it and then fill it in with cement.

'Oh, Marco,' Cassandra murmured. Handing the baby over to the midwife to put in the cot that had been made ready nearby, she reached out to him as she had done when he'd first entered the room. 'Don't be afraid,' she whispered, so that only he could hear.

He stiffened and stared down at her as if she were a stranger. 'I should go now.'

'Must you?' Her eyes implored him to stay.

'Yes. Yes, I must. I didn't realise how long this would take. I have appointments—'

'Yes, I see,' she said. 'I'm sorry I took so long.'

She was apologising to him? He was deeply ashamed. He had to get out of there or he would ruin her life. He needed time—space—the opportunity to counsel himself, so he could accept the truth—that he was afraid of love, terrified of it—terrified of losing it, terrified of losing Cassandra. He had kept his feelings bottled up since he was a child, and now they were threatening to drown him, just when Cassandra was at her most vulnerable—when she needed him most.

'I'll arrange the DNA test as soon as I can.'

'You'll…' Cassandra's mouth dropped open.

'Haven't you said enough?' the midwife hissed, glancing pointedly at the door.

He hadn't moved. Cassandra had gone white with shock, but then her shock turned to fury and, pulling herself up in the bed, she flung at him in anger, 'Get your court order first! Then you can have your DNA test!'

As a nurse rushed across the room to calm her, the midwife ushered him to the door. 'Get out,' she murmured coldly.

She was right. He was a monster. He'd always known it. He was a monster who didn't deserve to love or be loved.

He stood motionless outside the door, barely aware of the concerned murmurings inside the room. He couldn't be sure whose life he was ruining—maybe all of them. He couldn't bear to overhear Cassandra making excuses for him. But now he'd said this terrible thing he had to get it over and done with. He placed a call and asked the question. The Christmas holidays had produced a backlog in the lab, but for Marco di Fivizzano, anything was possible. And, yes, the answer would be with him within hours.

They would be the longest hours of his life.

Turning up the collar of his jacket, he walked out of

the building, only to find an army of paparazzi waiting for him. He pushed his way through them, hardly knowing where he was going. He wanted to be with Cassandra and the baby, but he knew that he didn't deserve to stay.

'No comment,' he flared when the photographers chased him down the street.

'Is it a boy?'

'Will you make him your heir?'

'Will you marry your gardener?'

'What did you buy her for Christmas, Marco—or have you already given her your best?'

Normally, he would stand and fight, but he had no fight left in him, and to a chorus of cruel laughter he kept on walking. It was just past four in the afternoon and already winter dark. He walked on past his car with no idea of where he was heading. Realising they'd get no response from him, the following pack dropped away. The streets were full of last-minute shoppers carrying unwieldy packages, and while he could slip through the scrum with relative ease, the reporters with all their equipment soon got left behind. He turned his mind to practicalities. That seemed to help. He would have security put in place for Cassandra and the baby. Pulling out his phone, he made the arrangements and walked on. Store windows were ablaze with Christmas cheer, but he felt numb—until a young girl and her boyfriend danced out of a large department store and the boy flung his scarf around the girl's neck.

'Here, take mine,' the boy insisted as they laughed happily into each other's eyes. 'I don't want you getting cold.'

'What about you?' the girl demanded, tightening her hold on the scarf.

The boy brought her close. 'I don't need it. I've got my love to keep me warm.'

He couldn't believe he'd been gripped by such a cheesy

display, and for a moment he couldn't understand why, but then he remembered, and tears stung his eyes as he retraced his steps back to the store. Ducking inside the brilliantly lit warmth, he bought the warmest and most colourful scarf he could find. 'Yes. Gift-wrap it, please.' On the surface it didn't seem much, but the scarf was a vital link to him between the past and what had happened today, and some sane—or maybe it was insane—part of his brain wanted desperately for it to mean something to Cassandra. She was his life.

Cassandra was his only preoccupation as he left the store. He couldn't believe he'd walked out of that hospital ward, leaving Cassandra and her baby in the care of strangers. As he strode along he had to tell himself that she was in good hands. That fierce midwife wouldn't let anyone get past her. But leaving them still wasn't right. Dealing with the enormity of birth and the creation of life had proved him to be emotionally inadequate. Wasn't it time to do something about that? For over twenty years he had pushed the past away, but now he had the scarf and a link to the past that made sense to him. He could only hope that it would make sense to Cassandra.

It was slippery underfoot and bitterly cold. Snow was feathering down, and the wintry conditions reminded him of the night when his eight-year-old self had been thrown out into the street with his mother. He had been freezing cold, and she had stopped to take off her scarf so she could tie it around his neck. So she *had* cared for him. He tightened his hold on the package from the store, and then he remembered staring back at the house where the man who had turned out not to be his father—the man he had loved with all his heart—had turned his back on him without even saying goodbye.

Was that what he'd just done to Cassandra? The thought

appalled him. Far from avoiding the past, he had invited it back and had given it a home in his cold, unfeeling heart.

He stopped walking and found himself on a bridge. Looking down at the oily water, he watched its steady progress to the sea and accepted that life moved on, and he must move with it. Tucking his hands beneath his arms for warmth, he headed back to his car.

No one stayed in hospital for long after the birth of a child unless there were complications, and Cass's experience of birth had been straightforward. Her little boy was healthy, and it seemed no time at all before Cass was in a cab on her way home with a newborn baby in her arms. Her child. Her son. Her Luca. She had given him an Italian name for the father he so closely resembled—particularly when he frowned like this—though in Luca's case it was probably wind rather than general alienation from the world and everything beautiful and gentle and remarkable in that world.

She felt so sorry for Marco—sorry that he wouldn't allow himself to feel anything, not even love for his son. Yet Marco could feel emotion. She'd seen proof of that in the delivery room when he'd cried when he'd held Luca for the first time. But Marco had very quickly retreated behind his barricades, becoming once again a cold, distant man that not even his infant son had the power to reach.

As the cab slowed outside her door, Cass wondered what Marco was doing now. He should be here to enjoy this moment. Taking their son home was such a special time. He must have been even more badly hurt than she knew to rob himself of this opportunity and then to take such trouble to hide his feelings. Even moments after holding his son in his arms, Marco had somehow managed to switch off. She felt so desperately sorry for him. Marco had no idea what he was missing, she thought as she gazed down into Luca's face. Her heart was ready to burst with love. She could only think that Marco had given his heart as a child, only to have it trampled on and destroyed for good. Maybe that was why he had never settled down, Cass reflected as she paid the fare.

'You stay there, love. I'll help you out,' the cabbie insisted. 'You've got someone coming to look after you for the first few days, I hope?'

'Yes, of course,' she said quickly, seeing the cabby's concerned face. He was the type of kind-hearted man who would send his wife round to look after her if she so much as hinted that she could do with some help, and as much as she would have liked the reassurance of an experienced person to back up her scant knowledge of baby care, she was determined to do this on her own. Better to start as she meant to go on, rather than put unfair demands on other people.

But she was apprehensive, Cass accepted as the cabbie opened the front door for her. Thanking him, she said goodnight, knowing that once she stepped over the threshold she was truly on her own with her baby in the little house.

Yes, it was a tiny house, but it was tiny and snug, and she'd be fine here, and so would Luca. She gazed adoringly into his sleeping face, and silently promised her little boy all the love and care that she could give him. But whatever gloss she tried to put on her new life, her footsteps still echoed as she walked into the empty house. However cosy she'd made their tiny nest, they were still alone. She put her apprehension down to baby blues. She'd get over it, Cass told herself firmly as she carefully tucked Luca in to his Moses basket. They'd warned her in the hospital to expect a bit of a comedown. 'It's just the hormones regulating themselves,' the midwife had told her. 'You'll come out of it, and then you'll find that every day is a new adventure for you and your son.'

At the time she had agreed, not wanting to burst the midwife's kindly bubble, but right now alone was alone, and she had a long night ahead of her, with not much of a clue as to what to do.

Put the computer on and get some books out, do some research, prepare bottles, nappies and anything else you think you might need, and do it now, while the baby's sleeping.

She felt better now she'd got a plan. She was bone-weary and longing for her bed, but she had things to do first, and then she had plans for the future to make.

CHAPTER FIFTEEN

'YOU'RE JUST LIKE your papa,' she murmured, leaving Luca sleeping soundly in his Moses basket upstairs as she crept downstairs to make more bottles.

And Luca would probably be every bit as demanding as his father, Cass reflected as she switched on the all the lights to make the place look cheery. She put more logs on the smouldering fire and turned up the heating. It was still dark outside and snow was falling. There were so few hours of daylight in the winter...

She backed into the shadows of the room, seeing a sleek black four-wheeler parked outside beneath a streetlamp. Did Marco have people watching her even now?

She had just turned from the window when a rap on the door made her jump. Crossing the room, she stared through the security peephole and started back.

Marco!

She hesitated. Her initial instinct was not to let him in. She couldn't face a replay of the drama in the hospital. But she loved him. How could she say no when everything inside the house was warm and cosy, and Marco was standing on her doorstep, stamping his feet, with his shoulders hunched against the driving wind and snow?

Her emotions were still in turmoil as she undid the locks and swung the door wide. 'If this is about your DNA test—'

'It isn't,' he assured her.

With the streetlamp behind him and his face wreathed in shadows, Marco looked more intimidating than he ever had. 'How did you know I was home?'

'Inside information.'

'Your people?' She tightened her jaw.

'Your midwife. I finally managed to convince her that I have your best interests at heart.'

'And how did you do that?' she asked suspiciously.

'I talked to her. Something I should maybe have tried with you.'

This admission made her soften a little. 'I don't want any trouble, Marco.' She was still standing in his way. 'My baby's sleeping—'

'I'm not here to give you trouble, Cassandra. What happened in the hospital—'

'Was unforgivable,' she said.

'Yes,' he agreed grimly. 'It was.'

'So, why are you here now?'

'To explain. I don't want to disturb you, but…'

He looked so hopeful, though she was still wary. Marco was the biological father of her child, but his appalling behaviour in the hospital had shocked her out of thinking he might change. It took a large wedge of snow, falling from the roof and landing on his shoulders, to jolt her into action. When he laughed and exclaimed, 'Divine retribution!' she laughed too.

'You'd better come in,' she said. 'But let's get rid of this first.' Standing on tiptoe, she swiped the snow from one shoulder as Marco swept it from the other.

'Ever the practical girl, Cassandra,' he said dryly, turning his dark, compelling stare on her face. The stare she had missed…the stare she had so longed to see again.

She stood back to let him into the house. 'I'm a woman, not a girl, Marco—as I have been since the day we met.'

Cool words that she could congratulate herself for finding, but she shouldn't have touched him, because even that lightest and most innocent of touches had made her long to be in his arms again—to have him kiss her, warm her. At the end of the day it didn't matter what he did or he said, she loved him with all her heart, and she always would.

'Why are you here?' she asked as soon as Marco had closed the door on the cold.

Why was he here? Because he couldn't stay away from her.

'Marco?' Cassandra prompted him. 'Let me take your jacket. Go and make yourself warm by the fire...'

His fist tightened around the envelope he was carrying, the envelope he hadn't shown her yet. It was still unopened. It contained the results of the DNA test.

'Where's the baby?' he asked, glancing around. He was consumed by a ravening hunger to see the child he had so callously discarded in the hospital.

'He's upstairs, sleeping. You can...'

Was she going to invite him to see the baby? He would never know. Her voice had tailed off, as if she had thought better of that suggestion after his despicable behaviour in the labour ward. 'And you, Cassandra? How are you?' She looked 'fine', as Cassandra would say, but was she? And shouldn't she be resting?

'Me?' she queried with surprise. 'I'm very well, thank you.' Her face relaxed. 'It's early days, you know.'

He frowned. 'Don't you have anyone to help you?'

'Do I need anyone? I have friends who have promised to pop round, but I'm still getting used to being a mother and I'm happy with my own company for now.'

'Shouldn't you be resting in bed?'

'I'm not sure how much resting Luca is going to allow me. I will rest when I can.'

'Luca?' he queried.

'That's what I've named my son.'

A steely glint had returned to her eyes, as if she dared him to disagree, either with the name she had chosen or the fact that she had just put her stake in the ground, making it clear that she was a single parent and quite happy to go it alone without him.

'What's that?' she demanded as he stared down at the envelope in his hand.

'I think you know,' he said quietly.

'The test.' She met his gaze steadily, but her eyes had turned cold. 'You had a DNA test carried out on my son without my permission? Of course,' she murmured thoughtfully. 'Anything is possible for Marco di Fivizzano. But that doesn't make it right, Marco. When did you get this done? Did you have someone sneak into the maternity ward to take a sample from my baby?'

'There was nothing underhand about it,' he assured her calmly.

'You had someone prick my baby's heel and take a sample of Luca's blood, and that's not underhand?' Her eyes were like pinpoints of fury on his face.

'I was told that saliva does just as well.'

'Am I supposed to be reassured by the idea of someone sticking a foreign object into my newborn baby's mouth?'

She was on fire and magnificent. If he were in a position to choose a mother for his child, who better than Cassandra?

'Well?' she demanded, taking the tension between them to breaking point. 'Don't you have anything to say about it?'

'I had the midwife you trusted do it. It was all above board. She didn't like doing it, even with a court order, but for the sake of what she called a foregone conclusion she said that it was better she did it than anyone else.' Catching hold of Cassandra, he laced his fingers through her hair to bring her close. 'Forgive me?'

With a disbelieving laugh she pulled away. 'No. I won't forgive you.' She stared at him white-faced. 'Well? Aren't you going to open it?' She glanced at the envelope in his hand.

Slowly and deliberately he ripped it up in front of her and let the pieces drop.

'I don't need to look at it. I trust you, and I know our son,' he said.

As they stared at each other, a multitude of emotions flashed across her face, and then after what seemed to him like an eternity she said, 'Are you going to clear that up?'

Breath rushed out of him as the tension in the room subsided. His shoulders relaxed and his face creased in a grin. He wanted to drag her close, but he dropped to his knees instead and thought himself the luckiest man on earth as he gathered up the unnecessary proof that the child sleeping upstairs was his. He didn't need a piece of paper to tell him what he already knew. He had known the moment the midwife had put the baby in his arms. He just hadn't wanted to admit it—not to himself, not to Cass—and not because he didn't want the child but because he so desperately did. And for the first time in his life he had wondered then, as he wondered now, if he had what it took to be a father—and not just a father but a good father. The best. Though remembering what Cass had said about babies not coming with a manual, he thought he could learn to do this…they could learn together.

* * *

By the time she came downstairs after feeding Luca and putting him back to sleep, Marco had got the fire blazing.

'Sit,' she invited. 'Thanks for stoking the fire.'

'You want to talk,' he guessed.

'Yes, I do.' Sitting down with some space between them, she turned a concerned look on Marco's face. 'I believe childhood forms the foundation of our lives—makes us who we are.'

'Childhood certainly teaches us what we don't want,' he said.

'And what we do,' she countered gently.

'We strive for some things, and do our best to avoid others,' he said with a shrug.

'Is it that simple, Marco? It wasn't that simple for me. I look back and I see my parents differently now I'm older. But my past is well documented, while yours is equally well hidden.'

'And you want to know why?'

'You're the father of my son. It would be strange if I didn't, if only so I can understand you better.'

At one time she might have been surprised to see Marco's eyes darken with emotion, but not now. The birth of their baby had changed him in some deep fundamental way, unlocking some hidden part of him. 'Tell me about your mother. Can you remember her?'

'Of course I can.' He frowned as he thought back. 'As you said, I see things differently now, but as a child I felt burdened by her. Now I can see that she did care for me in her way, but she was weak.'

'You mustn't blame yourself for how you felt about her as a child. You've resolved that as an adult.'

'Have I? I used to blame her for everything—for taking me away from the man I thought was my father, and for not staying with the man who was my father by blood. I later learned that my real father had abandoned her, and the man she married had no interest in a bastard son once he found out the truth about my parentage. I thought my mother was a drunken slut who had slept with another man and who then tried to pass me off as the true son of her marriage. I refused to see that her descent into alcoholic rages and her dependency on drugs was a result of her sickness, and that she needed help, not blame—certainly not blame from her son.'

'And when she died?' Cass prompted gently.

'I was scavenging in bins outside restaurants for our food by that time, and it was a chef who took pity on me. He brought me into the warmth of his kitchen, cleaned me up and taught me how to cook. When I was orphaned he introduced me to the local priest who found me a place in a children's home and made sure I was educated. Education and a safe roof over my head proved to be the key to everything I am today. And in answer to your question, I don't have anything noble to offer by way of an explanation. I hated my mother for what she had done.'

'What happened to change your mind?'

He paused a moment and then he huffed an unsmiling laugh. 'A scarf,' he revealed with an incredulous shrug. 'It was when I was walking away from the hospital after you had given birth that I remembered the weather was very similar to the night my mother and I were thrown out on the street. I remembered shivering, and my mother taking off her scarf to tie it around my neck. So she did care for me...'

'Of course she did.' Reaching out impulsively, Cass put her arms around Marco to draw him close. 'Her life must have been a black pit of misery and she had no one to help her climb out.'

Marco lifted his dark stare to hers. 'It took the birth of a baby for me to remember what my mother did for me that night, and then I remembered all the other little things she'd done before she became too sick to do anything.'

'But you have remembered,' Cass pointed out. 'Learning to love again is a slow, risky business Marco.'

'As you should know,' he murmured, brushing a strand of hair from her eyes. 'I wish you'd rest,' he murmured. 'You'll need all your strength to look after our son.'

Hearing Marco refer to *our* son sounded so good, but she needed more from him before she could be sure that he had put the past behind him. 'And you, Marco? What about you?'

'What about me?'

He would never admit to any weakness, she knew that. 'I've always believed that admitting weakness is a sign of strength. You've helped me to understand you. And you're doing everything you can to help me and our son, which tells me that you *are* reconciled with the past, but you haven't recognised that fact yet.'

'I can't just turn on a switch and make everything right.'

'But you can take one step at a time—as you have already done, and as you are doing, but now I need a commitment from you, going forward, or you will have to leave.'

She paused to give that time to sink in.

'You're throwing me out?' he demanded incredulously.

'To a stranger this might look like the traditional family scene, with all of us snug in our tiny house, but that's all it is, Marco—a scene, and I need more from you than that. We need a plan. Luca needs security, and so do I. And before I make any plan I have to know if we're going forward together or separately as individuals. We've talked about the past, and now we have to talk about the future.'

'What do you want me to say?'

She felt a cold chill of fear, knowing that Marco had always been able to go so far but no further, and she couldn't risk him slipping back into his cold-hearted past now they had Luca to consider. 'You're not the only one risking your heart here. I am too, but more importantly so is our son. And if you're serious about not wanting history to repeat itself, you need to think about your place in Luca's life, because I won't allow you to step in and out of it on a whim.'

She felt desperately sorry for Marco after what he'd told her, but she had a child to think about now. 'Luca's birth has changed you, but I need to be sure of you, Marco. Luca needs to be sure of you.'

'You can't stop me seeing him.'

Marco stood, and he towered over her in a menacing reminder of the power he wielded. 'What's to stop me taking him with me right now?'

'I will,' she said, standing to bar Marco's way to his son.

CHAPTER SIXTEEN

'BE REASONABLE, CASSANDRA. Let me go to my son.'

'No. You can't have it all, Marco,' she said, standing at the foot of the stairs. 'You think everyone wants you for the basest of reasons, even the mother of your son. If you think your worth lies solely in your money and power, then all I can say is that you must have a very low opinion of yourself.'

'You make it all sound so straightforward, Cassandra.'

'Because it *is* straightforward!' she exclaimed with frustration. 'You might be the master of all you survey at Fivizzano Inc., but this is my territory, my home, and I'm still waiting for an answer to my question. What part do you intend to play in Luca's life?'

'A full part if you come back to Rome with me. What?' He frowned. 'I don't understand why you're looking at me like that. You'll be living in the lap of luxury...'

Cass shook her head in desperation. 'If you don't know what's wrong with that statement, I can't help you. Why would I exchange my cosy home here for your sterile penthouse—where I never see you, and where I'm waited on by strangers who won't let me lift a finger, whether I want to or not, and where I'm hounded every time I leave the building by the paparazzi? Is that what you want for your son? Why on earth would either of us want that for

Luca? I may be the first woman in the world to say this to you, Marco, but you've got nothing to offer me that I don't have right here ten times over. When I was a little girl I lived in a mansion not too dissimilar from your home in Tuscany, but it was the unhappiest place I can ever remember living in. I was always hungry, always afraid—'

'That wouldn't happen in Rome,' Marco stated with absolute confidence.

'No,' Cass agreed. 'But I would be exchanging one set of problems for another—isolation instead of hunger, and uncertainty instead of fear. The end result wouldn't be happiness, or even progress—and I'm not just talking about me. I'm thinking about all three of us. I don't want Luca to experience the constant uncertainty that you and I grew up with. Have we learned nothing from that experience? You must have longed for a different life. I know I did. And you have built a successful and very different life for yourself, so why take your son back to the past? Let's move on. Let's take this chance to move forward.'

'That's all I've ever wanted.'

'But on your terms!' Cass exclaimed with exasperation. 'You want everything on your terms.'

'As you do on yours,' he argued.

'I am defensive,' she admitted. 'That's my legacy from the past, but now I have a son to consider, and my main job is to protect Luca. I have to do everything I can for him, and I believe I can do that best here, not in Rome.'

He laughed bitterly.

'Do you expect me to throw up everything and come to live here?'

'No. I'm a realist. I know you can't do that.'

'What, then?' he demanded. 'What's your solution, Cassandra?'

'I don't know,' she admitted, shaking her head.

Something in her dejection touched him. He'd never seen Cassandra in this mood. Had he reduced her to this? Had he stolen away all her certainty and confidence? If he had, he would never forgive himself. It was like taking one of Cassandra's precious plants and crushing the life out of it beneath his heel. 'I will do whatever you want,' he said.

'Anything?' she murmured.

'I won't lose you. I can't,' he said softly and intently.

They were silent for a long time, until he remembered what he'd left in the car. 'I've got something for you.'

'For me?'

He had never bought her anything, he realised. 'For Christmas,' he explained. 'It isn't much.'

Cassandra shook her head with concern. 'But I haven't got anything for you.'

He shook his head and laughed with sheer happiness. 'Are you sure about that? I think you just gave me the most precious gift in the world. The gift of a son?' he prompted. 'That's a gift beyond price. Do you want to see the small thing I got for you?'

'Why don't we check on our son first?'

The expression on Marco's face told Cass everything she needed to know. He was every bit as invested in their future as she was, and though the nuts and bolts for a couple who lived in different countries still had to be ironed out, he was one hundred per cent behind her, and they would find a way to make it work.

It was the first time that they had stood together as a couple, staring down at their infant son. 'You're right,' Marco said. 'He's beautiful.'

Cass smiled with pure happiness as she ruffled their son's soft, fluffy black hair. Luca's face was still wrinkled and pink, with a frowning, puzzled expression, as he grew accustomed to life.

'He looks like my son.' Marco's eyes were steel bright as he smiled at her.

She angled her chin to give him a wry look. 'I suppose if he grows up to look like you, it won't be too bad.'

They left their son sleeping and went downstairs again.

'Do you want me to get your gift?' Marco suggested.

'I'd like that very much.'

'I'll be right back,' he promised.

He felt as if he'd got wings on his heels as he ran out to the car. He delved onto the back seat, and brought out the gift-wrapped package he'd bought for Cassandra. Coming back into the house, he handed it to her.

She opened it and fell silent.

'You see, I do understand,' he said. 'I'm on the same steep learning curve you are, and I don't always get it right.'

'You got it right this time,' she said, caressing the scarf.

'Shall I...?'

'Please,' she said.

He took the length of soft cashmere from its ivory tissue paper and draped the colourful scarf around her neck.

'I love it,' she whispered. 'Thank you.'

'Thank you,' he said, as he dipped his head to brush her lips lightly with his. Cassandra leaned against him, and when he put his arms around her she lifted her face to his.

'I love you,' he said.

'I love you too,' she said, smiling, 'but you don't always make it easy.'

His eyes brightened. 'And you're so easy,' he commented, smiling soft and slow.

'Will you help me to bathe Luca?'

'Of course I will.' Putting his arm around her shoulder, he led her back upstairs.

He only had to take Luca in his arms and lower him

into the lukewarm water, keeping him safe in the crook of his arm, to know that without Luca and Cassandra he was nothing—he had nothing. But could he convince this spirited, vexing, complex woman to join him in a life that would be challenging from day one? Every move she made would be scrutinised and picked over, and every day would present them both with a new mountain to climb.

'You can pass him to me now.' She was holding out a towel.

He did so with the utmost care, and then he caught Cassandra looking at him with a little smile on her face.

'Do I look as soppy as you?' she asked him.

'I don't think you could ever look like me,' he reassured her, as she wrapped their infant son in a soft white towel.

'How do I look?' she asked.

'Fishing for compliments?'

She smiled. 'Why not?'

'You look like a woman in love.'

'How odd.' She pretended surprise. 'I can't imagine why that would be.'

Leaning against the door, he stopped her leaving the room, and bringing both Cassandra and Luca into his arms he murmured, 'If your imagination won't stretch that far, what hope is there for me?'

'None,' she agreed.

'Stay with me, Cass. My life doesn't mean anything without you. I want all three of us to live together, wherever you want to live. It doesn't have to be Rome... Tuscany,' he murmured. 'The countryside is so much better for a child to grow up in.'

'Tuscany,' she echoed softly, her face lighting up.

'I don't know why I didn't think of it before,' he admitted.

'You had other things on your mind?' she suggested.

'Maybe…' His eyes warmed as he smiled down at her.

'Do you think there will be more children?' she asked him thoughtfully.

'Why not? You're good at growing things, aren't you?'

She grinned. 'You're not so bad yourself.'

He was distracted for a moment as he pictured kicking a football about with his son in the beautiful gardens that Cassandra would design and care for on the country estate he'd always loved better than anywhere else on earth.

'Marco?'

'Marry me, Cassandra.'

'Marry you?' she exclaimed with surprise.

'Why not? No one else will do.'

'No one else would put up with you, don't you mean?' she suggested.

He curved a smile back at her and then turned serious. 'I don't want anyone else. I only care about you, and what you want, what you think…'

'What I want?' Cass said softly. 'I want what I've always wanted. You. I love you Marco. I've loved you since we first rolled a rug together.'

'So now we can be a real family and save rug-rolling for any spare moments we might have.'

'I doubt we'll have many.'

'Are you saying yes to my proposal?' Suddenly he wasn't sure of anything, and Cassandra's reply mattered more to him than anything else on earth.

'Luca has to know that love is for ever, and that his parents are for ever, and if you can promise me that…'

'For ever doesn't sound long enough to me.' Grabbing Cassandra close, he kissed her slowly and then with increasing passion until Luca got jealous of his parents' distraction and started to wail.

'Hold that thought,' Cassandra instructed as she headed for the bedroom. 'We have a little man who's hungry.'

'Shall I warm a bottle and bring it up?'

'No, thank you. I'll feed him myself. As soon as you arrived bottles became redundant.'

'So, I do have my uses,' he teased as he followed her upstairs.

'Luca thinks so,' Cass agreed wryly, making space for Marco on the bed.

EPILOGUE

Three years have passed...

'WHAT ARE YOU THINKING?' Marco murmured, looping his arms around Cass's waist.

'Right now? Or a few minutes ago? You have to be more specific,' she teased him, arching a brow as she stared into the face of a man who had only grown more ruggedly good looking in the time she'd known him.

'Right now?' Marco's powerful shoulders eased in a shrug in response to this part of her query. 'I know what you're thinking right now.'

'How?' Cass demanded, though she knew the answer. She just wanted to hear him say it.

'I can feel you softening in my arms.'

'Interesting that I *soften*,' she exclaimed, shivering with desire, 'when the opposite happens to you. You make me so hungry for you. How do you do that?' she groaned, pressing against him.

'Consistent results?' he suggested.

She smiled and rolled her head back, inviting more kisses.

'So, tell me,' Marco coaxed. 'What were you thinking just now to put that dreamy look on your face?'

'I was thinking that this was inevitable,' she admitted, pressing closer.

'You and me?' Marco rocked his body into hers.

'Our family, living here on your Tuscan estate. I don't know why I didn't think of it right away.' She glanced up. 'And Quentin and Paolo visiting on a regular basis. That crazy makeover you insisted I have for the party has certainly produced unexpected results.'

'Quentin and Paolo are good friends?'

'More than that, I think,' she said, smiling.

'Are they with the baby now?'

'My godmother and our two fairy godmothers are with our baby daughter and Luca now.' Cass laughed. 'Last time I looked all five of them were taking a nap before the gardens open at two o'clock.'

'That gives us plenty of time.'

'No, Marco—there's no time! Where are you taking me?' Marco had her firmly by the wrist and was leading her through the rose arbour she had designed in the gardens they had started opening to the public the previous year. 'Marco, I have to look respectable,' she protested when he pulled her down on the grass.

'It won't hurt for my gardener to have a little grass in her hair,' he said, looming over her. 'I just want to tell you how much I love you. And I want to tell you how much my family means to me, and that I owe all this to you.'

'I think you had some part to play in the creation of our family—an equal part, I do believe.'

'If you insist,' he murmured, slanting a grin.

'I do insist.'

'I never pictured myself with any of this—happiness, and a family.'

'And I never imagined I'd find someone like you. When

I was up to my elbows in mud and you arrived in that flashy helicopter, my first thought was to grab my pitch-fork and run you through.'

Marco laughed. 'Such a waste of a warm afternoon and a firm, grassy bank,' he murmured, dragging her close. 'But you're right—it is time to get ready to greet our guests...'

She followed his glance to the main gates and the road beyond, where, in the far distance, she could just see a haze of dust heralding the first visitors to the estate. With a cry of alarm she shot up. 'They're here! You've got to stop them—I forgot the time. I'm not properly dressed!'

Marco grinned at her. 'Go,' he said. 'I'll handle the visitors.'

'We make a good team,' she called back as she raced to the house.

'The best,' Marco murmured happily.

With three-year-old Luca sitting on his shoulders and baby Cristina sleeping in the shade at his side, Marco looked on with pride as his beautiful wife, the woman who had given his life meaning, took the local dignitaries and other avid gardeners on a guided tour around the beautiful garden she had created. Her seedlings were fully grown, and had burst into flower right on cue.

He glanced down at their baby daughter, and jiggled the legs of the son they adored. All their seedlings were growing nicely, thanks to the love and care of a woman who was a natural mother, as well as his lover and clos-est friend. Cass designed gardens for other people now, which gave her an interesting and varied life but allowed her to spend plenty of time with the children. Maria and Giuseppe were more a part of the family than they had ever been, thanks to Cass, as were Quentin and Paolo, and

Cass's godmother, who was home briefly from Australia, where she would return each winter to live with her son. He could safely say that the past and all its demons had finally been laid to rest.

When the visitors had gone she gave the children tea, while he set about the necessary job of splitting logs. Winters could be cold in Tuscany, and he had a family to keep warm.

When the children were in bed, Cass came outside in the burnished light of early evening to find Marco dressed in faded denim, stripped to the waist. She would never get used to seeing him half-naked. He was such a magnificent sight, bronzed and lean, with his muscles rippling. She indulged herself by just standing and watching him for a while, until he looked up and smiled, sensing she was there. He was glistening with sweat and covered in mud, as she had been on the day they'd first met...

Planting his axe, he strode towards her.

They went inside where the house was quiet. The children were sleeping, and a low buzz of conversation was coming from the kitchen where everyone else was happily chewing over the events of the day. They went straight up to their suite of rooms, where Marco headed for the shower. Snatching hold of her wrist, he took a laughing Cass in with him beneath the spray.

'Marco—I'm fully dressed!'

'Not for long, *cara*...'

Cupping her face, Marco kissed her long and slow. 'Do you have any idea how much I love you?'

'Not half as much as I love you. I must do to put up with you—I'm soaked.'

The look in Marco's eyes reduced her in an instant to

a trembling mass of need, and the smile on his firm, sexy mouth effortlessly completed the task.

'My wife,' he whispered against her ear. 'The mother of my children. My friend. My lover. The woman I love more than life itself.'

* * * * *

THE ITALIAN'S
CHRISTMAS SECRET

SHARON KENDRICK

For the vivacious and beautiful Amelia Tuttiett – who
is a great raconteur and always fun to be with.
She is also a brilliant ceramic artist.

Thanks for all the inspiration, Mimi!

CHAPTER ONE

'Mr Valenti?'

The woman's soft voice filtered into Matteo's thoughts and he made no effort to hide his exasperation as he leaned back against the leather seat of the luxury car. He'd been thinking about his father. Wondering if he intended carrying out the blustering threat he'd made just before Matteo had left Rome—and if so, whether or not he could prevent it. He gave a heavy sigh, forcing himself to accept that the ties of blood went deeper than any others. They must do. He certainly wouldn't have tolerated so much from one person if they hadn't been related. But family were difficult to walk away from. Difficult to leave. He felt his heart clench. Unless, of course, they left you.

'Mr Valenti?' the soft voice repeated.

Matteo gave a small click of irritation and not just because he loathed people talking to him when it was clear he didn't want to be disturbed. It was more to do with the fact that this damned trip hadn't gone according to plan, and not just because he hadn't seen a single hotel he'd wanted to buy. It was as much to do with the small-boned female behind the steering wheel who was irritating the hell out of him.

'Cos' hai detto?' he demanded until the ensuing silence reminded him that the woman didn't speak Italian, that he was a long way from home—in fact, he was in the middle of the infernal English countryside with a woman driver.

He frowned. Having a woman chauffeur was a first for him and when he'd first seen her slender build and startled blue eyes, Matteo had been tempted to demand a replacement of the more burly male variety. Until he reminded himself that the last thing he needed was to be accused of sexual prejudice. His aristocratic nostrils flared as he glanced into the driver's mirror and met her eyes. 'What did you say?' he amended, in English.

The woman cleared her throat, her slim shoulders shifting slightly—though the ridiculous peaked cap she insisted on wearing over her shorn hair stayed firmly in place. 'I said that the weather seems to have taken a turn for the worse.'

Matteo turned his head to glance out of the window where the deepening dusk was almost obscured by the violent swirl of snowflakes. He'd been so caught up in his thoughts that he'd paid scant attention to the passing countryside but now he could see that the landscape was nothing but a bleached blur. He scowled. 'But we'll be able to get through?'

'I certainly hope so.'

'You hope so?' he echoed, his voice growing harder. 'What kind of an answer is that? You do realise that I have a flight all geared up and ready to go?'

'Yes, Mr Valenti. But it's a private jet and it will wait for you.'

'I am perfectly aware that it's a *private jet* since I happen to own it,' he bit out impatiently. 'But I'm due at a party in Rome tonight, and I don't intend being late.'

With a monumental effort Keira stifled a sigh and kept her eyes fixed on the snowy road ahead. She needed to act calm and stay calm because Matteo Valenti was the most important customer she'd ever driven, a fact her boss had drummed into her over and over again. Whatever happened, she mustn't show the nerves she'd been experiencing for the past few days—because driving a client of this calibre was a whole new experience for her. Being the only woman and the more junior driver on the payroll, she usually got different sorts of jobs. She collected urgent packages and delivered them, or picked up spoilt children from their prep school and returned them to their nanny in one of the many exclusive mansions which were dotted around London. But even mega-rich London customers paled into insignificance when you compared them with the wealth of Matteo Valenti.

Her boss had emphasised the fact that this was the first time the Italian billionaire had ever used their company and it was her duty to make sure he gave them plenty of repeat business. She thought it was great that such an influential tycoon had decided to give Luxury Limos his business, but she wasn't stupid. It was obvious he was only using them because he'd decided on the trip at the last minute—just as it was obvious she'd only been given the job because none of the other drivers were available, this close to Christmas. According to her boss, he was an important hotelier looking to buy a development site in England, to expand his growing empire of hotels. So far they had visited Kent, Sussex and Dorset—though they'd left the most far-flung destination of Devon until last, which wouldn't have been how *she* would have arranged it, especially not with the pre-holiday traffic being what it was. Still, she wasn't being employed to sort out his schedule for him—she was here to get him safely from A to B.

She stared straight ahead at the wild flurry of snowflakes. It was strange. She worked *with* men and *for* men and knew most of their foibles. She'd learnt that in order to be accepted it was better to act like one of the boys and not stand out. It was the reason she wore her hair short—though not the reason she'd cut it in the first place. It was why she didn't usually bother with make-up, or wearing the kind of clothes which invited a second look. The tomboy look suited her just fine, because if a man forgot you were there, he tended to relax—though unfortunately the same rule didn't seem to apply to Matteo Valenti. She'd never met a less relaxed individual.

But that wasn't the whole story, was it? She clutched the steering wheel tightly, unwilling to admit the real reason why she felt so self-conscious in his company. Because wasn't the truth that he had blown her away the moment they'd met, with the most potent brand of charisma she'd ever encountered? It was disturbing and exciting and scary all at the same time and it had never happened to her before—that thing of looking into someone's eyes and hearing a million violins start playing inside your head. She'd gazed into the darkest eyes she'd ever seen and felt as if she could drown in them. She'd found herself studying his thick black hair and wondering how it would feel to run her fingers through it. Failing that, having a half-friendly working relationship would have satisfied her, but that was never going to happen. Not with a man who was so abrupt, narrow-minded and *judgmental*.

She'd seen his expression when she'd been assigned to him, his black gaze raking over her with a look of incredulity he hadn't bothered to disguise. He'd actually had the nerve to ask whether she felt *confident* behind the wheel of such a powerful car and she had been tempted to coolly inform him that yes, she was, thank you very much. Just as she was confident about getting underneath the bonnet and taking the engine to pieces, should the need arise. And now he was snapping at her and making no attempt to hide his irritation—as if she had some kind of magical power over the weather conditions which had suddenly hit them from out of the blue!

She shot a nervous glance towards the heavy sky and felt another tug of anxiety as she met his hooded dark eyes in the driver's mirror.

'Where are we?' he demanded.

Keira glanced at the sat-nav. 'I think we're on Dartmoor.'

'You think?' he said sarcastically.

Keira licked her lips, glad he was now preoccupied with staring out of the window instead of glaring so intently at her. Glad he was ignorant of the sudden panicked pounding of her heart. 'The sat-nav lost its signal a couple of times.'

'But you didn't think to tell me that?'

She bit back her instinctive response that he was unlikely to be an expert on the more rural parts of the south-west since he'd told her he hardly ever visited England. Unless, of course, he was implying that his oozing masculinity was enough to compensate for a total lack of knowledge of the area.

'You were busy with a phone call at the time and I didn't like to interrupt,' she said. 'And you said…'

'I said what?'

She gave a little shrug. 'You mentioned that you'd like to travel back by the scenic route.'

Matteo frowned. Had he said that? It was true he'd been distracted by working out how he was going to deal with his father, but he didn't remember agreeing to some guided tour of an area he'd already decided wasn't for him, or his hotels. Hadn't it simply been a case of agreeing to her hesitant suggestion of an alternative route, when she'd told him that the motorways were likely to be busy with everyone travelling home for the Christmas holiday? In which case, surely she should have had the sense and the knowledge to anticipate something like this might happen.

'And this snowstorm seems to have come from out of nowhere,' she said.

With an effort Matteo controlled his temper, telling himself nothing would be achieved by snapping at her. He knew how erratic and *emotional* women could be—both in and out of the workplace—and had always loathed overblown displays of emotion. She would probably burst into tears if he reprimanded her, followed by an undignified scene while she blubbed into some crumpled piece of tissue and then looked at him with tragic, red-rimmed eyes. And scenes were something he was at pains to avoid. He liked a life free of drama and trauma. A life lived on his terms.

Briefly, he thought about Donatella waiting for him at a party he wasn't going to be able to make. At the disappointment in her green eyes when she realised that several weeks of dating weren't going to end up in a swish Roman hotel bedroom, as they'd planned. His mouth hardened. He'd made her wait to have sex with him and he could tell it had frustrated the hell out of her. Well, she would just have to wait a little longer.

'Why don't you just get us there as safely as possible?' he suggested, zipping shut his briefcase. 'If I miss the party, it won't be the end of the world—just so long as I get home for Christmas in one piece. You can manage that, can't you?'

Keira nodded, but inside her heart was still racing faster than it should have been considering her sedentary position behind the wheel. Because she was rapidly realising that they were in trouble. Real trouble. Her windscreen wipers were going like crazy but no sooner had they removed a thick mass of white flakes, there were loads more their place. She'd never known such awful visibility and found herself wondering why she hadn't just risked the crowds and the traffic jams and gone by the most direct route. Because she hadn't wanted to risk a displeasure she suspected was never very far from the surface with her billionaire client. Matteo Valenti wasn't the kind of person you could imagine sitting bumper to bumper on a road of stationary traffic while children in Santa hats pulled faces through the back windows. To be honest, she was surprised he didn't travel round by helicopter until he'd informed her that you got to see a lot more of the natural lie of the land from a car.

He seemed to have informed her about quite a lot of things. How he didn't like coffee from service stations and would rather go without food than eat something 'substandard'. How he preferred silence to the endless stream of Christmas songs on the car radio, though he didn't object when once she changed the station to some classical music, which she found strangely unsettling—particularly when a glance in the mirror showed her that he had closed his eyes and briefly parted his lips. Her heartbeat had felt *very* erratic after that particular episode.

Keira slowed down as they drove past a small house on which an illuminated Santa Claus was driving his sleigh above a garish sign proclaiming *Best Bed & Breakfast on Dartmoor!* The trouble was that she wasn't used to men like Matteo Valenti—she didn't imagine a lot of people were. She'd watched people's reactions whenever he emerged from the limousine to cast his eye over yet another dingy hotel which was up for sale. She'd witnessed women's gazes being drawn instinctively to his powerful physique. She'd watched their eyes widen—as if finding it hard to believe that one man could present such a perfect package, with those aristocratic features, hard jaw and sensual lips. But Keira had been up close to him for several days and she realised that, although he looked pretty perfect on the surface, there was a brooding quality underneath the surface which hinted at danger. And weren't a lot of women turned on by danger? As she clamped her fingers around the steering wheel, she wondered if that was the secret of his undeniable charisma.

But now wasn't the time to get preoccupied about Matteo Valenti, or even to contemplate the holidays which were fast approaching and which she was dreading. It was time to acknowledge that the snowstorm was getting heavier by the second and she was losing control of the big car. She could feel the tyres pushing against the weight of the accumulating drifts as the road took on a slight incline. She could feel sweat suddenly beading her brow as the heavy vehicle began to lose power and she realised that if she wasn't careful…

The car slid to a halt and Keira's knuckles whitened as she suddenly realised there were no distant tail lights in front of them. Or lights behind them. She glanced in the mirror as she turned off the ignition and forced herself to meet the furious black stare which was being directed at her from the back seat.

'What's going on?' he questioned, his tone sending a shiver rippling down Keira's spine.

'We've stopped,' she said, turning the key again and praying for them to start moving but the car stayed exactly where it was.

'I can see that for myself,' he snapped. 'The question is, *why* have we stopped?'

Keira gulped. He must have realised why. Did he want her to spell it out for him so he could shovel yet more blame on her? 'It's a heavy car and the snow is much thicker than I thought. We're on a slight hill, and...'

'And?'

Face facts, she told herself fiercely. You know how to do that. It's a difficult situation, but it's not the end of the world. She flicked the ignition and tried moving forward again but despite her silent prayers, the car stubbornly refused to budge. Her hands sliding reluctantly from the wheel, she turned round. 'We're stuck,' she admitted.

Matteo nodded, biting back the angry exclamation which was on the tip of his tongue, because he prided himself on being good in an emergency. God knew, there had been enough of those over the years to make him an expert in crisis management. Now was not the time to wonder why he hadn't followed his instincts and demanded a male driver who would have known what he was doing, instead of some slip of a girl who didn't look strong enough to control a pushbike, let alone a car this size. Recriminations could come later, he thought grimly—and they would. First and foremost they needed to get out of here—and to do that, they needed to keep their wits about them.

'Where exactly are we?' he said, speaking slowly as if to a very small child.

She swivelled her head to look at the sat-nav for several silent seconds before turning to meet his gaze again.

'The signal has cut out again. We're on the edge of Dartmoor.'

'How close to civilisation?'

'That's the trouble. We're not. We're miles from anywhere.' He saw her teeth dig into her lower lip as if she were trying to draw blood from it. 'And there's no Wi-Fi connection,' she finished.

Matteo wanted to slam the flat of his hand against the snow-covered window but he sucked in an unsteady breath instead. He needed to take control.

'Move over,' he said roughly as he unclipped his seat belt.

She blinked those great big eyes at him. 'Move over where?'

'Onto the passenger seat,' he gritted out as he pushed open the car door to brace himself against a flurry of snowflakes. 'I'm taking over.'

He was pretty much covered in ice by the time he got into the car and slammed the door shut, and the bizarre thought which stuck in his mind was how deliciously warm the seat felt from where her bottom had been sitting.

Furious for allowing himself to be distracted by something so basic and inappropriate at a time like this, Matteo reached for the ignition key.

'You do know not to press down too hard on the accelerator, don't you?' she said nervously. 'Or you'll make the wheels spin.'

'I don't think I need any driving lessons from someone as incompetent as you,' he retorted. He started the engine and tried moving forward. Nothing. He tried until he was forced to surrender to the inevitable, which deep down he'd known all along. They were well and truly stuck and the car wasn't going anywhere. He turned to the woman sitting beside him who was staring at him nervously from beneath her peaked cap.

'So. Bravo,' he said, his words steeped in an anger he could no longer contain. 'You've managed to get us stranded in one of the most inhospitable parts of the country on one of the most inhospitable nights of the year—just before Christmas. That's some feat!'

'I'm so sorry.'

'Saying sorry isn't going to help.'

'I'll probably get the sack,' she whispered.

'You will if I have anything to do with it—that's if you don't freeze to death first!' he snapped. 'If it were down to me, I would never have employed you in the first place. But the consequences to your career are the last thing on my mind right now. We need to start working out what we're going to do next.'

She reached into the glove compartment for her mobile phone but he wasn't surprised to see her grimace as she glanced down at the small screen. 'No signal,' she said, looking up.

'You don't say?' he said sarcastically, peering out of the window where the howling flakes showed no signs of abating. 'I'm guessing there's no nearby village?'

She shook her head. 'No. Well, we did pass a little B&B just a while back. You know, one of those places which offer bed and breakfast for the night.'

'I'm in the hotel trade,' he said silkily. 'And I'm perfectly aware of what a B&B is. How far was it?'

She shrugged. 'Less than a mile, I'd guess—though it wouldn't be easy to reach in this kind of conditions.'

'No kidding?' Matteo eyed the virtual white-out which was taking place outside the window and his heart thundered as he acknowledged the real danger of their situation. Because suddenly this was about more than just missing his flight or disappointing a woman who had been eager to make him her lover; this was about survival. Venturing outside in this kind of conditions would be challenging—and dangerous—and the alternative was to hunker down in the car for the night and wait for help to arrive tomorrow. Presumably she would have blankets in the boot and they could continue to run the heater. His lips curved into a grim smile. And wasn't the traditional method of generating heat to huddle two bodies together? But he gave the idea no more than a few seconds' thought before dismissing it—and not just because she didn't look as if she had enough flesh on her bones to provide any degree of comfort. No. To take the risk of staying put while the snow came down this fast would be nothing short of madness, for there was no guarantee anyone would find them in the morning.

He ran his gaze over her uniform of navy blue trousers and the sturdy jacket which matched her cap. The material curved over the faint swell of her breasts and brushed against her thighs and was hardly what you would call *practical*—certainly not appropriate to face the elements at their worst. He sighed. Which meant he would have to give her his overcoat and freeze to death himself. 'I don't suppose you have any warmer clothes with you?'

For a few seconds, she seemed to brighten. 'I've got an anorak in the boot.'

'An anorak?'

'It's a waterproof jacket. With a hood.' She removed her peaked chauffeur's cap and raked her fingers through her short dark hair and Matteo felt inexplicably irritated by the brief smile which had lightened her pale face.

Was she expecting praise for having had the foresight to pack a coat? he wondered acidly.

'Just get it and put it on,' he bit out. 'And then let's get the hell out of here.'

CHAPTER TWO

KEIRA HAD TO work hard to keep up with Matteo as he battled his way through the deep snow because his powerful body moved much faster than hers, despite the fact that he'd insisted on bringing his suitcase with him. Thick, icy flakes were flying into her eyes and mouth and at times she wondered if she was imagining the small lighted building in the distance—like some bizarre, winter version of an oasis.

Despite putting on the big pair of leather gloves he'd insisted she borrow, her fingers felt like sticks of ice and she gave a little cry of relief when at last they reached the little house. Thank heavens she *hadn't* imagined it because she didn't like to think about Matteo Valenti's reaction if she'd brought him here on a wild goose chase. He might have insisted on her borrowing his gloves, but even that had been done with a terse impatience. She saw his unsmiling look as he kicked a pile of snow away from the wooden gate and pushed it open, and she stumbled after him up the path to stand beneath the flashing red and gold lights of the illuminated sign overhead. She was shivering with cold by the time he'd jammed his finger on the doorbell and they heard some tinkly little tune playing in the distance.

'Wh-what if…wh-what if nobody's in?' she questioned from between teeth which wouldn't seem to stop chattering.

'The light's on,' he said impatiently. 'Of course somebody's in.'

'They m-might have gone away for Christmas and left the lights on a timer to deter burglars.'

'You really think burglars are going to be enticed by a place like *this*?' he demanded.

But their bad-tempered interchange was brought to a swift halt by the sound of a lumbering movement from within the house and the door was pulled open by a plump, middle-aged woman wearing a flowery apron which was smeared with flour.

'Well, bless my soul!' she said, opening the door wider as she peered out into the gloom. 'You're not carol singers, are you?'

'We are not,' answered Matteo grimly. 'I'm afraid our car has got snowed in a little way down the road.'

'Oh, you poor things! What a night to be outside! Come in, come in!'

Keira felt like bursting into tears of gratitude as Matteo's palm positioned itself in the small of her back and propelled her inside the bright little hallway. During the seemingly endless journey here, she'd been convinced they weren't going to make it, and that their two frozen figures would be discovered the next day, or the day after that. And hadn't she been unable to stop herself from wondering whether anyone would have actually *cared* if she died?

But now they were standing dripping in a small hallway which had boughs of holly and strands of glittery tinsel draped absolutely everywhere. A green plastic tree was decked with flashing rainbow lights and from a central light hung a huge bunch of mistletoe. Keira's eyes were drawn in fascination to the row of small, fluffy snowmen waddling in a perfectly symmetrical line along a shelf—her attention only distracted by the realisation that puddles of water were growing on the stone tiles beneath their feet. Years of being told to respect property—especially when it *wasn't your own*—made Keira concentrate on the mess they were making, rather than the glaringly obvious fact that she and her bad-tempered Italian client were gate-crashing someone else's Christmas.

'Oh, my goodness—look at the floor!' she said, aware of the faint look of incredulity which Matteo Valenti was slanting in her direction. 'We're ruining your floor.'

'Don't you worry about that, my dear,' said the woman in her warm West Country accent. 'We get walkers coming in here all the time—that'll soon clean up.'

'We'd like to use your phone if that's okay,' said Matteo, and Keira watched as the woman looked at him, her mouth opening and closing comically as if she'd only just realised that she had six feet three inches of brooding masculine gorgeousness in her house, with melting snow sliding down over his black cashmere coat.

'And why would you want to do that, dear?' questioned the woman mildly.

Matteo did his best not to flinch at the overfamiliar response, even though he despised endearments from complete strangers. Actually, he despised endearments generally. Didn't they say that you always mistrusted what you weren't used to? Suppressing a frustrated flicker of anger at having found himself in this intolerable situation, he decided he needed to own it. Better to calmly spell out their needs, since his driver seemed incapable of doing anything with any degree of competence. 'Our car has become imbedded in the snow just down the road a little,' he said, directing an accusing glare at the woman who was currently pulling off her bulky waterproof jacket and shaking her short dark hair. 'We should never have taken this route, given the weather. However, what's done is done and we can't do anything about that now. We just need to get out of here, as quickly as possible, and I'd like to arrange that immediately.'

The woman nodded, her bright smile remaining unfaltering. 'I don't think that's going to be possible, dear. You won't get a rescue truck to dig you out—not tonight. Why, nothing's going to get through—not in these conditions!'

It was the confirmation of his worst fears and although Matteo was tempted to vent his rage, he was aware it would serve no useful purpose—as well as insulting the woman who'd been kind enough to open her house to them. And she was right. Who could possibly get to them tonight—in weather like this? He needed to face facts and accept that he was stuck here, in the middle of nowhere—with his incompetent driver in tow. A driver who was staring at him with eyes which suddenly looked very dark in her pale face. He frowned.

Of all the females in the world to be stranded with—it had to be someone like her! Once again his thoughts drifted to the luxurious party he would be missing, but he dismissed them as he drew in a deep breath and forced himself to say the unimaginable. 'Then it looks as if we're going to have to stay here. I assume you have rooms for hire?'

The woman's wide smile slipped. 'In December? Not likely! All my rooms are fully booked,' she added proudly. 'I get repeat trade all through the year, but especially at this time of year. People love a romantic Christmas on Dartmoor!'

'But we need somewhere to stay,' butted in Keira suddenly. 'Just until morning. Hopefully the snow will have stopped by then and we can get on our way in the morning.'

The woman nodded, her gaze running over Keira's pale cheeks as she took the anorak from her and hung it on a hook. 'Well, I'm hardly going to turn you out on a night like this, am I? Especially not at this time of the year—I'm sure we can find you room at the inn! I can put you in my daughter's old bedroom at the back of the house. That's the only space I have available. But the dining room is completely booked out and so I'm afraid I can't offer you dinner.'

'The meal doesn't matter,' put in Matteo quickly.

'Maybe if you could send something to the room when you have a moment?'

Keira felt numb as they were shown up some rickety stairs at the back of the house, and she remained numb as the landlady—who informed them that her name was Mary—opened the door with a flourish.

'You should be comfortable enough in here,' she said. 'The bathroom is just along the corridor though there's not much water left, and if you want a bath, you'll have to share. I'll just go downstairs and put the kettle on. Make yourselves at home.'

Mary shut the door behind her and Keira's heart started racing as she realised that she was alone in a claustrophobic space with Matteo Valenti. Make themselves at home? How on earth were they going to do that in a room this size with *only one bed*?

She shivered. 'Why didn't you tell her that we didn't want to share?'

He shot her an impatient look. 'We are two people and she has one room. You do the math. What alternative did I have?'

Keira could see his point. Mary couldn't magic up another bedroom from out of nowhere, could she? She looked around. It was one of those rooms which wasn't really big enough for the furniture it contained. It was too small for a double bed, but a double bed had been crammed into it nonetheless, and it dominated the room with its homemade patchwork quilt and faded pillow cases on which you could just about make out some Disney characters, one of which just happened to be Cinderella.

There were no signs of Christmas in here but on every available surface seemed to be a photo. Photos of someone who was recognisably Mary, looking much younger and holding a series of babies, then toddlers, right through gangly teenagers until the inevitable stiff wedding photos—and then yet more babies. Keira licked her lips. It was a life played out in stills. A simple life, probably—and a happy life, judging by the smile which was never far from Mary's face. Keira was used to cramped and cluttered spaces but she wasn't used to somewhere feeling homely—and she could do absolutely nothing about the fierce pang of something which felt like envy, which clutched at her heart like a vice.

She lifted her eyes to meet Matteo's flat gaze. 'I'm sorry,' she said.

'Spare me the platitudes,' he snapped, pulling out the mobile phone from the pocket of his trousers and staring at it with a barely concealed lack of hope. 'No signal. Of course there isn't. And no Wi-Fi either.'

'She said you could use the landline any time.'

'I know she did. I'll call my assistant once I've removed some of these wet clothes.' He loosened his tie before tugging it off and throwing it over the back of a nearby chair, where it dangled like some precious spiral of gunmetal. His mouth hardened with an expression of disbelief as he looked around. '*Per amor del cielo!* Who even uses places like this? We don't even have our own bathroom.'

'Mary told us we could use the one along the corridor.'

'She also told us that we'd need to share a bath because there wasn't enough hot water!' he flared. '*Sharing a bath? Not enough hot wate*r? Which century are
we supposed to be living in?'

Keira shrugged her shoulders awkwardly, suspecting
that Matteo Valenti wasn't used to the vagaries of small-
town English landladies, or the kind of places where
ordinary people stayed. Of course he wasn't. According to her boss, he owned luxury hotels all over his own
country—he even had some scattered over America, as
well as some in Barbados and Hawaii. What would he
know about having to traipse along a chilly corridor to
a bathroom which, like the rest of the house, obviously
hadn't been modernised in decades?

'It's an English eccentricity. Part of the place's
charm,' she added lamely.

'Charm I can do without,' he responded acidly.
'Good plumbing trumps charm every time.'

She wondered if he was deliberately ignoring something even more disturbing than the bathroom facilities…or maybe she was just being super-sensitive about
it, given her uneasy history. Awkwardly she raked her
fingers through her spiky hair, wondering what it was
which marked her out from other women. Why was it
that on the only two occasions she'd shared a bed with
a man, one had been passed out drunk—while the other
was looking at her with nothing but irritation in his
hard black eyes?

He was nodding his head, as if she had spoken out
loud. 'I know,' he said grimly. 'It's my idea of a night-

mare, too. Sharing a too-small bed with an employee wasn't top of my Christmas wish list.'

Don't react, Keira told herself fiercely. And don't take it personally. Act with indifference and don't make out like it's a big deal.

'I expect we'll survive,' she said coolly, then began to rub at her arms through the thin jacket as she started to shiver.

He ran a speculative gaze over her and an unexpected note of consideration crept into his voice. 'You're cold,' he said, his eyes lingering on her thighs just a fraction too long. 'And your trousers are soaking.'

'You don't say?' she said, her voice rising a little defensively, because she'd never been very good at dealing with unsolicited kindness.

'Don't you have anything else you can wear?' he persisted.

Embarrassment made her even more defensive and Keira glared at him, aware of the heat now staining her cheeks. 'Yes, of course I do. I always make sure I carry an entire change of clothes with me whenever I embark on a drive from London to Devon,' she said. 'It's what every driver does.'

'Why don't you skip the sarcasm?' he suggested. 'And go and take a hot bath? You can borrow something of mine.'

Keira looked at him suspiciously, taken aback by the offer and not quite sure if he meant it. Without his cashmere coat he stood resplendent in a dark charcoal suit which, even to her untutored eye, she could tell was made-to-measure. It must have been—because surely your average suit didn't cater for men with shoulders as broad as his, or legs that long. What on earth could Matteo Valenti have in his suitcase which would fit *her*? 'You carry women's clothes around with you, do you?'

An unexpected smile lifted the corners of his mouth and the corresponding race of Keira's heart made her hope he wasn't going to do a lot of smiling.

'Funnily enough, no,' he said drily, unzipping the leather case. 'But I have a sweater you can use. And a soap bag. Here. Go on. Take it.'

He was removing the items from his case and handing them to her and Keira was overcome by a sudden gratitude. 'Th-thanks. You're very kind—'

'*Basta!* Spare me the stumbling appreciation. I'm not doing it out of any sense of *kindness*.' His mouth hardened. 'This day has already been a disaster—I don't want to add to the misery by having you catch pneumonia and finding myself with a wrongful death suit on my hands.'

'Well, I'll do my best not to get sick then,' she bit back. 'I'd hate to inconvenience you any more than I already have done!'

Her fingers digging into his sweater, Keira marched from the room to the bathroom along the corridor, trying to dampen down her rising feelings of anger. He really was the most hateful person she'd ever met and she was going to have to endure a whole night with him.

Hanging his sweater on the back of the door, she quickly assessed the facilities on offer and for the first time that day, she smiled. Good thing *she* was used to basics. To her the avocado-coloured sink and bath were nothing out of the ordinary, though she shuddered to think how Mr Cynical was going to cope. When she'd been growing up, she and her mother had lived in places with far worse plumbing than this. In fact, this rather tatty bathroom felt almost *nostalgic*. A throwback to tougher times, yes, but at least it had been one of those rare times when she'd known emotional security, before Mum had died.

Clambering into the tiny bath, she directed the leaking shower attachment over her head and sluiced herself with tepid water before lathering on some of Matteo's amazing soap. And then the strangest thing started happening. Beneath her massaging fingers she could feel her nipples begin to harden into tight little nubs and for a moment she closed her eyes as she imagined her powerful client touching her there, before pulling her hands away in horror. What on earth was *wrong* with her?

Leaving the plug in situ and climbing out of the tub, she furiously rubbed herself dry. Wasn't the situation bad enough without her fantasising about a man who was probably going to make sure she got fired as soon as they reached civilisation?

She put on her bra, turned her knickers inside out and slithered Matteo's grey sweater over her head. It was warm and very soft—it was just unfortunate that it only came to mid-thigh, no matter how hard she tugged at the hem. She stared into the mirror. And the problem with that was, what? Was she really naïve enough to think that the Italian tycoon would even *notice* what she was wearing? Why, judging from his attitude towards her up until now, she could probably waltz back in there completely naked and he wouldn't even bat those devastatingly dark eyelashes.

But about that Keira was wrong—just as she'd been wrong in making the detour via Dartmoor—because when she walked back into the bedroom Matteo Valenti turned around from where he had been standing gazing out of the window and, just like the weather outside, his face froze. It was extraordinary to witness, that unmistakable double take when he saw her, something which never normally happened when Keira walked into a room. His eyes narrowed and grew smoky and something in the atmosphere seemed to subtly shift, and change. She wasn't used to it, but she wasn't going to deny that it made her skin grow warm with pleasure. Unless, of course, she was totally misreading the situation. It wouldn't be the first time, would it?

'Is everything okay?' she asked uncertainly.

Matteo nodded in response, aware that a pulse had begun to hammer at his temple. He'd just finished a telephone conversation with his assistant and as a consequence he'd been miles away, staring out of the window at the desolate countryside and having the peculiar sensation of realising that nobody could get hold of him—a sensation which had brought with it a surprising wave of peace. He had watched his driver scuttle off towards the bathroom in her unflattering navy trouser suit, only now she had returned and…

He stared and swallowed down the sudden lump which had risen in his throat. It was inexplicable. What the hell had she done to herself?

Her short, dark hair was still drying and the heat

of the shower must have been responsible for the rosy flush of her cheeks, against which her sapphire eyes looked huge and glittery. But it was his sweater which was responsible for inflicting a sudden sexual awakening he would have preferred to avoid. A plain cashmere sweater which looked like a completely different garment when worn by her. She was so small and petite that it pretty much swamped her, but it hinted at the narrow-hipped body beneath and the most perfect pair of legs he had ever seen. She looked…

He shook his head slightly. She looked *sexy,* he thought resentfully as lust arrowed straight to his groin, where it hardened and stayed. She looked as if she wanted him to lay her down on the bed and start kissing her. As if she were tantalising him with the question of whether or not she was wearing any panties. He felt he was in a schoolboy's fantasy, tempted to ask her to bend down to pick up some imaginary object from the carpet so he could see for himself if her bottom was bare. And then he glared because the situation was bad enough without having to endure countless hours of frustration, daydreaming about a woman he couldn't have—even if he was the kind of man to indulge in a one-night stand, which he most emphatically wasn't.

'*Sì,* everything is wonderful. *Fantastico,*' he added sarcastically. 'I've just made a phone call to my assistant and asked her to make my apologies for tonight's party. She asked if I was doing something nice instead and I told her that no, I was not. In fact, I was stuck on a snowy moor in the middle of nowhere.'

'I've left you some hot water,' she said stiffly, deciding to ignore his rant.

'How will I be able to contain my excitement?' he returned as he picked up the clothes he had selected from his case and slammed his way out of the room.

But he'd calmed down a little by the time he returned, dressed down in jeans and a sweater, to find her stirring a pot of tea which jostled for space on a tray containing sandwiches and mince pies. She turned her face towards him with a questioning look.

'Are you hungry?' she said.

It was difficult to return her gaze when all he wanted to do was focus on her legs and that still tantalising question of what she was or wasn't wearing underneath his sweater. Matteo shrugged. 'I guess.'

'Would you like a sandwich?'

'How can I refuse?'

'It's very kind of Mary to have gone to the trouble of making us some, especially when she's trying to cook a big turkey dinner for eight people,' she admonished quietly. 'The least we can do is be grateful.'

'I suppose so.'

Keira tried to maintain her polite smile as she handed him a cup of tea and a cheese sandwich, telling herself that nothing would be gained by being rude herself. In fact, it would only make matters worse if they started sparring. She was the one in the wrong and the one whose job was on the line. If she kept answering him back, who was to say he wouldn't ring up her boss and subject him to a blistering tirade about her incompetence? If she kept him sweet, mightn't he be persuaded not to make a big deal out of the situation, maybe even to forget it had ever happened and put it down to experience? She needed this job because she loved it and things to love in Keira's life happened too rarely for her to want to give them up without a fight.

She noticed that he said nothing as he ate, his expression suggesting he was merely fuelling his impressive body rather than enjoying what was on offer—but Keira's hunger had completely deserted her and that was a first. She normally had a healthy appetite, which often surprised people who commented on her tiny frame. But not today. Today food was the last thing on her mind. She broke off the rim of one of the mince pies and forced herself to chew on it and the sugar gave her a sudden rush, but all she could think about was how on earth they were going to get through the hours ahead, when there wasn't even a radio in the room—let alone a TV. She watched the way the lamplight fell on her client's face—the hardness of his features contrasting with the sensual curve of his lips—and found herself wondering what it might be like to be kissed by a man like him.

Stop it, she urged herself furiously. Just *stop* it. You couldn't even maintain the interest of that trainee mechanic you dated in the workshop—do you really fancy your chances with the Italian billionaire?

A note of desperation tinged her voice as she struggled to think of something they could do which might distract her from all that brooding masculinity. 'Shall I go downstairs and see if Mary has any board games we could play?'

He put his empty cup down and his eyes narrowed. 'Excuse me?'

'You know.' She shrugged her shoulders helplessly. 'Cards, or Scrabble or Monopoly. Something,' she added. 'Because we can't just spend the whole evening staring at each other and dreading the night ahead, can we?'

He raised his dark eyebrows. 'You're dreading the night ahead, are you, Keira?'

A shimmer of amusement had deepened his voice and Keira realised that, not only was it the first time he'd actually used her name, but that he'd said it as no one had ever said it before. She could feel colour flushing over her cheekbones and knew she had to stop coming over as some kind of unworldly idiot. 'Well, aren't you?' she challenged. 'Don't tell me your heart didn't sink when you realised we'd have to spend the night here.'

Matteo considered her question. Up until a few moments ago he might have agreed with her, but there was something about the girl with the spiky black hair which was making him reconsider his original assessment. It was, he thought, a novel situation and he was a man whose appetites had been jaded enough over the years to be entertained by the novel. And Keira whatever-her-name-was certainly wasn't your average woman. She wasn't behaving as most women would have done in the circumstances. She had suggested playing a game as if she actually meant it, without any purring emphasis on the word *playing*, leaving him in no doubt how she intended the 'game' to progress—with him thrusting into her eager body. People called him arrogant, but he preferred to think of himself as a realist. He'd never been guilty of under-assessing his own attributes—and one of those was his ability to make the opposite sex melt, without even trying.

He focussed his gaze on her, mildly amused by the competitive look in her eyes which suggested that her question had been genuine. 'Sure,' he said. 'Let's play games.'

Picking up the tray, she went downstairs, reappearing after a little while with a stack of board games, along with a bottle of red wine and two glasses.

'There's no need to be snobby about the vintage,' she said, noticing his expression as he frowningly assessed the label on the bottle. 'It was very sweet of Mary to offer us a festive drink and I'm having a glass even if you aren't. I'm not driving anywhere tonight and I don't want to offend her, not when she's been so kind.'

Feeling surprisingly chastened, Matteo took the bottle and opened it, pouring them each a glass and forcing himself to drink most of his in a single draught as he lowered himself into the most uncomfortable chair he'd ever sat in.

'Ready?' she questioned as she sat cross-legged on the bed, with a blanket placed discreetly over her thighs as she faced him.

'I guess,' he growled.

They played Monopoly, which naturally he won—but then, he'd spent all his adult life trading property and had learnt early that there was no commodity more precious than land. But he was surprised when she sug-

gested a quick game of poker and even more surprised
by her skill with the cards.

Matteo wondered afterwards if he'd been distracted
by knowing her legs were bare beneath the blanket. Or
if he'd just spent too long gazing at her curling black
lashes, which remarkably didn't carry a trace of mascara. Because wasn't the truth that he was finding his
pocket-sized driver more fascinating with every moment which passed? She was certainly managing to
keep her face poker-straight as she gazed at her cards
and inexplicably he found himself longing to kiss those
unsmiling lips.

He swallowed. Was she aware that her coolness towards him was fanning a sexual awareness which was
growing fiercer by the second? He didn't know—all he
did know was that by the time they'd drunk most of the
bottle of wine, she had beaten him hands-down and it
was an unfamiliar experience.

He narrowed his eyes. 'Who taught you to play like
that?'

She shrugged. 'Before I became a driver, I worked
as a car mechanic—mostly with men,' she added airily. 'And they liked to play cards when the workshop
was quiet.'

'You worked as a *car mechanic*?'

'You sound surprised.'

'I am surprised. You don't look strong enough to
take a car to pieces.'

'Appearances can be deceptive.'

'They certainly can.' He picked up the bottle and
emptied out the last of the wine, noticing her fingers

tremble as he handed her the glass. She must be feeling it too, he thought grimly—that almost tangible buzz of *electricity* when his hand brushed against hers. He crossed one leg over the other to hide the hard throb of his erection as he tried—and failed—to think of something which didn't involve his lips and her body.

'Mr Valenti,' she said suddenly.

'Matteo,' he instructed silkily. 'I thought we agreed we should be on first-name terms, given the somewhat *unusual* circumstances.'

'Yes, we did, but I...

Keira's words tailed away as he fixed her with a questioning look, not quite sure how to express her thoughts. The alcohol had made her feel more daring than usual—something which she'd fully exploited during that game of cards. She'd known it probably wasn't the most sensible thing to defeat Matteo Valenti and yet something had made her want to show him she wasn't as useless as he seemed to think she was. But she was now aware of her bravado slipping away. Just as she was aware of the tension which had been building in the cramped bedroom ever since she'd emerged from the bathroom.

Her breasts were aching and her inside-out panties were wet. Did he realise that? Perhaps he was used to women reacting that way around him but she wasn't one of those women. She'd been called frigid by men before, when really she'd been scared—scared of doing what her mother had always warned her against. But it had never been a problem before, because close contact with the opposite sex had always left her cold and the one time she'd ended up in bed with a man he had been snoring in a drunken stupor almost before his head had hit the pillow. So how was Matteo managing to make her feel like this—as if every pore were screaming for him to touch her?

She swallowed. 'We haven't discussed what we're going to do about sleeping arrangements.'

'What did you have in mind?'

'Well, it looks as if we've got to share a bed—so obviously we've got to come to some sort of compromise.' She drew a deep breath. 'And I was thinking we might sleep top and tail.'

'Top and tail?' he repeated.

'You know.'

'Obviously I don't,' he said impatiently. 'Or I wouldn't have asked.'

Awkwardly, she wriggled her shoulders. 'It's easy. I sleep with my head at one end of the bed and you sleep with yours at the other. We used to do it when I was in the Girl Guides. Sometimes people even put pillows between them, so they can keep to their side and there's no encroaching on the other person's space.' She forged on but it wasn't easy when he was staring at her with a growing look of incredulity. 'Unless you're prepared to spend the night in that armchair?'

Matteo became aware of the hardness of the overstuffed seat which made him feel as if he were sitting on spirals of iron. 'You honestly think I'm going to spend the night sitting in this damned chair?'

She looked at him uncertainly. 'You want *me* to take the chair?'

'And keep me awake all night while you shift around trying to get comfortable? No. I do not. I'll tell you exactly what's going to happen, *cara mia*. We're going to share that bed as the nice lady suggested. But don't worry, I will break the habit of a lifetime by not sleeping naked and you can keep the sweater on. *Capisci?* And you can rest assured that you'll be safe from my intentions because I don't find you in the least bit attractive.'

Which wasn't exactly true—but why make a grim situation even worse than it already was?

He stood up and as he began to undo the belt of his trousers, he saw her lips fall open. 'Better close those big blue eyes,' he suggested silkily, a flicker of amusement curving his lips as he watched all the colour drain from her cheeks. 'At least until I'm safely underneath the covers.'

CHAPTER THREE

KEIRA LAY IN the darkness nudging her tongue over lips which felt as dry as if she'd been running a marathon. She'd tried everything. Breathing deeply. Counting backwards from a thousand. Relaxing her muscles from the toes up. But up until now nothing had worked and all she could think about was the man in bed beside her. *Matteo Valenti. In bed beside her.* She had to keep silently repeating it to herself to remind herself of the sheer impossibility of the situation—as well as the undeniable temptation which was fizzing over her.

Sheer animal warmth radiated from his powerful frame, making her want to squirm with an odd kind of frustration. She kept wanting to fidget but she forced herself to lie as still as possible, terrified of waking him up. She kept telling herself that she'd been up since six that morning and should be exhausted, but the more she reached out for sleep, the more it eluded her.

Was it because that unwilling glimpse of his body as he was about to climb into bed had reinforced all the fantasies she'd been trying not to have? And yes, he'd covered up with a T-shirt and a pair of silky boxers—

but they did nothing to detract from his hard-packed abdomen and hair-roughened legs. Each time she closed her eyes she could picture all that hard, honed muscle and a wave of hunger shivered over her body, leaving her almost breathless with desire.

The sounds coming from downstairs didn't help. The dinner which Mary had mentioned was in full flow and bothering her in ways she'd prefer not to think about. She could hear squeals of excitement above the chatter and, later, the heartbreaking strains of children's voices as they started singing carols. She could picture them all by a roaring log fire with red candles burning on the mantle above, just like on the front of a Christmas card, and Keira felt a wave of wistfulness overwhelm her because she'd never had that.

'Can't sleep?' The Italian's silky voice penetrated her spinning thoughts and she could tell from the shifting weight on the mattress that Matteo Valenti had turned his head to talk to her.

Keira swallowed. Should she pretend to be asleep? But what would be the point of that? She suspected he would see through her ruse immediately—and wasn't it a bit of a relief not to have to keep still any more? 'No,' she admitted. 'Can't you?'

He gave a short laugh. 'I wasn't expecting to.'

'Why not?'

His voice dipped. 'I suspect you know exactly why not. It's a somewhat *unusual* situation to be sharing a bed with an attractive woman and having to behave in such a chaste manner.'

Keira was glad of the darkness which hid her sudden

flush of pleasure. Had the gorgeous and arrogant Matteo Valenti actually called her *attractive*? And was he really implying that he was having difficulty keeping his hands off her? Of course, he might only be saying it to be polite—but he hadn't exactly been the model of politeness up until now, had he?

'I thought you said you didn't find me attractive.'

'That's what I was trying to convince myself.'

In the darkness, she gave a smile of pleasure. 'I could go downstairs and see if I could get us some more tea.'

'Please.' He groaned. 'No more tea.'

'Then I guess we'll have to resign ourselves to a sleepless night.' She plumped up her pillow and sighed as she collapsed back against it. 'Unless you've got a better suggestion?'

Matteo gave a frustrated smile because her question sounded genuine. She wasn't asking it in such a way which demanded he lean over and give her the answer with his lips. Just as she wasn't accidentally brushing one of those pretty little legs against his and tantalising him with her touch. He swallowed. Not that her virtuous attitude made any difference because he'd been hard from the moment he'd first slipped beneath the covers, and he was rock-hard now. Hard for a woman with terrible hair whose incompetence was responsible for him being marooned in this hellhole in the first place! A different kind of frustration washed over him as the lumpy mattress dug into his back until he reminded himself that apportioning blame would serve little purpose.

'I guess we could talk,' he said.

'What about?'

'What do women like best to talk about?' he questioned sardonically. 'You could tell me something about yourself.'

'And what good will that do?'

'Probably send me off to sleep,' he admitted.

He could hear her give a little snort of laughter. 'You do say some outrageous things, Mr Valenti.'

'Guilty. And I thought we agreed on Matteo—at least while we're in bed together.' He smiled as he heard her muffled gasp of outrage. 'Tell me how you plan to spend Christmas—isn't that what everyone asks at this time of year?'

Beneath the duvet, Keira flexed and unflexed her fingers, thinking that of all the questions he *could* have asked, that was the one she least felt like answering. Why hadn't he asked her about cars so she could have dazzled him with her mechanical knowledge? Or told him about her pipedream of one day being able to restore beautiful vintage cars, even though realistically that was never going to happen. 'With my aunt and my cousin, Shelley,' she said grudgingly.

'But you're not looking forward to it?'

'Is it that obvious?'

'I'm afraid it is. Your voice lacked a certain…enthusiasm.'

She thought that was a very diplomatic way of putting it. 'No, I'm not.'

'So why not spend Christmas somewhere else?'

Keira sighed. In the darkness it was all too easy to forget the veneer of nonchalance she always adopted when people asked questions about her personal life.

She kept facts to a minimum because it was easier that way. If you made it clear you didn't want to talk about something, then eventually people stopped asking.

But Matteo was different. She wasn't ever going to see him again after tomorrow. And wasn't it good to be able to say what she felt for once, instead of what she knew people expected to hear? She knew she was lucky her aunt had taken her in when that drunken joy-rider had mown down her mother on her way home from work, carrying the toy dog she'd bought for her daughter's birthday. Lucky she hadn't had to go into a foster home or some scary institution. But knowing something didn't always change the way you felt inside. And it didn't change the reality of being made to feel like an imposition. Of constantly having to be grateful for having been given a home, when it was clear you weren't really wanted. Trying to ignore all the snide little barbs because Keira had been better looking than her cousin Shelley. It had been the reason she'd cut off all her hair one day and kept it short. Anything for a quiet life. 'Because Christmas is a time for families and they're the only one I have,' she said.

'You don't have parents?'

'No.' And then, because he seemed to have left a gap for her to fill, she found herself doing exactly that. 'I didn't know my father and my aunt brought me up after my mother died, so I owe her a lot.'

'But you don't like her?'

'I didn't say that.'

'You didn't have to. It isn't a crime to admit it. You

don't have to like someone, just because they were kind to you, Keira, even if they're a relative.'

'She did her best and it can't have been easy. There wasn't a lot of money sloshing around,' she said. 'And now my uncle has died, there's only the two of them and I think she's lonely, in a funny kind of way. So I shall be sitting round a table with her and my cousin, pulling Christmas crackers and pretending to enjoy dry turkey. Just like most people, I guess.'

There was a pause so long that for a moment Keira wondered if he *had* fallen asleep, so that when he spoke again it startled her.

'So what *would* you do over Christmas?' he questioned softly. 'If money were no object and you didn't have to spend time with your aunt?'

Keira pulled the duvet up to her chin. 'How much money are we talking about? Enough to charter a private jet and fly to the Caribbean?'

'If that's what turns you on.'

'Not particularly.' Keira looked at the faint gleam of a photo frame glowing in the darkness on the other side of the room. It was a long time since she'd played make-believe. A long time since she'd dared. 'I'd book myself into the most luxurious hotel I could find,' she said slowly, 'and I'd watch TV. You know, one of those TVs which are big enough to fill a wall—big as a cinema screen. I've never had a TV in the bedroom before and it would be showing every cheesy Christmas film ever made. So I'd lie there and order up ice cream and popcorn and eat myself stupid and try not to blub too much.'

Beneath the thin duvet, Matteo's body tensed and not just because of the wistfulness in her voice. It had been a long time since he'd received such an uncomplicated answer from anyone. And wasn't her simple candour refreshing? As refreshing as her lean young body and eyes which were *profundo blu* if you looked at them closely—the colour of the deep, dark sea. The beat of his heart had accelerated and he felt the renewed throb of an erection, heavy against his belly. And suddenly the darkness represented danger because it was cloaking him with anonymity. Making him forget who he was and who she was. Tempting him with things he shouldn't even be thinking about. Because without light they were simply two bodies lying side by side, at the mercy of their senses—and right then his senses were going into overdrive.

Reaching out his arm, he snapped on the light, so that the small bedroom was flooded with a soft glow, and Keira lay there with the duvet right up to her chin, blinking her eyes at him.

'What did you do that for?'

'Because I'm finding the darkness…distracting.'

'I don't understand.'

He raised his eyebrows. 'Don't you?'

There was a pause. Matteo could see wariness in her eyes as she shook her head, but he could see the flicker of something else, something which made his heart pound even harder. Fraternising with the workforce was a bad idea—everyone knew that. But knowing something didn't always change the way you felt. It didn't stop your body from becoming so tight with lust that it felt like a taut bow, just before the arrow was fired.

No,' she said at last. 'I don't.'

'I think I'd better go and sleep in that damned armchair after all,' he said. 'Because if I stay here any longer I'm going to start kissing you.'

Keira met his mocking black gaze in astonishment. Had Matteo Valenti just said he wanted to *kiss* her? For a moment she just lay there, revelling in the sensation of being the object of attraction to such a gorgeous man, while common sense pitched a fierce battle with her senses.

She realised that despite talking about the armchair he hadn't moved and that an unspoken question seemed to be hovering in the air. Somewhere in a distant part of the house she heard a clock chiming and, though it wasn't midnight, it felt like the witching hour. As if magic could happen if she only let it. If she listened to what she wanted rather than the voice of caution which had been a constant presence in her life ever since she could remember. She'd learnt the hard way what happened to women who fell for the wrong kind of man—and Matteo Valenti had *wrong* written on every pore of his body. He was dangerous and sexy and he was a billionaire who was way out of her league. Shouldn't she be turning away from him and telling him yes, to please take the armchair?

Yet she wasn't doing any of those things. Instead of her eyes closing, the tip of her tongue was sliding over her bottom lip and she was finding it impossible to drag her gaze away from him. She could feel a molten heat low in her belly, which was making her ache in a way which was shockingly exciting. She thought about the holidays ahead. The stilted Christmas lunch with her aunt beaming at Shelley and talking proudly of her daughter's job as a beautician, while wondering how her only niece had ended up as a car mechanic.

Briefly Keira closed her eyes. She'd spent her whole life trying to be good and where had it got her? You didn't get medals for being good. She'd made the best of her dyslexia and capitalised on the fact that she was talented with her hands and could take engines apart, then put them back together. She'd found a job in a man's world which was just about making ends meet, but she'd never had a long-term relationship. She'd never even had sex—and if she wasn't careful she might end up old and wistful, remembering a snowy night on Dartmoor when Matteo Valenti had wanted to kiss her.

She stared at him. 'Go on, then,' she whispered. 'Kiss me.'

If she thought he might hesitate, she was wrong. There was no follow-up question about whether she was sure. He framed her face in his hands and the moment he lowered his lips to hers, that was it. The deal was done and there was no going back. He kissed her until she was dizzy with pleasure and molten with need. Until she began to move in his arms—restlessly seeking the next stage, terrified that any second now he would guess how laughingly inexperienced she was and push her away. She heard him laugh softly as he slid his fingers beneath the sweater to encounter the bra which curved over her breasts.

'Too much clothing,' he murmured, slipping his hand round her back to snap open the offending article and shake it free.

She remembered thinking he must have done this lots of times before and maybe she should confess how innocent she was. But by then he'd started circling her nipples with the light caress of his thumb and the moment passed. Desire pooled like honey in her groin and Keira gave a little cry as sensation threatened to overwhelm her.

'*Sta' zitto,*' he urged softly as he pulled the sweater over her head and tossed it aside, the movement quickly followed by the efficient disposal of his own T-shirt and boxers. 'Stay quiet. We don't want to disturb the rest of the house, do we?'

Keira shook her head, unable to answer because now he was sliding her panties down and a wild flame of hunger was spreading through her body. 'Matteo,' she gasped as his fingers moved down over her belly and began to explore her molten flesh. He stoked her with a delicacy which was tantalising—each intimate caress making her slide deeper into a brand-new world of intimacy. Yet strangely, it felt familiar. As if she knew exactly what to do, despite being such a novice. Did he tell her to part her legs or were they opening of their own accord? She didn't know. All she knew was that once he started stroking his fingertip against those hot, wet folds, she thought she might pass out with pleasure. 'Oh,' she whispered, on a note of wonder.

'Oh, what?' he murmured.

'It's…incredible.'

'I know it is. Now, touch me,' he urged against her mouth.

Keira swallowed. Did she dare? He was so big and proud and she didn't really know what to do. Swallowing down her nerves, she took him between her thumb and forefinger and began to stroke him up and down with a featherlight motion which nearly made him shoot off the bed.

'*Madonna mia!* Where did you learn to do *that*?' he gasped.

She guessed it might destroy the mood if she explained that car mechanics were often blessed with a naturally sensitive touch. Instead, she enquired in a husky voice which didn't really sound like her voice at all, 'Do you like it?'

'Do I like it?' He swallowed. 'Are you crazy? I love it.'

So why was he halting her progress with the firm clamp of his hand around her wrist, if he loved it so much? Why was he was blindly reaching for the wallet which he'd placed on the nightstand? He was pulling out a small foil packet and Keira shivered as she realised what he was about to do. This might be the craziest and most impulsive thing which had ever happened to her—but at least she would be protected.

He slid on the condom and she was surprised by her lack of fear as she wound her arms eagerly around his neck. Because it felt right. Not because he was rich and powerful, or even because he was insanely good-looking and sexy, but because something about him had touched her heart. Maybe it was the way his voice had softened when he'd asked her those questions about Christmas. Almost as if he *cared*—and it had been a long time since anybody had cared. Was she such a sucker for a few crumbs of affection that she would give herself completely to a man she didn't really know? She wasn't sure. All she knew was that she wanted him more than she'd ever wanted anything.

'Matteo,' she said as he pulled her into his body.

His eyes gleamed as he looked down at her. 'You want to change your mind?'

His consideration only made her want him more. 'No,' she whispered, her fingertips whispering over his neck. 'No way.'

He kissed her again—until she'd reached that same delicious melting point as before and then he moved to straddle her. His face was shadowed as he positioned himself and she tensed as he made that first thrust and began to move, but although the pain was sharp it was thankfully brief. She saw his brow darken and felt him grow very still before he changed his rhythm. His movements slowed as he bent her legs and wrapped them tightly around his waist so that with each long thrust he seemed to fill her completely.

As her body relaxed to accommodate his thickness, Keira felt the excitement build. Inch by glorious inch he entered her, before pulling back to repeat the same sweet stroke, over and over again. She could feel her skin growing heated as all her nerve-endings bunched in exquisitely tight anticipation. She could feel the inexorable build-up of excitement to such a pitch that she honestly didn't think she could take it any more. And then it happened. Like a swollen dam bursting open, waves of intense pleasure began to take her under. She felt herself shatter, as if he needed to break her apart before she could become whole again, and she pressed her mouth against his sweat-sheened shoulder. Dimly, she became aware of his own bucked release as he shuddered above her and was surprised by the unexpected prick of tears to her eyes.

He pulled out of her and rolled back against the pillows to suck in a ragged breath. With a sudden shyness, Keira glanced across at him but his eyes were closed and his olive features shuttered, so that suddenly she felt excluded from the private world in which he seemed to be lost. The room was quiet and she didn't dare speak—wondering what women usually said at moments like this.

Eventually he turned to her, his eyebrows raised in question and an expression on his face she couldn't quite work out.

'So?'

She wanted to hang on to the pleasure for as long as possible—she didn't want it all to evaporate beneath the harsh spotlight of explanation—but he seemed to be waiting for one all the same.

She peered up at him. 'You're angry?'

He shrugged. 'Why should I be angry?'

'Because I didn't tell you.'

'That you were a virgin?' He gave an odd kind of laugh. 'I'm glad you didn't. It might have shattered the mood.'

She tucked a strand of hair behind her ear. 'Aren't you going to ask me why?'

'You chose me to be your first?' His smile now held a faint trace of arrogance. 'I could commend you for your excellent judgment in selecting someone like me to be your first lover, but it's not really any of my business, is it, Keira?'

For some reason, that hurt, though she wasn't going to show it. Had she been naïve enough to suppose he might exhibit a chest-thumping pride that she had chosen him, rather than anyone else? 'I suppose not,' she said, her toes moving beneath the rumpled bedclothes in a desperate attempt to locate her only pair of panties.

'I just hope you weren't disappointed.'

'You must know I wasn't,' she said, in a small voice.

He seemed to soften a little at that, and brushed back a few little tufts of hair which had fallen untidily over her forehead. '*Sì*, I know. And for what it's worth, it was pretty damned amazing for me, too. I've never had sex with a virgin before but I understand it's uncommon for it to be as good as that the first time. So you should feel very pleased with yourself.' He began to stroke her hair. 'And you're tired.'

'No.'

'Yes,' he said firmly. 'And you need to sleep. So why don't you do that? Lie back and let yourself drift off.'

His words were soothing but Keira didn't want to sleep, she wanted to talk. She wanted to ask him about himself and his life. She wanted to know what would happen now—but there was something in his voice which indicated he didn't feel the same. And mightn't stilted conversation destroy some of this delicious afterglow which felt so impossibly fragile—like a bubble which could be popped at any moment? So she nodded obediently and shut her eyes and within seconds she could feel herself drifting off into the most dreamy sleep she'd ever known.

Matteo watched as her eyelashes fluttered down and waited until her breathing was steady before removing his arm from where it had been resting around her shoulders, but, although she stirred a little, she didn't waken. And that was when the reality of what he'd done hit him.

He'd just seduced a member of staff. More than that, he'd taken her innocence.

Silently, he cursed. He'd broken two fundamental rules in the most spectacular way. His chest was tight as he switched off the lamp and his mind buzzed as he attempted to ignore the naked woman who lay sleeping beside him. Yet that was easier said than done. He wanted nothing more than to push his growing erection inside her tight body again, but he needed to work out the most effective form of damage limitation. For both of them.

He stared up at the shadowy ceiling and sighed. He didn't want to hurt her and he could so easily hurt her. Hurting was something he seemed to do to women without even trying, mainly because he couldn't do love and he couldn't do emotion—at least that was what he'd been accused of, time after time. And Keira didn't deserve that. She'd given herself to him with an openness which had left him breathless and afterwards there had been no demands.

But none of that detracted from the reality of their situation. They came from worlds which were poles apart, which had collided in this small bedroom on the snowy outreaches of Devon. For a brief time they had come together in mindless pleasure but in truth they were nothing more than mismatched strangers driven by the stir of lust. Back in Italy he had been given an ultimatum which needed addressing and he needed to consider the truth behind his father's words.

'*Give me an heir, Matteo,*' he had breathed. '*Continue the Valenti name and I will give you your heart's desire. Refuse and I will sign the estate over to your stepbrother and his child.*'

Matteo's heart kicked with pain. He had to decide how much he was willing to sacrifice to maintain his links to the past. He needed to return to his world. And Keira to hers.

His jaw tightened. Would he have stopped if he'd known he was her first? He might have *wanted* to stop but something told him he would have been powerless to pull back from the indescribable lure of her petite body. His throat dried as he remembered that first sweet thrust. She had seemed much too small to accommodate him, but she had taken him inside her as if he had been intended to fit into her and only her. He remembered the way she'd touched him with that tentative yet sure touch. She'd made him want to explode. Had the newness of it been responsible for her joyful response—and for the tears which had trickled against his shoulder afterwards, but which she'd hastily blotted away?

Suddenly he could understand the potent power wielded by virgins but he could also recognise that they were a responsibility. They still had dreams—because experience hadn't yet destroyed them. Would she be expecting him to take her number? For him to fly her out to Rome for a weekend of sex and then see what happened? Hand in hand for a sunset stroll along Trastevere, Rome's supposedly most romantic neighbourhood? Because that was never going to happen. His jaw tightened. It would only raise up her hopes before smashing them.

He heard her murmur something in her sleep and felt the heavy weight of his conscience as he batted possibilities back and forth. What would be the best thing he could do for Keira—this sexy little driver with the softest lips he'd ever known? Glancing at his watch, he saw from the luminous dial that it was just before midnight and the rest of the house had grown silent. Could he risk using the landline downstairs without waking everyone? Of course he could. Slipping from the sex-scented bed, he threw on some clothes and made his way downstairs.

He placed the call without any trouble, but his mood was strangely low after he'd terminated his whispered conversation and made his way back to the bedroom. With the light from the corridor flooding in, he stared at Keira's face, which was pillowed on a bent elbow. Her lips were curved in a soft smile and he wanted to kiss them. To take her in his arms and run his hands over her and do it all over again. But he couldn't. Or rather, he shouldn't.

He was careful not to touch her as he climbed into bed, but the thought of her out-of-bounds nakedness meant that he lay there sleeplessly for a long, long time.

CHAPTER FOUR

A PALE LIGHT woke her and for a moment Keira lay completely still, her head resting against a lumpy pillow as her eyes flickered open and she tried to work out exactly where she was. And then she remembered. She was in a strange bedroom on the edge of a snowy Dartmoor—and she'd just lost her virginity to the powerful billionaire she'd been driving around the country!

She registered the sweet aching between her legs and the delicious sting of her nipples as slowly she turned her head to see that the other half of the bed was empty. Her pulse speeded up. He must be in the bathroom. Quickly, she sat up, raking her fingers through her mussed hair and giving herself a chance to compose herself before Matteo returned.

The blindingly pale crack of light shining through the gap in the curtains showed that the snow was still very much in evidence and a smile of anticipation curved her lips. Maybe they'd be stuck here today too—and they could have sex all over again. She certainly hoped so. Crossing her arms over her naked breasts, she hugged herself tightly as endorphins flooded through her warm body. Obviously, she'd need to reassure him that although she was relatively inexperienced, she certainly wasn't naïve. She knew the score—she'd heard the men in the workshop talking about women often enough to know what they did and didn't like. She would be very grown up about what had happened. She'd make it clear that she wasn't coming at this with any *expectations*—although, of course, if he wanted to see her again when the snow had been cleared she would be more than happy with that.

And that was when she noticed the nightstand—or rather, what was lying on top of it. Keira blinked her eyes in disbelief but as her vision cleared she realised this was no illusion as she stared in growing horror at the enormous wad of banknotes. She felt as if she were taking part in some secretly filmed reality show. As if the money might suddenly disintegrate if she touched it, or as if Matteo would suddenly appear from out of hiding. She looked around, realising there *was* nowhere to hide in this tiny room.

'Matteo?' she questioned uncertainly.

Nobody came. Of course they didn't. She stared at the money and then noticed the piece of paper which was lying underneath it. It took several seconds before she could bring herself to pick it up and as she began to read it she was scarcely able to believe what she was seeing.

Keira, he had written—and in the absence of any affectation like *Dear* or *Darling*, she supposed she ought to be grateful that he'd got her name right, because Irish names were notoriously difficult to spell.

I just wanted to tell you how much I enjoyed last night and I hope you did, too. You looked so peaceful sleeping this morning that I didn't want to wake you—but I need to be back in Italy as soon as possible.

You told me your dream was to spend Christmas in a luxury hotel and I'd like to make this possible, which is why I hope you'll accept this small gift in the spirit with which it was intended.

And if we'd been playing poker for money, you would certainly have walked away with a lot more than this!

I wish you every good thing for your future.
Buon Natale.
Matteo.

Keira's fingers closed tightly around the note and her feeling of confusion intensified as she stared at the money—more money than she'd ever seen. She allowed herself a moment of fury before getting up out of bed, acutely aware that for once she wasn't wearing her usual nightshirt, and the sight of her naked body in the small mirror taunted her with memories of just what she and the Italian had done last night. And once the fury had passed she was left with hurt, and disappointment. Had she really been lying there, naïvely thinking that Matteo was going to emerge from the bathroom and take her in his arms when the reality was that he couldn't even bear to face her? What a stupid fool she'd been.

She washed and dressed and went downstairs, politely refusing breakfast but accepting a mug of strong tea from Mary, who seemed delighted to relay every-thing which had been happening while Keira had been asleep.

'First thing I know, there's a knock on the door and it's a man in one of those big four-wheel drives,' she announced.

'Which managed to get through the snow?' questioned Keira automatically.

'Oh, yes. Because Mr Valenti ordered a car with a snow plough. Apparently he got on the phone late last night while everyone was asleep and organised it. Must have been very quiet because nobody heard him.'

Very quiet, thought Keira grimly. He must have been terrified that she would wake up and demand he take her with him.

'And he's ordered some men to dig your car out of the snow. Said there was no way you must be stranded here,' said Mary, with a dreamy look on her careworn face. 'They arrived about an hour ago—they should be finished soon.'

Keira nodded. 'Can I pay you?'

Mary beamed. 'No need. Your Mr Valenti was more than generous.'

Keira's heart pounded; she wanted to scream that he wasn't 'her' anything. So the cash wasn't there to pay for the B& B or help her make her own journey home, because he'd already sorted all that out. Which left only one reason for leaving it. Of course. How could she have been so dense when the bland words of the accompanying letter had made it perfectly clear? The comment about the poker and the disingenuous suggestion she take herself off to a luxury hotel were just a polite way of disguising the very obvious. A wave of sickness washed over her.

Matteo Valenti had *paid her for sex*.

Operating on a dazed kind of autopilot, Keira made her way back to her newly liberated car, from where she slowly drove back to London. After dropping the car off at Luxury Limos, she made her way to Brixton, acutely aware of the huge wad of cash she was carrying. She'd thought of leaving it behind at Mary's, but wouldn't the kindly landlady have tried to return it and just made matters a whole lot worse? And how on earth would she have managed to explain what it was doing there? Yet it felt as if it were burning a massive hole in her pocket—haunting her with the bitter reminder of just what the Italian really thought of her.

The area of Brixton where she rented a tiny apartment had once been considered unfashionable but now, like much of London, the place was on the up. Two days before Christmas and the streets had a festive air which was bordering on the hysterical, despite the fact that the heavy snows hadn't reached the capital. Bright lights glittered and she could see Christmas trees and scarlet-suited Santas everywhere she looked. On the corner, a Salvation Army band was playing 'Silent Night' and the poignancy of the familiar tune made her heart want to break. And stupidly, she found herself missing her mother like never before as she thought about all the Christmases they'd never got to share. Tears pricked at the backs of her eyes as she hugged her anorak around her shivering body, and never had she felt so completely alone.

But self-pity would get her nowhere. She was a survivor, wasn't she? She would get through this as she had got through so much else. Dodging the crowds, she started to walk home, her journey taking her past one of the area's many charity shops and as an idea came to her she impulsively pushed open the door of one. Inside, the place was full of people trying on clothes for Christmas parties and New Year—raiding feather boas and old-fashioned shimmery dresses from the crowded rails. The atmosphere was chaotic and happy but Keira was grim-faced as she made her way to the cash desk. Fumbling around in her pocket, she withdrew the wad of cash and slapped it down on the counter in front of the startled cashier.

'Take this,' Keira croaked. 'And Happy Christmas.'

The woman held up a hand. 'Whoa! Wait a minute! Where did you—?'

But Keira was already pushing her way out of the shop, the cold air hitting the tears which had begun streaming down her cheeks. Her vision blurred and she stumbled a little and might have fallen if a steady arm hadn't caught her elbow.

'Are you okay?' a female voice was saying.

Was she okay? No, she most definitely was not. Keira nodded, looking up at a woman with platinum hair who was wearing a leopard-skin-print coat. 'I'm fine. I just need to get home,' she husked.

'Not like that, you're not. You're not fit to go anywhere,' said the woman firmly. 'Let me buy you a drink. You look like you could use one.'

Still shaken, Keira allowed herself to be led into the bright interior of the Dog and Duck where music was playing and the smell of mulled wine filled her nostrils. The woman went up to the bar and returned minutes later with a glass of a brown mixture resembling medicine, which was pushed across the scratched surface of the table towards her.

'What's this?' Keira mumbled, lifting the glass and recoiling from the fumes.

'Brandy.'

'I don't like brandy.'

'Drink it. You look like you're in shock.'

That much was true. Keira took a large and fiery swallow and the weird thing was that she *did* feel better afterwards. Disorientated, yes—but better.

'So where did you get the money from?' the blonde was asking. 'Did you rob a bank or something? I was in the charity shop when you came in and handed it over. Pretty dramatic gesture, but a lovely thing to do, I must say—especially at this time of the year.'

Afterwards Keira thought that if she hadn't had the brandy then she might not have told the sympathetic blonde the whole story, but the words just started tumbling out of her mouth and they wouldn't seem to stop. Just like the tears which had preceded them. It was only when the woman's eyes widened when she came out with the punchline about how Matteo had left her a stack of money and done a runner that she became aware that something in the atmosphere had changed.

'So he just disappeared? Without a word?'

'Well, he left a note.'

'May I see it?'

Keira put the brandy glass down with a thud. 'No.'

There was a pause. 'He must be very rich,' observed the blonde. 'To be able to be carrying around that kind of money.'

Keira shrugged. 'Very.'

'And good-looking, I suppose?'

Keira swallowed. 'What does that have to do with anything?'

The blonde's heavily made-up eyes narrowed. 'Hunky Italian billionaires don't usually have to pay women for sex.'

It was hearing someone else say it out loud which made it feel a million times worse—something Keira hadn't actually thought possible. She rose unsteadily to her feet, terrified she was going to start gagging. 'I… I'm going home now,' she whispered. 'Please forget I said anything. And…thanks for the drink.'

Somehow she managed to get home unscathed, where her cold, bare bedsit showed no signs of the impending holiday. She'd been so busy that she hadn't even bought herself a little tree, but that now seemed like the least of her worries. She realised she hadn't checked her phone messages since she'd got back and found a terse communication from her aunt, asking her what time she was planning on turning up on Christmas Day and hoping she hadn't forgotten to buy the pudding.

The pudding! Now she would have to brave the wretched shops again. Keira closed her eyes as she pictured the grim holiday which lay ahead of her. How was she going to get through a whole Christmas, nursing the shameful secret of what she'd done?

Her phone began to ring, the small screen flashing an unknown number; in an effort to distract herself with the inevitable sales call, Keira accepted the call with a tentative hello. There was an infinitesimal pause before a male voice spoke.

'Keira?'

It was a voice she hadn't known until very recently but she thought that rich, Italian accent would be branded on her memory until the end of time. Dark and velvety, it whispered over her skin just as his fingers had done. Matteo! And despite everything—the wad of money and the blandly worded note and the fact that he'd left without even saying goodbye—wasn't there a great lurch of hope inside her foolish heart? She pictured his ruffled hair and the dark eyes which had gleamed with passion when they'd looked at her. The way he'd crushed his lips hungrily down on hers, and that helpless moment of bliss when he'd first entered her.

'Matteo?'

Another pause—and if a silence could ever be considered ominous, this one was. 'So how much did she pay you?' he questioned.

'Pay me?' Keira blinked in confusion, thinking that bringing up money wasn't the best way to start a conversation, especially in view of what had happened. 'What are you talking about?'

'I've just had a phone call from a…a *journalist*.'

He spat out the word as if it were poison. 'Asking me whether I make a habit of paying women for sex.'

Keira's feeling of confusion intensified. 'I don't...' And then she realised and hot colour flooded into her cheeks. 'Was her name Hester?'

'So you *did* speak to her?' He sucked in an unsteady breath. 'What was it, Keira—a quickly arranged interview to see what else you could squeeze out of me?'

'I didn't plan on talking to her—it just happened.'

'Oh, really?'

'Yes, really. I was angry about the money you left me!' she retorted.

'Why? Didn't you think it was enough?' he shot back. 'Did you imagine you might be able to get even more?'

Keira sank onto the nearest chair, terrified that her wobbly legs were going to give way beneath her. 'You bastard,' she whispered.

'Your anger means nothing to me,' he said coldly. 'For *you* are nothing to me. I wasn't thinking straight. I couldn't have been thinking straight. I should never have had sex with you because I don't make a habit of having one-night stands with strangers. But what's done can't be undone and I have only myself to blame.'

There was a pause before he resumed and now his voice had taken on a flat and implacable note, which somehow managed to sound even more ominous than his anger.

'I've told your journalist friend that if she prints one word about me, I'll go after her and bring her damned publication down,' he continued. 'Because I'm not someone you can blackmail—I'm just a man who allowed himself to be swayed by lust and it's taught me a lesson I'm never going to forget.' He gave a bitter laugh. 'So, goodbye, Keira. Have a good life.'

CHAPTER FIVE

Ten months later

'I HOPE THAT baby isn't going to cry all the way through lunch, Keira. It would be nice if we were able to eat a meal in peace for once.'

Tucking little Santino into the crook of her arm, Keira nodded as she met her aunt's accusing stare. She would have taken the baby out for a walk if the late October day hadn't been so foul and blustery. Or she might have treated him to a long bus ride to lull him to sleep if he hadn't been so tiny. As it was, she was stuck in the house with a woman who seemed determined to find fault in everything she did, and she was tired. So tired. With the kind of tiredness which seemed to have seeped deep into her bones and taken up residence there. 'I'll try to put him down for his nap before we sit down to eat,' she said hopefully.

Aunt Ida's mouth turned down at the corners, emphasising the deep grooves of discontentment which hardened her thin face. 'That'll be a first. Poor Shelley says she hasn't had an unbroken night since you moved in. He's obviously an unsettled baby if he cries so much. Maybe it's time you came to your senses and thought about adoption.'

Keira's teeth dug into her bottom lip as the word lodged like a barb in her skin.

Adoption.

A wave of nausea engulfed her but she tried very hard not to react as she stared down into the face of her sleeping son. Holding onto Santino even tighter, she felt her heart give a savage lurch of love as she told herself to ignore the snide comments and concentrate on what was important. Because only one thing mattered and that was her baby son.

Everything you do is for him, she reminded herself fiercely. *Everything.* No point in wishing she hadn't given away Matteo's money, or tormenting herself by thinking how useful it might have been. She hadn't known at the time that she was pregnant—how could she have done? She'd handed over that thick wad of banknotes as if there were loads more coming her way—and now she just had to deal with the situation as it was and not what it could have been. She had to accept that she'd lost her job and her home in quick succession and had been forced to take the charity of a woman who had always disapproved of her. Because how else would she and Santino have managed to cope in an uncaring and hostile world?

You know exactly how, prompted the ever-present voice of her conscience but Keira pushed it from her mind. She could *not* have asked Matteo for help, not when he had treated her like some kind of *whore*. Who had made it clear he never wanted to see her again.

'Have you registered the child's birth yet?' Aunt Ida was asking.

'Not yet, no,' said Keira. 'I have to do it within the first six weeks.'

'Better get a move on, then.'

Keira waited, knowing that there was more.

Her aunt smiled slyly. 'Only I was wondering whether you were going to put the mystery father's name on the birth certificate—or whether you were like your poor dear mother and didn't actually know who he was?'

Keira's determination not to react drained away. Terrified of saying something she might later regret, she turned and walked out of the sitting room without another word, glad she was holding Santino because that stopped her from picking up one of her aunt's horrible china ornaments and hurling it against the wall. Criticism directed against her she could just about tolerate—but she wouldn't stand to hear her mother's name maligned like that.

Her anger had evaporated by the time she reached the box-room she shared with Santino, and Keira placed the baby carefully in his crib, tucking the edges of the blanket around his tiny frame and staring at him. His lashes looked very long and dark against his olive skin but for once she found herself unable to take pleasure in his innocent face. Because suddenly, the fear and the guilt which had been nagging away inside her now erupted into one fierce and painful certainty.

She couldn't go on like this. Santino deserved more than a mother who was permanently exhausted, having to tiptoe around a too-small house with people who didn't really like her. She closed her eyes, knowing there was somebody else who didn't like her—but someone she suspected wouldn't display a tight-lipped intolerance whenever the baby started to cry. Because it was *his* baby, too. And didn't all parents love their children, no matter what?

A powerful image swam into her mind of a man whose face she could picture without too much trying. She knew what she had to do. Something she'd thought about doing every day since Santino's birth, and in the nine months preceding it, until she'd forced herself to remember how unequivocally he'd told her he never wanted to see her again. Well, maybe he was going to have to.

Her fingers were shaking as she scrolled down her phone's contact list and retrieved the number she had saved, even though the caller had hung up on her the last time she'd spoken to him.

With a thundering heart, she punched out the number. And waited.

Rain lashed against the car windscreen and flurries of falling leaves swirled like the thoughts in Matteo's mind as his chauffeur-driven limousine drove down the narrow suburban road. As they passed houses which all looked exactly the same, he tried to get his head round what he'd learned during a phone call from a woman he'd never thought he'd see again.

He was a father.

He had a child.

A son. His heart pumped. In a single stroke he had been given exactly what he needed—though not necessarily what he wanted—and could now produce the grandson his father yearned for.

Matteo ordered the driver to stop, trying to dampen down the unfamiliar emotions which were sweeping through his body. And trying to curb his rising temper about the way Keira had kept this news secret. How *dared* she keep his baby hidden and play God with his future? Grim-faced, he stepped out onto the rain-soaked pavement and a wave of determination washed over him as he slammed the car door shut. He was here now and he would fix this—to his advantage. Whatever it took, he would get what he wanted—and he wanted his son.

He hadn't told Keira he was coming. He hadn't wanted to give her the opportunity to elude him. He wanted to surprise her—as she had surprised him. To allow her no time to mount any defences. If she was unprepared and vulnerable then surely that would aid him in his determination to get his rightful heir. Moving stealthily up the narrow path, he rapped a small bronze knocker fashioned in the shape of a lion's head and moments later the door was opened by a woman with tight, curly hair and a hard, lined face.

'Yes?' she said sharply. 'We don't buy from the doorstep.'

'Good afternoon,' he said. Forcing the pleasantry to his unwilling lips, he accompanied it with a polite smile. 'I'm not selling anything. I'd like to see Keira.'

'And you are?'

'My name is Matteo Valenti,' he said evenly. 'And I am her baby's father.'

The woman gasped, her eyes scanning him from head to toe, as if registering his cashmere coat and handmade shoes. Her eyes skated over his shoulder and she must have observed the shiny black car parked so incongruously among all the sedate family saloons. Was he imagining the look of calculation which had hardened her gimlet eyes? Probably not, he thought grimly.

'You?' she demanded.

'That's right,' he agreed, still in that same even voice which betrayed nothing of his growing irritation.

'I had no idea that...' She swallowed. 'I'll have to check if she'll see you.'

'No,' Matteo interrupted her, only just resisting the desire to step forward and jam his foot in the door, like a bailiff. 'I *will* see Keira—and my baby—and it's probably best if we do it with the minimum of fuss.' He glanced behind him where he could see the twitching of net curtains on the opposite side of the road and when he returned his gaze to the woman, his smile was bland. 'Don't you agree? For everyone's sake?'

The woman hesitated before nodding, as if she too had no desire for a scene on the doorstep. 'Very well. You'd better come in.' She cleared her throat. 'I'll let Keira know you're here.'

He was shown into a small room crammed with porcelain figurines but Matteo barely paid any attention to his surroundings. His eyes were trained on the door as it clicked open and he held his breath in anticipation—

expelling it in a long sigh of disbelief and frustration when Keira finally walked in. Frustration because she was alone. And disbelief because he scarcely recognised her as the same woman whose bed he had shared almost a year ago—though that lack of recognition certainly didn't seem to be affecting the powerful jerk of his groin.

Gone was the short, spiky hair and in its place was a dark curtain of silk which hung glossily down to her shoulders. And her body. He swallowed. What the hell had happened to *that*? All the angular leanness of before had gone. Suddenly she had hips—as well as the hint of a belly and breasts. It made her look softer, he thought, until he reminded himself that a woman with any degree of softness wouldn't have done what she had done.

'Matteo,' she said, her voice sounding strained—and it was then he noticed the pallor and the faint circles which darkened the skin beneath her eyes. In those fathomless pools of deepest blue he could read the vulnerability he had wanted to see, yet he felt a sudden twist of something like compassion, until he remembered what she had done.

'The very same,' he agreed grimly. 'Pleased to see me?'

'I wasn't—' She was trying to smile but failing spectacularly. 'I wasn't expecting you. I mean, not like this. Not without any warning.'

'Really? What did you imagine was going to happen, Keira? That I would just accept the news you finally saw fit to tell me and wait for your next instruction?' He walked across the room to stare out of the window and saw that a group of small boys had gathered around his limousine. He turned around and met her eyes. 'Perhaps you were hoping you wouldn't have to see me at all. Were you hoping I would remain a shadowy figure in the background and become your convenient benefactor?'

'Of course I wasn't!'

'No?' He flared his nostrils. 'Then why *bother* telling me about my son? Why now after all these months of secrecy?'

Keira tried not to flinch beneath the accusing gaze which washed over her like a harsh ebony spotlight. It was difficult enough seeing him again and registering the infuriating fact that her body had automatically started to melt, without having to face his undiluted fury.

Remember the things he said to you, she reminded herself. But the memory of his wounding words seemed to have faded and all she could think was the fact that here stood Santino's father and that, oh, the apple didn't fall far from the tree.

For here was the adult version of the little baby she'd just rocked off to sleep before the doorbell had rung. Santino was the image of his father, with his golden olive skin and dark hair, and hadn't the midwife already commented on the fact that her son was going to grow up to be a heartbreaker? Keira swallowed. Just like Matteo.

She felt an uncomfortable rush of awareness because it wasn't easy to acknowledge the stir of her body, or the fact that her senses suddenly felt as if they'd been kicked into life. Matteo's hair and his eyes seemed even blacker than she remembered and never had his sensual lips appeared more kissable. Yet surely that was the last thing she should be thinking of right now. Her mind-set should be fixed on practicalities, not foolish yearnings. She felt disappointed in herself and wondered if nature was clever enough to make a woman desire the father of her child, no matter how contemptuously he was looking at her.

She found herself wishing he'd given her some kind of warning so she could at least have washed her hair and made a bit of effort with her appearance. Since having a baby she'd developed curves and she was shamefully aware that her pre-pregnancy jeans were straining at the hips and her baggy top was deeply unflattering. But the way she looked had been the last thing on her mind. She knew she needed new clothes but she'd been forced to wait, and not just because of a chronic shortage of funds.

Because how could she possibly go shopping for clothes with a tiny infant in tow? Asking her aunt to babysit hadn't been an option—not when she was constantly made aware of their generosity in providing a home for her and her illegitimate child, and how that same child had disrupted all their lives. The truth was she hadn't wanted to spend her precious pennies on new clothes when she could be buying stuff for Santino. Which was why she was wearing an unflattering outfit, which was probably making Matteo Valenti wonder what he'd ever seen in her. Measured against his made-to-measure sophistication, Keira felt like a scruffy wrongdoer who had just been dragged before an elegant high court judge.

She forced a polite smile to her lips. 'Would you like to sit down?'

'No, I don't want to *sit down*. I want an answer to my question. Why did you contact me to tell me that I was a father? Why now?'

She flushed right up to the roots of her hair. 'Because by law I have to register his birth and that brought everything to a head. I've realised I can't go on living like this. I thought I could but I was wrong. I'm very...grateful to my aunt for taking me in but it's too cramped. They don't really want me here and I can kind of see their point.' She met his eyes. 'And I don't want Santino growing up in this kind of atmosphere.'

Santino.

As she said the child's name Matteo felt a whisper of something he didn't recognise. Something completely outside his experience. He could feel it in the icing of his skin and sudden clench of his heart. 'Santino?' he repeated, wondering if he'd misheard her. He stared at her, his brow creased in a frown. 'You gave him an Italian name?'

'Yes.'

'Why?'

'Because when I looked at him—' her voice faltered as she scraped her fingers back through her hair and turned those big sapphire eyes on him '—I knew I could call him nothing else but an Italian name.'

'Even though you sought to deny him his heritage and kept his birth hidden from me?'

She swallowed. 'You made it very clear that you never wanted to see me again, Matteo.'

'I didn't know you were pregnant at the time,' he bit out.

'And neither did I!' she shot back.

'But you knew afterwards.'

'Yes.' How could she explain the sense of alienation she'd felt—not just from him, but from everyone? When everything had seemed so *unreal* and the world had suddenly looked like a very different place. The head of Luxury Limos had said he didn't think it was a good idea if she carried on driving—not when she looked as if she was about to throw up whenever the car went over a bump. And even though she hadn't been sick—not once—and even though Keira knew that by law she could demand to stay where she was, she didn't have the energy or the funds to investigate further. What was she going to do—take him to an industrial tribunal?

She'd been terrified her boss would find out who the father of her unborn child was—because having sex with your most prestigious client was definitely a sacking offence. He'd offered her a job back in the workshop, but she had no desire to slide underneath a car and get oil all over her hands, not when such a precious bundle was growing inside her. Eventually she'd accepted a mind-numbingly dull job behind the reception desk, becoming increasingly aware that on the kind of wages she was being paid, she'd never be able to afford childcare after the birth. She'd saved every penny she could and been as frugal as she knew how, but gradually all her funds were running out and now she was in real trouble.

'Yes, I knew,' she said slowly. 'Just like I knew I ought to tell you that you were going to be a father. But every time I picked up the phone to call you, something held me back. Can't you understand?'

'Frankly, no. I can't.'

She looked him straight in the eye. 'You think those cruel words you said to me last time we spoke wouldn't matter? That you could say what you liked and it wouldn't hurt, or have consequences?'

His voice grew hard. 'I haven't come here to argue the rights and wrongs of your secrecy. I've come to see my son.'

'He's sleeping.'

'I won't wake him.' His voice grew harsh. 'You've denied me all this time and you will deny me no longer. I want to see my son, Keira, and if I have to search every room in the house to find him, then that's exactly what I'm going to do.'

It was a demand Keira couldn't ignore and not just because she didn't doubt his threat to search the small house from top to bottom. She'd seen the brief tightening of his face when she'd mentioned his child and another wave of guilt had washed over her. Because she of all people knew what it was like to grow up without a father. She knew about the gaping hole it left—a hole which could never be filled. And yet she had sought to subject her own child to that.

'Come with me,' she said huskily.

He followed her up the narrow staircase and Keira

was acutely aware of his presence behind her. You couldn't ignore him, even when you couldn't see him, she thought despairingly. She could detect the heat from his body and the subtle sandalwood which was all his and, stupidly, she remembered the way that scent had clung to her skin the morning after he'd made love to her. Her heart was thundering by the time they reached the box-room she shared with Santino and she held her breath as Matteo stood frozen for a moment before moving soundlessly towards the crib. His shoulders were stiff with tension as he reached it and he was silent for so long that she started to get nervous.

'Matteo?' she said.

Matteo didn't answer. Not then. He wasn't sure he trusted himself to speak because his thoughts were in such disarray. He looked down at the baby expecting to feel the instant bolt of love people talked about when they first set eyes on their own flesh and blood, but there was nothing. He stared down at the dark fringe of eyelashes which curved on the infant's olive-hued cheeks and the shock of black hair. Tiny hands were curled into two tiny fists and he found himself leaning forward to count all the fingers, nodding his head with satisfaction as he registered each one. He felt as if he were observing himself and his reaction from a distance and realised it was possession he felt, not love. The sense that this was someone who belonged to him in a way that nobody ever had before.

His son.

He swallowed.

His *son*.

He waited for a moment before turning to Keira and he saw her dark blue eyes widen, as if she'd read something in his face she would prefer not to have seen.

'So you played God with all our futures,' he observed softly. 'By keeping him from me.'

Her gaze became laced with defiance.

'You paid me for sex.'

'I did not *pay you for sex*,' he gritted out. 'I explained my motivation in my note. You spoke of a luxury you weren't used to and I thought I would make it possible. Was that so very wrong?'

'You know very well it was!' she burst out. 'Because offering me cash was insulting. Any man would know that.'

'Was that why you tried to sell your story to the journalist, because you felt "insulted"?'

'I did not *sell my story* to anyone,' she shot back. 'Can't you imagine what it was like? I'd had sex for the first time and woke to find you gone, leaving that wretched pile of money. I walked into a charity shop to get rid of it because it felt…well, it felt tainted, if you must know.'

He grew very still. 'You gave it away?'

'Yes, I gave it away. To a worthy cause—to children living in care. Not realising I was pregnant at the time and could have used the money myself. The journalist just happened to be in the shop and overheard—and naturally she was interested. She bought me a drink and I hadn't eaten anything all day and…' She shrugged. 'I guess I told her more than I meant to.'

Matteo's eyes narrowed. If her story was true it

meant she hadn't tried to grab some seedy publicity from their brief liaison. *If it was true.* Yet even if it was—did it really change anything? He was here only because her back was up against the wall and she had nowhere else to turn. His gaze swept over the too-tight jeans and baggy jumper. And this was the mother of his child, he thought, his lips curving with distaste.

He opened his mouth to speak but Santino chose that moment to start to whimper and Keira bent over the crib to scoop him up, whispering her lips against his hair and rocking him in her arms until he had grown quiet again. She looked over his head, straight into Matteo's eyes. 'Would you…would you like to hold him?'

Matteo went very still. He knew he *should* want that, but although he thought it, he still couldn't *feel* it. There was nothing but an icy lump where his heart should have been and as he looked at his son he couldn't shift that strange air of detachment.

His lack of emotional empathy had never mattered to him before—only his frustrated lovers had complained about it and that had never been reason enough to change, or even *want* to change. But now he felt like someone on a beach who had inadvertently stepped onto quicksand. As if matters were spinning beyond his control.

And he needed to assert control, just as he always did.

Of course he would hold his son when he'd got his head round the fact that he actually *had* a son. But it would be in conditions favourable to them both—not in some tiny bedroom of a strange house while Keira stood studying him with those big blue eyes.

'Not now,' he said abruptly. 'There isn't time. You need to pack your things while I call ahead and prepare for your arrival in Italy.'

'What?'

'You heard me. He isn't staying here. And since a child needs a mother, then I guess you will have to come, too.'

'What are you talking about?' She rocked the child against her breast. 'I know it's not perfect here but I can't just walk out without making any plans. We can't just go to *Italy.*'

'You can't put out a call for help and then ignore help when it comes. You telephoned me and now you must accept the consequences,' he added grimly. 'You've already implied that the atmosphere here is intolerable so I'm offering you an alternative. The only sensible alternative.' He pulled a mobile phone from the pocket of his cashmere overcoat and began to scroll down the numbers. 'For a start, you need a nursery nurse to help you.'

'I don't *need* a nurse,' she contradicted fiercely. 'Women like me don't have nurses. They look after their babies themselves.'

'Have you looked in the mirror recently?'

It was an underhand blow to someone who was already feeling acutely sensitive and once again Keira flushed. 'I'm sorry I didn't have a chance to slap on a whole load of make-up and put on a party dress!'

He shook his head. 'That wasn't what I meant. You look as if you haven't had a decent night's sleep in weeks and I'm giving you the chance to get some rest.' He forced himself to be gentle with her, even though his instinct was always to push for exactly what he wanted. And yet strangely, he felt another wave of compassion as he looked into her pale face. 'Now, we can do this one of two ways. You can fight me or you can make the best of the situation and come willingly.' His mouth flattened. 'But if you choose the former, it will be fruitless because I want this, Keira. I want it very badly. And when I want something, I usually get it. Do you believe me?'

The mulish look which entered her eyes was there for only a second before she gave a reluctant nod. 'Yes,' she said grudgingly. 'I believe you.'

'Then pack what you need and I'll wait downstairs.' He turned away but was halted by the sound of her voice.

'And when we get there, what happens then, Matteo?' she whispered. 'To Santino?' There was a pause. 'To us?'

He didn't turn back. He didn't want to look at her right then, or tell her he didn't think there was an 'us'. 'I have no crystal ball,' he ground out. 'We'll just have to make it up as we go along. Now pack your things.'

He went downstairs, and, despite telling himself that this was nothing more than a problem which needed solving, he could do nothing about the sudden and inexplicable wrench of pain in his heart. But years of practice meant he had composed himself long before he reached the tiny hallway and his face was as hard as granite as he let himself out into the rainy English day.

CHAPTER SIX

GOLDEN SUNLIGHT DANCED on her closed eyelids and warmed her skin as Keira nestled back into the comfortable lounger. The only sounds she could hear were birdsong and the buzz of bees and, in the far distance, the crowing of a cock—even though it was the middle of the day. Hard to believe she'd left behind a rain-washed English autumn to arrive in a country where it was still warm enough to sit outside in October. And even harder to believe that she was at Matteo Valenti's Umbrian estate, with its acres of olive groves, award-winning vineyards and breathtaking views over mountains and lake. In his private jet, he'd announced he was bringing her here, to his holiday home, to 'acclimatise' herself before he introduced her to his real life in Rome. She hadn't been sure what he meant by that but she'd been too exhausted to raise any objections. She'd been here a week and much of that time had been spent asleep, or making sure that Santino was content. It felt like being transplanted to a luxury spa cleverly hidden within a rustic setting—with countless people working quietly in the background to maintain the estate's smooth running.

At first she'd been too preoccupied with the practical elements of settling in with her baby to worry about the emotional repercussions of being there. She'd worried about the little things, like how Matteo would react when he discovered she wasn't feeding Santino herself. Whether he would judge her negatively, as the whole world seemed to do if a woman couldn't manage to breastfeed. Was that why, in a rare moment of candour, she'd found herself explaining how ill she'd been after the birth—which meant breastfeeding hadn't been possible? She thought she'd glimpsed a brief softening of the granite-like features before his rugged features resumed their usual implacable mask.

'It will be easier that way,' he'd said, with a shrug. 'Easier for the nursery nurse.'

How *cold* he could be, she thought. Even if he was right. Because despite her earlier resistance, she was now hugely appreciative of the nursery nurse they'd employed. The very day after they'd arrived, he had produced three candidates for her to interview—top-notch women who had graduated from Italy's finest training establishment and who all spoke fluent English. After asking them about a million questions—but more importantly watching to see how well they interacted with her baby—Keira had chosen Claudia, a serene woman in her mid-thirties whom she instinctively trusted. It meant Keira got all the best bits of being a mother—cuddling and bathing her adorable son and making goo-goo noises at him as she walked him around the huge estate—while Claudia took over the dreaded three o'clock morning feed.

Which meant she could catch up with the sleep she so badly needed. She'd felt like a complete zombie when she arrived—a fact not helped by the disorientating experience of being flown to Italy on Matteo's luxury jet then being picked up by the kind of limousine which only a year ago she would have been chauffeuring. The drive to his Umbrian property had passed in a blur and Keira remembered thinking that the only time emotion had entered Matteo's voice was when they drove through the ancient gates and he began to point out centuries-old landmarks, with an unmistakable sense of pride and affection.

She almost wished Santino had been a little older so he could have appreciated the silvery ripple of olive trees, heavy with fruit and ready for harvest, and the golden pomegranates which hung from the branches like Christmas baubles. She remembered being greeted by a homely housekeeper named Paola and the delicious hot bath she took once the baby had been settled. There had been the blissful sensation of sliding between crisp, clean sheets and laying her head on a pillow of goose-down, followed by her first full night's sleep since before the birth. And that was pretty much how she'd spent the last seven days, feeling her vitality and strength returning with each hour that passed.

'You're smiling,' came a richly accented voice from above her as a shadow suddenly blotted out the sun.

Shielding her eyes with the edge of her hand, Keira peered up to see Matteo towering over her and her smile instantly felt as if it had become frozen. She could feel her heart picking up speed and the tug of silken hunger in the base of her belly and silently she cursed the instinctive reaction of her body. Because as her strength had returned, so too had her desire for Matteo—a man who she couldn't quite decide was her jailer or her saviour. Or both.

Their paths hadn't crossed much because he'd spent much of the time working in a distant part of the enormous farmhouse. It was as if he'd unconsciously marked out different territories for them, with clear demarcation lines which couldn't be crossed. But what she'd noted above all else was the fact that he'd kept away from the nursery, using the *excuse* that his son needed to settle in before getting used to too many new people. Because that was what it had sounded like. An excuse. A reason not to touch the son he had insisted should come here.

She'd seen him, of course. Glimpses in passing, which had unsettled her. Matteo looking brooding and muscular in faded denims and a shirt as he strode about the enormous estate, conversing in rapid Italian with his workers—or wearing a knockout charcoal suit just before driving to Rome for the day and returning long after she'd gone to bed.

Another image was burnt vividly into her mind, too. She'd overslept one morning and gone straight to the nursery to find Claudia cradling Santino by the window and telling him to watch 'Papa' going down the drive. *Papa.* It was a significant word. It emphasised Matteo's importance in their lives yet brought home how little she really knew about the cold-hearted billionaire. Yet that hadn't stopped her heart from missing a beat as he'd speeded out of the estate in his gleaming scarlet sports car, had it?

'It makes me realise how rarely I see you smile,' observed Matteo, still looking down at her as he stood silhouetted by the rich October sun.

'Maybe that's because we've hardly seen one another,' said Keira, flipping on the sunglasses which had been perched on top of her head, grateful for the way they kept her expression hidden. Not for the first time, she found it almost impossible to look at the man in front of her with any degree of impartiality, but she disguised it with a cool look. 'And you're a fine one to talk about smiling. You don't exactly go around the place grinning from ear to ear, do you?'

'Perhaps our forthcoming trip to Rome might bring a smile to both our faces,' he suggested silkily.

Ah yes, the trip to Rome. Keira felt the anxious slam of her heart. She licked her lips. 'I've been meaning to talk to you about that. Do we really have to go?'

In a movement which distractingly emphasised the jut of his narrow hips, he leaned against the sun-baked wall of the farmhouse. 'We've agreed to this, Keira. You need to see the other side of my life, not just this rural idyll. And I'm mainly based in Rome.'

'And the difference is what?'

'It's a high-octane city and nothing like as relaxed as here. When I'm there I go to restaurants and theatres. I have friends there and get invited to parties—and as the mother of my baby, I will be taking you with me.'

She sat up on the lounger, anxiety making her heart thud even harder against her ribcage. 'Why bother?

Why not just leave me somewhere in the background and concentrate on forming a relationship with your son?'

'I think we have to examine all the possibilities,' he said carefully. 'And number one on that list is to work out whether we could have some kind of life together.' He lifted his brows. 'It would certainly make things a whole lot easier.'

'And you're saying I'll let you down in my current state, is that it?'

He shrugged his broad shoulders with a carelessness which wasn't very convincing. 'I think we're both aware that you don't have a suitable wardrobe for that kind of lifestyle. You can't wear jeans all the time and Paola mentioned that you only seem to have one pair of boots.'

'So Paola's been spying on me, has she?' Keira questioned, her voice dipping with disappointment that the genial housekeeper seemed to have been taking her inventory.

'Don't be absurd. She was going to clean them for you and couldn't find any others you could wear in the meantime.'

Keira scrambled up off the lounger and stared into his hard and beautiful features. He really came from a totally different planet, didn't he? One which was doubtless inhabited by women who had boots in every colour of the rainbow and not just a rather scuffed brown pair she'd bought in the sales. 'So don't take me with you,' she said flippantly. 'Leave me behind while you go out to all your fancy places and I can stay home and look after Santino, wearing my solitary pair of boots.'

A flicker of a smile touched the corners of his lips, but just as quickly it was gone. 'That isn't an option, I'm afraid,' he said smoothly. 'You're going to have to meet people. Not just my friends and the people who work for me, but my father and stepmother at some point. And my stepbrother,' he finished, his mouth twisting before his gaze fixed her with its ebony blaze. 'The way you look at the moment means you won't fit in. Not any-where,' he continued brutally. 'And there's the chance that people will talk about you if you behave like some kind of hermit, which won't make things easy for you. Apart from anything else, we need to learn more about each other.' He hesitated. 'We are parents, with a child and a future to consider. We need to discuss the options open to us and that won't be possible if we continue to be strangers to one another.'

'You haven't bothered coming near me since we got here,' she said quietly. 'You've been keeping your dis-tance, haven't you?'

'Can you blame me? You were almost on your knees with exhaustion when you arrived.' He paused as his eyes swept over her again. 'But you look like a differ-ent person now.'

Keira was taken aback by the way her body re-sponded to that slow scrutiny, wondering how he could make her feel so many different things, simply by look-ing at her. And if that was the case, shouldn't she be protecting herself from his persuasive power over her, instead of going on a falsely intimate trip to Rome?

'I told you. I don't want to leave the baby,' she said stubbornly.

'Is that what's known as playing your trump card?' he questioned softly. 'Making me out to be some cruel tyrant who's dragging you away from your child?'

'He's only little! Not that you'd know, of course.' She paused and lifted her chin. 'You've hardly gone near him.'

Matteo acknowledged the unmistakable challenge in her voice and he felt a sudden chill ice his skin, despite the warmth of the October day. How audacious of her to interrogate him about his behaviour when her own had hardly been exemplary. By her keeping Santino's existence secret he had been presented with a baby, instead of having time to get used to the idea that he was to become a father.

Yet her pointed remark about his lack of interaction struck home, because what she said was true. He *had* kept his distance from Santino, telling himself that these things could not be rushed and needed time. And she had no right to demand anything of him, he thought bitterly. He would do things according to *his* agenda, not hers.

'Rome isn't far,' he said coolly. 'It is exactly two hundred kilometres. And I have a car constantly on standby.'

'Funnily enough that's something I *do* remember— being at your beck and call!'

'Then you will know there's no problem,' he said drily. 'Particularly as my driver is solid and reliable and not given to taking off to remote areas of the countryside in adverse weather conditions.'

'Very funny,' she said.

'We can be back here in an hour and a half should the need arise. We'll leave here at ten tomorrow morning—and be back early the next day. Less than twenty-four hours in the eternal city.' He gave a faintly cynical laugh. 'Don't women usually go weak at the knees at the prospect of an unlimited budget to spend on clothes?'

'Some women, maybe,' she said. 'Not me.'

But Keira's stubbornness was more than her determination not to become a rich man's doll. She didn't *know* about fashion—and the thought of what she might be expected to wear scared her. Perhaps if she'd been less of a tomboy, she might have flicked through glossy magazines like other women her age. She might have had some idea of what did and didn't suit her and would now be feeling a degree of excitement instead of dread. Fear suddenly became defiance and she glared at him.

'You are the bossiest man I've ever met!' she declared, pushing a handful of hair over her shoulder.

'And you are the most difficult woman I've ever encountered,' he countered. 'A little *gratitude* might go down well now and again.'

What, gratitude for his high-handedness and for making her feel stuff she'd rather not feel? Keira shook her head in frustration as she tugged her T-shirt down over her straining jeans.

'I'll be ready at ten,' she said, and went off to find Santino.

She put the baby in his smart new buggy to take him for a walk around the estate, slowly becoming aware that the weather had changed. The air had grown heavy and sultry and heavy clouds were beginning to accumulate on the horizon, like gathering troops. When eventually they returned to the farmhouse, Santino took longer than usual to settle for his sleep and Keira was feeling out of sorts when Paola came to ask whether she would be joining Signor Valenti for dinner that evening.

It was the first time she'd received such an invitation and Keira hesitated for a moment before declining. Up until now, she'd eaten her supper alone or with Claudia and she saw no reason to change that routine. She was going to be stuck with Matteo in Rome when clearly they were going to have to address some of the issues confronting them. Why waste conversation during a stilted dinner she had no desire to eat, especially when the atmosphere felt so close and heavy?

Fanning her face with her hand, she showered before bed but her skin still felt clammy, even after she'd towelled herself dry. Peering up into the sky, she thought she saw a distant flash of lightning through the thick curtain of clouds. She closed the shutters and brushed her hair before climbing into bed, but sleep stubbornly eluded her. She wished the occasional growl of thunder would produce the threatened rain and break some of the tension in the atmosphere and was just drifting off into an uneasy sleep when her wish came true. A loud clap of thunder echoed through the room and made her sit bolt upright in bed. There was a loud whoosh and heavy rain began to hurl down outside her window and quickly she got up and crept into Santino's room but, to her surprise, the baby was sound asleep.

How did he manage to do that? she thought enviously—feeling even more wide awake than before. She sighed as she went back to bed and the minutes ticked by, and all she could think about was how grim she was going to look, with dark shadowed eyes and a pasty face. Another clap of thunder made her decide that a warm drink might help relax her. And wasn't there a whole stack of herb teas in the kitchen?

To the loud tattoo of drumming rain, she crept downstairs to the kitchen with its big, old-fashioned range and lines of shiny copper pots hanging in a row. She switched on some low lighting and not for the first time found herself wistfully thinking how *homely* it looked—and how it was unlike any place she had imagined the urbane Matteo Valenti would own.

She had just made herself a cup of camomile tea when she heard a sound behind her and she jumped, her heart hammering as loudly as the rain as she turned to see Matteo standing framed in the doorway. He was wearing nothing but a pair of faded denims, which were clinging almost indecently to his long and muscular thighs. His mouth was unsmiling but there was a gleam in his coal-dark eyes, which made awareness drift uncomfortably over her skin and suddenly Keira began to shiver uncontrollably, her nipples tightening beneath her nightshirt.

CHAPTER SEVEN

THE WALLS SEEMED to close in on her and Keira was suddenly achingly conscious of being alone in the kitchen with a half-naked Matteo, while outside she could hear the rain howl down against the shuttered windows.

With a shaking hand she put her mug down, her eyes still irresistibly drawn to the faded jeans which hugged his long and muscular thighs. He must have pulled them on in a hurry because the top button was undone, displaying a line of dark hair which arrowed tantalisingly downwards. Soft light bathed his bare and gleaming torso, emphasising washboard abs and broad shoulders.

She realised with a start that she'd never seen his naked torso before—or at least hadn't really noticed it. She'd been so blown away when they'd been having sex that her eyes hadn't seemed able to focus on anything at all. But now she could see him in all his beauty— a dark and forbidding beauty, but beauty all the same. And despite all the *stuff* between them, despite the fact that they'd been snapping at each other like crocodiles this afternoon, she could feel herself responding to him, and there didn't seem to be a thing she could do about it.

Beneath her nightshirt her nipples were growing even tighter and her breasts were heavy. She could feel a warm melting tug at her groin and the sensation was so intense that she found herself shifting her weight uncomfortably from one bare foot to the other. She opened her mouth to say something, but no words came.

He stared at her, a strange and mocking half-smile at his lips, as if he knew exactly what was happening to her. 'What's the matter, Keira?' he queried silkily. 'Can't sleep?'

She struggled to find the correct response. To behave as anyone else would in the circumstances.

Like a woman drinking herb tea and not wishing that he would put his hand between her legs to stop this terrible aching.

'No. I can't. This wretched storm is keeping me awake.' She forced a smile. 'And neither could you, obviously.'

'I heard someone moving around in the kitchen, so I came to investigate.' He stared down at her empty cup. 'Is the tea working?'

She thought about pretending but what was the point? 'Not really,' she admitted as another crash of thunder echoed through the room. 'I'm still wide awake and I'm probably going to stay that way until the storm dies down.'

There was a pause while Matteo's gaze drifted over her and he thought how pale she looked standing there with her nightshirt brushing against her bare thighs and hair spilling like dark silk over her shoulders. Barefooted, she looked *tiny*—a tantalising mixture of vulnerability and promise—and it felt more potent than anything he'd ever experienced. She was trying to resist him, he knew that, yet the look in her eyes told him that inside she was aching as much as he was. He knew what he was going to do because he couldn't put it off any longer, and although the voice of his conscience was sounding loud in his ears, he took no notice of it. She needed to relax a little—for all their sakes.

'Maybe you should try a little distraction technique,' he said.

Her eyes narrowed. 'Doing what?'

'Come and look at the view from my study,' he suggested evenly. 'It's spectacular at the best of times, but during a storm it's unbelievable.'

Keira hesitated because it felt as if he were inviting her into the lion's lair, but surely anything would be better than standing there feeling totally out of her depth. What else was she going to do— go back to bed and lie there feeling sorry for herself? And they were leaving for Rome tomorrow. Perhaps she should drop her guard a little. Perhaps they should start trying to be friends.

'Sure,' she said, with a shrug. 'Why not?'

His study was in a different wing of the house, which hadn't featured in the guided tour he'd given her at the beginning of the week—an upstairs room sited at the far end of a vast, beamed sitting room. She followed him into the book-lined room, her introspection vanishing the instant she saw the light show taking place outside the window. Her lips fell open as she stood watching the sky blindingly illuminated by sheet lightning, which lit up the dark outlines of the surrounding mountains. Each bright flash was reflected in the surface of the distant lake, so that the dramatic effect of what she was seeing was doubled. 'It's…amazing,' she breathed.

'Isn't it?'

He had come to stand beside her—so close that he was almost touching and Keira held her breath, wanting him to touch her, *praying* for him to touch her. Did he guess that? Was that why he slid his arm around her shoulders, his fingers beginning to massage the tense and knotted muscles?

She looked up into the hard gleam of his eyes, startled by the dark look of hunger on his face.

'Shall we put a stop to all this right now, Keira?' he murmured. 'Because we both know that the damned storm has nothing to do with our inability to sleep. It's desire, isn't it? Two people lying in their lonely beds, just longing to reach out to one another.'

His hands had slipped to her upper arms, and as his hard-boned face swam in and out of focus Keira told herself to break away and escape to the sanctuary of her room. Yet her body was stubbornly refusing to obey. All she could seem to focus on were his lips and how good it felt to have him touching her like this. She'd never stood in a storm-lit room with a half-dressed man, completely naked beneath her frumpy nightshirt, and yet she knew exactly what was going to happen next. She could feel it. Smell it. She swayed. Could almost *taste* the desire which was bombarding her senses and making her pounding heart the only thing she could hear above the loud hammer of the rain.

'Isn't that so?' he continued, brushing hair away from

her face as the pad of his thumb stroked its way over her trembling lips. 'You want me to kiss you, don't you, Keira? You want it really quite badly.'

Keira resented the arrogance of that swaggering statement—but not enough to make her deny the truth behind it. 'Yes,' she said. 'Yes, I do.'

Matteo tensed, her whispered assent sharpening his already keen hunger, and he pulled her against his body and crushed his mouth over hers. And, oh, she tasted good. Better than good. Better than he remembered— but maybe that was because her kiss had lingered in his memory far longer than it should have done. He tried to go slowly but his usual patience fled as his hands began to rediscover her small and compact body. Before she had been incredibly lean—he remembered narrow hips and the bony ladder of her ribcage. But now those bones had disappeared beneath a layer of new flesh, which was soft and tempting and just ripe for licking.

Her head tipped back as he rucked up her nightshirt, his hand burrowing beneath the bunched cotton until he had bared her breast. He bent his head to take one taut rosebud in between his lips and felt her fingers digging into his bare shoulders as he grazed the sensitive areola between his teeth. Already he felt as if he wanted to explode—as if he would die if he'd didn't quickly impale her. Was the fact that she'd borne his child the reason why he was feeling a desire which felt almost *primitive* in its intensity? Was that why his hands were trembling like this?

'Do you know how long I've been wanting to do this?' he husked, his fingers sliding down between her breasts and caressing their silken weight. 'Every second of every day.'

Her reply was a muffled gasp against his mouth. 'Is that why you've stayed away from me?'

'That's exactly why.' He let his fingertips trickle down over her belly and heard her catch her breath as they travelled further downwards. 'You needed to rest and I was trying to be a...*gentleman*,' he growled.

'And how does this qualify as being...*oh*!' Her words faded away as he slid his hand between her legs, brushing over the soft fuzz of hair to find the molten heat beneath.

'You were saying?' he breathed as he dampened his finger in the soft, wet folds before starting to stroke the little bud which was already so tight.

He heard her give a shaky swallow. 'Matteo, this is...is...'

He knew exactly what it was. It was arousing her to a state where she was going to come any second, and while it was turning him on to discover how close to the edge she was—it was also making his own frustration threaten to implode. With a necessary care which defied his hungry impatience, he eased the zip of his jeans down over his straining hardness—breathing a sigh of relief as his massive erection sprang free. The denim concertinaed around his ankles but he didn't care. He knew propriety dictated he should take them off, but he couldn't. He couldn't wait, not a second longer.

Impatiently he pushed her back against his desk, shoving aside his computer and paperwork with uncharacteristic haste. And the moment the moist tip of his penis touched her, she seemed to go wild, clawing eagerly at his back—and it took more concentration than he'd ever needed to force himself to pull back. Through the distracting fog of desire, he recalled the condom concealed in a drawer of his desk and by the time it was in place he felt as excited as a teenage boy as his hungry gaze skated over her.

Like a sacrifice she lay on the desk, her arms stretched indolently above her head as he leaned over to make that first thrust deep inside her. And this time there was no pain or hesitation. This time there was nothing but a gasped cry of pleasure as he filled her. Greedily, he sank even deeper and then he rode her— and even the crash of something falling from the desk wasn't enough to put him off his stroke. Or maybe it was just another crash of thunder from the storm outside. Who cared? He rode her until she came, her frantic convulsions starting only fractionally before his own, so that they moved in perfect time before his ragged groan heralded the end and he slumped on top of her, her hands clasped around the sweat-sheened skin of his back.

He didn't say anything at first, unwilling to shatter the unfamiliar peace he felt as he listened to the quietening of his heart. He felt spent. As if she had milked him dry. As if he could have fallen asleep right there, despite the hardness of the wooden surface. He forced himself to open his eyes and to take stock of their surroundings. Imagine if they were discovered here in the morning by one of the cleaners, or by Paola—already surprised that, not only had he brought a woman here, but he had a baby son.

A son he had barely seen.

Guilt formed itself into an icy-cold knot deep in his chest and was enough to dissolve his lethargy. Untwining himself from Keira's arms, he moved away from the desk, bending to pull up his jeans and zip them. Only then did he stare down at her, where she lay with her eyes closed amid the debris of his wrecked desk. Her cotton nightshirt was rucked right up to expose her beautiful breasts and her legs were bent with careless abandon. The enticing gleam between her open thighs was making him grow hard again but he fought the feeling—telling himself he needed to start taking control. He would learn about his son in time—he *would*—but for now his primary purpose was to ensure that Santino remained a part of his life, and for that to happen he needed Keira onside.

So couldn't their powerful sexual chemistry work in his favour—as effective a bargaining tool as his vast wealth? Couldn't he tantalise her with a taste of what could be hers, if only she was prepared to be reasonable? Because Keira Ryan was unpredictable. She was proud and stubborn, despite the fact that she'd been depending on other people's charity for most of her life, and he was by no means certain that she would accede to his wishes. So maybe it was time to remind her just who was calling the shots. He bent and lifted her into his arms, cradling her against his chest as her eyelashes fluttered open.

'What are you doing?' she questioned drowsily.

'Taking you back to bed.'

She yawned. 'Can't we just stay here?'

He gave an emphatic shake of his head. 'No.'

Keira closed her eyes again, wanting to capture this feeling for ever—a feeling which went much deeper than sexual satisfaction, incredible though that side of it had been. She had felt so close to Matteo when he'd been deep inside her. *Scarily* close—almost as if they were two parts of the same person. Had he felt that, too? Her heart gave a little leap of hope. Couldn't they somehow make this work despite everything which had happened? Couldn't they?

Resting her head against his warm chest, she let him carry her through the house to her own room, not pausing until he had pulled back the duvet and deposited her in the centre of the soft bed. Only then did her eyelids flutter open, her heart missing a beat as she took in his gleaming torso and powerful thighs. She stared up at him hopefully. Was he going to lose the jeans and climb in beside her, so she could snuggle up against him as she so desperately wanted to do and stroke her fingers through the ruffled beauty of his black hair?

She watched as his gaze swept over her, the hectic glitter of hunger in their ebony depths unmistakable. And she waited, because surely it should be *him* asking her permission to stay? She didn't know very much about bedroom etiquette, but instinct told her that. She recognised that she'd been a bit of a pushover back there, and it was time to show the Italian tycoon that he might need to work a little harder this time.

'So?' She looked at him with what she hoped was a welcoming smile.

'That's better. You don't smile nearly enough.' His finger traced the edges of her lips as he leaned over her. 'All the bad temper of this afternoon banished in the most pleasurable way possible.' He stroked an exploratory finger over the tightening nipple beneath her nightshirt. 'Was that what you needed all along, Keira?'

It took a few moments for his meaning to sink in and when it did, Keira could hardly believe her ears. A powerful wave of hurt crashed over her. Was that all it had been? Had he made love to her as a way of soothing her ruffled emotions and making her more *amenable*? As if he were some kind of *human sedative*? She wanted to bite down hard on her clenched fist. To demand how someone so cold-blooded could possibly live with himself. But she forced herself to remain silent because only that way could she cling onto what was left of her battered pride. Why give him the satisfaction of knowing he'd hurt her? If he was going to act so carelessly, then so would she. And why be so surprised by his callous behaviour when he hadn't shown one fraction of concern for his baby son. Matteo Valenti was nothing but a manipulative and cold-blooded *bastard*, she reminded herself.

Hauling the duvet up to her chin, she closed her eyes. 'I'm tired, Matteo,' she said. 'Would you mind turning off the light as you go?'

And then, deliberately manufacturing a loud yawn, she turned her back on him.

CHAPTER EIGHT

KEIRA DIDN'T SAY a word to Matteo next morning, not until they were halfway to Rome and his powerful car had covered many miles. The fierce storm had cleared the air and the day had dawned with a sky of clear, bright blue—but the atmosphere inside the car was heavy and fraught with tension. She was still feeling the painful tug of saying goodbye to Santino, though he'd been happily cradled in Claudia's arms when the dreaded moment had arrived. But as well as the prospect of missing her baby, Keira was still smarting from what had happened the night before.

She'd woken up with a start soon after dawn, wondering why her body felt so…

Slowly she had registered her lazy lethargy and the sweet aching between her legs.

So…*used.*

Yes, used, that was it. *Used.* Vivid images had flashed through her mind as she remembered what had happened while the storm raged outside. Matteo unzipping his jeans and pushing her onto his desk. Matteo rucking up her nightdress before thrusting into her and making her cry out with pleasure. It had hardly been the stuff of fairy tales, had it? So why not concentrate on the reality, rather than the dumb romantic version she'd talked herself into when she was lying quivering beneath his sweat-sheened body?

He had cold-bloodedly seduced her after days of acting as if she didn't exist. He had invited her to witness the storm from the best vantage point in the house and, although it had been the corniest request in the world, she had agreed. Trotting behind him like some kind of puppy dog, she'd had sex with him. Again. Keira closed her eyes in horror as she remembered the way she'd clawed at his bare back like some kind of wildcat. Did her inexperience explain the fierce hunger which had consumed her and made her unable to resist his advances? Or was it just that Matteo Valenti only had to touch her for her to come apart in his arms?

And now the trip to Rome, which she'd already been dreading, was going to be a whole lot worse. Bad enough being in the kind of car she'd lusted after during her days as a mechanic—and having it driven by *someone else*—without the knowledge of how smug Matteo must be feeling. Why, he hadn't even wanted to spend the night with her! He'd just deposited her in her bed like some unwanted package and behaved as if what had happened had been purely functional. Like somebody scratching an itch. Was that how it had been for him, she wondered bitterly? Had he seen her as a body rather than a person?

'So, are you going to spend the next twenty-four hours ignoring me?' Matteo's voice broke into her rebellious thoughts as they passed a signpost to a pretty-looking place called Civita Castellana.

Keira wanted to pretend she hadn't heard him but that was hardly the way forward, was it? She mightn't be happy with the current state of affairs, but that didn't mean she had to lie down and passively accept it. Unless she was planning on behaving like some sort of victim—allowing the powerful tycoon to pick her up and move her around at will, without her having any say in the matter. It was time she started asserting herself and stopped beating herself up. They'd had sex together as two consenting adults and surely that put them on some kind of equal footing.

So *ask* him.

Take some of the control back.

She turned her head to look at his profile, trying not to feel affected by that proud Roman nose and the strong curve of his shadowed jaw. His silk shirt was unbuttoned at the neck, offering a tantalising glimpse of olive skin, and he exuded a vitality which made him seem to glow with life. She could feel a trickle of awareness whispering over her body and it made her want to fidget on the plush leather car seat.

She wanted him to touch her all over again. And when he touched her she went to pieces.

Firmly pushing all erotic possibilities from her mind, she cleared her throat. 'So why this trip, Matteo?'

There was a pause. 'You know why. We've discussed this. We're going to buy you some pretty clothes to wear.'

His words were deeply patronising and she wondered

if that had been his intention—reminding her that she fell way short of his ideal of what a woman should be. 'I'm not talking about your determination to change my appearance,' she said. 'I mean, why bring me to Italy in the first place? That's something we haven't even discussed. What's going to happen once you've waved your magic wand and turned me into someone different? Are you planning to return me to England in your fancy plane and make like this was all some kind of dream?'

His mouth hardened into a flat and implacable line. 'That isn't an option.'

'Then what *are* the options?' she questioned quietly.

Matteo put his foot down on the accelerator and felt the powerful engine respond. It was a reasonable question, though not one he particularly wanted to answer. But he couldn't keep on putting off a conversation they needed to have because he was wary of all the stuff it might throw up. 'We need to see whether we can make it work as a couple.'

'A *couple*?'

He saw her slap her palms down on her denim-covered thighs in a gesture of frustration.

'You mean, living in separate parts of the same house? How is that in any way what a *couple* would do?' She sucked in a breath. 'Why, we've barely *seen* one another—and when we have, it isn't as if we've done much talking!'

'That can be worked on,' he said carefully.

'Then let's start working on it right now. Couples aren't complete strangers to one another and we are. Or at least, you are. I told you a lot about my circumstances on the night we...' Her voice wavered as she corrected herself before growing quieter. 'On that night we spent together in Devon. But I don't know you, Matteo. I still don't really know anything about you.'

Matteo stared at the road ahead. Women always asked these kinds of questions and usually he cut them short. With a deceptively airy sense of finality, he'd make it clear that he wouldn't tolerate any further interrogation because he didn't want anyone trying to 'understand' him. But he recognised that Keira was different and their situation was different. She was the mother of his child and she'd given birth to his heir—not some socially ambitious woman itching to get his ring on her finger. He owed her this.

'What do you want to know?' he questioned.

She shrugged. 'All the usual stuff. About your parents. Whether or not you have any brothers or sisters. That kind of thing.'

'I have a father and a stepmother. No siblings,' he said, his voice growing automatically harsher and there wasn't a damned thing he could do to stop it. 'But I have a stepbrother who's married, with a small child.'

He could feel her eyes on him. 'So your parents are divorced?'

'No. My mother is dead.'

'Like mine,' she said thoughtfully.

He nodded but didn't say anything, his attention fixed on the road ahead, trying to concentrate on the traffic and not on the bleak landscape of loss.

'Tell me about your father,' she said. 'Do you get on well with him?'

Some of the tension left his body as he overtook a truck and he waited until he had finished the manoeuvre before answering. He wondered if he should give her the official version of his life, thus maintaining the myth that all was well. But if she stayed then she would soon discover the undercurrents which surged beneath the surface of the powerful Valenti clan.

'We aren't close, no. We see each other from time to time, more out of duty than anything else.'

'But you mentioned a stepmother?'

'You mean the latest stepmother?' he questioned cynically. 'Number four in a long line of women who were brought in to try to replace the wife he lost.'

'But…' She hesitated. 'None of them were able to do that?'

'That depends on your definition. I'm sure each of them provided him with the creature comforts most men need, though each marriage ended acrimoniously and at great financial cost to him. That's the way it goes, I guess.' His hands tightened around the steering wheel. 'But my mother would have been a hard act for any woman to follow—at least according to the people who knew her.'

'What was she like?' she prompted, and her voice was as gentle as he'd ever imagined a voice could be.

Matteo didn't answer for a long time because this was something nobody ever really asked. A dead mother was just that. History. He couldn't remember anyone else who'd ever shown any interest in her short life.

He could feel the tight squeeze of his heart. 'She was beautiful,' he said eventually. 'Both inside and out. She was training to be a doctor when she met my father—an only child from a very traditional Umbrian family who owned a great estate in the region.'

'The farmhouse where we've been staying?' she questioned slowly. 'Is that…?'

He nodded. 'Was where she grew up, *sì*.'

Keira nodded as slowly she began to understand. She gazed out of the window at the blue bowl of the sky. Did that explain his obvious love for the estate? she wondered. The last earthly link to his mum?

'Does your father know?' she questioned suddenly. 'About Santino?'

'Nobody knows,' he said harshly. 'And I won't let it be known until we've come to some kind of united decision about the future.'

'But a baby isn't really the kind of thing you can keep secret. Won't someone from the farm have told him? One of the staff?'

He shook his head. 'Discretion is an essential quality for all the people who work for me and their first loyalty is to me. Anyway, my father isn't interested in the estate, only as…'

'Only as what?' she prompted, her curiosity sharpened by the harsh note which had suddenly entered his voice.

'Nothing. It doesn't matter. And I think we've had enough questions for today, don't you?' he drawled. He lifted one hand from the steering wheel to point straight ahead. 'We're skirting Rome now and if you look over there you'll soon be able to see Lake Nemi.'

Her gaze followed the direction of his finger as she tried to concentrate. 'And that's where you live?'

'That's where I live,' he agreed.

They didn't say much for the rest of the journey, but at least Keira felt she knew a little more about him. And yet it was only a little. He had the air of the enigma about him. Something at the very core of him which was dark and unknowable and which seemed to keep her at arm's length. Behind that formidable and sexy exterior lay a damaged man, she realised—and something about his inner darkness made her heart go out to him. *Could* they make it as a couple? she wondered as they drove through a beautiful sheltered valley and she saw the silver gleam of the lake. Would she be a fool to want that?

But the stupid thing was that, yes, she did want that, because if Santino was to have any kind of security— the kind she'd always longed for—then it would work best if they *were* a couple. Her living with Matteo Valenti as his lover and mother to his son…would that be such a bad thing?

Her daydreaming was cut short by her first sight of Matteo's villa and she began to wonder if she was crazy to ever imagine she would fit in here. Overlooking Lake Nemi, the apricot-coloured house was three storeys high, with high curved windows overlooking acres of beautifully tended gardens. And she soon discovered that inside were countless rooms, including a marble-floored dining room and a ballroom complete with a lavish hand-painted ceiling. It felt more like being shown round a museum than a house. Never had her coat felt more threadbare or the cuffs more frayed as it was plucked from her nerveless fingers by a stern-faced butler named Roberto, who seemed to regard her with complete indifference. Was he wondering why his powerful employer had brought such a scruffy woman to this palace of a place? Keira swallowed. Wasn't she wondering the same thing herself?

After ringing the farmhouse and being told by Paola that Santino was lying contentedly in his pram in the garden, Keira accepted the tiny cup of espresso offered by a maid in full uniform and sat down on a stiff and elegant chair to drink it. Trying to ignore the watchful darkness of Matteo's eyes, she found herself thinking about the relaxed comfort of the farmhouse and felt a pang as she thought about her son, wondering if he would be missing his mama. As she drank her coffee she found herself glancing around at the beautiful but cavernous room and suppressed a shiver, wondering how much it must cost to heat a place this size.

'Why do you live here?' she questioned suddenly, lifting her gaze to the dark figure of the man who stood beside the vast fireplace.

He narrowed his eyes. 'Why wouldn't I? It has a fresher climate than the city, particularly in the summer months when it can get very hot. And it's a valuable piece of real estate.'

'I don't doubt it.' She licked her lips. 'But it's *enormous* for just one person! Don't you rattle around in it?'

'I'm not a total hermit, Keira,' he said drily. 'Sometimes I work from here—and, of course, I entertain.'

The question sprang from her lips before she could stop it. 'And bring back loads of women, I expect?'

The look he shot her was mocking. 'Do you want me to create the illusion that I've been living a celibate life all these years?' he asked softly. 'If sexual jealousy was the reason behind your question?'

'It wasn't!' she denied, furious with herself for having asked it. Of *course* Matteo would have had hundreds of women streaming through these doors—and it wasn't as if he were her *boyfriend*, was it? Her cheeks grew red. He never had been. He was just a man who could make her melt with a single look, no matter how much she fought against it. A man who had impregnated her without meaning to. And now he was observing her with that sexy smile, as if he knew exactly what she was thinking. As if he was perfectly aware that beneath her drab, chain-store sweater her breasts were hungering to feel his mouth on them again. She could feel her cheeks growing warm as she watched him answer his mobile phone to speak in rapid Italian and when he'd terminated the call he turned to look at her, his hard black eyes scanning over her.

'The car is outside waiting to take you into the city centre,' he said. 'And the stylist will meet you there.'

'A stylist?' she echoed, her gaze flickering uncertainly to her scuffed brown boots.

'A very famous stylist who's going to take you shopping.' He shrugged. 'I thought you might need a little guidance.'

His condescension only intensified Keira's growing feelings of inadequacy and she glared at him. 'What, in case I opt for something which is deeply unsuitable?'

His voice was smooth. 'There is a different way of looking at it, Keira. I don't expect you've been given unlimited use of a credit card before, have you?'

Something in the way he said it was making Keira's blood boil. 'Funnily enough, no!'

'So what's the problem?'

'The problem is *you*! I bet you're just loving this,' she accused. 'Does flashing your wealth give you a feeling of power, Matteo?'

He raised his eyebrows. 'Actually, I was hoping it might give you a modicum of pleasure. So why don't you go upstairs and freshen up before the car takes you into the city?'

Keira put her empty cup down on a spindly gold-edged table and rose to her feet. 'Very well,' she said, forcing her stiff shoulders into a shrug.

'By the way,' he said as he gestured for her to precede him, 'I notice you didn't make any comment about my driving on the way here.'

'I thought it might be wise, in the circumstances.'

'But as a professional, you judged me favourably, I hope?'

She pursed her lips together. 'You were okay. A little heavy on the clutch, perhaps—but it's a great car.'

She took a stupid and disproportionate pleasure from the answering humour which gleamed from his eyes before following him up a sweeping staircase into a sumptuous suite furnished in rich brocades and velvets, where he left her. Alone in the ballroom-sized bathroom, where water gushed from golden taps, Keira dragged the hairbrush through her hair, wondering what on earth the stylist was going to think about being presented with such unpromising raw material.

But the stylist was upbeat and friendly—even if the store on the Via dei Condotti was slightly terrifying. Keira had never been inside such an expensive shop before—although in her chauffeuring days she'd sat outside places like it often enough, waiting for her clients. A slim-hipped woman named Leola came forward to greet her, dressed in an immaculate cream dress accessorised with gleaming golden jewellery and high-heeled patent shoes. Although she looked as if she'd stepped straight off the catwalk, to her credit, she didn't seem at all fazed by Keira's appearance, as she led her around the shop and swished her fingertips over rail after rail of clothes.

In the chandelier-lit changing room, she whipped a tape measure around Keira's newly abundant curves. 'You have a fantastic figure,' she purred. 'Let's show it off a little more, shall we?'

'I'd rather not, if you don't mind,' said Keira quickly. 'I don't like to be stared at.'

Leola raised perfectly plucked black eyebrows by a centimetre. 'You are dating one of the city's most eligible bachelors,' she observed quietly. 'And Matteo will expect people to stare at you.'

Keira felt a shimmer of anxiety as she tugged a blue cashmere dress over her head and pulled on some navy-blue suede boots. What possible response could she make to that? What would the stunning Leola say if she explained that she and Matteo weren't 'dating', but simply parents to a darling little boy? And even that wasn't really accurate, was it? You couldn't really describe a man as a parent when he regarded his newborn infant with the caution which an army expert might display towards an unexploded bomb.

Just go with the flow, she told herself. Be amenable and do what's suggested—and after you've been dressed up like a Christmas turkey, you can sit down with the Italian tycoon and talk seriously about the future.

She tried on hip-hugging skirts with filmy blouses, flirty little day dresses and sinuous evening gowns, and Keira was reeling by the time Leola had finished with her. She wanted to protest that there was no way she would wear most of these—that she and Matteo hadn't even discussed how long she would be staying—but Leola seemed to be acting on someone else's orders and it wasn't difficult to work out whose orders they might be.

'I will have new lingerie and more shoes sent by courier to arrive later,' the stylist explained, 'since I understand you're returning to Umbria tomorrow. But you certainly have enough to be going on with. Might I suggest you wear the red dress this evening? Matteo was very specific about how good he thought you would look in vibrant colours. Oh, and a make-up artist will be visiting the house later this afternoon. She will also be able to fix your hair.'

Keira stared at the slippery gown of silk-satin which was being dangled from Leola's finger and shook her head. 'I can do my own hair,' she said defensively, wondering if dressing up in all this finery was what Matteo usually expected for dinner at home on a weekday evening. 'And I can't possibly wear that—it's much too revealing.'

'Yes, you can—and you must—because you look amazing in it,' said Leola firmly, before her voice softened a little. 'Matteo must care for you a great deal to go to so much trouble. And surely it would be unwise to displease him when he's gone to so much trouble.'

It was a candid remark which contained in it a trace of warning. It was one woman saying to another—don't look a gift horse in the mouth. But all it did was to increase Keira's sensation of someone playing dress-up. Of being moulded for a role in the billionaire's life which she wasn't sure she was capable of filling. Her heart was pounding nervously as she shook the stylist's hand and went outside to the waiting car.

And didn't she feel slightly ashamed at the ease with which she allowed the chauffeur to open the door for her as she slid onto the squishy comfort of the back seat? As if already she was turning into someone she didn't recognise.

CHAPTER NINE

THE CLOCK WAS striking seven and Matteo gave a click of impatience as he paced the drawing room, where an enormous fire crackled and burned. Where the hell *was* she? He didn't like to be kept waiting—not by anyone, and especially not by a woman who ought to have been bang on time and full of gratitude for his generosity towards her. He wondered how long it would have taken Keira to discover how much she liked trying on lavish clothes. Or how quickly she'd decided it was a turn-on when a man was prepared to buy you an entire new wardrobe, with no expense spared. He was just about to send Roberto upstairs to remind her of the time, when the door opened and there she stood, pale-faced and slightly uncertain.

Matteo's heart pounded hard in his chest because she looked… He shook his head slightly as if to clear his vision, but the image didn't alter. She looked *unrecognisable*. Light curls of glossy black tumbled over her narrow shoulders and, with mascara and eyeliner, her sapphire eyes looked enormous. Her lips were as red as her dress and he found himself wanting to kiss away her unfamiliar lipstick. But it was her body which commanded the most attention. *Santo cielo!* What a body! Scarlet silk clung to the creamy curve of her breasts, the material gliding in over the indentation of her waist, then flaring gently over her hips. Sheer stockings encased her legs and skyscraper heels meant she looked much taller than usual.

He swallowed because the transformation was exactly what he'd wanted—a woman on his arm who would turn heads for all the *right* reasons—and yet now he was left with intense frustration pulsing through his veins. He wanted to call their host and cancel and to take her straight to bed instead, but he was aware that such a move would be unwise. He had less than twenty-four hours to get Keira Ryan to agree to his plan—and that would not be achieved by putting lust before logic.

'You look…beautiful,' he said unsteadily, noticing how pink her cheeks had grown in response to his compliment, and he was reminded once again of her innocence and inexperience.

She tugged at the skirt of the dress as if trying to lengthen it. 'I feel a bit underdressed, to be honest.'

He shook his head. 'If that were the case then I certainly wouldn't let you leave the house.'

She raised her eyebrows. 'What, you mean you'd keep me here by force? Prisoner of the Italian tycoon?'

He smiled. 'I've always found persuasion to be far more effective than force. I assume Leola organised a suitable coat for you to wear?'

'A coat?' She stared at him blankly.

'It's November, Keira, and we're going to a party in

the city. It might be warmer than back in England, but you'll still need to wrap up.'

Keira's stomach did a flip. 'You didn't mention a party.'

'Didn't I? Well, I'm mentioning it now.'

She gave the dress another tug. 'Whose party is it?'

'An old friend of mine. Salvatore di Luca. It's his birthday—and it will be the perfect opportunity for you to meet people. It would be a pity for you not to have an audience when you look so very dazzling.' His gaze travelled over her and his voice thickened. 'So why not go and get your coat? The car's waiting.'

Keira felt nerves wash over her. She was tempted to tell him she'd rather stay home and eat a *panino* in front of the fire, instead of having to face a roomful of strangers—but she was afraid of coming over as some kind of social misfit. Was this some strange kind of interview to assess whether or not she would be up to the task of being Matteo's partner? To see if she was capable of making conversation with his wealthy friends, of getting through a whole evening without dropping a canapé down the front of her dress?

Her black velvet swing coat was lined with softest cashmere and Keira hugged it around herself as the driver opened the door of the waiting limousine, her heart missing a beat as Matteo slid onto the seat beside her. His potent masculinity was almost as distracting as the dark suit which fitted his muscular body to perfection and made him look like some kind of movie star on his way to an awards ceremony. 'You aren't driving, then?' she observed.

'Not tonight. I have a few calls I need to make.' His black eyes gleamed. 'After that I'm exclusively yours.'

The way he said it sent ripples of excitement whispering over her skin and she wondered if that had been deliberate. But there was apprehension too because Keira wasn't sure she would be able to cope with the full blaze of his undivided attention. Not when he was being so… *nice* to her.

She suspected he was on his best behaviour because he wanted her to agree to his masterplan—whenever he got around to unveiling it. And although he hadn't shown any desire to parent their son, something told her that he saw Santino as his possession, even if so far he had exhibited no signs of love. Because of that, she suspected he wouldn't let her go easily and the stupid part was that she didn't want him to. She was beginning to recognise that she was out of her depth—and not just because he was a billionaire hotelier and she a one-time car mechanic. She didn't have any experience of relationships and she didn't have a clue how to react to him. Part of her wished she were still in the driver's seat, negotiating the roads with a slick professionalism she'd been proud of until she'd ruined her career in the arms of the man who sat beside her, his long legs stretched indolently in front of him.

She forced herself to drag her eyes away from the taut tension of his thighs—and at least there was plenty to distract her as she gazed out of the window at the lights of the city and the stunning Roman architecture, which made her feel as if she'd fallen straight into the pages of a guide book.

Salvatore de Luca's apartment was in the centre of it all—a penthouse situated close to the Via del Corso and offering commanding views of the city centre. Keira was dimly aware of a maid taking her coat and a cocktail being pressed into her hand and lots of people milling around. To her horror she could see that every other woman was wearing elegant black and her own expensive scarlet dress made her feel like something which had fallen off the Christmas tree. And it wasn't just the colour. She wasn't used to displaying a hint of cleavage, or wearing a dress which came this high above the knee. She felt like an imposter—someone who'd been more at home with her hair hidden beneath that peaked hat, instead of cascading over her shoulders like this.

She saw a couple of the men give her glances which lingered more than they should have done—or was that just something Italian men did automatically? Certainly, Matteo seemed to be watching her closely as he introduced her to a dizzying array of friends and she couldn't deny the thrill it gave her to feel those dark eyes following her every move.

Keira did her best to chat animatedly, hugely grateful that nearly everybody spoke perfect English, but conversation wasn't easy. She was glaringly aware of not mentioning the one subject which was embedded deeply in her heart and that was Santino. She wondered when Matteo was planning to announce that he was a father and what would happen when he did. Did any of his friends have children? she wondered. This apartment certainly didn't look child-friendly and she couldn't imagine a toddler crawling around on these priceless rugs, with sticky fingers.

Escaping from the growing pitch of noise to the washroom, Keira took advantage of the relative calm and began to peep into some of the rooms on her way back to the party. Entering only those with open doors, she discovered a bewildering number of hand-painted salons which reminded her of Matteo's villa. His home wasn't exactly child-friendly either, was it?

The room she liked best was small and book-lined— not because she was the world's greatest reader but because it opened out onto a lovely balcony with tall green plants in pots and fabulous views over the glittering city. She stood there for a moment with her arms resting on the balustrade when she heard the clip-clop of heels enter the room behind her and she turned to see a tall redhead who she hadn't noticed before. Maybe she was a late arrival, because she certainly wasn't the kind of woman you would forget in a hurry. Her green gaze was searching rather than friendly and Keira had to concentrate very hard not to be fixated on the row of emeralds which gleamed at her slender throat and matched her eyes perfectly.

'So *you're* the woman who's been keeping Matteo off the scene,' the woman said, her soft Italian accent making her sound like someone who could have a very lucrative career in radio voice-overs.

Keira left the chilly balcony and stepped into the room. 'Hello, I'm Keira.' She smiled. 'And you are?'

'Donatella.' Her green eyes narrowed, as if she was

surprised that Keira didn't already know this. 'Your dress is very beautiful.'

'Thank you.'

There was a pause as Donatella's gaze flickered over her. 'Everyone is curious to know how you've managed to snare Italy's most elusive bachelor.'

'He's not a rabbit!' joked Keira.

Either Donatella didn't get the joke or she'd decided it wasn't funny because she didn't smile. 'So when did you two first meet?'

Aware of the sudden race of her heart, Keira suddenly felt *intimidated*. As if she was being backed into a corner, only she didn't know why. 'Just under a year ago.'

'When, exactly?' probed the redhead.

Keira wasn't the most experienced person when it came to social etiquette, but even she could work out when somebody was crossing the line. 'Does it really matter?'

'I'm curious, that's all. It wouldn't happen to have been two nights before Christmas, would it?'

The date was burned so vividly on Keira's memory that the affirmation burst from her lips without her even thinking about it. 'Yes, it was,' she said. 'How on earth did you know that?'

'Because he was supposed to be meeting me that night,' said Donatella, with a wry smile. 'And then I got a call from his assistant to say his plane couldn't take off because of the snow.'

'That's true. The weather was terrible,' said Keira.

'And then, when he got back—nothing. Complete

radio silence—even though the word was out that there was nobody else on the scene.' Donatella's green eyes narrowed thoughtfully. 'Interesting. You're not what I expected.'

Even though she hadn't eaten any of the canapés which had been doing the rounds, Keira suddenly felt sick. All she could think about was the fact that another woman had been waiting for Matteo while he'd been in bed with *her*. He must have had his assistant call Donatella while she'd been in the bath and then preceded to seduce *her*. Had it been a case of *any* woman would do as a recipient of all that hard hunger? A man who'd been intent on sex and was determined not to have his wishes thwarted? What if all that stuff about not finding her attractive had simply been the seasoned technique of an expert who'd recognised that he needed to get her to relax before leaping on her. She swallowed. Had he been imagining it was Donatella beneath him instead of her?

'Well, you know what they say…there's no accounting for taste.' From somewhere Keira dredged up a smile. 'Great meeting you, Donatella.'

But she was trembling by the time she located Matteo, surrounded by a group of men and women who were hanging onto his every word, and maybe he read something in her face because he instantly disengaged himself and came over to her side.

'Everything okay?' he questioned.

'Absolutely lovely,' she said brightly, for the benefit of the onlookers. 'But I'd like to go now, if you wouldn't mind. I'm awfully tired.'

His dark brows lifted. '*Certamente.* Come, let us slip away, *cara.*'

The practised ease with which the meaningless endearment fell from his lips made Donatella's words seem even more potent and in the car Keira sat as far away from him as possible, placing her finger on her lips and shaking her head when he tried to talk to her. She felt stupidly emotional and close to tears but there was no way she was going to break down in front of his driver. She knew better than most how domestic upsets could liven up a sometimes predictable job and that a chauffeur had a front-row seat to these kinds of drama. It wasn't until they were back in the villa, where a fire in the drawing room had obviously been kept banked for their return, that she turned to Matteo at last, trying to keep the edge of hysteria from her voice.

'I met Donatella,' she said.

'I wondered if you would. She arrived late.'

'I don't give a damn when she arrived!' She flung her sparkly scarlet clutch bag down onto a brocade sofa where it bounced against a tasselled cushion. 'She told me you were supposed to be meeting her the night we got stuck in the snow!'

'That much is true.'

She was so horrified by his easy agreement that Keira could barely choke out her next words. 'So you were in a sexual relationship with another woman when you seduced me?'

He shook his head. 'No, I was not. I'd been dating her for a few weeks, but it had never progressed beyond dinner and the occasional trip to the opera.'

'And you expect me to believe that?'

'Why wouldn't you believe it, Keira?'

'Because...' She sucked in a deep breath. 'Because you didn't strike me as the kind of man who would chastely court a woman like that.'

'Strangely enough, that's how I like to operate.'

'But not with me,' she said bitterly. 'Or maybe you just didn't think I was worth buying dinner for.'

Matteo tensed as he read the hurt and shame which clouded her sapphire eyes and was surprised how bad it made him feel. He knew he owed her an explanation but he sensed that this went deeper than anything he'd had to talk his way out of in the past, and part of him rebelled at having to lay his thoughts open. But he sensed there was no alternative. That despite the ease with which she had fallen into his arms, Keira Ryan was no pushover.

'Oh, you were worth it, all right,' he said softly. 'Just because we didn't do the conventional thing of having dinner doesn't change the fact that it was the most un-forgettable night of my life.'

'Don't tell me lies!'

'It isn't a lie, Keira,' he said simply. 'It was amazing. We both know that.'

He saw her face working, as if she was struggling to contain her emotions.

'And then,' she said, on a gulp, 'when you got back—she says you didn't see her again.'

'Again, true.'

'Why not?' she demanded. 'There was nothing stopping you. Especially after you'd given me the heave-ho.'

If he was surprised by her persistence he didn't show it and Matteo felt conflicted about how far to go with his answer. Mightn't it be brutal to explain that he'd been so appalled at his recklessness that night that he'd decided he needed a break from women? If he told her that he'd never had a one-night stand before, because it went against everything he believed in, mightn't it hurt her more than was necessary? He didn't believe in love—not for him—but he believed in passion and, in his experience, it was always worth the wait. Deferred gratification increased the appetite and made seduction sweeter. And delaying his own pleasure reinforced his certainty that he was always in control.

Yet his usual fastidiousness had deserted him that snowy night when he'd found himself in bed with his petite driver, and it had affected him long after he'd returned to Italy. It wasn't an admission he particularly wanted to make but something told him it would work well in his favour if he did. What was it the Americans said? Ah, *sì*. It would buy him brownie points. 'I haven't had sex with anyone since the night I spent with you. Well, until last night,' he said.

Her eyes widened and the silence of the room was broken only by the loud ticking of the clock before she blurted out a single word.

'Why?' she breathed.

He bent to throw an unnecessary log onto the already blazing fire before straightening up to face the dazed disbelief which had darkened her eyes. He had tried convincing himself it had been self-disgust which had made him retreat into his shell when he'd returned to Rome, but deep down he'd known that wasn't the whole story.

'Because, annoyingly, I couldn't seem to shift you from my mind,' he drawled. 'And before you start shaking your head like that and telling me I don't mean it, let me assure you I do.'

'But why?' she questioned. 'I mean, why me?'

He paused long enough to let her know that he'd asked himself the same question. 'Who knows the subtle alchemy behind these things?' He shrugged, his gaze roving over her as he drank in the creamy curves of her flesh. 'Maybe because you were different. Because you spoke to me in a way that people usually don't. Or maybe because you were a virgin and on some subliminal level I understood that and it appealed to me. Why are you looking at me that way, Keira? You think that kind of thing doesn't matter? That a man doesn't feel an incomparable thrill of pleasure to discover that he is the first and the only one? Then you are very wrong.'

Keira felt faint and sank down onto the brocade sofa, next to her discarded clutch bag. His words were shockingly old-fashioned but that didn't lessen their impact on her, did it? It didn't stop her from feeling incredibly *desired* as his black gaze skated over her body and hinted at the things he might like to do to her.

Did her lips open of their own accord or did he somehow orchestrate her reaction from his position by the fireplace—like some puppet master twitching invisible strings? Was that why a hard gleam suddenly entered his eyes as he walked towards her and pulled her to her feet.

'I think we're done with talking, don't you?' he questioned unsteadily. 'Haven't I answered all your questions and told you everything you need to know?'

'Matteo, I—'

'I'm going to make love to you again,' he said, cutting right through her protest. 'Only this time it's going to be in a bed and it's going to be all night long. And please don't pretend you're outraged by the idea, when the look on your face says otherwise.'

'Or maybe you're just going to do it to pacify me?' she challenged. 'Like you did last night.'

'Last night we were in the middle of a howling storm and I wasn't really thinking straight, but today I am.'

And with that he lifted her up into his arms and swept her from the room and it occurred to Keira that no way would she have objected to such masterful treatment, even if he *had* given her the option. Because wasn't he making her feel like a woman who was completely desired—a woman for whom nothing but pleasure beckoned? Up the curving marble staircase he carried her, her ear pressed closely to his chest so she could hear the thundering of his heart. It felt like something from a film as he kicked the bedroom door shut behind them. Unreal. Just as the excitement coursing through her body felt unreal. Was it wrong to feel this rush of hungry pleasure as Matteo unzipped the scarlet dress and let it fall carelessly onto the silken rug? Or for her to gasp out words of encouragement from lips soon swollen by the pressure of his kiss?

Her bra swiftly followed and she gave a squeal of protesting pleasure as he hooked his fingers into the edges of her panties and ripped them apart and didn't that thrill her, too? Showing similar disregard for his own clothes, he tore them from his body like a man with the hounds of hell snapping at his ankles. But once they were both naked on the bed, he slowed things right down.

'These curves,' he said unevenly as his fingertips trickled over her breasts and hips.

'You don't like them?' she questioned breathlessly.

'Whatever gave you that idea? I seem to like you lean and I seem to like you rounded. Any way at all is okay with me, Keira.'

Slowly, he ran his fingertip from neck to belly before sliding it down between her thighs, nudging it lightly against her wet heat in a lazy and rhythmical movement. She shivered and had to stifle a frustrated moan as he moved his hand away. But then his mouth began to follow the same path as his fingers and Keira held her breath as she felt his lips acquainting themselves with the soft tangle of hair at her groin before he burrowed his head deep between her legs and made that first unbelievable flick of his tongue against her slick and heated flesh.

'Matteo!' she gasped, almost shooting off the bed with pleasure. 'What…what are you doing?'

He lifted his head and she saw pure devilry in his black eyes. 'I'm going to eat you, *cara mia*,' he purred, before bending his head to resume his task.

Keira let her head fall helplessly back against the pillow as he worked sweet magic with his tongue, loving the way he imprisoned her wriggling hips with the firm clamp of his hands. She came so quickly that it took her by surprise—as did the sudden way he moved over her to thrust deep inside her, while her body was still racked with those delicious spasms. She clung to his shoulders as he started a sweet, sure rhythm which set senses singing.

But suddenly his face hardened as he grew still inside her. 'How long do you think I can stop myself from coming?' he husked.

'Do you…?' She could barely get the words out when he was filling her like this. 'Do you *have* to stop yourself?'

'That depends. I do if you're going to have a second orgasm, which is my intention,' he murmured. 'In fact, I'm planning to make you come so often that you'll have lost count by the morning.'

'Oh, Matteo.' She closed her eyes as he levered himself to his knees and went even deeper.

She moaned as the finger moved between their joined bodies to alight on the tight nub between her legs and began to rub against her while he was deep inside her. The pleasure it gave her was almost too much to bear and it felt as if she were going to come apart at the seams. She gasped as pleasure and pressure combined in an unstoppable force. Until everything splintered around her. She heard him groan as his own body starting to convulse before eventually collapsing on top of her, his head resting on her shoulder and his shuddered breath hot and rapid against her neck.

His arms tightened around her waist and for countless seconds Keira felt as if she were floating on a cloud.

Had he really told her he hadn't slept with anyone else because he hadn't been able to get her out of his mind? Yes, he had. With a sigh of satisfaction, she rested her cheek against his shoulder and he murmured something soft in Italian in response.

She lay there for a long time after he'd fallen asleep, thinking that sex could blind you to the truth. Or maybe lull you into such a stupefied state that you stopped seeking the truth. He'd commented on her curves and admired them with his hands, but he'd made no mention of *why* her body had undergone such a dramatic transformation. She bit her lip. Because she'd carried his son and given birth to him—a fact he seemed to find all too easy to forget.

And she thought how—despite the heart-stopping intimacy of what had just taken place—she still didn't know Matteo at all.

CHAPTER TEN

SHE HAD TO say something. She *had* to. She couldn't keep pretending nothing was wrong or that there weren't still a million questions buzzing around in her head which needed answering.

Keira turned her head to look at the face of the man who lay sleeping beside her. It was a very big bed, which was probably a good thing since Matteo Valenti's naked body was taking up most of it. Morning light flooded in from the two windows they hadn't bothered closing the shutters on before they'd tumbled into bed the night before. From here she could see the green of the landscape which spread far into the distance and, above it, the endless blue of the cloudless sky. It was the most perfect of mornings, following the most perfect of nights.

She hugged her arms around herself and gave a wriggle of satisfaction. She'd never thought she could feel the way Matteo had made her feel. But the clock was ticking away and she needed to face reality. She couldn't keep pretending everything was wonderful just because they'd spent an amazing night together. He'd said he wanted to explore the possibility of them becoming a couple but there was more to being a couple than amazing sex. How could they keep ignoring the gaping hole at the centre of their relationship which neither of them had addressed? He for reasons unknown and she...

She turned her attention from the distraction of the view to the dark head which lay sleeping beside her. Was she too scared to ask him, was that it?

Because the most important thing was all out of kilter and the longer it went on, the worse it seemed. Matteo acted as if Santino didn't exist. *As if he didn't have a son.* To her certain knowledge, he'd never even cuddled him—why, he'd barely even asked after him.

It didn't matter how many boxes the Italian ticked—she could never subject Santino to a life in which he was overlooked. And trying to compensate for his father's lack of regard with her own fierce love wouldn't work. She'd grown up in a house where she had been regarded as an imposition and no way was she going to impose that on her darling son.

Which left her with two choices. She could carry on being an ostrich and ignore what was happening—or rather, what wasn't happening. Or she could address the subject when Matteo woke and make him talk about it. She wouldn't accuse him or judge him. Whatever he told her, she would try to understand—because something told her that was very important.

Quietly, she slipped from the bed and went to the bathroom and when she returned with brushed teeth and hair, Matteo was awake—his black gaze following her as she walked back towards the bed.

'Morning,' she said shyly.

'Is this the point where I ask whether you slept well and you lower your eyelids and say, *not really*?' he murmured.

Blushing like a schoolgirl, Keira slipped rapidly beneath the covers so that her naked body was no longer in the spotlight of that disturbingly erotic stare. It was all very well being uninhibited when the room was in darkness but the bright morning light was making her feel awfully vulnerable. Especially as she sensed that Matteo wasn't going to like what she had to say, no matter how carefully she asked the question. He drew her into his arms but she gave him only the briefest of kisses before pulling her lips away. Because she needed to hear this, and the sooner, the better.

'Matteo,' she said, rubbing the tip of her finger over the shadowed angle of his jaw.

His brows knitted together. 'Why does my heart sink when you say my name that way?' he questioned softly.

She swallowed. 'You know we have to go back to Umbria soon.'

'You think I'd forgotten? Which is why I suggest we don't waste any of the time we have left.'

He had begun to stroke a light thumb over one of her nipples and although it puckered obediently beneath his touch, Keira pushed his hand away. 'And we need to talk,' she said firmly.

'And that was why my heart sank,' he drawled, shifting his body to lie against the bank of pillows and fixing her with a hooded look. 'Why do women always want to talk instead of making love?'

'Usually because something needs to be said.' She

pulled in a breath. 'I want to tell you about when I was growing up.'

The look on his face said it all. Wrong place; wrong time. 'I met your aunt,' he said impatiently. 'Over-strict guardian, small house, jealous cousin. I get it. You didn't have such a great time.'

Keira shook her head as uncomfortable thoughts flooded into her mind. She needed to be completely honest, else how could she expect complete honesty in return? Yet what she was about to tell him wasn't easy. She'd never told anyone the full story. Even her aunt. Especially her aunt. 'I told you my mother wasn't mar-ried and that I didn't know my father. What I didn't tell you was that she didn't know him either.'

His gaze was watchful now. 'What are you talking about?'

Keira flushed to the roots of her hair because she could remember her mother's shame when she'd finally blurted out the story, no longer able to evade the curi-ous questions of her young daughter. Would her mother be appalled if she knew that Keira was now repeating the sorry tale, to a man with a trace of steel running through his veins?

'My mother was a student nurse,' she said slowly, 'who came to London and found it was nothing like the rural farm she'd grown up on in Ireland. She was quite shy and very naïve but she had those Irish looks. You know, black hair and blue eyes—'

'Like yours?' he interrupted softly.

She shook her head. 'Oh, no. She was much prettier than me. Men were always asking her out but usually she preferred to stay in the nurses' home and watch something on TV, until one night she gave in and went to a party with a group of the other nurses. It was a pretty wild party and not her kind of thing at all. People were getting wasted and Mum decided she didn't want to stay.' She swallowed. 'But by then it was too late because someone had…had…'

'Someone had what, Keira?' he questioned as her words became strangled and his voice was suddenly so gentle that it made her want to cry.

'Somebody spiked her drink,' she breathed, the words catching like sand in her throat because even now, they still had the power to repulse her. 'She…she woke up alone in a strange bed with a pain between her legs, and soon after that she discovered she was pregnant with me.'

He gave a terse exclamation and she thought he was going to turn away in disgust but to her surprise he reached out to push away the lock of hair which had fallen over her flushed cheeks, before slipping his hand round her shoulder and pulling her against the warmth of his chest. *'Bastardo,'* he swore softly and then repeated it, for added emphasis.

She shook her head and could feel the taste of tears nudging at the back of her throat and at last she gave into them, in a way she'd never done before. 'She didn't know how many men had been near her,' she sobbed. 'She had to go to the clinic to check she hadn't been given some sort of disease and of course they offered her…' She swallowed away the tears because she saw from the tightening of his jaw that she didn't actually need to spell it out for him. 'But she didn't want that. She wanted me,' she said simply. 'There wasn't a moment of doubt about that.'

He waited until she had composed herself before he spoke again, until she had brushed the remaining tears away with the tips of her fingers.

'Why are you telling me all this, Keira?' he questioned softly. 'And why now?'

'Because I grew up without a father and for me there was no other option—but I don't want the same for my baby. For... Santino.' Her voice wavered as she looked into the hardness of his eyes and forced herself to continue, even though the look on his face would have intimidated stronger people than her. 'Matteo, you don't... you don't seem to feel anything for your son.' She sucked in a deep breath. 'Why, you've barely *touched* him. It's as if you can't bear to go near him and I want to try to understand why.'

Matteo released his hold on her and his body tensed because she had no right to interrogate him, and he didn't *have* to answer her intrusive question. He could tell her to mind her own damned business and that he would interact with his son when he was good and ready and not according to *her* timetable. Just because she wanted to spill out stuff about her own past, didn't mean he had to do the same, did it? But in the depths of her eyes he could read a deep compassion and something in him told him there could be no going forward unless she understood what had made him the man he was.

He could feel a bitter taste coating his throat. Maybe everyone kept stuff hidden away inside them—the stuff which was truly painful. Perhaps it was nature's way of trying to protect you from revisiting places which were too dark to contemplate. 'My mother died in childbirth,' he said suddenly.

There was a disbelieving pause as the words sank in and when they did, her eyes widened. 'Oh, Matteo. That's terrible,' she whispered.

Matteo instantly produced the self-protective clause which enabled him to bat off unwanted sympathy if people *did* find out. 'What is it they say?' He shrugged. 'That you can't miss what you've never had. And I've had thirty-four years to get used to it.'

Her muffled 'But...' suggested she was about to disagree with him, but then she seemed to change her mind and said nothing. Leaving him free to utter the next words from his set-piece statement. 'Maternal death is thankfully rare,' he bit out. 'My mother was just one of the unlucky ones.'

'I'm so sorry.'

'Yes,' he said. 'I think we've established that.' He chose his words carefully. 'I've never come into contact with babies before. To be honest, I've never even held one, but you're right—it isn't just inexperience which makes me wary.' His jaw tightened. 'It's guilt.'

'Guilt?' she echoed, in surprise.

He swallowed and the words took a long time in coming. 'People say they feel instant love for their own child but that didn't happen to me when I looked at Santino for the first time. Oh, I checked his fingers and his toes and was relieved that he was healthy, but I didn't *feel* anything.' He punched his fist against his heart and the words fell from his lips, heavy as stones. 'And I don't know if I ever can.'

Keira nodded as she tried to evaluate what he'd told her. It all made sense now. It explained why he'd thrown a complete wobbly when she'd kept her pregnancy quiet. What if history had grimly repeated itself and she'd died in childbirth as his mother had done? Nobody had known who the father of her baby was because she'd kept it secret. Wasn't it possible that Santino could have been adopted by her aunt and her cousin and grown up without knowing anything of his roots?

She felt another wrench as she met the pain in his eyes. What must it have been like for him—this powerful man who had missed out on so much? He had never experienced a mother's love. Never even felt her arms hugging him in those vital hours of bonding which followed birth. Who had cradled the tiny Matteo as the cold corpse of his mother was prepared for her silent journey to the grave, instead of a joyous homecoming with her newborn baby? No wonder he'd been so reluctant to get close to his little boy—he didn't know *how*.

'Didn't your father make up for the fact that you didn't have a mother?'

His mouth twisted and he gave a hollow laugh. 'People cope in their own way—or they don't. He left my care to a series of young nannies, most of whom he apparently slept with—so then they'd leave—or the new stepmother would fire them. But it didn't seem to matter how much sex he had or how many women he married, he never really got over my mother's death. It left a hole in his life which nothing could ever fill.'

Keira couldn't take her eyes away from his ravaged face. Had his father unconsciously blamed his infant son for the tragic demise of his beloved wife—would that explain why they weren't close? And had Matteo been angry with his father for trying to replace her? She wondered if those different stepmothers had blamed the boy for being an ever-present reminder of a woman they could never compete with.

And blame was the last thing Matteo needed, Keira realised. Not then and certainly not now. He needed understanding—and love—though she wasn't sure he wanted either. Reaching out, she laid her hand on his bunched and tensed biceps but the muscle remained hard and stone-like beneath her fingers. Undeterred, she began to massage her fingertips against the un-yielding flesh.

'So what do we do next, now we've brought all our ghosts into the daylight?' she questioned slowly. 'Where do we go from here, Matteo?'

His gaze was steady as he rolled away from her touch, as if reminding her that this was a decision which needed to be made without the distraction of the senses. 'That depends. Where do you want to go from here?'

She recognised he was being open to negotiation and on some deeper level she suspected that this wasn't usual for him in relationships. Because this *was* a relationship, she realised. Somehow it had grown despite their wariness and private pain and the unpromising beginning. It had the potential to grow even more—but only if she had the courage to give him the affection he needed, without making any demands of her own in return. She couldn't *demand* that he learn to love his son, she could only pray that he would. Just as she couldn't demand that he learn to love *her*. 'I'll go anywhere,' she whispered. 'As long as it's with Santino. And you.'

She leaned forward to kiss him and Matteo could never remember being kissed like that before. A kiss not fuelled by sexual hunger but filled with the promise of something he didn't recognise, something which started his senses humming. He murmured something in objection when she pulled back a little, her eyes of *profondo blu* looking dark and serious, but at least when she wasn't kissing him he was able to think straight. He didn't understand the way she made him feel, but maybe that didn't matter. Because weren't the successes of life—and business—based on gut feeling as much as understanding? Hadn't he sometimes bought a hotel site even though others in the business had told him he was crazy—and turned it into a glittering success because deep down he'd known he was onto a winner? And wasn't it a bit like that now?

'I will learn to interact with my son,' he said.

'That's a start,' she said hesitantly.

The look on her face suggested that his answer had fallen short of the ideal—but he was damned if he was going to promise to love his son. Because what if he failed to deliver? What if the ice around his heart was so deep and so frozen that nothing could ever penetrate it? 'And I want to marry you,' he said suddenly.

Now the look on her face had changed. He saw surprise there and perhaps the faint glimmer of delight, which was quickly replaced by one of suspicion, as if perhaps she had misheard him.

'Marry me?' she echoed softly.

He nodded. 'So that Santino will have the security you never had, even if our relationship doesn't last,' he said, his voice cool but certain. 'And so that he will be protected by my fortune, which one day he will inherit. Doesn't that make perfect sense to you?'

He could see her blinking furiously, as if she was trying very hard to hold back the glitter of disappointed tears, but then she seemed to pull it all together and nodded.

'Yes, I think marriage is probably the most sensible option in the circumstances,' she said.

'So you will be my wife?'

'Yes, I'll be your wife. But I'm only doing this for Santino. To give him the legitimacy I never had. You do understand that, don't you, Matteo?'

She fixed him with a defiant look, as if she didn't really care—and for a split second it occurred to him that neither of them were being completely honest. 'Of course I understand, *cara mia*,' he said softly.

CHAPTER ELEVEN

KEIRA HEARD FOOTSTEPS behind her and turned from the mirror to see Claudia in a pretty flowery dress, instead of the soft blue uniform she usually wore when she was working.

'Is everything okay with Santino?' Keira asked the nursery nurse immediately, more out of habit than fear because she'd been cradling him not an hour earlier as she had dressed her baby son in preparation for his parents' forthcoming marriage.

Claudia smiled. 'He is well, *signorina*. His father is playing with him now. He says he is teaching him simple words of Italian, which he is certain he will remember when eventually he starts to speak.'

Keira smiled, turning back to her reflection and forcing herself to make a final adjustment to her hair, even though she kept telling herself that her bridal outfit was pretty irrelevant on what was going to be a purely functional wedding day. But Matteo's father and stepmother were going to be attending the brief ceremony, so she felt she had to make *some* sort of effort. And surely if she did her best it might lessen their

inevitable disbelief that he was going to marry someone like her.

'What kind of wedding would you like?' Matteo had
asked during that drive back from Rome after she'd
agreed to be his wife.

Keira remembered hedging her bets. 'You first.'

She remembered his cynical laugh, too.

'Something small. Unfussy. I'm not a big fan of weddings.'

So of course Keira had agreed that small and unfussy would be perfect, though deep down that hadn't
been what she'd wanted at all. Maybe there was a part
of every woman which wanted the whole works—the
fuss and flowers and clouds of confetti. Or maybe that
was just her—because marriage had always been held
up as the perfect ideal when she'd been growing up.
There had been that photo adorning her aunt's side-
board—the bouquet-clutching image which had stared
out at her over the years. She recalled visiting for Sun-
day tea when her mother was still alive, when attention
would be drawn to Aunt Ida's white dress and stiff veil.
'Wouldn't you have loved a white wedding, Bridie?' Ida
used to sigh, and Keira's mother would say she didn't
care for pomp and ceremony.

And Keira had thought she was the same—until
she'd agreed to marry Matteo and been surprised by
the stupid ache in her heart as she realised she must play
down a wedding which wasn't really a wedding. It was
a legal contract for the benefit of their son—not something inspired by love or devotion or a burning desire to

want to spend the rest of your life with just one person, so it didn't really count. At least, not on Matteo's part.

And hers?

She smoothed down her jacket and sighed. Because even more disturbing than her sudden yearning to wear a long white dress and carry a fragrant bouquet was the realisation that her feelings for Matteo had started to change. Was that because she understood him a little better now? Because he'd given her a glimpse of the vulnerability and loss which lay beneath the steely exterior he presented to the world? Maybe. She told herself not to have unrealistic expectations. Not to wish for things which were never going to happen, but concentrate on being a good partner. To give Matteo affection in quiet and unobtrusive ways, so that maybe the hard ice around his heart might melt a little and let her in.

He was doing his best to change, she knew that. In the busy days which followed their return from his Roman villa, he had meticulously paid his son all the attention which had been lacking before. Sometimes he would go to Santino if he woke in the night—silencing Keira's sleepy protests with a kiss. Occasionally, he gave the baby a bottle and, once, had even changed his nappy, even though he'd protested that this was one task surely better undertaken by women.

But as Keira had watched him perform these fatherly duties she had been unable to blind herself to the truth. That it *was* simply a performance and Matteo was just going through the motions. He was being a good father, just as he was a good lover—because he was a man who excelled in whatever he did. But it was duty which motivated him. His heart wasn't in it, that much was obvious. And as long as she accepted that, then she'd be fine.

She turned away from the mirror, wondering if there was anything she'd forgotten to do. Matteo's father, Massimo, and his wife, Luciana, had arrived only a short while ago because the traffic from Rome had been bad. Since they were due at the town hall at noon, there had been little opportunity for Keira to exchange more than a few words of greeting and introduce them to their new grandson. She'd been nervous—of course she had—she suspected it was always nerve-racking meeting prospective in-laws, and most people didn't have to do it on the morning of the wedding itself.

Massimo was a bear of a man, his build bulkier than Matteo's, though Keira could see a likeness around the jet-dark eyes. Her prospective stepmother-in-law, Luciana, was an elegant woman in her fifties, who had clearly embraced everything facial surgery had to offer, which had resulted in a disturbingly youthful appearance.

Keira picked up her clutch bag and went downstairs, her heart pounding with an anxiety which seemed to be increasing by the second. Was that because she'd seen Luciana's unmistakable look of disbelief when they'd been introduced? Was she wondering how this little Englishwoman from nowhere had wrested a proposal of marriage from the Italian tycoon?

But the expression on Matteo's face made Keira's stomach melt as she walked into the hallway, where everyone was waiting. She saw his eyes darken and the edges of his lips curve into an unmistakable smile of appreciation as he took her cold hand in his and kissed it.

'*Sei bella, mia cara,*' he had murmured softly. '*Molta bella.*'

Keira told herself he was only saying it because such praise was expected of the prospective groom, but she couldn't deny the feeling of satisfaction which rippled down her spine in response. Because she *wanted* him to look at her and find her beautiful, of course she did. She wasn't stupid and knew she couldn't take his desire for granted. Someone like her was always going to have to work to maintain it. Leola the stylist had been dispatched from Rome with a selection of wedding outfits and Keira had chosen the one she felt was the most flattering but also the most *appropriate*. Steadfastly pushing away the more floaty white concoctions, she had opted for functional rather than fairy tale. The silvery-grey material of the dress and jacket reminded her of a frosty winter morning but there was no doubt that it suited her dark hair and colouring. Only the turquoise shoes and matching clutch bag provided a splash of colour—because she had refused all Leola's inducements to carry flowers.

At least Massimo Valenti seemed enchanted by his grandson. Keira travelled in one of the cars with him to the nearly town and watched as he spent the entire journey cooing at the baby in delight. It made her wonder why he hadn't been close to his own son—but there was no time for questions because they were drawing up outside the town hall where Matteo was waiting to introduce her to the interpreter, which Italian law demanded.

Twenty minutes later she emerged from the building as a married woman and Matteo was pulling her into his arms, his hands resting on either side of her waist—but even that light touch was enough to make her want to dissolve with lust and longing.

'So. How does it feel to be Signora Valenti?' he questioned silkily.

Her heart was pounding as she stared up into the molten darkness of his eyes. 'Ask me again next week,' she said breathlessly. 'It feels a little unreal right now.'

'Maybe this will help you accept the reality,' he said, *'mia sposa.'*

And there, beneath the fluttering Italian flag of the town hall, his lips came down to claim hers with a kiss which left her in no doubt that he would rather they were somewhere private, preferably naked and horizontal. It set off an answering hunger and reminded Keira of the slightly incredible fact that he couldn't seem to get enough of her. Didn't he demonstrate that every night when he covered her trembling body with his own? And wasn't that *enough*? she wondered as they drove back to the farmhouse together, her golden ring glinting as she fussed around with Santino's delicate shawl. Was it just her inherently cautious nature which made her wonder if her relationship with Matteo was as superficial as the icing sugar sprinkled over the top of the chocolate wedding cake which Paola had baked?

Yet when he carried her over the threshold, it felt real. And when she returned from putting Santino down for a nap, having removed the silvery-grey jacket to reveal the filmy chiffon dress beneath, Matteo had been waiting in the shadowed hallway for her.

Pulling her into a quiet alcove, he placed his palm over her hammering heart and she licked her lips as her nipple automatically hardened beneath his touch.

'Ever wish you could just wave a magic wand and make everyone disappear?' he drawled.

She shivered as the light stroking of her nipple increased. 'Isn't that a little...anti-social?'

'I'm feeling anti-social,' he grumbled, his lips brushing over the curve of her jaw before moving upwards to tease her now trembling lips. 'I want to be alone with my new wife.'

Keira kissed him back as his words set off another whisper of hope inside her and she wondered if it was wrong to allow herself to hope, on this, her wedding day.

'You were the man who once told me about the benefits of waiting,' she teased him. 'Won't this allow you to test out your theory?'

Matteo laughed as she pulled away from him, the prim twitch of her lips contradicting the hunger in her eyes, and he shook his head slightly, wondering what kind of spell she had cast over him. He was used to the wiles of women yet Keira used none of them. She wasn't deliberately provocative around him and didn't possess that air of vanity of someone who revelled in her sexual power over a man. On the contrary, in public she was almost demure—while in private she was red-hot. And that pleased him, too. She pleased him and unsettled him in equal measure. She left him wanting more—but more of *what*, he didn't know. She was like a drink you took when your throat was dry yet when you'd finished it, you found that your thirst was just as intense.

He stroked his fingers down over her belly, his gaze steady as they stood hidden by the shadows of the staircase. Hard to believe that a child had grown beneath its almost-flat curve. 'I want you to know you are an amazing mother,' he said suddenly. 'And that Santino is blessed indeed.'

He saw the surprise behind the sudden brightness in her eyes, her mouth working as she struggled to contain herself.

'Don't make me get all emotional, Matteo,' she whispered. 'I've got to go in there and make conversation with your father and stepmother and I'm not going to make a very good impression if I've been blubbing.'

But he disregarded her soft plea, knowing he needed to express something which had slowly become a certainty. He owed her that, at least. 'I shouldn't have taken you to Rome when I did and made you leave the baby behind,' he admitted slowly. 'No matter how good the childcare we had in place. I can see now that it was a big ask for a relatively new mother in a strange country.'

He saw her teeth working into her bottom lip and he thought she might be about to cry, when suddenly she smiled and it was like the bright summer sun blazing all over him with warmth and light, even though outside it was cold and wintry.

'Thank you,' she said, a little shakily. 'I love you for saying that.'

He stilled. 'Really?'

A look of horror crossed her face as she realised what she'd said. 'I didn't mean—'

'Didn't you?' he murmured. 'How very disappointing.'

Keira told herself he was only teasing as he led her into the salon, but she felt as if she were floating on air as she took a grizzling Santino from Massimo's bear-like arms and rocked him dreamily against her chest. Had Matteo really just admitted he'd been in the wrong by taking her to Rome and told her she was a good mother? It wasn't so much the admission itself, more the fact he was beginning to accept that each and every one of them got it wrong sometimes—and that felt like a major breakthrough.

And had she really just let her guard down enough to tell him she loved him? It hadn't been in a dramatic way or because she'd expected an instant reciprocal response. She'd said it affectionately and Matteo needed that, she reckoned. How many times had he been told he'd been loved when he was growing up? Too few, she suspected.

Still high from the impact of their conversation, Keira refused the glass of vintage champagne which was offered and accepted a glass of some bittersweet orange drink instead.

But unusually, Santino grizzled in her arms and she wondered if it was the excitement of the day which was making him so fractious. Discreetly, she slipped away to the nursery to feed and change him before rocking him until he was sound asleep and carefully putting him in his crib.

She picked up the empty bottle and was just on her way out when she was startled by the sight of Luciana, who suddenly appeared at the nursery door in a waft of expensive scent. Keira wondered if she'd wandered into the wrong room or if she'd been hoping for a cuddle with Santino. But there was an odd smile on her new stepmother's face and, for some reason, whispers of trepidation began to slide over Keira's spine.

'Is everything okay, Luciana?' she questioned, hoping she sounded suitably deferential towards the older woman.

Luciana shrugged. 'That depends what you mean by *okay*. I was a little disappointed that my son and his family were not invited to the ceremony today.'

'Oh, well—you can see how it is.' Keira gave a nervous smile, because Matteo had hinted that there was no love lost between him and his stepbrother, Emilio. 'We just wanted a very small wedding.'

'*Sì.*' Luciana picked up a silver-framed photo of Santino and began to study it. 'And naturally, it would have been very *difficult* for Emilio.'

'Difficult?'

Luciana put the photograph down. 'In the circumstances.'

Keira blinked. 'What circumstances?'

Elegantly plucked eyebrows were raised. 'Because of the clause in my husband's will, of course.'

Keira's heart began to pound as some nameless dread crept over her. 'What clause?'

'Surely Matteo has told you?' Luciana looked surprised. 'Though perhaps not. He has always been a man who gives very little away.' Her expression became sly. 'You are aware that this house belonged to Massimo's first wife?'

'To Matteo's mother?' questioned Keira stiffly. 'Yes, I knew that. It's where she was born and where she grew up. It's one of the reasons he loves it so much.'

Luciana shrugged. 'Ever since Matteo reached the age of eighteen, Massimo has generously allowed his son to use the estate as his own. To all intents and purposes, this *was* Matteo's home.' She paused. 'But a strange thing happens to men as they grow older. They want to leave something of themselves behind.' Her surgically enhanced eyes gleamed. 'I'm talking, of course, about continuing the Valenti name. I am already a grandmother. I understand these desires.'

Keira's head was spinning. 'I honestly don't understand what you're getting at, Luciana.'

'Ah, I can see you know nothing of this.' Luciana gave a hard smile. 'It's very simple. He loves this house for obvious reasons, but he does not *own* it. And Massimo told him he intended bequeathing the entire estate to his stepson, unless Matteo produced an heir of his own with the Valenti name.' She shrugged her bony shoulders. 'I wondered if he would be prepared to sacrifice his freedom for an heir, not least because he has always shown a certain…*disdain* for women. And yet here you are—a pretty little English girl who arrived with a baby in her arms and got a wedding ring for her troubles. The perfect solution to all Matteo's problems!'

'You're saying that…that Matteo would have lost this house unless he produced an heir?'

'That's exactly what I'm saying. His gain, my son's loss.' Luciana shrugged. *'C'est la vie.'*

Keira felt so shocked that for a moment her limbs felt as if they were completely weightless. With a shaking hand, she put the empty bottle down on a shelf and swallowed, trying to compose herself—and knowing that she had to get away from Luciana's toxic company before she did or said something she regretted. 'Please excuse me,' she said. 'But I must get back to the wedding party.'

Did she imagine the look of disappointment which flickered across Luciana's face, or did she just imagine it? It didn't matter. She was going to get through this day with her dignity intact. Matteo had married her to get his hands on this property, so let him enjoy his brief victory. What good would come of making a scene on her wedding day?

Somehow she got through the rest of the afternoon, meeting Matteo's questioning stare with a brittle smile across the dining table, while everyone except her tucked into the lavish wedding breakfast. Did he sense that all was not well, and was that the reason why his black gaze seemed fixed on her face?

She was relieved when finally Massimo and Luciana left—though her father-in-law gave her the most enormous hug, which brought an unexpected lump to her throat. Leaving Matteo to dismiss Paola and the rest of the staff, Keira hurried to tend to Santino, spending far longer than necessary as she settled her baby son for the night.

At last she left the nursery and went into the bedroom but her hands were clammy as she pulled off her wedding outfit and flung it over a chair. Spurred on by Leola, she had been planning on surprising Matteo with the shortest dress she'd ever worn. A bottom-skimming dress for his eyes and no one else's. She'd wanted to wear it in anticipation of the appreciative look on his face when he saw it and to hint at a final farewell to her residual tomboy. But now she tugged on a functional pair of jeans and a sweater because she couldn't bear the thought of dressing up—not when Matteo's motives for marrying her were making her feel so *ugly* inside.

Although she would have liked nothing better than to creep into bed on her own and pull the duvet over her head to blot out the world, she knew that wasn't an option. There was only one acceptable course of action which lay open to her, but she couldn't deny her feeling of dread as she walked into the room which overlooked the garden at the back of the house, where Matteo stood beside the fire, looking impossibly handsome in his charcoal wedding suit. Don't touch me, she prayed silently, even though her body desperately wanted him to do just that—and maybe something had alerted him to her conflicted mood because his eyes narrowed and he made no attempt to approach her.

His face was sombre as he regarded her. 'Something is wrong.'

It was a statement, not a question, but Keira didn't answer straight away. She allowed herself a few more seconds before everything changed for ever. A final few seconds where she could pretend they were newly-weds about to embark on a shared life together. 'You could say that. I had a very interesting conversation with Luciana earlier.' She inhaled deeply and then suddenly the words came spilling out, like corrosive acid leaking from a car battery. 'Why didn't you tell me you were only marrying me to get your hands on an inheritance?' she demanded. 'And that this house would only become yours if you produced a legitimate child? I would have understood, if only you'd had the guts to tell me.'

He didn't flinch. His gaze was hard and steady. 'Because the inheritance became irrelevant. I married you because I care for you and my son and because I want us to make a future together.'

Keira wanted to believe him. The child-woman who had yearned for a long white dress and big bouquet of flowers longed for it to be the truth. But she couldn't believe him—it was a stretch too far. Once she'd thought he sounded like someone reading from a script when he'd been addressing a subject which would make most people emotional—and he was doing it again now.

I care for you and my son.

He sounded like a robot intoning the correct response, not someone speaking from the heart. And his lack of emotion wasn't the point, was it? She'd known about that from the start. She'd known the reason he was made that way and, filled with hope and with trust, had been prepared to make allowances for it. She bit her lip. When all the time he'd been plotting away and using her as a pawn in his desire to get his hands on this estate.

'I understand that you're known as an elusive man who doesn't give anything away,' she accused shakily. 'But how many more people are going to come out of the woodwork and tell me things about you that I didn't know? Can you imagine how it made me feel to hear that from Luciana, Matteo? To know you'd been buttering me up to get me to marry you? I thought... I thought you were doing it for your son's future, when all the time it was because you didn't want to lose a piece of land you thought of as rightfully yours! You don't want a family—not really—you've just used me as some kind of incubator!'

'But there's a fundamental flaw in your argument,' he grated. 'If inheriting the estate meant so much to me, then why hadn't I fathered a child with someone else long before I met you?'

'Because I don't think you really like women,' she said slowly. 'Or maybe you just don't understand them. You never knew your mother and she died so tragically that it's inevitable you idealised her. She would have had flaws, just like we all do—only you never got to see them. No woman could ever have lived up to her and maybe that's one of the reasons why you never settled down.' She sucked in a deep breath. 'And then I came along and took the decision away from you. A stolen night, which was never meant to be any more, suddenly produced an heir. You didn't have to go through the whole tedious ritual of courting a woman you didn't care for in order to get yourself a child. Fate played right into your hands, didn't it, Matteo? Suddenly you had everything you needed, without any real effort on your part.'

His face blanched. 'You think I am so utterly ruthless?'

She shrugged. 'I don't know,' she said, and there was

a crack in her voice. 'Maybe you do care—a little. Or as much as you ever can. But you're missing the point. I thought growing up without a father was difficult, but at least I knew where I stood. It may have been grim at times but it was honest and you haven't been honest with me.' She swallowed. 'It feels like I'm in the shadows of your life—like someone in the wings watching the action on stage. I see the way you are with the baby—and with me—and it comes over as a performance, not real. How could it be, when Santino and I were only ever a means to an end?'

Matteo flinched as he met the accusation in her eyes, because nobody had ever spoken quite so candidly to him. 'For someone so tiny, you certainly don't pull any punches, do you, Keira?'

'What's the point in pulling punches? All we have left is the truth,' she said wearily. 'You've got what you wanted, Matteo. We're married now and your son has been legitimised. You have continued the Valenti name and will therefore inherit the estate. You don't need me any more.'

Matteo felt his chest tighten and his instinct was to tell her that she was right—and that he *didn't* need anyone. He'd spent his whole life not needing anyone because there had been nobody there to lean on, nobody to get close to—why change that pattern now? But some unknown emotion was nudging at his conscience as something deep inside him told him this was different.

'And what if I say I do need you?' he said hoarsely as he attempted to articulate the confusion of thoughts which were spinning around inside his head.

Her eyes widened, but he could see a wariness in their depths of *profondo blu*. 'You do?' she queried uncertainly.

The moment it took for her to ask the question was all Matteo needed to shift things into perspective, because he knew he mustn't offer her false promises or false hope. She deserved more than that. So stick to the facts, he urged himself grimly. You're good with facts. Allow her to consider all the advantages of remaining here, as his wife.

'Of course,' he said. 'And logistically it makes perfect sense.'

'Logistically?' she echoed, her voice a little faint.

'Sure.' He shrugged. 'If we're all living together under one roof as a family, it will be much better for Santino. Better than having a father who just jets in and sees him on high days and holidays.'

'There is that, of course,' she said woodenly.

'And I've married you now, Keira,' he said softly. 'I have given you the security of bearing my name and wearing my ring. Your future is assured. You don't need to worry about money ever again.'

'You think that's what it's all about?' she questioned, her voice trembling. 'Money?'

'Not all of it, no—but a big part of it. And we have plenty of other reasons to keep our marriage going.' He curved her a slow smile. 'What about the sexual chemistry which exists between us? That fact that you are the hottest woman I've ever had in my bed?'

She gasped as if she had been winded before staring at him—as if she were looking at someone she'd never seen before. 'You just don't get it, do you, Matteo? You list all the reasons I should stay with you and yet you haven't mentioned anything which really *matters*!'

He flinched with pain as he met the undiluted anger in her gaze, but at the same time a strange sense of relief washed over him as he realised that he no longer had to try. She was going and taking their child with him and he would just have to learn how to deal with that. And anyway, he thought grimly—why would he want to prolong a relationship when it could hurt like this? Hadn't he vowed never to let anyone hurt him, ever again?

'Okay, I get it. What do you want?'

With an effort he held up the palms of his hands, in silent submission, and the sudden wobble of her lips made him think she might be about to backtrack— maybe to soften the blows which she'd just rained on him, but all she said was, 'I'd like us to separate.'

He told himself it was better this way. Better to go back to the life he was used to and be the person he knew how to be, rather than chase after the glimmer of gold which Keira Ryan had brought shimmering into his life.

'Tell me what you want, in practical terms,' he said flatly.

He could see her throat constricting as she nodded.

'I'd like to return to London as soon as possible and to rent somewhere before I decide to buy,' she said, before sucking in a deep breath. 'But I want you to know that I'll take only what is necessary for our needs and you're not to worry. I don't intend to make a great hole in your wealth, Matteo.'

And even that got to him, because he couldn't even level the charge of greed against her. She wasn't interested in his money, he realised, and she never had been. She'd taken the cash he'd thoughtlessly left beside the bed and had given it away to charity. She'd fought like mad against him buying her a fancy wardrobe. She was a jewel of a woman, he realised—a bright and shining jewel. But it was too late for them. The cold, pinched look on her beautiful face told him that. So let her go, he told himself. Set her free. At least you can give her that.

'That can all be arranged,' he said. 'But in turn, I need your reassurance that I can continue to see my son.'

There was surprise on her face now and he wondered if secretly she had expected him to cut all ties with his own flesh and blood.

'Of course. You can see as much of Santino as you wish,' she said quietly. 'I will never deny you your son, Matteo, and I hope you will see him very often, because he…he needs you. You're his daddy.'

A lump rose in his throat as he moved away from the blaze of the fire.

'I'd like to say goodnight to him now,' he said and she nodded and made as if to follow him.

'Alone,' he gritted out.

But Matteo's heart was heavy as he walked towards the nursery—as if a dark stone had lodged itself deep inside his chest. The night light made the room appear soft and rosy and Matteo stared down at the sleeping child. He remembered the first time he had seen him. When he had counted his fingers and toes like someone learning basic mathematics, and had felt nothing.

But not this time.

This time he could barely make out any detail of his sleeping son, his vision was so blurred. Too late, his heart had cracked open and left room for emotion to come flooding in, powerfully and painfully. And Santino stirred as Matteo's tears fell like rain onto the delicate white shawl.

CHAPTER TWELVE

IT WAS RAINING by the time Keira got back from her walk and she had just let Charlie off his lead when she noticed the letter lying in the centre of the hall table, where Claudia must have left it. She pulled a face. Another one.

The envelope carried an Italian stamp and the airmail sticker seemed to wink at her. Quickly, she slid it into a drawer to lie on top of all the others, because she couldn't quite bring herself to throw them away. Her reluctance to dispose of the growing pile of correspondence was just about equal to her reluctance to read them, because they were from Matteo—she recognised his handwriting. And why would she wish to read them and risk making the hole in her heart even bigger? Why was he even *writing* to her when she'd told him it was better if all correspondence took place between their respective solicitors? Why had he arrogantly elected to take no notice?

Because she was fighting like crazy not to go under. Not to give into the tears which pricked at her eyes at night when she lay in bed missing the warm embrace of her estranged husband. She was determined to pour all her energies into being there for Santino—into being the best mother she possibly could—and she couldn't manage that if her heart stayed raw and aching from thinking about Matteo all the time.

She'd wondered whether his determination to keep in close contact with his son would have faded once she and Santino had left Umbria but to her surprise, it hadn't. He'd already paid two visits and they'd only been back in England a little over a fortnight. On both those occasions she had absented herself from the house, leaving Claudia in charge of the baby—Claudia who had been happy to accompany her from Umbria when Keira had made the emotional return to her homeland.

She supposed people might think it a form of cowardice that she couldn't bear the thought of confronting the man with whom she hadn't even shared a wedding night. But that was too bad. It didn't matter what anyone else thought, only what was right for her and her son. Sooner or later she hoped she'd be able to greet him with a genuine air of indifference but for now she didn't trust herself not to burst into noisy howls of sorrow and to tell him how much she was missing him.

With the money he'd settled on her, she was renting a house. A house with a garden and a front door which wasn't shared—the kind of house in Notting Hill where she used to drop off her prep-school charges when she was working at Luxury Limos. And she'd bought a dog, too. A scruffy little thing with a lopsided ear and the saddest eyes she'd ever seen. The staff at the rescue centre had told her he'd been badly beaten and was fearful and shy, but he had taken one look at Keira and hurled himself at her with a series of plaintive yelps. Charlie was the best thing to have happened to them since they'd returned to England and had reinforced her intention to give Santino a proper childhood. The kind she'd never had—with a dog and a mother who was always waiting for him when he got home from school.

Pulling off her rain-soaked coat, she went upstairs to the nursery where Claudia was just putting Santino down to sleep. The nursery nurse straightened up as Keira entered the room and she found herself wondering why Claudia's cheeks were so pink. Walking over to the crib, Keira stared down into the sleepy eyes of her son, her heart turning over with love.

'He looks happy,' she murmured as she leaned over to plant a soft kiss on his silken cheek.

'He should be!' said Claudia. 'After you took him out for such a long walk this morning.'

'Good thing I did. At least we missed the rain,' said Keira, with an idle glance out of the window as she drew the curtains.

There was a pause. 'Would you mind if I went out earlier than planned?' asked Claudia.

'Of course I don't mind.' Keira smiled because she knew that Claudia had struck up a close friendship with a man she'd met at the Italian Embassy. 'Hot date?'

Claudia smiled as she put her forefinger over her lips and Keira was so preoccupied with tidying up the nursery that she barely registered the nursery nurse leaving the room, though she did hear the distant bang of the front door. She turned the light out and was just about to make her way downstairs when her mobile phone began to ring and she pulled it from the pocket of her jeans, frowning when she saw Matteo's name flashing up on the screen.

Fury began to bubble up inside her. She'd asked him not to write and he had ignored that. She'd asked him not to call her and he was ignoring that too! So why now, coming straight after yet another unwanted letter from him? She clicked the connection.

'This had better be urgent,' she said.

'It is.'

She frowned as she registered a curious echo-like quality to his voice. 'And?'

'I need to see you.'

She needed to see him too, but no good would come of it. Wouldn't it make her hunger for what she could never have and certainly didn't need—a man who had lured a woman into marriage just because he wanted to inherit a house? 'I thought we'd decided that wasn't a good idea.'

'No, Keira…*you* decided.'

Still that curious echo. Keira frowned. Shouldn't she just agree to see him once and get it over with? Steel her heart against her own foolish desires and listen to what he had to say? 'Very well,' she said. 'We'll put an appointment in the diary.'

'Now,' he bit out.

'What do you mean…*now*?'

'I want to see you now,' he growled.

'Matteo, you're in Italy and I'm in England and unless you've discovered the secret of teleportation, that's not going to happen.'

'I'm downstairs.'

She froze. '*What* did you say?'

'I'm downstairs.' The echo began to get louder. 'Coming up.'

Her heart slamming against her ribcage, Keira rushed from the nursery to see Matteo with his mobile phone held against his ear, making his way up the stairs towards her. His face was more serious than she'd ever seen it as he cut the connection and slid the phone into the pocket of his jeans.

'Hi,' he said, the casual greeting failing to hide the tension and the pain which were written across his ravaged features.

She wanted to do several things all at once. To drum her fists against his powerful chest, over and over again. And she wanted to pull his darkly handsome face to hers and kiss him until there was no breath left in her body.

'What are you doing here?' she demanded.

'I need to speak to you.'

'Did you have to go about it so dramatically? You scared me half to death!' She looked at him suspiciously. 'You don't have a key, do you?'

'I don't,' he agreed.

'So how did you get in?'

'Claudia let me in before she left.'

'*Claudia let you in?*' she repeated furiously. 'Why would she do something like that?'

'Because I asked her to.'

'And what you say goes, I suppose, because you're the one with the money,' she said contemptuously.

'No.' He sucked in a ragged breath. 'I'm the one with the broken heart.'

It was such an unbelievable thing for him to say that Keira assumed she'd misheard him, and she was too busy deciding that they needed to move out of Santino's earshot in case they woke him to pay very much attention to her husband's words. 'You'd better come with me,' she said.

Matteo followed the denim-covered sway of her bottom as they went downstairs, watching her long black ponytail swinging against her back with every determined stride she took. Her body language wasn't looking promising and neither was her attitude. But what had he expected—that she would squeal with delight when she saw him again? Welcome him into the embrace he had so missed—as if that whole great betrayal had never happened? His throat thickened. He had tried playing it slow and playing by her rules but he'd realised she would be prepared to push him away for ever if he let her.

And he couldn't afford to let her.

They reached a beautiful, high-ceilinged sitting room dominated by a tall Christmas tree, which glittered in front of one of the tall windows. Fragrant and green, it was covered with lights and tiny stars and on the top stood an angel with gossamer-fine wings. A heap of presents with ribbons and bows stood at the base of the giant conifer and Matteo thought it looked so homely. And yet he wasn't connected to any of it, was he? He was still the outsider. The motherless boy who had never really felt part of Christmas.

So what are you going to do about it, Valenti? he asked himself as she turned to face him and they stood looking at one another like two combatants.

'You wanted to talk,' she said, without preamble. 'So talk. Why did you sneak into my house like this?'

'You've been ignoring my letters.'

She nodded and the glossy black ponytail danced around her shoulders. 'I told you I wanted to keep all written communication between our respective solicitors.'

'You really think that my lawyer wants to hear that I love you?' he demanded, his breath a low hiss.

Her lips opened and he thought she might be about to gasp, before she closed them again firmly, like an oyster shell clamping tightly shut.

'And that I miss you more than I ever thought possible?' he continued heatedly. 'Or that my life feels empty without you?'

'Don't waste my time with your lies, Matteo.'

'They aren't lies,' he said unevenly. 'They're the truth.'

'I don't believe you.'

'I didn't think you would.' He sucked in a deep breath. 'Which is why I wrote you the letters.'

'The letters,' she repeated blankly.

'I know you got them, because I asked Claudia. What did you do with them, Keira—did you throw them away? Set light to them and watch them go up in flames?'

She shook her head. 'No. I didn't do that. I have them all.'

'Then, I wonder, could you possibly fetch them?'

Was it the word 'fetch' which brought Charlie bounding into the room, his tail wagging furiously and his once sad eyes bright and curious as he looked up at the strange man? Keira glared as she saw Matteo crouch down and offer his hand to the little dog, furious yet somehow unsurprised when the terrier edged cautiously towards him. The shock of seeing Matteo again had shaken her and weakened her defences, making her realise that she was still fundamentally shaky around him—and so she nodded her agreement to his bizarre request. At least leaving the room and his disturbing presence would give her the chance to compose herself and to quieten the fierce hammering of her heart.

Slowly she walked into the hallway to retrieve the pile of envelopes from the drawer and went back into the sitting room, holding them gingerly between her fingers, like an unexploded bomb. By now Charlie's tail was thrashing wildly, and as Matteo straightened up from stroking him the puppy gave a little whine of protest and she wondered how he had so quickly managed to charm the shy little dog. But the terrier had been discovered wriggling in a sack by the side of the road, she remembered, the only survivor among all his dead brothers and sisters. Charlie had also grown up without a mother, she thought—and a lump lodged in her throat.

'Here,' she croaked, holding the letters towards him.

'Don't you want to open them?' he said.

She shook her head. 'Not really.'

'Then maybe I'd better tell you what's in them,' he said, his eyes not leaving her face as he took them from her. 'They are all love letters. With the exception of one.'

He saw her eyes widen before dark lashes came shuttering down to cloak their sapphire hue with suspicion.

'What's that? A hate letter?' she quipped.

'I'm serious, Keira.'

'And so am I. Anyone can write down words on a piece of paper and not mean them.'

'Then how about I summarise them for you out loud?'

'No.'

But that one word was so whispered that he barely heard it and Matteo had no intention of heeding it anyway. 'Four words, actually,' he husked. 'I love you, Keira. So how about I say it again, just so there can be no misunderstanding? I love you, Keira, and I've been a fool. *Uno scemo!* I should have been honest with you from the start, but...' He inhaled deeply through his nostrils and then expelled the air on a shuddered breath. 'Keeping things locked away inside was the way I operated. The only way I knew. But believe me when I tell you that by the time I asked you to marry me, I wasn't thinking about the house any more. My mind was full of you. It still is. I can't stop thinking about you and I don't want to. So I'm asking you to give me another chance, Keira. To give *us* another chance. You, me and Santino. That's all.'

She didn't say anything for a moment and when she spoke she started shaking her head, as if what he was demanding of her was impossible.

'That's *all*?' she breathed. 'After everything that's happened? You don't know what you're asking, Matteo.'

'Oh, but I do,' he demurred. 'I'm asking you to be my wife for real. With nothing but total honesty between us from now on, because I want that. I want that more than anything.' His voice lowered. 'But I realise it can only work if you love me too. Once, in a shadowed hallway after we had taken our wedding vows, you whispered to me that you did, but you may not have meant it.'

Keira clamped her lips together to try to contain the stupid tremble of emotion. Of course she had meant it. Every single word. The question was whether he did, too. Was it possible that he really loved her, or was this simply a means to an end—the manipulative declaration of a man determined to get his rightful heir back into his life? Or maybe just pride refusing to let a woman walk away from him.

Yet something was stubbornly refusing to allow her to accept the bleaker version of his reasons for coming here today. Was it the anguish she could see in his black eyes—so profound that even she, in her insecurity, didn't believe she was imagining it? She flicked the tip of her tongue over her mouth, wondering if it was too late for them, until she realised what the reality of that would mean. Matteo gone from her life and free to make another with someone else, while she would never be able to forget him.

And she wasn't going to allow that to happen. Because how could she ignore the burning inside her heart and the bright spark of hope which was beginning to flood through her veins?

'I've tried not to love you,' she admitted slowly. 'But it doesn't work. I think about you nearly all the time and I miss you. I love you, Matteo, and I will be your wife, but on one condition.'

His body grew very still. 'Anything,' he said. 'Name it.'

She had been about to ask him never knowingly to hurt her, but she realised that was all part of the package. That hurt and pain were the price you paid for love and you just had to pray they didn't rear their bitter heads too often in a lifetime. She knew also that if they wanted to go forward, then they had to leave the bitterness of the past behind. So instead of demanding the impossible, she touched her fingertips to his face, tracing them slowly down over his cheek until they came to rest on his beautiful lips.

'That you make love to me,' she said, her voice softened by tears of joy. 'And convince me this really is happening.'

His voice was unsteady. 'You mean, right now?'

She swallowed and nodded, rapidly wiping underneath her eyes with a bent finger. 'This very second,' she gulped.

Framing her face within the palms of his hands, he looked at her for one long moment before he spoke. 'To the woman who has given me everything, because without you I am nothing. *Ti amo, mia sposa.* My beautiful, beautiful wife,' he husked, and crushed his lips down hard on hers.

EPILOGUE

OUTSIDE THE WINDOW big white flakes floated down from the sky, adding to the dazzling carpet which had already covered the vast sweep of lawn. Keira gazed at it and gave a dreamy sigh. It was unusual for snow to settle in this part of Umbria and she thought she'd never seen anything quite so magical, or so beautiful. She smiled. Well, except maybe one other time...

Looking up from where she was crouched beside the Christmas tree where she'd just placed a couple of presents, she saw Matteo walk into the room—with snowflakes melting against his dark hair. He'd been outside, putting the finishing touches to a snowman, which would be the first thing Santino saw when he looked out of his window tomorrow morning. Their son's first real Christmas, Keira thought, because last year he'd been too young to realise what was going on and she...

Well, if she was being honest, she could hardly remember last Christmas herself. She and Matteo had been busy discovering each other all over again—and finding out that things were different from how they'd been before. They couldn't have been anything *but* different once the constraints of the past were lifted and they'd given themselves the freedom to say exactly what was on their minds. Or in their hearts.

Matteo had given her the option of living in London, Rome or Umbria—and she'd opted for the sprawling Umbrian estate which had once belonged to his mother's family. She figured it was healthier for Santino to grow up in the glorious Italian countryside, especially now that they had acquired a beautiful black cat named Luca who, against all odds, had become a devoted companion to Charlie the terrier.

But it was more than that. This estate was Matteo's link with his roots. It represented continuity and stability—something which had been lacking in both their lives until now. One day Santino might listen to the call of his forebears and decide he didn't want to be a businessman, like his daddy. He might want to grow up and farm the fertile acres of this beautiful place. A place which might so nearly have disappeared from the family.

Because Keira had discovered that the very first letter Matteo had sent during their separation contained estate agent details marketing the property. He'd put it up for sale to demonstrate that the house meant nothing, if he didn't have her. They had quickly aborted the prospective sale, despite the frantic bidding war which had been taking place at the time. And had decided to make the estate their permanent home.

'What are you smiling at?' questioned Matteo softly as he walked over to the Christmas tree and pulled her to her feet.

Her contented expression didn't change. 'Do I need a reason?' She sighed. 'I'm just so happy, Matteo. Happier than I ever thought possible.'

'Well, isn't that a coincidence? Because I feel exactly the same way,' he said, his fingers beginning to massage her shoulders, their practised caress never failing to arouse her. 'Have I told you lately that I love you, Mrs Valenti?'

She pretended to frown. 'I think you might have mentioned it before you went out to build Santino's snowman. And just for the record, I love you, too. So very much.'

He bent his head and kissed her, deeply and passionately and it was some time before she broke off to graze her lips against the dark stubble of his angled jaw.

'Did you speak to your father?' she said.

'I did. And he's looking forward to Christmas lunch tomorrow. He says he'll be here soon after eleven and is bringing his new girlfriend.' His eyes gleamed down at her. 'And that we should prepare ourselves for what he calls a *significant* age gap.'

Keira giggled as she rested her head on Matteo's shoulder. Massimo had divorced Luciana in the spring and although Keira had tried to feel sad about it, she just couldn't. Not only had the older woman been a trouble-maker—it transpired that she'd been unfaithful to her husband as well. And one night, soon after the decree nisi had come through and Matteo had been away on business, Keira and her father-in-law had dined together in Rome. He'd told her it wasn't a desire to manipulate which had made him threaten to disinherit Matteo if he didn't produce an heir—but concern that his son was becoming emotionally remote and would end up a rich and lonely old man.

'And then you stepped in and saved him and made him happy. Truly happy—and I cannot thank you enough for that, Keira,' he had whispered, his voice cracking a little. 'I know I wasn't a good father when he was growing up.' He had fallen silent for a moment and his eyes had grown reflective. 'I missed his mother so much and he...well, he looked so much like her, that sometimes it was painful to be around him.'

'Have you told him that, Massimo?' she had said quietly, pressing her hand over his across the table. 'Because I think you should.'

And he had. Keira closed her eyes, remembering the long overdue heart-to-heart between father and son, and the growing closeness of their relationship which had resulted.

Her mind flicked back to the present as Matteo began to caress her bottom, murmuring his appreciation that these days she almost always wore a dress. She liked wearing dresses, although she could still resurrect her inner tomboy when needed—and she suspected she was going to need to do that a lot if Santino played as much football as Matteo intended he should. 'Would you like part of your Christmas present tonight?' she whispered, snuggling up to him.

He pulled away to look at her and raised his eyebrows. 'Is that an offer I shouldn't refuse?'

'Put it this way—I'm wearing it underneath this dress and I need you to unwrap it for me. Matteo!' She giggled as he began to lead her towards the bedroom. 'I didn't mean *now*—I meant later.'

'Too bad,' he murmured, not lessening his pace by a fraction. 'Because I have something for you which can't wait.'

Actually, that wasn't quite true—he had two things for her. The first was sitting in the garage wrapped in a giant red bow ready to be untied on Christmas morning. A neglected Ferrari 1948 Spider sports car which he'd tracked down with great difficulty and at considerable expense, because she'd once told him it was her dream to restore beautiful vintage cars—and Matteo was rather partial to making his wife's dreams come true.

The second gift was rather different and he didn't give it to her until after he'd dealt with her outrageous panty thong with its matching boned bodice, which he damaged beyond repair in his eagerness to unhook it. And once he had her naked, he was distracted for quite some time...

His throat thickened with unexpected emotion as he pulled the small box from his discarded trousers and flipped open the lid to reveal a flawless white solitaire which sparkled like a giant star against dark velvet.

'What's this?' she questioned breathlessly, from among the sheets which were rumpled around her.

He lifted her left hand and slid the solitaire in place above her wedding band. 'I never gave you an engagement ring, did I? And I didn't give you a dream wedding either. A civil ceremony in a town hall was never something we were going to enjoy telling our grandchildren about.' He lifted her hand to his lips and kissed her fingertips. 'So I wondered if you'd like to renew our vows in my favourite church in Rome. You could wear a big white dress and do it properly this time, and we could throw a party afterwards. Or not—whichever you prefer. What I'm asking is, would you like to marry me again, Keira Valenti?'

Keira opened her mouth to say that she didn't care about pomp or ceremony, but that wasn't quite true. And weren't she and Matteo all about the truth, these days? She thought about something else, too, something which had been niggling away at her for a while now. Because weddings could bring people together and heal old wounds, couldn't they? Motherhood had changed her. Softened her. She realised now that her aunt might have been strict when she was growing up, but she'd given an orphaned little girl the home she'd badly needed and had stopped her from being taken into care. And didn't she owe her aunt Ida a great deal for that? Wasn't it time to invite her and Shelley to Italy, to share in her good fortune and happiness and to introduce Santino to some of *her* roots?

She wound her arms around Matteo's neck and looked into his beautiful black eyes, her heart turning over with emotion. 'Yes, Matteo,' she said breathlessly. 'I'll be proud to marry you. To stand before our family and friends and say the thing I'll never tire of saying, which is that I love you—and I'll love you for the rest of my life.'

* * * * *

THE ITALIAN'S
CHRISTMAS CHILD

LYNNE GRAHAM

Christmas is one of my favourite times of year.

It's about family and friends, so this is dedicated
to you.

CHAPTER ONE

THE MOORLAND LANDSCAPE on Dartmoor was cold and crisp with ice. As the four-wheel drive turned off the road onto a rough lane, Vito saw the picturesque cottage sheltering behind winter-bare trees with graceful frosted branches. His lean, strong face grim with exhaustion, he got out of the car ahead of his driver, only tensing as he heard the sound of yet another text hitting his phone. Ignoring it, he walked into the property while the driver emptied the car.

Instant warmth greeted him and he raked a weary hand through the dense blue-black hair that the breeze had whipped across his brow. There was a welcome blaze in the brick inglenook fireplace and he fought the sense of relief threatening to engulf him. He was not a coward. He had not run away as his ex-fiancée had accused him of doing. He would have stood his ground and stayed in Florence had he not finally appreciated that the pursuit of the paparazzi and outrageous headlines were only being fuelled by his continuing presence.

He had grudgingly followed his best friend Apollo's advice and had removed himself from the scene, recognising that his mother had quite enough to deal with when her husband was in hospital following a serious heart attack without also having to suffer the embarrassment of her son's newly acquired notoriety. Undeniably, his friend had much more experience than Vito had of handling scandals and bad publicity. The Greek playboy had led a far less restricted life than Vito, who had known from an early age that he would become the next CEO of the Zaffari Bank. His grandfather had steeped him in the history and traditions of a family that could trace its beginnings back to the Middle Ages when the Zaffari name had stood shoulder to shoulder with words like *honour* and *principle*. No more, Vito reflected wryly. Now he would be famous for ever as the banker who had indulged in drugs and strippers.

Not his style, not his style at all, Vito ruminated ruefully, breaking free of his thoughts to lavishly tip his driver and thank him. When it came to the drug allegations, he could only suppress a groan. One of his closest friends at school had taken something that had killed him at a party and Vito had never been tempted by illegal substances. And the whores? In truth Vito could barely remember when he had last had sex. Although he had been engaged until a week earlier, Marzia had always been cool in that department.

'She's a lady to her backbone.' His grandfather had sighed approvingly, shortly before his passing. 'A Ravello with the right background and breeding. She will make a superb hostess and future mother for your children.'

Not now, though, Vito thought, glancing at his phone to discover that his ex had sent him yet another text. *Dio mio*, what did she want from him now? He had perfectly understood her decision to break off their engagement and he had wasted no time in putting the house she had been furnishing for their future occupation back on the market. That, however, had proved to be a move that had evidently rankled, even though he had assured Marzia that she was welcome to keep every stick of furniture in the place.

What about the Abriano painting? she'd texted.

He pointed out that his grandfather's engagement gift would have to be returned. It was worth millions—how much more compensation was he to pay in terms of damages? He had offered her the house but she had refused it.

But in spite of his generosity, he still felt guilty. He had messed up Marzia's life and embarrassed her. For probably the first time in his life he had wronged someone. On the spur of the moment he had made a decision that had hit Marzia very hard and even the sincerest apology could not lessen the impact of it. But he could not have told his former fiancée the truth because he could not have trusted her to keep it secret. And if the truth came out, his sacrifice would be pointless and it would plunge the only woman he had ever loved into gross humiliation and heartbreak. Vito had made a very tough choice and he was fully prepared to take the heat for it.

That, indeed, was why vanishing off-grid for a couple of weeks over Christmas *still* felt disturbingly gutless to Vito, whose natural instincts were pre-emptive and forceful.

'Ritchie's a lying, cheating scumbag!' Holly's flatmate and best friend, Pixie, ranted furiously down the phone.

Holly grimaced and pushed her hand through her

heavy mane of black curling hair, her big blue eyes red-rimmed and sad as she checked her watch to see that she was still safely within her lunch hour. 'You're not going to get any argument from me on that score,' she said ruefully.

'He's as bad as that last guy who borrowed all the money from you,' Pixie reminded her with a typical lack of tact. 'And the one before that who wanted to marry you so that you could act as a carer for his in-valid mother!'

Wincing at her disheartening past history with men, Holly reflected that she could not have done worse in the dating stakes had she drawn up a specific list of self-ish, dishonest losers. 'Let's not look back,' she urged, keen to move on to more positive subjects.

Pixie refused to cooperate, saying, 'So, what on earth are you planning to do now for your festive break with me, stuck in London and Ritchie out of the picture?'

A sudden grin lit Holly's oval face with surprising enthusiasm. 'I'm going to make Christmas for Sylvia instead!'

'But she's staying with her daughter in Yorkshire over the holiday...*isn't she*?'

'No, Alice had to cancel Sylvia at the last minute. Her house has been flooded by a burst pipe. Sylvia was horribly disappointed when she found out and then when I walked in on Ritchie with his floozy today, I re-alised that I could take two pieces of bad luck and make something good out of them...'

'I really hate it when you pick yourself up off the floor and come over all optimistic again.' Pixie sighed dramatically. 'Please tell me you at least *thumped* Ritchie...'

'I told him what I thought of him...briefly,' Holly qualified with her innate honesty, for really she had been too squeamish to linger in the presence of her half-naked boyfriend and the woman he had chosen to cheat on her with. 'So, is it all right for me to borrow your car to go to Sylvia's?'

'Of course it is. How else would you get there? But watch out: there's snow forecast—'

'They always like to talk about snow this close to Christmas,' Holly demurred, unimpressed by the threat. 'By the way, I'm taking our Christmas tree and ornaments with me and I'd already bought and made all the trimmings for a festive lunch. I'm going to put on that Santa outfit you wore for the Christmas party at the salon last year. Sylvia loves a laugh. She'll appreciate it.'

'Sylvia will be over the moon when she finds you on the doorstep,' her friend predicted warmly. 'Between losing her husband and having to move because she couldn't manage the farmhouse alone any more, she's had a horrible year.'

Holly held firmly on to the inspiring prospect of her foster mother's happiness at her arrival while she finished her afternoon shift at the busy café where she worked. It was Christmas Eve and she adored the festive season, possibly because she had grown up mainly in foster care and had always been painfully conscious that she did not have a real family to share the experience with. In an effort to comfort her, Pixie had assured her that family Christmases could be a nightmare and that she was in love with an ideal of Christmas rather than the reality. But some day, somehow, Holly was determined to turn fantasy into reality with a husband and children of her own That was her dream and in spite of recent setbacks she understood that it was hanging on to her dream that essentially kept her going through more challenging times.

Both she and Pixie had been fostered by Sylvia Ware from the age of twelve and the older woman's warm acceptance and understanding had been far superior to the uncaring and occasionally neglectful homes Holly and Pixie had endured as younger children caught up in the care system. Holly had long regretted not paying more heed to Sylvia's lectures about studying harder at school. Over the years Holly had attended so many different schools and made so many moves that she had simply drifted through her education, accepting that she would always be behind in certain subjects. Now at almost twenty-four, Holly had redressed that adolescent mistake by attending night classes to achieve basic qualifications but the road ahead to further education seemed so long and complex that it daunted her and she had instead chosen to study for a qualification in interior design online.

'And what use is that to you?' Pixie, who was a hairdresser, had asked baldly.

'I'm really interested in it. I love looking at a room and thinking about how I can improve it.'

'But people from our sort of background don't get hired as interior designers,' Pixie had pointed out. 'I mean, we're just ordinary workers trying to pay our bills, not people with fancy careers.'

And Holly had to acknowledge as she donned her friend's Santa outfit that there *was* nothing fancy or impressive about her likely to combat that discouraging assurance. Fortunately the short dress had been far too generously sized on her infinitely more slender friend.

Pixie might envy Holly's curves but Pixie could eat whatever she liked and never put on a pound while Holly was engaged in a constant struggle to prevent her curves from taking over. Her golden skin tone hailed from an unknown father. He might or might not have been someone her erratic mother had met abroad. On the other hand he might simply have been a man who lived in the same street. Her only parent had told her so many lies that Holly had long accepted that the truth of her fatherhood would never be known.

At four feet ten inches tall, Holly, like her mother, lacked height. She pulled on warm black winter tights under the bright red satin and corseted dress. Thrusting her feet into cowboy boots rather than the heels Pixie had sported for her party a year earlier, Holly scowled at her gaudy, busty reflection in the mirror and jammed on the Santa hat in a defiant move. OK, she looked comical, she acknowledged, but her appearance would make Sylvia laugh and overlook the disappointment of not having her own daughters around her to celebrate Christmas Day with, and that was what was truly important.

Planning to spend the night on the sofa in Sylvia's tiny living area, she packed her rucksack and carefully placed what remained of the decorations and the food into a box heavy enough to make her stagger on her final trip to the car. *At least the food wouldn't be going to waste*, she thought with determined positivity, until a flashback of the ugly scene she had interrupted with Ritchie and the receptionist at his insurance office cut through her rebellious brain.

Her tummy rolled with nausea and her battered heart clenched. *In the middle of the day as well*, she thought with a shudder. She couldn't imagine even having sex, never mind going at it on a desk in broad daylight. Possibly she wasn't a very adventurous person. In fact both she and Pixie were probably pretty strait-laced. At twelve years old they had shuddered over the ugly chaos of broken relationships in their mothers' lives and had solemnly decided to swear off men altogether. Of course once puberty had kicked in, with all its attendant confusing hormones, that rule had failed. At fourteen they had ditched their embargo on men while deciding that sex was the real danger and best avoided outside a serious relationship. *A serious committed relationship.* Holly's eyes rolled at the memory of their mutual innocence. And so far neither she nor her friend had managed to have a serious committed relationship with a man.

All that considered thought about steering clear of sexual relationships hadn't done her many favours either, Holly reflected with helpless insecurity. There had been men she really liked who ran a mile from what they saw as her outdated expectations and then there had been the others who stayed around for a few weeks or months, eager to be the first into her bed. Had she only ever been a sexual challenge to Ritchie? How long, for instance, had he been messing around with other women?

'Did you expect me to wait for you for ever?' Ritchie had shouted back at her, blaming her for his betrayal because she had held back on having sex with him. 'What's so special about you?'

Holly flinched at that ugly recollection because she had always known that there was nothing particularly special about her.

It was snowing as she drove off in the battered little hatchback that Pixie had christened Clementine, and she groaned. She loved the look of snow but she didn't like to drive in it and she hated being cold. Thank goodness for the car, she acknowledged, as she rattled out of the small Devon town where she lived and worked.

Snow was falling fast by the time she reached Sylvia's home, which was dismayingly dark. Perhaps the older woman was out at a church service or visiting a neighbour. Jamming down her hat over the mass of hair fighting to escape its confines, Holly rapped on the door and waited, stamping her feet to keep warm. After a couple of minutes she knocked again and then she followed the communal path to the little house next door, which was brightly lit, and knocked there instead.

'I'm sorry to bother you but I wondered if you knew where Mrs Ware has gone and if she'll be home soon,' Holly asked with a friendly smile.

'Sylvia left this afternoon. I helped her pack—she was in such a tizzy because she wasn't expecting anyone,' the elderly little woman at the door told her.

Holly frowned, her heart sinking. 'So, she went to her daughter's after all, then?'

'Oh, no, it wasn't the daughter who came, it was her son. Big tall chap in a suit. He's taking her back to Bruges or Belgium or some place,' the neighbour told her less certainly.

'Brussels. That's where Stephen lives. Do you know how long she'll be away?'

'A couple of weeks at least, she seemed to think…'

As deflated as a pricked balloon, Holly walked back to her car.

'You watch yourself driving home,' the old lady called after her. 'There's to be heavy snow tonight.'

'Thanks, I will,' Holly promised, forcing a smile. 'Merry Christmas!'

And a very merry Christmas it was going to be on her own, she thought unhappily, annoyed to find that her eyes were prickling with tears. After all, Sylvia was going to have the best possible Christmas with her son and the grandchildren she rarely saw. Holly was really, really pleased that Stephen had swooped in from abroad to save the day. He and his wife were rare visitors but he had at least made the effort and now his mother wouldn't have to spend her first Christmas as a widow alone. Holly sniffed and blinked back the tears, scolding herself for being so selfish. She was young and healthy and employed. She had nothing to complain about, nothing at all.

Maybe she was simply missing Pixie, she reasoned, as she drove with care on the steep, icy road that climbed up over the moors. Pixie's kid brother was in some sort of trouble and Pixie had taken time off to go and stay with him and sort it out. It was probably financial trouble but Holly wouldn't ask any awkward questions or offer unwelcome advice because she didn't want to hurt her friend, who was deeply attached to her horribly self-centred sibling. Everyone had problems, she reminded herself doggedly, tensing as she felt the tyres of the car shift into a near skid on the slippery surface and slowing her speed even more. She had far fewer problems than most people and had no excuse whatsoever for feeling sorry for herself.

Ritchie? Well, that wasn't an excuse. So, she had got hurt but then Pixie would point out that she was too soft in that line, too prone to thinking well of people and being knocked back hard when they let her down. Pixie was more of a cynic, strong on distrust as a means of self-defence, except when it came to her own brother.

Holly peered out of the windscreen because visibility was fading fast with the wipers unable to keep up with the heavy snow. She wasn't the dramatic type, she assured herself, as the car coasted down a hill that seemed steeper than it had seemed when she drove over it earlier that evening, but the weather was foul and the light snowfall she had dimly expected now bore a closer resemblance to a blizzard.

And then without the smallest warning, and to the accompaniment of her strangled scream, the car glided in the most terrifying slow motion off the road into a ditch where it tilted over and wedged fast with a loud, nerve-racking crunch of metal. After switching off the engine, Holly breathed in slow and deep to calm herself. She was alive, no other car was involved and nobody was hurt. There was much to be thankful for, she told herself bracingly.

Sadly that was a conviction that took a beating once she climbed out with some difficulty, owing to the angle the car had crashed at, to inspect the damage. The side wing of Pixie's elderly vehicle was crushed up against a large rock, which had presumably been placed to mark the entrance to the lane. *My goodness, how much will the repairs cost?* was her first fearful thought. It was *her* responsibility, not Pixie's.

A spark of fear assailed her only after she had examined her surroundings. The road was deserted and lay under a covering of unbroken snow. It was a bad night and it was Christmas Eve and she didn't think there

would be much passing traffic, if any. As she stood
there nursing her mobile phone and wondering what
she was going to do, Holly had never felt more lonely.
She had no close friend she could ring and drag out in
such dreadful weather on such a special night. No, she
was on her own, sink or swim. Consternation gripped
her when she couldn't get a signal on her phone to use
it. Only then did she turn round to look again at the
lane she stood beside and there, like a faint beacon in
the darkness, she saw the lights of what could only be
a house and relief filled her to overflowing. Hopefully
it was occupied and the occupant had a landline she
could use to call for a breakdown truck.

Vito was savouring a glass of award-winning wine
and wondering what to do with the evening when the
knocker on the door sounded. Taken aback, he frowned
because he hadn't heard a car and there were no lights
outside. Did the local caretaker live within walking distance? He peered out through the spyhole and saw a
red-and-white Santa hat. Someone was definitely at the
wrong house because Vito hated Christmas. He yanked
open the door and enormous blue eyes like velvet pan-
sies looked up at him. At first he thought his visitor
was a child and then his eyes dropped and took in the
swell of breasts visible between the parted edges of her
coat and he registered that, although she might be very
small, she was all woman.

Holly stared up in wonderment at the male who appeared in the doorway. He looked like every fantasy
male she had ever dreamt about meeting all rolled into
one spectacular package. In fact he was so gorgeous
with his black hair, designer stubble and dark, deep-set,

mysterious eyes that he made her teeth clench in dismay because he didn't look approachable or helpful or anything that might have encouraged her. That he wore a very formal dark business suit with a white shirt and natty gold tie didn't help to relax her either.

'If you're looking for a party, you're at the wrong house,' Vito told her loftily, recalling his friend's warnings about how sneaky the paparazzi could be. If he'd thought about that risk, he wouldn't have answered the door at all.

'I'm looking for a phone. Mine has no reception here and my car went off the road at the foot of your lane,' Holly explained in a rush. 'Do you have a landline?'

Exasperation flashed through Vito, who had far too much sensitive information on his cell phone to consider loaning it to anyone. 'This isn't my house. I'll look and see,' he fielded drily.

As he turned on his heel without inviting her in out of the heavily falling snow, Holly grimaced and shivered because she wasn't dressed for bad weather, having only thrown on a raincoat to cover her outfit because she had known she would be warm inside the car. *Not Mr Nice Guy, anyway*, she thought ruefully. She had recognised the impatience in those electrifyingly dark magnetic eyes, watched the flare of his nostrils and the tightening of his wide, sculpted mouth as he'd bit back a withering comment. She was good at reading faces, even gorgeous ones, she conceded, as she shifted her feet in a vain effort to heat the blood freezing in her veins. She didn't think she had ever seen a more handsome man, no, not even on a movie screen, but personality-wise she reckoned that there was a good chance that he was chillier than an icicle.

'There is a phone… You may step inside to use it,' he invited grudgingly, his foreign accent edging every syllable in a very attractive way.

Holly reddened with discomfiture, already well aware that she was not a welcome visitor. She dug out her phone to scroll through numbers for Pixie's car mechanic, Bill, who ran a breakdown service. As she did so, she missed seeing the step in front of her and tripped over it, falling forward with a force that would have knocked the breath from her body had not strong arms snapped out to catch her before she fell.

'Watch out…' Taken aback by a level of clumsiness utterly unknown to a male as surefooted as a cat, Vito virtually lifted her into the porch. As her hair briefly brushed his face he was engulfed by the scent of oranges, sweet and sun-warmed. But it was only by touching her and seeing her face below the lights that he registered that she was almost blue with cold. '*Maledizione*, you're freezing! Why didn't you tell me that?'

'It's enough of an imposition coming to the door—'

'Yes, I would surely have been happier to trip over your frozen corpse on my doorstep in the morning!' Vito fielded scathingly. 'You should've told me—'

'You've got eyes of your own and an off-putting manner. I don't like bothering people,' Holly said truthfully while she frantically rubbed her hands over her raincoat in an effort to get some feeling back into her fingers before she tried to work her phone again.

Vito gazed down at her from his height of six foot one. He was bemused by her criticism when he was trying to be pleasant and when he could not recall when a woman had last offered him a word of criticism. Even in the act of breaking their engagement, Marzia had contrived not to speak a word of condemnation. Either a woman of saintly tolerance or one who didn't give a damn who he might have slept with behind her back? It was a sobering thought.

An off-putting manner? Could that be true about him? His grandfather had taught him to maintain distance between himself and others and he had often thought that a useful gift when it came to commanding a large staff, none of whom dared to take liberties with their authoritarian CEO.

Thoroughly irritated by the thoughts awakened by his visitor and that unfamiliar self-questioning mode, he swiped the phone from between her shaking fingers and said firmly, 'Go and warm up first by the fire and then make the call.'

'Are you sure you don't mind?'

'I will contrive to bear it.'

Halfway towards the wonderful blaze of the log fire illuminating the dim interior, Holly spun round with a merriment in her eyes that lit up her whole face and she laughed. 'You're a sarky one, aren't you?'

In the firelight her eyes were bright as sapphires and that illuminating smile made the breath catch in his throat because it lent her incredible appeal. And Vito was not the sort of male who noticed women very often and when he did he usually swiftly stifled the impulse. But for a split second that playful tone and that radiant smile knocked him sideways and he found himself staring. He scanned the glorious dark hair that fell free of the Santa hat as she whipped it off, before lowering his appreciative gaze to the wonderfully generous thrust of her breasts above a neat little waist, right down to the hem of the shimmering dress that revealed slim knees and shapely calves incongruously encased in cowboy boots. He threw his shoulders back, bracing as the pulse at his groin beat out a different kind of tension.

Holly connected momentarily with eyes of gold semi-veiled by the lush black sweep of his lashes and something visceral tightened low in her pelvis as she let her attention linger on his lean, hard bone structure, which was stunningly hard and male from his level dark brows to his arrogant classic nose and his strong, sculpted jawline. Just looking at him sent the oddest flash of excitement through her and she reddened uneasily, and deliberately spun back to the fire to hold her hands out to the heat. So, he was very good-looking. That didn't mean she had to gape like an awestruck fan at a rock star, did it? She was only inside his house to use the phone, she reminded herself in embarrassment.

She flexed her fingers. 'Where did you put my phone?'

As she half turned it was settled neatly into her hand and she opened it and scrolled through the numbers. He handed her the handset of the house phone and she pressed out Bill's number, lifting it to her ear while carefully not glancing again in her host's direction.

Vito was engaged in subduing his sexual arousal and reeling in shock from the need to do so. What was he? A teenager again? She wasn't his type...if he had a type. The women in his life had invariably been tall, elegant blondes and she was very small, very curvy and very, *very* sexy, he conceded involuntarily as she moved about the room while she talked, her luxuriant hair rippling across her shoulders, her rounded hips swaying. She was apologising for disturbing someone on Christmas Eve and she apologised at great length instead of getting straight to the point of her problem with her car.

What were the chances that she was a particularly clever member of the paparazzi brigade? Vito had flown into the UK on a private plane to a private airfield and travelled to the cottage in a private car. Only Apollo and his mother, Concetta, knew where he was. But Apollo had warned him that the paps went to extraordinary lengths to steal photos and find stories they could sell. His perfect white teeth gritted. At the very least, he needed to check that there was a broken-down car at the foot of the lane.

'Boxing Day?' Holly was practically whispering in horror.

'And possibly only if the snowplough has been through ahead of me,' Bill told her apologetically. 'I'm working flat out tonight as it is. Where exactly is the car?'

The older man was local and, knowing the road well, was able to establish where she was. 'Aye, I know the house down there—foreign-owned holiday home as far as I know. And you're able to stay there?'

'Yes,' Holly said in as reassuring a tone as she could contrive while wondering if she was going to have to bed down in Pixie's car. 'Do you know anyone else I could ring?'

She tried the second number but there was no response at all. Swallowing hard, she set the digital phone down. 'I'll go back to the car now,' she told Vito squarely.

'I'll walk down with you… See if there's anything I can do—'

'Unless you have a tractor to haul it out of the ditch I shouldn't think so.' Holly buttoned her coat, tied the belt and braced herself to face the great outdoors again.

As she straightened her shoulders she looked round the room with belated admiration, suddenly noticing that the opulent décor was an amazing and highly effective marriage of traditional and contemporary styles. In spite of the ancient brick inglenook fireplace, the staircase had a glass surround and concealed lights. But she also noticed that there was one glaring omission: there were no festive decorations of any kind.

Vito yanked on his cashmere coat and scarf over the suit he still wore.

'If you don't have boots, I can't let you go down there with me… You'll get your shoes soaked,' Holly told him ruefully, glancing at the polished, city-type footwear he sported with his incredibly stylish suit, which moulded to his well-built, long-legged frame as though specifically tailored to do so.

Vito walked into the porch, which boasted a rack of boots, and, picking out a pair, donned them. Her pragmatism had secretly impressed him. Vito was extremely clever but, like many very clever people, he was not particularly practical and the challenges of rural living in bad weather lay far outside his comfort zone.

'My name is Holly,' she announced brightly on the porch.

'Vito…er… Vito Sorrentino,' Vito lied, employing his father's original surname.

His mother had been an only child, a daughter when his grandfather had longed for a son. At his grandfather's request, Vito's father had changed his name to Zaffari when he married Vito's mother to ensure that the family name would not die out. Ciccio Sorrentino had been content to surrender his name in return for the privilege of marrying a fabulously wealthy banking heiress. There was no good reason for Vito to take the risk of identifying himself to a stranger. Right now the name Zaffari was cannon fodder for the tabloids across Europe and the news of his disappearance and current location would be worth a great deal of money to a profiteer. And if there was one gift Vito had in spades it was the gilded art of making a profit and ensuring that nobody got to do it at his expense.

His grandfather would have turned in his grave at the mere threat of his grandson plunging the family name and the family bank into such a sleazy scandal. Vito, however, was rather less naive. Having attended a board meeting before his departure, Vito was aware that he could virtually do no wrong. All the Zaffari directors cared about was that their CEO continued to ensure that the Zaffari bank carried on being the most successful financial institution in Europe.

CHAPTER TWO

'YOU SAID THIS wasn't your house,' Holly reminded him through chattering teeth as they walked out into the teeth of a gale laced with snow.

'A friend loaned it to me for a break.'

'And you're staying here alone?'

'*Sì*...yes.'

'By choice...*alone*...at Christmas?' Holly framed incredulously.

'Why not?' Vito loathed Christmas but that was none of her business and he saw no need to reveal anything of a personal nature. His memories of Christmas were toxic. His parents, who rarely spent time together, had squabbled almost continuously through the festive break. His mother had made a real effort to hide that reality and make the season enjoyable, but Vito had always been far too intelligent even as a child not to understand what was happening around him. He had seen that his mother loved his father but that her love was not returned. He had watched her humiliate herself in an effort to smooth over Ciccio's bad moods and even worse temper. He had listened to her beg for five minutes of her husband's attention. He had eventually grasped that the ideal goal composed of marriage, family and respectability could be a very expensive shrine to worship at. Had he not been made aware that it was his inherent duty to carry on the family line, nothing would have persuaded Vito into matrimony.

He studied the old car in the ditch with an amount of satisfaction that bemused him. It was a shabby ancient wreck of a vehicle. It had to mean that Holly was not a plant, not a spy or a member of the paparazzi, but a genuine traveller in trouble. Not that that reality softened his irritation over the fact that he was now stuck with her for at least one night. He had listened to the phone call she had made. Short of it being a matter of life or death, nobody was willing to come out on such a night. Of course he could have thrown his wealth at the problem to take care of it but nothing would more surely advertise his presence than the hiring of a helicopter to remove his unwanted guest, and he was doubtful that even a helicopter could fly in such poor conditions.

'As you see…it's stuck,' Holly pointed out unnecessarily while patting the bonnet of the car as if it were a live entity in need of comfort. 'It's my friend's car and she's going to be really upset about this.'

'Accidents happen…particularly if you choose to drive without taking precautions on a road like this in this kind of weather.'

In disbelief, Holly rounded on him, twin spots of high colour sparking over her cheekbones. 'It wasn't snowing this bad when I left home! There were no precautions!'

'Let's get your stuff and head back to the house.'

Suppressing the anger his tactless comment had roused with some difficulty, Holly studied him in astonishment. 'You're inviting me back to the house? You don't need to. I can—'

'I'm a notoriously unsympathetic man but even I could not leave you to sleep in a car in a snowstorm on Christmas Eve!' Vito framed impatiently. 'Now, may we cut the conversation and head back to the heat? Or do you want to pat the car again?'

Face red now with mortification, Holly opened the boot and dug out her rucksack to swing it up onto her back.

The rucksack was almost as big as she was, Vito saw in disbelief. 'Let me take that.'

'No…I was hoping you'd take the box because it's heavier.'

Stubborn mouth flattening, Vito reached in with reluctance for the sizeable box and hefted it up with a curled lip. 'Do you really need the box as well?'

'Yes, it's got all my stuff in it…*please*,' Holly urged.

Her amazingly blue eyes looked up at him and he felt strangely disorientated. Her eyes were as translucent a blue as the Delft masterpieces his mother had conserved from his grandfather's world-famous collection. They trudged back up the lane with Vito maintaining a disgruntled silence as he carried the bulky carton.

'*Porca miseria!* What's in the box?'

'My Christmas decorations and some food.'

'Why are you driving round with Christmas decorations and food? Of course, you were heading to a party,' he reasoned for himself, thinking of what she wore.

'No, I wasn't. I intended to spend the night with my foster mother because I thought she was going to be on her own for Christmas. *But*…turns out her son came and collected her and she didn't know I was planning to surprise her, so when I went off the road I was driving home again.'

'Where's home?'

She named a town Vito had never heard of.

'Where are you from?'

'Florence…in Italy,' he explained succinctly.

'I do know where Florence is…it *is* famous,' Holly countered, glancing up at him while the snow drifted down steadily, quietly, cocooning them in the small space lit by his torch. 'So, you're Italian.'

'You do like to state the obvious, don't you?' Vito derided, stomping into the porch one step behind her.

'I hate that sarcasm of yours!' Holly fired back at him angrily, taking herself almost as much by surprise as she took him because she usually went out of her way to avoid conflict.

An elegant black brow raised, Vito removed the boots, hung his coat and scarf and then lifted the rucksack from her bent shoulders. 'What have you got in here? Rocks?'

'Food.'

'The kitchen here is packed with food.'

'Do you always know better than everyone else about everything?' Holly, whose besetting fault was untidiness, carefully hung her wet coat beside his to be polite.

'I very often *do* know better,' Vito answered without hesitation.

Holly spread a shaken glance over his lean, darkly handsome and wholly serious features and groaned out loud. 'No sense of humour either.'

'Knowing one's own strengths is not a flaw,' Vito informed her gently.

'But it is if you don't consider your faults—'

'And what are *your* faults?' Vito enquired saccharine smooth, as she headed for the fire like a homing pigeon and held her hands out to the heat.

Holly wrinkled her snub nose and thought hard. 'I'm untidy. An incurable optimist. Too much of a people-pleaser… That comes of all those years in foster care and trying to fit in to different families and different schools.' She angled her head to one side, brown hair lying in a silken mass against one creamy cheek as she pondered. In the red Santa get-up, she reminded him of a cheerful little robin he had once seen pacing on a fence. 'I'm too forgiving sometimes because I always want to think the best of people or give them a second chance. I get really cross if I run out of coffee but I don't like conflict and avoid it. I like to do things quickly but sometimes that means I don't do them well. I fuss about my weight but I *still* don't exercise…'

As Vito listened to that very frank résumé he almost laughed. There was something intensely sweet about that forthright honesty. 'Strengths?' he prompted, unable to resist the temptation.

'I'm honest, loyal, hardworking, punctual…I like to make the people I care about happy,' she confided. 'That's what put me on that road tonight.'

'Would you like a drink?' Vito enquired.

'Red wine, if you have it…' Moving away from the fire, Holly approached her rucksack. 'Is it all right if I put the food in the kitchen?'

She walked through the door he indicated and her eyebrows soared along with the ceiling. Beyond that door the cottage changed again. A big extension housed an ultra-modern kitchen diner with pale sparkling granite work surfaces and a fridge large enough to answer the storage needs of a restaurant. She opened it up. It was already generously packed with goodies, mainly of the luxury version of ready meals. She arranged her offerings on an empty shelf and then walked back into the main room to open the box and extract the food that remained.

Obviously, she was stuck here in a strange house with a strange man for one night at the very least, Holly reflected anxiously. A slight frisson of unease trickled down her spine. Vito hadn't done or said anything threatening, though, she reminded herself. Like her, he recognised practicalities. He was stuck with her because she had nowhere else to go and clearly he wasn't overjoyed by the situation. Neither one of them had a choice but to make the best of it.

'You brought a lot of food with you,' Vito remarked from behind her.

Holly flinched because she hadn't heard him approach and she whipped her head around. 'I assumed I would be providing a Christmas lunch for two people.'

Walking back out of the kitchen when she had finished, she found him frowning down at the tree ornaments visible in the box.

'What is all this stuff?' he asked incredulously.

Holly explained. 'Would it be all right if I put up my tree here? I mean, it is Christmas Eve and I won't get another opportunity for a year,' she pointed out. 'Christmas is special to me.'

Vito was still frowning. 'Not to me,' he admitted flatly, for he had only bad memories of the many disappointing Christmases he had endured as a child.

Flushing, Holly closed the box and pushed it over to the wall out of the way. 'That's not a problem. You're doing enough letting me stay here.'

Dio mio, he was relieved that she was only a passing stranger because her fondness for the sentimental trappings of the season set his teeth on edge. Of course she wanted to put up her Christmas tree! Anyone who travelled around wearing a Santa hat was likely to want a tree on display as well! He handed her a glass of wine, trying not to feel responsible for having doused her chirpy flow of chatter.

'I'm heading upstairs for a shower,' Vito told her, because even though he had worn the boots, his suit trousers were damp. 'Will you be all right down here on your own?'

'Of course... This is much better than sitting in a crashed car,' Holly assured him before adding more awkwardly, 'Do you have a sweater or anything I could borrow? I only have pyjamas and a dress with me. My foster mum's house is very warm so I didn't pack anything woolly.'

Vito had not a clue what was in his luggage because he hadn't packed his own case since he was a teenager at boarding school. 'I'll see what I've got.'

Through the glass barrier of the stairs, Holly watched his long, powerful legs disappear from view and a curious little frisson rippled through her tense body. She heaved a sigh. So, no Christmas tree. What possible objection could anyone have to a Christmas tree? Did Vito share Ebenezer Scrooge's loathing for the festive season? Reminding herself that she was *very* lucky not to be shivering in Pixie's car by the side of the road, she settled down on the shaggy rug by the hearth and simply luxuriated in the warmth emanating from the logs glowing in the fire.

Vito thought about Holly while he took a shower. It

was a major mistake. Within seconds of picturing her sexy little body he went hard as a rock, his body reacting with a randy enthusiasm that astonished him. For months, of course, his libido had very much taken a back seat to the eighteen-hour days he was working. This year the bank's revenues would, he reminded himself with pride, smash all previous records. He was doing what he had been raised to do and he was doing it extremely well, so why did he feel so empty, so joyless? Vito asked himself in exasperation.

Intellectually he understood that there was more to life than the pursuit of profit but realistically he was and always had been a workaholic. An image of Holly chattering by the fire assailed him. Holly with her wonderful curves and her weird tree in a box. She was unusual, not remotely like the sort of women Vito usually met, and her originality was a huge draw. He had no idea what she was likely to say next. She wasn't wearing make-up. She didn't fuss with her appearance. She said exactly what she thought and felt—she had no filter. Towelling off, he tried to stop thinking about Holly. Obviously she turned him on. Equally obviously he wasn't going to do anything about it.

Why the hell not? The words sounded in the back of his brain. That battered old car, everything about her spelled out the message that she came from a different world. Making any kind of a move would be taking advantage, he told himself grimly. Yet the instant he had seen Holly he had wanted her, *wanted* her with an intensity he hadn't felt around a woman since he was a careless teenager. It was the situation. He could relax with a woman who had neither a clue who he was nor any idea of the sleazy scandal currently clinging to his name. And why wouldn't he want her? After all, he was very probably sex-starved, he told himself impatiently as he tossed out the contents of one of his suitcases and then opened a second before finding a sweater he deemed suitable.

Holly watched Vito walk down the stairs with the fluid, silent grace of a panther. He had looked amazing in his elegant business suit, but in black designer jeans and a long-sleeved red cotton tee he was drop-dead gorgeous and, with those high cheekbones and that full masculine mouth, very much in the male-model category. She blinked and stared, feeling the colour rise in her cheeks, her self-consciousness taking over, for she had literally never ever been in the radius of such a very handsome male and it was just a little like bumping into a movie star without warning.

'Here… You can roll up the sleeves.' Vito tossed the sweater into her lap. 'If you want to freshen up, there's a shower room just before you enter the kitchen.'

Holly scrambled upright and grabbed her rucksack to take his advice. A little alone time to get her giddy head in order struck her as a very good idea. When she saw herself in the mirror in the shower room she was affronted by the wind-tousled explosion of her hair and the amount of cleavage she was showing in the Santa outfit. Stripping off, she went for a shower, exulting in the hot water and the famous-name shower gel on offer. Whoever owned the cottage had to be pretty comfortably off, she decided with a grimace, which probably meant that Vito was as well. He wore a very sleek gold-coloured watch and the fit of his suit had been perfection. But then what did she know about such trappings or the likely cost of them? Pixie would laugh to hear such musings when the closest Holly had ever got to even dating an office worker was Ritchie, the cheating insurance salesman.

She pulled on the blue sweater, which plunged low enough at the neck to reveal her bra. She yanked it at the back to raise it to a decent level at the front and knew she would have to remember to keep her shoulders back. She rolled up the sleeves and, since the sweater covered her to her knees, left off her tights. Her hair she rescued with a little diligent primping until it fell in loose waves round her shoulders. Frowning at her bunny slippers, she crammed them back in her rucksack, deciding that bare feet were preferable. Cosmetics-wise she was pretty much stuck with the minimal make-up she had packed for Sylvia's. Sighing, she used tinted moisturiser, subtle eyeliner and glossed her lips. Well, at short notice that was the best she could do. In any case it was only her pride that was prompting her to make the effort. After all, a male as sophisticated as Vito Sorrentino wouldn't look at her anyway, she thought with a squirming pang of guilty disappointment. Why on earth was she thinking about him that way?

And thinking about Vito that way put her back in mind of Ritchie, which was unfortunate. But it also reminded her that she hadn't taken her pill yet and she dug into her bag to remedy that, only to discover that she had left them at home. As to why a virgin was taking contraceptive precautions, she and Pixie both did on a 'better safe than sorry' basis. Both of their mothers had messed up their lives with early unplanned pregnancies and neither Holly nor Pixie wanted to run the same risk.

Of course a couple of years back Holly had had different and more romantic expectations. She had fondly imagined that she would eventually meet a man who would sweep her away on a tide of passion and she had believed that she had to protect herself in the face of such temptation. Sadly, nothing any boyfriend had yet made her feel could have fallen into a category that qualified as being *swept away*. Since then Holly had wondered if there was a distinct possibility that she herself simply wasn't a very passionate woman. Still, Holly reasoned wryly, there was nothing wrong with living in hope, was there?

Somehow Vito had been fully expecting Holly to reappear with a full face of make-up. Instead she appeared with her face rosy and apparently untouched, his sweater drooping round her in shapeless, bulky folds, her tiny feet bare. And Vito almost laughed out loud in appreciation and relief. What remained of his innate wariness was evaporating fast because no woman he had ever yet met could possibly have put less effort into trying to attract him than Holly. Before his engagement and even since it he had been targeted so often by predatory women that he had learned to be guarded in his behaviour around females, both inside and outside working hours. His rare smile flashed across his lean, strong face.

Holly collided involuntarily with molten gold eyes enhanced by thick black lashes and then that truly heart-stopping smile that illuminated his darkly handsome features, and her heart not only bounced in her chest but also skipped an entire beat in reaction. She came to an abrupt halt, her fingers dropping from her rucksack. 'Do you want me to make something to eat?' she offered shakily, struggling to catch her breath.

'No, thanks. I ate before you arrived,' Vito drawled

lazily, watching her shrug back the sweater so that it didn't slip too low at the front. No, she really *wasn't* trying to pull him and he was captivated as he so rarely was by a woman.

'Then you won't mind if *I* eat? I brought supper with me,' she explained, moving past him towards the kitchen.

She's not even going to try to entertain me, Vito reflected, positively rapt in admiration in receipt of that clear demonstration of indifference.

When had he become so arrogant that he expected every young woman he came into contact with to make a fuss of him and a play for him?

It wasn't arrogance, he reasoned squarely. He was as rich as Midas and well aware that that was the main reason for his universal appeal. He poured Holly a fresh glass of wine and carried it into the kitchen for her. She closed the oven, wool stretching to softly define her heart-shaped derrière.

'Do you have a boyfriend?' he heard himself enquire, seemingly before his brain had formed the question, while his attention was still lodged on the sweater that both concealed and revealed her lush curves.

'No. As of today I have an ex,' Holly told him. 'You?'

'I'm single.' Vito lounged back against the kitchen island, the fine fabric of his pants pulling taut to define long, muscular thighs *and*...the noticeable masculine bulge at his crotch. Heat surging into her cheeks, Holly dragged her straying attention off him and stared down at her wine. Since when had she looked at a man *there*? Her breath was snarled up in her throat and her entire body felt super sensitive.

'What happened today?' Vito probed.

'I caught Ritchie having sex with his receptionist on his lunch break,' Holly told him in a rush before she could think better of that humiliating admission. Unfortunately looking at Vito had wrecked her composure to such an extent that she barely knew what she was saying any more.

CHAPTER THREE

IN RECEIPT OF that startling confession, Vito had the most
atrocious desire to laugh, but he didn't want to hurt
Holly's feelings. Her cheeks had gone all pink again and
her eyes were evasive as if that confession had simply
slipped accidentally from her lips. He breathed in deep.
'Tough. What did you do?'

'Told him what I thought of him in one sentence,
walked out again.' Holly tilted her chin, anger darkening her blue eyes as she remembered the scene she had
interrupted. 'I hate liars and cheats.'

'I'm shockingly well behaved in that line. Too busy
working,' Vito countered, relieved that she had not a
clue about the scandal that had persuaded him to leave
Florence and even less idea of who he was. In recent
days he had been forced to spend way too much time
in the company of people too polite to say what they
thought but not too polite to stare at him and whisper.
Anonymity suddenly had huge appeal. He finally felt
that he could relax.

'So, why are you staying here all alone?' Holly asked,
sipping her wine, grateful he had glossed over her gaffe
about Ritchie without further comment.

'Burnout. I needed a break from work.' Vito gave

her the explanation he had already decided on in the shower. 'Obviously I wasn't expecting weather like this.'

He was unusually abstracted, however, ensnared by the manner in which the blue of his sweater lit up her luminous eyes. He was also wondering how she could possibly look almost irresistibly cute in an article of his clothing when the thick wool draped her tiny body like a blanket and only occasionally hinted at the treasures that lay beneath. What was the real secret of her appeal? he was asking himself in bewilderment, even though the secret was right in front of him. She had a wonderfully feminine shape, amazing eyes and a torrent of dark hair that tumbled round her shoulders in luxuriant loose curls. But what was most different about Holly was that she was genuine as so few people dared to be. She put on no show and said nothing for effect; indeed she followed a brand of candour that was blunt to the point of embarrassing.

'Why are you staring at me?' Holly asked baldly, straightening her spine and squaring her little shoulders for all the world as though she was bracing herself for him to say something critical.

'Am I?' Vito fielded, riveting dark eyes brimming with amusement as he straightened to leave the kitchen. 'Sorry... I didn't mean to make you uncomfortable.'

He was setting up a games console when Holly joined him with her plate of savoury snacks. 'I thought I'd have a game,' he told her, 'but perhaps you would rather watch TV—'

'No, what game is it?'

It was a war game Holly knew well. 'I'll play you,' she told him.

Vito shot her a startled glance. 'You play?'

'Of course I do. Every foster family had a console and you learned to play with the other kids to fit in,' she pointed out wryly.

'*Dio mio*...how many different families did you live with?'

'I never counted but there were a lot of them. I'd get settled somewhere and then someone somewhere would decide I should have another go at bonding with my mother, and I'd be shot back to her again for a few months.'

Vito was frowning as he set up the game. 'Your mother was still alive?'

'Just not a good parent. It never worked out with her,' Holly completed wryly, keen to gloss over the facts with as little detail as possible while she watched Vito, lean hips flexing down into powerful thighs as he bent down.

From her position kneeling on the floor, she could admire the fluidity of his long-fingered brown hands as he leant over the console. His every movement was incredibly graceful, she acknowledged. And when she glanced up at him she noticed the black density of his eyelashes and the definition that dark luxuriance lent to his already stunning dark eyes. Her nipples were tight little buds inside her bra and she felt hot.

'Your father?' Vito queried.

'I had no idea who my father was so he didn't come into the picture. But my mother still being around was the reason why I moved around so much, because she refused to allow me to be put up for adoption. Every time I went back to my mother and then had to leave her again to go back into care, I ended up with a new foster family.' Holly grimaced and shrugged. 'It was a messy way to grow up.'

Vito had always thought he had it rough with a tyrannical grandfather, warring parents and being an only child on whom huge expectations rested. But his glimpse at what lay on Holly's side of the fence sobered him and gave him an unsettling new perspective. He had always had security and he had always known he was loved. And although Holly had enjoyed neither advantage, she wasn't moaning about it, he thought with grudging appreciation.

As Vito lounged back on the sofa his six-pack abs rippled below the soft cotton stretched over his broad chest and Holly's mouth ran dry. He was amazingly beautifully built and the acknowledgement sent colour surging into her cheeks because she had never looked at a man's body and thought that before. But she couldn't take her eyes off him and it mortified her. It was as if she had been locked back into a teenager's body again because there was nothing sensible or controlled about what she was experiencing.

'We'll set the timer for a ten-minute challenge,' Vito told her lightly, doubting that she would last the game that long.

Fortunately, Holly didn't even have to think while she played him. In dark times the engrossing, mindless games had been her escape from the reality of a life that hurt too much. With the weapon she had picked she made kill after kill on screen and then the challenge was over and she had won.

'You're very fast,' Vito conceded with a slashing grin of appreciation, because once again he could not think of a single woman who, having chosen to play him, would not have then allowed him to win even though she was a better player. Of course that was a debatable point when he didn't actually know any other woman who could play.

'Lots of practice over the years,' Holly conceded, still recovering from the raw charisma of that wolfish grin that cracked right through his essential reserve. Gaming had relaxed him, warmed him up, melted that cool façade he wore to show the real man underneath. And now he didn't just strike her as heartbreakingly handsome, he was downright irresistible. She shifted uneasily in her seat, her body tense and so weirdly super sensitive that even her clothes seemed to chafe her tender skin.

'And the prize is…' Vito's attention locked like a missile to the soft pink fullness of her mouth and her nipples pinched into tight little points. 'You get to put your Christmas tree up.'

Holly sprang off the seat. 'Seriously?' she exclaimed in surprise.

'Seriously.' Vito focused on that sparkling smile and gritted his teeth in a conscious attempt to cool off and quell his hard-on. He didn't know what it was about her but one look from those melting blue eyes and he was hotter than hell. 'Go ahead…' He pinched one of the snacks on her plate by his feet. 'Any more of these?'

Holly laughed. 'I'll put more on before I get the tree sorted.'

Vito watched her rush about full of energy, and suppressed a rueful sigh. It didn't take a lot to make her happy. 'Why does Christmas mean so much to you?'

'I didn't have it when I was very small,' she admitted.

'How can you *not* have Christmas?'

'Mum didn't celebrate it. Well, not in the family sense. There was no tree, no present, nothing. She went out partying but I didn't know what the day was supposed to be until I went into care for the first time.'

Vito frowned. 'And how did that happen?'

Holly hesitated, eyes troubled as her oval face stiffened. 'You know, this is all very personal…'

'I'm curious…I've never met anyone who grew up in care before,' Vito told her truthfully, revelling in every fleeting expression that crossed her expressive little face. She was full to the brim with emotional responses. She was his exact opposite because she felt so much and showed even more. It shook him that he could find that ingenuousness so very appealing in a woman that he was challenged to look away from her.

Holly compressed her lips, those full pink lips with that dainty little cupid's bow that called to him on a far more primitive level. 'When I was six years old, Mum left me alone for three days over Christmas. I went to a neighbour because I was hungry and she called the police.'

Taken aback by that admission, Vito sat up very straight, dark-as-night eyes locked to her as she finished that little speech in an emotive surge. 'Your mother abandoned you?'

'Yes, but eventually she probably would have come back, as she'd done it before. I was put into a short-term foster home and the family gave me Christmas even though it was already over,' Holly told him with a fond smile of remembrance.

'And you've been making up for that loss ever since,' Vito said drily, shrugging off the pangs of sympathy assailing him, taking refuge in edgy cynicism instead. He didn't do emotion, avoiding such displays and feelings whenever he could because the memories of his mother's raw pain in the face of his father's rejections still disturbed him. As far as he was concerned, if you put your feelings out on display you were asking to be kicked in the teeth and it was not a risk he was prepared to take for anyone. Yet just looking at Holly he could tell that she had taken that same risk time and time again.

'Probably. As obsessions go, Christmas is a fairly harmless one,' Holly fielded before she got up to hurry into the kitchen and retrieve the snacks from the oven. After handing him the plate, she returned to winding the fairy lights round the small tree.

He watched the firelight flicker over her, illuminating a rounded cheekbone, a tempting stretch of gleaming thigh as she bent down, and the provocative rise of her curvy behind. 'How old are you, Holly?'

Holly attached an ornament to a branch and glanced over her shoulder at him. As soon as she collided with his spellbinding dark golden eyes, her heart raced, her mouth ran dry and her mind went blank. 'I'm twenty-four...tomorrow.'

Vito's gaze glittered in the firelight. 'It's both Christmas *and* your birthday.'

'Now it's your turn. Tell me about you,' Holly urged with unconcealed eagerness because everything about Vito Sorrentino made her insanely curious.

It should not have been an unexpected question but it hit Vito like a brick and he froze on the reality that having questioned her so thoroughly he could hardly refuse to respond in kind. He breathed in deep, squaring his broad shoulders, fighting his tension. 'I'm the only child of ill-matched parents. Holiday periods when my father was expected to play his part as a family man were always very stressful because he hated being forced to spend time with us. Christmas fell into that category.'

'Why haven't they separated?' He was so on edge talking about his family situation that it touched her heart. Such a beautiful man, so sophisticated and cool in comparison to her, so seemingly together and yet he too bore the damage of a wounding childhood. Holly was fascinated.

'My mother was raised to believe that divorce is wrong...and she loves my father. She's incredibly loyal to the people she loves.' Vito spoke very stiffly because he had never in his life before shared that much about his family dynamics. He had been taught to live by the same code of secretive silence and polite denial that his mother had always observed. Even if the roof was falling in, appearances still had to be conserved. Breaking that code of silence with an outsider filled him with discomfiture.

'That must've put a lot of pressure on you,' Holly remarked, soulful big blue eyes pinned to him with an amount of sympathy far beyond what he considered necessary.

And yet inexplicably there was something in Vito that was warmed by that show of support. He came up off the sofa as though she had yanked a chain attached to his body, and pulled her up into his arms, and in neither of those moves did he recognise conscious thought or decision. It was instinct, pure instinct to reach for Holly.

He tugged her close, long brown fingers flying up to tilt her chin, and gazed down into those inviting clear eyes of hers. A split second later, he kissed her.

In shock, Holly simply stood there, conflicting feelings pulling her in opposing directions. *Push him away, back off* now, one voice urged. *He finds me attractive, find out what it's like*, the other voice pleaded while she brimmed with secret pride. He touched her mouth slow and soft, nipping her lips lightly and teasingly, and she could hardly breathe. Her heart was thumping like a jackhammer inside her ribcage. His tongue eased apart the seam of her lips and flickered and a spasm of raw excitement thrilled down into her pelvis. With a hungry groan he tightened his arms round her.

Nothing had ever tasted as good as Vito's mouth on hers and she trembled in reaction, her whole body awakening. Her hands linked round his neck as the hard, demanding pressure of his mouth sent a delicious heat spiralling down through her. She felt wonderfully warm and safe for the first time ever. In that moment of security she rejoiced in the glorious feel of his mouth and the taste of the wine on his tongue. His fingers splayed to mould to her hips and trailed down the backs of her thighs. Tiny little shivers of response tugged at her as she felt a tightening sensation at her core and her breasts felt achingly full.

Vito lifted his dark head. Dark golden eyes sought hers. 'I want you,' he husked.

'I want you,' Holly framed shakily and it was the very first time she understood the need to say that to someone.

In all the years she had thought about having sex it had always been because sex was expected of her in a relationship, never because she herself was tempted. In the face of those expectations, her body had begun to seem like something to cede, and not fully her own. And that had been wrong, *so* wrong, she finally saw. It should be her choice and her choice alone. But she was learning that only now in Vito's arms and recognising the difference because she was finally experiencing a genuine desire for something more. And it was a heady feeling that left her bemused and giddy.

Staring up into Vito's dark, dangerous eyes, she stretched up on tiptoe to reach him, simply desperate to feel his beautiful mouth on hers again. And the sheer strength of that physical connection, the locking in of every simultaneous sensation that assailed her, only emphasised how right it felt to be with him that way.

This was what all the fuss was about, she thought joyously, the thrumming pulse of need that drove her, the tiny little tremors of desire making her tremble, the overwhelming yearning for the hard, muscular feel of his body against hers. And as one kiss led into another he drew her down onto the rug again and the heat of the fire on her skin burned no more fiercely than the raw hunger raging through her with spellbinding force.

With her willing collusion he extracted her from the sweater and released the catch on her bra. He studied the full globes he had bared with unhidden hunger. 'You have a totally amazing body, *gioia mia*.'

A deep flush lit Holly's cheeks and the colour spread because she was not relaxed about nudity. Yet there in the firelight with Vito looking at her as though he were unveiling a work of art, she was horribly self-conscious but she felt no shame or sense of inadequacy. Indeed, the more Vito looked, the more the pulse of heat humming between her thighs picked up tempo. Long fingers shaping the plump curves of her breasts, Vito flicked a tongue over a straining pink nipple and a hungry groan of appreciation was wrenched from him as he dallied there, toying with her sensitive flesh in a caress that made her hips squirm while a new sense of urgency gripped her.

'Kiss me,' she urged breathlessly as he tugged at the tender buds of her breasts and an arrow of burning heat pierced her feminine core, only increasing her agitation.

He crushed her ripe mouth beneath his again, his tongue plunging deep, and for a split second it satisfied the craving pulling at her, and then somehow even that wasn't enough any more. She shifted position restively, her legs sliding apart to let his hips slide between as she silently, instinctively sought more. Her hips rocked. She wanted and she *wanted*...

And then at last, as if he knew exactly what she needed, he smoothed his passage up a silken inner thigh and tugged off her panties. He stroked her, found the most needy place of all, and a current of almost unbearable excitement shot through Holly's veins. Suddenly in the hold of her own explosive response she was all heat and light and sensation. A long finger tested her slick, damp core and she whimpered, her teeth clenching, the ferocious need clawing cruelly at her as her spine arched, her body all too ready to take charge.

There was no room for thought in the passion that had swept her away in the way she had always dreamed. But it wasn't the same as her dream because what she was feeling was much more basic, much more wild and out of control than she had ever allowed herself to be. He moved to one side, yanking off his top, revealing an abdomen grooved with lean, hard muscle, and her hand slid greedily up over his chest, rejoicing in his sleek bronzed skin and the manner in which every muscle jerked taut the instant she touched him.

'I have no condoms,' Vito bit out in sudden frustration. 'But I had a health check a few weeks ago and I'm clean.'

'I'm on the pill,' Holly framed shakily, belatedly jolted into rational thought by the acknowledgement that she wasn't about to call a halt to their activities. And why was that? She had never wanted anything or anyone the way she wanted him and surely that was the way it was supposed to be? It felt right. *He* felt right.

Vito hauled in a shuddering breath of relief and came back down to her again, tasting her reddened mouth again with devouring appetite. Her hands smoothed over him, caressing every part of him she could reach from his wide brown shoulders to the satin-smooth expanse of his back. Desire drove her like an addictive drug. Beneath his touch she writhed, her reactions pitching her desire higher and higher until the mushroom of liquid-honey heat inside her flared up in ecstasy before spreading to every part of her. She gasped, shaken by an almost out-of-body feeling, her entire being singing with the potent rush of pleasure.

And then she felt him pushing at the heart of her, tilting her back for his entrance and she was wildly impatient, needing more, ready to try anything that he could give her. He filled her completely, thrusting deep with a slick, sure forcefulness that took her by surprise. The bite of pain was an equal surprise and she blinked back tears and sank her teeth into her lower lip, grateful that her face was against his shoulder where he couldn't see her reaction.

'You're incredibly wet and tight,' Vito growled in a roughened undertone. 'It's a hell of a turn-on, *gioia mia*.'

The pinch of discomfort evaporated as he moved

and she arched up to receive him. He vented a groan of all-male satisfaction as she joined in, no longer separate in thought and behaviour. That overpowering hunger kicked back in as his fluid, insistent thrusts filled her with renewed enthusiasm. In fact the wild, sweet rhythm of his sensual possession fired a blinding, pulsing excitement inside her. Locked with his, her body was snatched up into a passionate climax that flooded her with exquisite sensation.

Coiling back from her, Vito saw the blood on her thighs. '*Maledizione*...you're bleeding? Did I hurt you? Why didn't you stop me?'

Brutally summoned back to reality without warning, Holly snaked back from him and hugged her knees in sudden mortification. 'It's all right—'

'No, you being hurt is *not* all right in any way,' Vito shot back at her grimly.

Holly could feel a beetroot-red flush start at her toes and slowly burn up over her whole body. Lifting her head, she clashed reluctantly with glittering dark eyes of angry concern. 'I wasn't hurt...at least not the way you mean,' she explained grudgingly. 'I was a virgin... and obviously there was some physical evidence of it... which I wasn't expecting...'

'A virgin?' Vito exclaimed in raw disbelief. 'You were a *virgin*?'

Snatching up the sweater he had taken off her, Holly pulled it over her again, struggling to slide her arms back into the sleeves. 'Don't make such a big deal of it,' she urged while she was still safely submerged in the wool.

'It *is* a big deal!' Vito grated, springing upright to zip his trousers again and reach for his shirt.

Flushed and uncomfortable, Holly glanced at him

unwillingly. 'Maybe to me but I don't see why it should bother you!'

'Don't you indeed?' Vito riposted.

'No, I don't,' Holly countered on a rising note of anger because his reaction was the very last thing she had expected from him and the topic mortified her.

Dark eyes flashing gold, Vito studied her. 'You should've warned me. Why didn't you?'

Holly stood her ground, her vexation stifling her embarrassment. 'Because it was a private matter and none of your business.'

'Nothing of that nature stays private when you're having sex with someone!'

In discomfited retreat, Holly headed towards the shower room she had used earlier. 'Well, I'll take your word for that since it was my first experience.'

Vito was inflamed by her refusal to understand and chose to be blunt. 'I feel like I took advantage of you!' he admitted harshly.

Holly whirled back at the door. 'That's nonsense. I'm not a kid. My body, my choice.'

Vito snatched in a ragged breath, still reeling from the shock of her innocence. He hadn't told her who he was or indeed anything important about himself. She didn't, *couldn't* understand that in his position he was innately suspicious of anything as unexpected as their encounter and on top of it the very tardy revelation that she was a virgin. With his experience, that revelation had smacked of a possible sting of some kind and he had immediately wondered if she had some kind of hidden agenda. Now gazing into her troubled face, belatedly recognising the hurt and sadness there, he wanted to kick himself for treating her like some sort of scam artist.

'I'm sorry...' Vito breathed abruptly. 'I let my surprise push me into an overreaction, Holly. Of course, it's your choice...'

Some of her tension evaporated but her eyes remained guarded. 'I didn't even think of warning you. And if I *had* thought of it, I probably would've been too embarrassed to mention it.'

'I wrecked the moment,' Vito groaned in acknowledgement. He moved forward to close his arms round her and somehow, even after that uneasy exchange, it felt like the best thing in the world to Holly. Her stiffness slowly ebbing, she rested against him, drinking in the heat and the comfortingly hard, masculine contours of his lean, muscular body against hers. 'I also neglected to tell you that what we shared...it was amazing.'

'You're just saying that,' she mumbled.

'No. It *was* amazing, *cara mia*. Now let's go upstairs and shower,' Vito urged, easing her in a different direction, inexplicably keen to keep her close even though something in his brain was urging him to step back.

Amazing? Was that a polite lie? Just something a man said for the sake of it? He had flipped the situation on its head again and she didn't know how he had achieved that. She blinked in surprise as the lights illuminated a much bigger bedroom than she had expected, airily furnished in stylish tones of grey.

Vito pushed open the door of a very spacious en-suite. 'You first...unless you'd like company in the shower?'

Holly gave him a startled look. 'I don't think I'm ready for that yet.'

Vito laughed in appreciation and bent down to claim her swollen pink mouth with his own in a searing kiss that made every skin cell in her body sit up and take notice. 'I'll ask you again in the morning,' he warned her.

Holly's attention skated to the giant bed. 'We're going to share the bed?'

'There is only one bedroom here. I was planning to take the sofa.'

'No, I won't banish you to the sofa,' Holly breathed with a sudden grin as she slid past him into the en-suite while barely recognising her own thoughts or feelings. She only knew she didn't want him to sleep downstairs on the sofa and away from her. That felt wrong.

She stood in the shower feeling astonishingly light-hearted for a woman who had strayed from values that were as ingrained in her as her usual honesty. But making love with Vito had felt right and it was hard to credit that anything that had felt so natural and right could possibly be wrong. After all, they were both single and nobody was being hurt by their being together. What harm could it possibly do for her to go with the flow for a change in a relationship instead of trying to plan everything or wait for some extraordinary special sign? And why on earth was she feeling guilty about Ritchie when *he* had cheated on *her*?

It wasn't as though she had ever imagined that she was in love with Ritchie. She had only been seeing him for a few weeks and, even though he had been full of himself, he had been good company. Was what she felt with Vito a rebound attraction?

But how could it be? Ritchie couldn't be compared to Vito on any level. Vito utterly overshadowed his predecessor in every way. And just like her secret fantasy,

Vito had swept Holly away in the tide of passion she had always dreamt of experiencing. Of course, it wasn't going anywhere, she reminded herself staunchly, suppressing a pang of sorrow at that acknowledgement. There would be no ongoing relationship with Vito. She didn't need Vito to spell that out. What they had now was time out of time, separate from their normal lives and associations. Attraction had sparked purely because they were stuck together in a snowbound cottage, and she wasn't foolish enough to try and make more of it, was she?

She wrapped a towel round herself rather than put on his sweater again and crept out of the bathroom. Clad only in his jeans, which were unbuttoned at the waistband, Vito was towelling his hair dry. He tossed aside the towel, finger-combing his black hair carelessly off his brow. 'I used the shower downstairs.'

Holly hovered, suddenly awkward. 'I could have done that. This is your room, after all.'

Vito saw the wary uncertainty in her blue eyes and knew he had put it there. Holly was nothing at all like the women he was accustomed to meeting. Nevertheless he had initially judged her by the cynical standards formed by years of experience with such women. Yet he sensed that she would have been very shocked by the scandal that he had been forced to leave behind him. He had wounded her by questioning her innocence yet that same innocence of hers ironically drew him like a beacon. He crossed the room and closed both arms round her, responding to the inbuilt drive to bridge the gap between them. 'Tonight it's *our* room. Let's go to bed...' he urged.

And Holly thought about saying no and heading

down to the sofa. After all, she had broken her own rules and just because she had done that once didn't mean she had an automatic excuse to keep on doing it. Indeed, if having sex with Vito had been a mistake, she was honour-bound to choose the sofa over him.

But sleeping alone wasn't what she wanted and needed right then. She wanted to be with Vito. She wanted to make the most of the time they had together. She was even feeling sensible enough to know that it was fortunate that she wouldn't be with Vito for much longer, for she reckoned that given the opportunity she would fall for him like a ton of bricks. That, of course, would be totally, unforgivably stupid. And she might be a little sentimental, but stupid she was not.

She looked at Vito, even though she knew she really shouldn't, but there he was, etched in her head in an image that would burn for all time, she thought dizzily. He was beautiful, drop-dead beautiful and tonight...tonight he was all *hers*...

CHAPTER FOUR

AT DAWN, HOLLY sneaked out of bed and crept into the bathroom to freshen up. She grimaced at her reflection. Her hair was a mess. Her face reddened in places by Vito's stubble. Her mouth was very swollen and pink. And when she stepped into the shower she swallowed a groan because every muscle she possessed complained as if she had overdone it in a workout.

But no workout, she thought dizzily, could possibly have been more demanding than the stamina required for a night in bed with Vito Sorrentino. He was insatiable and he had made her the same way, she conceded in stupefaction. She felt as though she had changed dramatically in less than twelve hours. She had learned so much about herself and even more about sex. Her body ached in intimate places and a bemused smile tilted her lips as she emerged from the en-suite again.

Vito was sprawled across the bed, a glorious display of bronzed perfection. Luxuriant black lashes flickered as he focused on her. 'I wondered where you were,' he muttered.

'Bathroom,' she whispered, barely breathing as she slid back under the duvet.

Vito reached for her with a sleepy hand and pulled

her back against him. She shivered in contact with the raw heat and scent of him. 'Go back to sleep,' he told her thickly.

He wanted her again. What the hell was wrong with him? How could he want her again when he had already had her so many times? She had to be sore too, he reminded himself in exasperation. He was being a selfish bastard. As soon as he heard the deep, even tenor of her breathing sink into sleep, he eased out of the bed, went for a cold shower and got dressed.

Nothing in Vito's mental rule book covered what had happened the night before. He hadn't had a one-night stand in many years and none had been extraordinary on any level. Sex was sex, a temporary release and pleasure. He was practical about sex, cool about sex. His desire had never controlled him and he would never let it do so. But then he had never ever been intimate with a woman he wanted over and over again, and his voracious hunger for Holly even after having her downright unnerved him. What was wrong with him? Was he in some weird frame of mind after the trying ordeal of the publicity fallout he had endured over the past week? In his opinion it certainly wasn't normal to want a woman *that* much. It smacked of unbalance, of unhealthy obsession. It was fortunate that their time together had a built-in closing date, he told himself grimly.

Even so, it was Christmas Day as well as being Holly's birthday and it bothered him that he had nothing to give her. Vito was so accustomed to gift-giving and other people's high expectations of his gifts that he felt very uncomfortable in that situation. In an effort to make the day special for Holly he decided to make her breakfast in bed. He couldn't cook but how difficult could it be to make breakfast? He could manage orange juice and toast, couldn't he?

Holly was stunned when she blinked into drowsy wakefulness because Vito was sliding a tray of food on to her lap. She stared down in wonderment at the charred toast. 'You made me breakfast?'

'It's your birthday. It's not much but it's the best I can do.'

Holly tried not to look at him as though he were the eighth wonder of the world but that was certainly how he struck her at that moment because nobody had ever given Holly breakfast in bed before, no, not even when she was ill. It was a luxury she could barely even imagine and that Vito should have gone to that much effort to spoil her thrilled her. So, she didn't make a sound when her first sip of tea gave her a mouthful of the teabag that had not been removed and she munched through the charred toast without complaint. It was the thought that counted, after all, and that Vito *had* thought touched her heart. In addition, the effect of having Vito carelessly sprawled at the foot of the same bed sent her pulse rate rocketing. She remembered all the things they had done and tried desperately to feel guilty about them. But it didn't work. One look into those inky-black-lashed dark golden eyes of his and she was shot off to another planet.

'Thanks,' she said even though it took great effort to locate her voice.

'I'm not great in the kitchen. If it had only been for me I would have cooked one of the ready meals,' he admitted.

'It was very thoughtful of you.' Holly was registering how very lucky she was not to be facing roast meat for breakfast and she gratefully drank her orange juice, which was so cold it froze her teeth. As she drained the glass she pushed the tray away and he swept it up and put it on the floor.

He came back to the bed and moved towards her with the sinuous grace of a stalking cat and her mouth ran dry, her heartbeat racing. 'I was going to get up, organise lunch,' she framed shakily.

'Way too early for that, *bellezza mia*,' Vito husked, up close, his breath fanning her cheek and his luxuriant black hair brushing her chin as he bent his head to press his mouth to the pulse point below her ear.

And her whole body went into free fall as though he had hit a button. Breath fled her parted lips as she sank back into the pillows and gazed up at him with luminous blue eyes. 'Vito—'

He closed her mouth with the onslaught of his own. 'No, we don't talk,' he told her after kissing her breathless. 'We already know all we need to know about each other.'

'I don't even know what you do,' she began.

'I'm in business…and you?'

'Waitress…well, waitress with aspirations,' she adjusted jerkily when he tensed against her. 'I want to be an interior designer but it's more a dream than reality.'

'It takes work to turn dreams into reality.'

Holly smiled up at him. 'Vito… I've had to work hard for everything in life but sometimes getting a break relates more to resources and luck than slaving away.'

'This is getting way too serious,' Vito objected when he found himself on the brink of offering her advice.

Holly let her fingers drift up to brush his black hair off his brow, her attention locked to his lean, darkly handsome features even as her heart had sunk because she was scarily well attuned to his body language. 'Agreed. Let's stay away from the real world.'

His long, lean body relaxed against hers again and tears stung her eyes as she blinked against his shoulder. The news that she was a waitress had been too sharp a stab of reality for Vito, highlighting as it did the difference in their statuses. His clothing, even the variety and expense of the food in the refrigerator, not to mention the stylish opulence of her surroundings all told Holly that Vito inhabited a rather more privileged place in society than she did. And while here at the cottage without other people around, that difference didn't really matter. She knew it would matter very much outside these walls.

'I still want you,' Vito confided thickly, running the tip of his tongue along her collarbone.

Her tummy flipped, her feminine core clenched and she stiffened. Reality was intruding whether she wanted it to or not because she was too tender to engage again in the kind of intimacy he was probably envisaging. 'I can't,' she whispered tightly, a small hand smoothing down a denim-clad thigh, feeling the ripple of his muscles tightening in response.

'Maybe later,' Vito murmured sibilantly, fingers spearing into her hair to lift her mouth to his. 'But in the short term there are other things we can do, *gioia mia*.'

Holly laughed and buried her face in his shoulder. 'You're so shameless.'

'Why wouldn't I be? You've been brilliant. I can't understand why you were still untouched.'

'It was a promise I made to myself when I was very young…to wait. It just seemed sensible to wait until I was an adult and then…' Holly sighed. 'Somewhere along the line it became a burden, a tripwire in relationships that held me back from who I could be.'

Vito gazed down at her with a frown of incomprehension. 'But why me? Why did you choose me?'

'Maybe it was because you let me put my Christmas tree up,' she teased, because there were all too many reasons why she had chosen him and very few she was prepared to share. There was no safe way to tell a man that he had been her fantasy without him getting the wrong idea and assuming that she was feeling more than she was supposed to feel in terms of attachment.

Her fingers slid up caressingly to the firm bulge at his crotch and exerted gentle pressure and he groaned, dark head falling back, wide sensual mouth tightening, his broad chest vibrating against her. Holly leant over him, staring down into lustrous eyes that glittered like precious gold. 'Maybe it's because you act as though I'm the most ravishing female you've ever met, even though I'm perfectly ordinary. But perhaps that's your true talent. Maybe you treat all women the same way.'

'No. I've never been with any woman the way I've been with you…' Vito surveyed her with frowning force, probing that statement, worrying about it because it was true. He had never felt so comfortable with a woman or so relaxed. He hadn't once thought about work or about the shocking scandal he had left behind him in Italy. Furthermore Holly was completely unique on his terms because for the first time ever he was with a woman who didn't know who he was, cherished no financial expectations and in truth attached no undue importance to him. He was Mr Anonymous with Holly and he liked the freedom of that one hell of a lot.

Holly unzipped his jeans with a sense of adventure.

Her most driving need was to give him pleasure and she didn't understand it. Shouldn't she be more selfish? The catch in his breathing was followed by a long, un-restrained sound of rising hunger. She had distracted him with sex, she thought guiltily. She didn't want to talk about being a waitress, about any of the things that separated them as people in the outside world, and his unashamed sexual response to her gave her a shocking sense of power.

Heaven for Vito was the gentle friction of her mouth and the teasing, erotic stroke of her tiny fingers. His hand knotted in her hair and he trembled on the edge of release, gruffly warning her, but she didn't pull away. Then the sheer liberating wash of pleasure engulfed him and wiped him out.

Holly watched Vito sleep with a rueful grin. She went for another shower, donned the dress she had packed and dried her hair. Downstairs, she switched on the television and tuned it to a channel playing Christmas carols before going into the kitchen and beginning to organise the lunch she had prepared with such care. It shook her to acknowledge that she hadn't even known Vito Sorrentino existed the day before.

The shame and embarrassment she had fought off at dawn began to creep up again through the cracks in her composure. She had broken all her rules and for what? A one-night stand with a male she would probably never hear from or see again? How could she be proud of that? But would it have been any better to lose her virginity with a sleazy, cheating liar like Ritchie, who had pre-tended that she meant much more to him than she did?

She thought not. Anyway, it was too late for regrets, she reminded herself unhappily. What was done was done and it made more sense to move on from that point than to torture herself over what could not be changed. How much, though, had all the wine she had imbibed contributed to her recklessness? Her loss of inhibition? *Stop it, stop it*, she urged herself fiercely, *stop dwelling on it*.

Vito came down the stairs when she was setting the table. 'You should have wakened me.'

'You were up much earlier than I was,' she pointed out as she retrieved the starters from the kitchen. 'Hungry?'

Vito reached for her instead of a chair. 'Only for you.'

Her bright blue eyes danced with merriment. 'Now, where did you get that old chestnut from?'

In answer Vito bent his tousled dark head and kissed her and it was like an arrow of fire shooting through her body to the heart of her. She quivered, taken aback all over again by the explosive effect he had on her. His sensual mouth played with hers and tiny ripples of arousal coursed through her. Her breasts swelled, their buds tightening while heat and dampness gathered between her legs. It took enormous willpower but she made herself step back from him, almost careening into the table in her haste to break their connection. Suddenly feeling out of control with him seemed dangerous and it *was* dangerous, she told herself, if it made her act out of character. And whether she liked it or not, everything she had done with Vito was out of character for her.

'We should eat before the food gets cold,' she said prosaically.

'I'll open a bottle of wine.'

'This is an incredibly well-equipped house,' Holly

remarked as he poured the wine he had fetched from the temperature-controlled cabinet in the kitchen.

'The owner enjoys his comforts.'

'And he's your friend?'

'We went to school together.' A breathtaking smile of amused recollection curled Vito's mouth. 'He was a rebel and although he often got me into trouble he also taught me how to enjoy myself.'

'Pixie's like that. We're very close.' Holly lifted the plates and set out the main course.

'You're a good cook,' Vito commented.

'My foster mother, Sylvia, was a great teacher. Cooking relaxes me.'

'I eat out a lot. It saves time.'

'There's more to life than saving time. Life is there to be savoured,' Holly told him.

'I savour it at high speed.'

The meal was finished and Holly was clearing up when Vito stood up. 'I feel like some fresh air,' he told her. 'I'm going out for a walk.'

From the window, Holly watched him trudge down the lane in the snow. There was an odd tightness in her chest and a lump in her constricted throat. Vito had just rebelled against their enforced togetherness to embrace his own company. He hadn't invited her to join him on his walk, but why should he have? Out of politeness? They weren't a couple in the traditional sense and he didn't have to include her in everything. They were two people who had shared a bed for the night, two *very* different people. Maybe she talked too much, maybe he was tired of her company and looking forward to the prospect of some silence. It was not a confidence-boosting train of thought.

Vito ploughed up the steep gradient, his breath steaming on the icy air. He had needed a break, had been relieved when Holly hadn't asked if she could accompany him. A loner long accustomed to his own company, he had felt the walls closing in while he'd sat surrounded by all that cosy Christmas spirit.

And that really wasn't Holly's fault, Vito conceded wryly. Even her cheerful optimism could not combat the many years of bad Christmas memories that Vito harboured. Sadly the stresses and strains of the festive season were more likely to expose the cracks in an unhappy marriage. His mother's resolute enthusiasm had never contrived to melt his father's boredom and animosity at being forced into spending time with his family.

They had never been a family, Vito acknowledged heavily, not in the truest sense of the word. His father had never loved him, had never taken the smallest interest in him. In fact, if he was honest with himself, his father sincerely disliked him. From an early age Vito had been treated like the enemy, twinned in his father's mind with the autocratic father-in-law he fiercely resented.

'He's like a bloody calculator!' Ciccio had condemned with distaste when his five-year-old son's brilliance at maths was remarked on. 'He'll be as efficient as a cash machine—just like his grandfather.'

Only days earlier, Vito's relationship with his father had sunk to an all-time low when Ciccio had questioned his son's visit to the hospital where he was recovering from his heart attack. 'Are you here to crow over my downfall?' his father had asked nastily while his mother had tried to intervene. 'My sins have deservedly caught up with me? Is that what you think?'

And Vito had finally recognised that there was no relationship left to rescue with his father. Ciccio bitterly resented his son's freedom from all financial constraints yet the older man's wild extravagance and greed had forced Vito's grandfather to keep his son-in-law on a tight leash. There was nothing Vito could do to change those hard facts. Even worse, after his grandfather had died it had become Vito's duty to protect his mother's fortune from Ciccio's demands, scarcely a reality likely to improve a father and son relationship.

For the first time Vito wondered what sort of relationship he would have with his son if he ever had one. Momentarily he was chilled by the prospect because his family history offered no encouragement.

Holly had just finished clearing up the dishes when the knocker on the front door sounded loudly. She was stunned when she opened the door and found Bill, who ran the breakdown service, standing smiling on the doorstep.

'I need the keys for Clementine to get her loaded up.'

'But it's Christmas Day… I mean, I wasn't expecting—'

'I didn't want to raise your hopes last night but I knew I'd be coming up this way some time this afternoon. My uncle joins us for lunch and he owns a smallholding a few fields away. He has to get back to feed his stock, so I brought the truck when I left him at home.'

'Thank you so much,' Holly breathed, fighting her consternation with all her might while turning away to reach into the pocket of her coat where she had left the car keys. She passed the older man the keys. 'Do you need any help?'

He shook his head. 'I'll come back up for you when I'm done.'

'I'll get my stuff together.' With a weak smile and with every sensitive nerve twanging, Holly shut the door again and sped straight upstairs to gather her belongings. She dug her feet into her cowboy boots and thrust her toiletries and make-up bag back into her rucksack.

And throughout that exercise she wouldn't let herself even think that she could be foolish enough to be disappointed at being picked up and taken home. Clearly, it was time to *leave*. She had assumed that she would have one more night with Vito but fate had decreed otherwise. Possibly a quick, unexpected exit was the best way to part after such a night, she thought unhappily. There would be neither the time nor the opportunity for awkward exchanges. She closed her rucksack and checked the room one last time. Reminding herself that she still had to pack the Christmas tree, she went back down wondering anxiously if Vito would make it back before she had to leave.

She flipped open her cardboard box and stripped the tree of ornaments and lights, deftly packing it all away while refusing to think beyond the practical. She raced into the kitchen to dump the foil containers she had used to transport the meal, pausing only to lift a china jug and quickly wash it before placing it in the box. That was that then, all the evidence of her brief stopover removed, she conceded numbly.

She didn't want to go home, she didn't *want* to leave Vito, and the awareness of that stupid, hopeless sense of attachment to him crushed and panicked her. He would probably be relieved to find her gone and he would have cringed if he saw tears in her eyes. Men didn't like messy and there could be nothing more messy or embarrassing than a woman who got too involved and tried to cling after one night. *This one-night-and-walk-away stuff is what you signed up for,* Holly scolded herself angrily. There had been no promises and no mention of a future of any kind. She would leave with her head held high and no backward glances.

All the same, she thought hesitantly, if Vito wasn't coming back in time to see her leave, shouldn't she leave a note? She dug into her rucksack and tore a piece of paper out of a notebook and leant on the table. She thanked him for his hospitality and then hit a brick wall in the creative department. What else was there to say? What else *could* she reasonably say?

After much reflection she printed her mobile-phone number at the foot of the note. Why not? It wasn't as if she was asking him to phone her. She was simply giving him the opportunity to phone if he wanted to. Nothing wrong with that, was there? She left the note propped against the clock on the shelf inside the inglenook.

Holly wore a determined smile when Bill's truck backed into the drive. She had her box and her rucksack on the step beside her in a clear face-saving statement that she was eager to get going but there was still no sign of Vito. She climbed into the truck with a sense of regret but gradually reached the conclusion that possibly it was preferable to have parted from Vito without any awkward or embarrassing final conversation. This way, nobody had to pretend or say anything they didn't mean.

Vito strode into the cottage and grimaced at the silence. He strode up the stairs, calling Holly's name while wondering if she had gone for a bath. He studied the empty bathroom with a frown, noting that she had removed her possessions. Only when he went downstairs again did he notice that the Christmas decorations had disappeared along with her. The table was clear, the kitchen immaculate.

Vito was incredulous. Holly had done a runner and he had no idea how. He walked out onto the doorstep and belatedly registered that the old car no longer lay at the foot of the lane in the ditch. So much for his observation powers! He had been so deep in his thoughts that he hadn't even noticed that the car had gone. Holly had walked out on him. Well, that hadn't happened to him before, he acknowledged grimly, his ego stung by her sudden departure. All his life women had chased after Vito, attaching strings at the smallest excuse.

But would he have wanted her to *cling*? Vito winced, driven to reluctantly admit that perhaps in the circumstances her unannounced disappearance was for the best. After all, what would he have said to her in parting? Holly had distracted him from more important issues and disrupted his self-control. Now he had his own space back and the chance to get his head clear. And that was exactly what he should want…

'When you're finished throwing up you can do the test,' Pixie said drily from the bathroom doorway.

'I'm not doing the test,' Holly argued. 'I'm on the pill. I *can't* be pregnant—'

'You missed a couple of pills *and* you had a course of antibiotics when you had tonsillitis,' her friend and flatmate reminded her. 'You know that antibiotics can interfere with contraception—'

'Well, actually I *didn't* know.' Holly groaned as she

freshened up at the sink, frowning at her pale face and dark-circled eyes. She looked absolutely awful and she felt awful both inside and out.

'Even the pill has a failure rating. I don't know…I leave you alone for a few weeks and you go completely off the rails,' the tiny blonde lamented, studying Holly with deeply concerned eyes.

'I can't be pregnant,' Holly said again as she lifted the pregnancy testing kit and extracted the instructions.

'Well, you've missed two periods, you're throwing up like there's no tomorrow and you have sore boobs,' Pixie recounted ruefully. 'Maybe it's chickenpox or something.'

'All right, I'll do it!' Holly exclaimed in frustration. 'But there is no way, just no way on earth that I could be pregnant!'

Some minutes later she slumped down on the side of the bath. Pixie was right and she was wrong. The test showed a positive. The door opened slowly and she looked wordlessly up at her friend and burst into floods of tears.

'Remember how we used to say that the babies we had would be precious gifts?' Pixie breathed as she hugged her sobbing friend. 'Well, this baby is a gift and we *will* manage. We don't need a man to survive.'

'I can't even knit!' Holly wailed, unable to concentrate, unable to think beyond the sheer immensity of the challenges she was about to face.

'That's OK. You won't have time to knit,' her friend told her, deadpan.

Holly was remembering when she and Pixie had talked innocently about their ideal of motherhood. Both of them had been born unwanted and had suffered at the hands of neglectful mothers. They had sworn that they would love and protect their own babies no matter what.

And the vague circumstances suggested by 'no matter what' had actually happened now, Holly reflected heavily, her sense of regret at that truth all-encompassing. Her baby would not be entering the perfect world as she had dreamt. Her baby was unplanned, however, but *not* unwanted. She would love her child, fight to keep him or her safe and if she had to do it alone, and it looked as though she would, she *would* manage.

'If only Vito had phoned...' The lament escaped Holly's lips before she could bite it back and she flushed in embarrassment.

'He's long gone. In fact, the more I think about him,' Pixie mused tight-mouthed, 'the more suspicious I get about the father of your child. For all you know he could be a married man.'

'No!' Holly broke in, aghast at that suggestion.

'Well, what was Vito doing spending Christmas alone out in the middle of nowhere?' Pixie demanded. 'Maybe the wife or girlfriend threw him out and he had nowhere better to go?'

'Don't make me feel worse than I already do,' Holly pleaded. 'You're such a pessimist, Pixie. Just because he didn't want to see me again doesn't make him a bad person.'

'He got you drunk and somehow persuaded you into bed. Don't expect me to think nice things about him. He was a user.'

'I *wasn't* drunk.'

'Let's not rehash it again.' Her flatmate sighed, her piquant face thoughtful. 'Let's see if we can trace him online.'

And while Pixie did internet searches on several potential spellings of Vito's surname and came up with precisely nothing, Holly sat on the sofa hugging her still-flat stomach and fretting about the future. She had already secretly carried out all those searches weeks earlier on Vito and was too proud to admit to the fact, even to her friend.

'I can't find even a trace of a man in the right age group. The name could be a fake,' her friend opined.

'Why would he give me a fake name? That doesn't make sense.'

'Maybe he didn't want to be identified. I don't know...you tell me,' Pixie said very drily. 'Do you think that's a possibility?'

Holly reddened. Of course it was a possibility that Vito had not wanted to be identified. As to why, how could she know? The only thing she knew with certainty was that Vito had decided he didn't want to see her again. Had he felt otherwise, he would have used the phone number she had left him and called her. In the weeks of silence that had followed her departure from the cottage, she had often felt low. But that was foolish, wasn't it? Vito had clearly made the decision that he had no desire to see her again.

And why should she feel hurt by that? Yes, he had said that night with her was amazing but wasn't that par for the course? The sort of thing a man thought a woman expected him to say after sex? How could she have been naive enough to actually believe that Vito had truly believed they were something special together? And now that little bit of excitement was over. What was done was done and what was gone, like her innocence, was gone. Much as her tidy, organised life had gone along with it, she conceded unhappily, because, although she would embrace motherhood wholeheartedly, she knew it would be incredibly tough to raise a baby alone without falling into the poverty trap.

CHAPTER FIVE

Fourteen months later

HOLLY SUPPRESSED A groan as she straightened her aching back. She hated parcelling up the unsold newspapers at the end of her evening shift in the local supermarket but it also meant she would be going home soon and seeing Angelo snugly asleep in his cot.

Picturing her son's little smiling face made her heart swell inside her. There was nothing Holly wouldn't do for her baby. The minute she had laid eyes on Angelo after his premature birth she had adored him with a fierce, deep love that had shaken her to the roots.

Without Pixie's help she would have struggled to survive, but, fortunately for Holly, her friend had supported her from the start. When waitressing had become impossible, Holly had taken a course to become a registered childminder and now by day she looked after her baby and two other children at home. She also worked in the shop on a casual basis. If evening or weekend work came up and Pixie was free to babysit, Holly did a shift to earn some extra cash.

And it was right then when she was thinking about how much she was looking forward to supper and her bed that it happened: she looked down at the bundle of newspapers she was tying up and saw a photograph on the front page of a man who reminded her of Vito. She stopped dead and yanked out the paper to shake it open. It was a financial broadsheet that she would never normally have even glanced at and the picture showed a man standing behind a lectern, a man who bore a remarkable resemblance to the father of her son.

'Are you nearly done, Holly?' one of her co-workers asked from the doorway.

'Almost.' Her shoulders rigid with tension, Holly was frantically reading the italicised print below the photograph. Vittore Zaffari, not Sorrentino. It was a man who resembled Vito—that was all. Her shoulders dropped again but just as she was about to put the newspaper back in the pile she hesitated and then extracted that particular page. Folding it quickly, she dug it into the pocket of her overall and hurriedly finished setting out the newspapers for collection.

It was after midnight before Holly got the chance to check out Vittore Zaffari online. Holly had studied the photograph again and again. He looked like her Vito but the newsprint picture wasn't clear enough for her to be certain. But the instant she did a search on Vittore Zaffari the images came rolling in and she knew without a doubt that she had finally identified her child's father.

'*My word,*' Pixie groaned, performing her own search on her tablet. 'Now I know why he gave you a fake name and was hiding out on Dartmoor. He was involved in some drugs-and-sex orgy. Hold on while I get this document translated into English.'

'Drugs and sex?' Holly repeated sickly. '*Vito?* It can't be the same man!'

But it was. The photos proved that he was *her* Vito, not some strange lookalike character. Of course, he had never been hers even to begin with, Holly reminded herself doggedly. And it was two in the morning before the two women finished digging up unwelcome facts about Vito, the billionaire banker ditched by his fabulously beautiful blonde fiancée only days before Holly had met him.

'Of course, you don't need to concern yourself with any of that nonsense,' Pixie told her ruefully. 'All you want from him now is child support and he seems to be wealthy enough that I shouldn't think that that will be a big deal.'

Holly lay sleepless in her bed, tossing and turning and at the mercy of her emotions. Vito had lied to her by deliberately giving her a false name. He too had been on the rebound but he hadn't mentioned that either. How would he react when she told him that he was a father? And did she really want to expose her infant son to a drug-abusing, womanising father? The answer to that was a very firm no. No amount of money could make a parent who was a bad influence a good idea.

But that really wasn't for her to decide, she reasoned over breakfast while she spooned baby rice into Angelo, who had a very healthy appetite. She studied her son with his coal-black curls and sparkling brown eyes. He was a happy baby, who liked to laugh and play, and he was very affectionate. Vito had been much more reserved, slow to smile and only demonstrative in bed. Holly winced at that unwelcome recollection. Regardless, Vito had a right to know that he was a father and in the same way she had a right to his financial help. She had to stop considering their situation from the

personal angle because that only muddied the waters
and upset her.

Angelo was the main issue. Everything came back to
her son. Set against Angelo's needs, her personal feelings had no relevance. She had to be practical for his
benefit and concentrate on what *he* needed. And the
truth was that financially she was really struggling to
survive and her baby was having to do without all the
extras that he might have enjoyed. That was wrong.
Her son didn't deserve to suffer because she had made
a bad choice.

On the other hand, if Vito truly was the sort of guy
who got involved in sex-and-drug orgies, he wasn't at
all the male she had believed him to be. How could she
have been so wrong about a man? She had honestly believed that Vito was a decent guy.

Even so, he was still Angelo's father and that was
important. She was very much aware of just how much
she had longed to know who her own father was. There
was no way she could subject Angelo to living in the
same ignorance. Nor could she somehow magically esti-
mate whether Vito would be a good or bad influence on
his son. The bottom line was that Angelo had the right
to know who his father was so that he did not grow up
with the same uncertainty that Holly had been forced
to live with.

Holly acknowledged the hurt she had felt when Vito
failed to make use of her phone number and contact her.
Naturally her pride had been wounded and she had been
disappointed. No woman wanted to feel that forgettable,
but Angelo's birth had cast a totally different light on
her situation. She had to forget her resentment and hurt
and move on while placing her son's needs first. That

would be a tall order but she believed that she loved her son enough to do it. She had to face Vito in the flesh and tell him that he was a father.

One week later, Holly handed over her package to the receptionist on the top floor of the Zaffari Bank in London. 'It's for Mr Zaffari. I would like to see him.'

The elegant receptionist set the small parcel down on the desktop and reached for something out of view. 'Mr Zaffari's appointments are fully booked weeks in advance, Miss...er...?'

'Cleaver. I believe he will want to see me,' Holly completed quietly while she wondered if that could possibly be true. 'I'll just wait over there until he's free.'

'There's really no point in you waiting,' the receptionist declared curtly, rising from her chair as two security guards approached. 'Mr Zaffari doesn't see anyone without a prior appointment.'

Stubbornly ignoring that assurance, Holly walked over to the waiting area and sat down, tugging her stretchy skirt down over her thighs. It had taken massive organisation for Holly to make a day trip to London but she knew that if she wanted to confront Vito she had to take advantage of his current presence in the UK. Her internet snooping had revealed that he was giving a speech at some fancy banking dinner that very evening and was therefore highly likely to be at the Zaffari Bank HQ throughout the day. Pixie had taken a day off to look after Angelo, and the children Holly usually minded were with their grandparents instead.

Holly had made a very early start to her day and had been appalled by the price of the train fare. Pixie had urged her to dress up to see Vito but, beyond abandoning her usual jeans and putting on a skirt with the knee boots Pixie had given her for Christmas, Holly had made no special effort. Why? As she continually reminded herself, this wasn't a *personal* visit and she wasn't trying to impress Vito. She was here to tell him about Angelo and that was all. Her restive fingers fiddled with the zip on her boots while she watched the two security guards carrying off her parcel with the absurdly cautious air of men who feared they could be carrying a bomb. Did she look like a terrorist? Like some kind of a madwoman?

Vito was in a board meeting and when his PA entered and slid a small package in front of him, which had already been unwrapped, he frowned in incomprehension, but when he pulled back the paper and saw the Santa hat and the small sprig of holly, he simply froze and gave his PA a shaken nod of immediate acceptance. Interrupting the proceedings to voice his apologies, he stood up, his cool dark eyes veiled.

What the hell was Holly doing here at the bank? Why now? And how had she tracked him down?

Hearing about that night, Apollo had scoffed. *With all your options you settled for a stranger? Are you crazy? You're one of the most eligible bachelors in the world and you picked up some random woman? A waitress?* he had scoffed in a tone of posh disbelief.

In fact, Apollo's comments had annoyed Vito so much that he had fiercely regretted confiding in his friend. He had told himself that it was for the best that Holly had walked away without fanfare, freeing them both from the threat of an awkward parting. He had also reminded himself that attempting to repeat a highly enjoyable experience invariably led to disappointment.

With the information he had had he could have traced her but he had resisted the urge with every atom of discipline he possessed. Self-control was hugely important to Vito and Holly had obliterated his self-control. He remembered that he had acted oddly with her and that memory made him uncomfortable. Even so he still hadn't forgotten her. In fact he was eager to see her because his memories of her had lingered to the extent that he had become disturbingly indifferent to other women and more particular than ever in his choices. He *wanted* to see Holly in full daylight, shorn of the schmaltzy sparkle of the festive season. He was suddenly convinced that such a disillusionment would miraculously knock him back to normality.

But why the hell would Holly be seeking him out now so long after the event? And in person rather than more tactfully by phone? And how had she linked him to the Zaffari Bank? Black brows lowering over cold dark eyes suddenly glittering with suspicion, Vito strode back into his office to await his visitor without an appointment.

Holly smiled and stood up when the receptionist approached her. In spite of her apprehension, Vito *had* remembered her and she was relieved. The Santa hat had been designed to jog his memory. After all, a male who indulged in sex parties might well not recall one night with an ordinary woman from over a year earlier. When it came to a question of morals he was a total scumbag, Holly reminded herself doggedly while walking down the corridor after another woman—even more thin and elegant—had asked her to follow her. She wondered why the other people working there seemed to be peering out of their offices in her direction and staring.

Suddenly she wondered what she was doing. Did she really want a man of Vito's dissolute proclivities in her life and Angelo's? Common sense warned her not to make snap judgements and to give Vito a chance for Angelo's sake. Her son would want to know who his dad was. Hadn't she wondered all her life who had fathered her? Hadn't that made her insecure? Made her feel less of a person than others because she didn't know that most basic fact about herself? No, Angelo deserved access to the truth of his parentage right from the start and that was what Holly would ensure her son had, no matter how unpleasant seeing Vito again proved to be.

Vito was a total scumbag, Holly reminded herself afresh while wondering why she was experiencing the strangest sense of...*elation*. Why was her heart pounding and her adrenaline buzzing? Her guide opened a door and stood back for her to enter. My goodness, he had a big office, *typical scumbag office*, she rephrased mentally. She would not be impressed; she *refused* to be impressed. And then Vito strode in through a side door and she was paralysed to the carpet because he simply looked so drop-dead amazing that she could not believe that she had ever slept with him and that he was the father of her child.

Her mouth ran dry. She felt dizzy. Butterflies danced in her tummy as she focused on those lean, darkly handsome features, and she knew that Pixie would have kicked her hard. *Total scumbag*, she told herself, but her brain would not engage with that fact and was much more interested in opening a back catalogue on Vito's sheer perfection. *To look at—perfect to* look *at*, she rephrased doggedly, striving to get back to the scumbag awareness. *Drugs...sex with hookers*, she fired at herself in desperation.

'The hat and the holly were an original calling card,' Vito drawled, the dark, deep accent tautening every muscle in her already tense body. 'But I *did* remember your name. I didn't need the prompt.'

Holly turned the red-hot colour of a tomato because she hadn't expected him to grasp the reasoning behind her introduction that easily.

'It would have been much easier to phone me,' Vito assured her silkily.

'And how could I have done that without your phone number?' Holly asked stiffly, because she was determined to make no reference to the fact that she had left her phone number with him and that he had decided not to make use of it. Discussing that would be far, far too humiliating.

'Well, maybe you shouldn't have run out on me before I got back to the cottage that day.' Vito smiled suddenly, brilliantly. It almost stopped her heart dead in its tracks as she stared at him. But it had not sat well with Vito that a night he had considered exceptional should have meant so much less to her that she'd walked out without a backward glance. Her reappearance satisfied him. He now felt free to study her with acute appreciation. She was wearing the most ordinary garments: a sweater, a shortish skirt, a jacket and boots, all black and all unremarkable but the glorious hourglass curves he cherished could not be concealed. His dark eyes flamed gold over the swell of her breasts below the wool and the lush curve of her hips before flying up to her full pink mouth, little snub nose and huge blue eyes. Shorn of the schmaltz and the sparkle and in full daylight, Holly was passing the test he had expected her to fail and for the first time in Vito's life, failure actually tasted sweet. He shifted almost imperceptibly as the hot swell of an erection assailed him and he almost smiled at that as well because his diminished libido had seriously bothered him.

'How did you find out who I was?' Vito enquired.

'Yes, that's right…you *lied*. You gave me a false name,' Holly was prompted to recall as she struggled to fight free of the spell he cast over her just by being in the same room.

'It wasn't a false name. I didn't lie. I was christened Vittore Sorrentino Zaffari,' he told her, smooth as glass. 'Sorrentino was my father's surname.'

That smoothness set Holly's teeth on edge. 'You lied,' she said again. 'You deliberately misled me. What I don't understand is why you did that.'

'You must appreciate that I am very well known in the business world. I prefer to be discreet. You coming here today in such a manner…' Vito shifted fluid brown fingers in an expressive dismissive gesture. 'That *was* indiscreet.' From his inside pocket he withdrew a business card and presented it to her. 'My phone number.'

Holly put the card into her jacket pocket because she didn't know what else to do with it. Indiscreet? Coming to see him in the flesh was indiscreet?

Dark golden eyes fringed by inky black, unfairly long lashes surveyed her and her tummy flipped, her heart rate increasing. 'Holly…I have the feeling that you don't understand where I'm going with this but I must be frank. I like to keep my private life *private*. I certainly do not want it to intrude when I'm at the bank. My working hours are sacrosanct.'

My word, he was literally telling her off for approaching him at his place of work, for coming to see him where other people would see her and notice her. A sense of deep humiliation pierced Holly because it had taken so much courage for her to come and confront him with the news she had. His case was not helped by the reality that she had seen a photo of him and his ex-fiancée, Marzia, posing outside the Zaffari Bank in Florence. Evidently, Marzia had enjoyed such privileges because she was someone he was *proud* to be seen with in public. Holly just could not get over Vito's nerve in daring to talk to her like that. Did he really think she was the sort of woman who would let a man talk down to her?

Her blue eyes widened and raked over him but it was pointless to try and put him down that way because she couldn't see a single flaw in his appearance. His dark grey suit fitted him like a tailored glove, outlining his height, breadth and long, powerful legs. And looking at him inevitably sent shards of mortifying memory flying through her already blitzed brain. She knew what he looked like out of his suit, she knew what he *felt* like, she also knew how he looked and sounded when he… *No, don't go there*, she urged herself and plunged straight into punitive speech because he had to be punished for putting such inappropriate thoughts into her head.

'I can't believe you're talking down to me as if you're a superior being,' Holly bit out tightly. 'Why? Because you've got money and a big fancy office? Certainly not because you've been shopped for taking drugs and sleeping with hookers!'

There was a flash of bemused surprise in Vito's brilliant dark eyes before he responded. 'That was a case of misidentification. I was not the man involved.'

'Of course you're going to say that,' Holly retorted with a roll of her eyes. 'Of course you're going to deny it to me but, as I understand it, you never once denied it in public.'

'I had a good reason for that. I never respond to tabloid journalists and I was protecting my family,' Vito returned levelly. 'I assure you…on my honour…that I was not the man involved and that I profoundly disapprove of such activities.'

Holly remained unimpressed. How did she credit that he had honour? How was she supposed to believe him? He had been protecting his family by remaining silent? How did that work?

'I do believe it would be wiser to take this meeting out of my big fancy office to somewhere more comfortable,' Vito continued, his smooth diction acidic in tone. 'I have an apartment in London. My driver will take you and you can relax there until I can join you for lunch.'

Knocked right off balance by that suggestion coming at her out of nowhere, Holly actually found herself thinking about the offer of lunch. Telling him about Angelo in an office setting felt wrong to her as well, and then a little voice in the back of her brain that sounded alarmingly like Pixie told her to wise up and think about the invitation he had made. And at that point the coin finally dropped for Holly and she grasped how Vito had chosen to interpret her sudden reappearance in his life. She wanted to kick herself for not foreseeing that likelihood, but she wanted to kick him even harder for daring to think that he could have a chance with her again. Certainly not with what she now knew about his partying habits!

'I haven't come here for another hook-up,' Holly stated with an embarrassed force that made her voice rise slightly. Behind her mortification lurked a great well of burning resentment.

Did he really think that she was so desperate for sex that she would travel all the way to London for it? How dared he assume that she was that keen, that easy? Well, she certainly hadn't taught him that she was a big challenge the night they first met, Holly conceded grudgingly. *But, my goodness, that one night must have been as good on his terms as he had said it was if he was willing to do it again.* Or maybe he was simply a sex addict? Anything was possible. When Holly had snapped back at him about his money and his fancy office and his debauched partying, she had also picked up on his surprise. He had assumed she was a quiet, easy-going little mouse but Holly wasn't quiet when her temper was roused. And right now her temper was rising like lava in a volcano. The past fourteen months had been very challenging, and working all day after a sleepless night had become her new norm. Having no way of contacting her son's father, who had handicapped her by giving her a false name, had only added to her stress.

Vito tensed. 'I didn't say anything about that. No expectations…' he murmured silkily, lean brown hands sketching an eloquent arc in the air as if to nullify her suspicions.

'Of course you have expectations…but, in this case, I'm afraid it's not going to happen. You had your chance and you blew it!' Holly snapped back, striving to hang on to her temper.

His brows drew together. 'What's that supposed to mean?'

Holly rolled her eyes, her lush mouth compressed. 'A timely little reminder that if you had really *wanted* to see me again I did leave you my phone number.'

'No, you didn't,' Vito insisted.

Holly tensed even more, angry that she had let that reminder fall from her mouth. 'I left a note thanking you for your hospitality and I printed my phone number at the bottom of it.'

Vito groaned. 'I didn't find a note when you left. Where did you leave it?'

'On the shelf in the fireplace.' Holly shrugged dismissively, keen to drop the subject.

'If there was a note, I didn't see it,' Vito assured her.

But then he would say that, wouldn't he? Holly thought, unimpressed. Of course he had found the silly note she had left behind and he had done nothing with it. And in doing nothing he had taught her all she needed to know about how he saw her. She had gone over the events of that morning in her mind many, many times. She was convinced that Vito had gone out for a walk to get a break from her. For him the fun of togetherness had already worn thin. He had ignored her note most probably because he'd been relieved to find her already gone. He had seen that night as a casual one-night stand that he had no desire to repeat.

'Whatever. It's pointless to discuss it after the amount of time that has passed. But let me spell out one fact,' Holly urged thinly. 'I *didn't* come to see you today for anything…er…physical. I came to see you about something much *more* important.'

At her emphasis, Vito raised a level dark brow in cool query mode, his wide sensual mouth tightening with impatience. And she could feel the whole atmosphere turning steadily colder and less welcoming. Naturally. She had taken sex off the lunch table, as it were, and he was no longer interested in anything she might have to say to him. And why would he be interested? She was poor and he was rich. He was educated and she was more of a self-educated person, which meant that she had alarming gaps in her knowledge. He was hugely successful and a high achiever while she worked in dead-end jobs without a career ladder for advancement. It was incredible, she finally conceded, that they had ever got involved in the first place.

'More important?' Vito prompted, his irritation barely hidden.

Defiance and umbrage combined inside Holly. She had held on to her temper but it was a close-run battle. His assumption that she was approaching him for another sexual encounter had shocked her, possibly because she had persuaded herself that they had shared something more than sex. Now she saw her illusions for the pitiful lies that they were, lies she had told herself to bolster her sagging self-esteem while she was waddling round with a massive tummy.

'Yes, much more important,' she confirmed, lifting her chin and simply spilling out her announcement. 'I got pregnant that night we were together.'

Vito froze as if she had threatened to fling a grenade at him. He turned noticeably pale, his strong bone structure suddenly clearly etched below his skin by raw tension. 'You said you were on the pill—'

Holly wasn't in the mood to go into the intricacies of missed pills and antibiotic treatment. 'You must know that every form of contraception has a failure rate and I'm afraid there was a failure. I got pregnant but I had no way of contacting you, particularly not when you had given me a fake name.'

Vito was in shock. Indeed Vito could never recall being plunged into such a state of shock before. Everything he had assumed had been turned upside down and inside out with those simple words...*I got pregnant.*

'And do you usually reintroduce yourself with a very evocative Santa hat and a sprig of holly when this happens?' he heard himself snap without even mentally forming the words. 'Is this some sort of a scam?'

Holly's small shoulders pushed up, along with her chin. 'No, Angelo is not a scam, Vito. He was born eight months after that night.'

'You come here without a word of warning and throw this announcement at me like a challenge,' Vito ground out in condemnation, no fan of major surprises in his life, as yet not even capable of thinking of what she was telling him. The prospect of having a child had long struck him as a possibility as remote as the moon. He had known fatherhood was on the cards somewhere down the line if he married Marzia but he had also known that neither of them were in any hurry to start a family.

'No, I did not. If I challenged you it would be an awful lot tougher!' Holly shot back at him furiously. 'Tough was waitressing until I was eight months pregnant and being in labour for two days before I got a

C-section. Tough is working as a childminder and a shelf-stacker and never getting enough sleep. You wouldn't know tough if it leapt on you and bit you...because in your whole blasted spoilt-rotten life you have had *everything* handed to you on a plate!'

A dark line of colour had delineated Vito's high cheekbones as he viewed her in growing disbelief. 'That is enough.'

'No, it's not enough, and you do *not* tell me when enough is enough!' Holly fired back at him, while pointing at him with an angry finger.

'Ranting at me is not getting us anywhere.'

'I'm entitled to rant if I want to rant!' Holly launched back at him an octave higher, shaking with rage and the distress she was fighting off while wondering if Vito ever lost his temper, because he was still so very controlled. 'And I don't *want* to get anywhere with you. I'm done here. I've told you that you're a father and that's why I came to see you. I saw your photo in a newspaper, incidentally...a *lovely* way to identify the father of your child! But if you want to think Angelo's a scam, you're welcome.'

'Holly...'

Holly yanked open the door and marched down the corridor very fast because she could not wait to get out of the building. She could feel the tears building up and she didn't want them to fall in front of an audience. She ignored Vito's voice when he repeated her name and stabbed the lift button with frantic force.

'Holly...*come back here*!' Vito shouted without warning.

So taken aback was she by that sudden rise in volume from him that she spun round and looked at him. He was only halfway down the corridor, evidently having expected her to return at his urging, and if looks could kill she would have been lying dead at his feet. He did have a temper, though, she registered belatedly, and it made his dark eyes glitter like gold ingots and gave his lean, darkly beautiful features a hard, forbidding edge.

Horribly aware of the number of people openly staring, Holly turned back to the lift just as the doors opened. She dived in as fast as she could but not fast enough to prevent Vito from joining her.

'You should've come back to my office.'

In silence, Holly contemplated his polished shoes because the tears were even closer now and stinging her eyes like angry wasps.

'I have to look into this situation. I need your phone number and your address,' Vito breathed in a raw undertone.

'I wasn't expecting you to be so offensive—funny, how you get the wrong idea about people. I really didn't want to get pregnant, Vito, but I love my son and he is never ever going to hear me admit that because now that he's here he's the *best* thing that ever happened to me,' she bit out shakily, hurriedly stepping out of the lift.

'Phone number. Address,' Vito said again, closing a hand to a slight shoulder to prevent her from walking away through the crowded concourse.

With a heavy sigh, Holly dug into her bag and produced a notebook. He handed her a gold pen. She squinted down at the pen, dimly wondering if it was real gold, and then scolded herself for that stupid thought. She printed out the requested details and ripped out the sheet to hand it back to him. 'Look,' she muttered uncomfortably. 'There's no pressure on you here. If I'm honest I don't really want you in our lives. You're not the sort of man I want around my son.'

And having deprived Vito of breath and speech with that damning final indictment of his character, Holly disappeared into the crowds.

CHAPTER SIX

WELL, YOU MADE a real screw-up of that, Vito reflected
for the first time in his life. But Holly hadn't given him
the smallest preparation for what was to come, so it was
scarcely surprising that everything that could go wrong
had gone wrong. He didn't react well to surprises and
the delivery of the Santa hat and the holly had seemed
suggestively sexual. Was it any wonder he had got the
wrong idea? His hard mouth compressed while he wondered about that note she had mentioned. Had she left
a note? He had looked in all the obvious places. There
had been nothing on the table or the door, and what did
it matter now anyway?

What really mattered was that without the smallest
warning he was apparently a father...

That was a mind-blowing concept but Vito was
primarily ruled by his very shrewd brain and his first
call was to his lawyer, who within the hour put him into
contact with a London-based specialist in family law.
Once all his questions had been answered, Vito was
frowning at the realisation that he didn't really have
any rights over his own son. Only marriage granted
such legal rights. He didn't consult Apollo because he
knew that his friend would start talking about demand-

ing DNA tests but he and Apollo lived very different lives and Vito was confident that if Holly had given birth to a baby eight months after that night, it could only be his baby.

He didn't know how he felt about becoming a father, and after he had organised travel to Holly's home town for the following day and informed her by text of his planned visit, he phoned his mother to break the news.

Concetta Zaffari's delight at learning that she was a grandmother tumbled through her every word and then there were questions about Holly that Vito found hard to answer, and some he skipped altogether.

'*Obviously* you'll be getting married,' Concetta trilled cheerfully, and Vito laughed that his mother should even feel the need to say that. Of course they would be getting married. No Zaffari in history had had an illegitimate child and Vito had every intention of being a better parent than his own father had proved to be, although how to go about achieving that ambition he had no very clear idea.

Holly did not respond to Vito's text because it annoyed her. Why did he assume that she was free to drop everything to make herself and Angelo available at a time that suited him? She was working an early morning shift the next day because it was a Saturday and Pixie was taking care of Angelo for her.

As a result, when Vito arrived in his limousine, having been picked up from the helicopter ride that had brought him from London, he was taken aback to be met by Pixie and informed that his son was having a nap.

'Where's Holly?' he demanded, frowning down at

the diminutive blonde, whose facial expression tele-
graphed her antagonism towards him.

'At work.'

'Where?'

'The supermarket fifty yards down the road,' Pixie
advanced reluctantly. 'You can wait in your car. Her
shift ends in an hour.'

Infuriated that Holly hadn't thought to warn him so
that he could adjust his arrival time accordingly, Vito
strode down the road. He was full of righteous indigna-
tion until he walked through the busy shop and caught
a glimpse of Holly wheeling a trolley bigger than she
was through the aisles and pausing to restock shelves.
*Tough is working as a shelf-stacker and never getting
enough sleep.* Abruptly, he spun on his heel and strode
back out of the busy shop again, shamed by the reality
that the mother of his child was being forced to work
so hard to survive.

Vito would have argued that he had not been spoilt
rotten, but he had been born rich and with a near-
genius-level IQ, and phenomenal success in almost
every field was a reward he took for granted. He had
never had to struggle, never had to make the best of
two bad choices, never had to do anything he didn't
want to do and the sheer undeniable luxury of those
realities about his life was finally sinking in on him.
With uncharacteristic patience he directed his driver to
take him away from the street of tiny terraced houses
where Holly lived to a hotel, where he had lunch while
imagining Holly going without food, which didn't improve his appetite.

'Vito came, then?' Holly exclaimed as she wriggled
out of her overall.

Pixie nodded confirmation. 'Cheese toastie for lunch?'

'Lovely. I should've texted him to say that time didn't suit me. I don't know what it is about Vito but he makes me act completely out of character!' Holly declared guiltily.

'Take it from me, anything other than awe and flattery is probably good for Vito's character. At least he's interested in meeting his son,' Pixie said cheerfully. 'That's good news.'

Holly scoffed down the cheese toastie and touched up her make-up. She couldn't sit down, and she couldn't concentrate either. She wanted to stand at the window waiting for Vito like a kid watching out for Santa Claus arriving. Embarrassment gripped her then and she sat down, only to fly up again when Angelo cried as he wakened from his nap. Changing her son, she gave him a hug and he drank down some water to quench his thirst. It was cold in the small sitting room and she lit the fire to warm it up.

'I'm off out now,' Pixie told her while Holly was strapping a wriggling Angelo into his infant seat.

'But—'

'This is about you and him and Angelo and it's private. Give me a text when he's gone,' Pixie suggested.

Only minutes later the bell went and Holly's heartbeat leapt into her throat, convulsing it. She raced to the front door and then paused to compose herself for several seconds before opening it.

'Holly…' Vito pronounced softly, staring broodingly down at her from his great height. Sheathed in jeans and a sweater teamed with a buttery soft brown leather jacket, he totally took her breath away.

'Come in…' Her wary glance was ensnared by black-fringed dark golden eyes that sent her heart racing. 'Don't stare,' she scolded breathlessly.

'I find you very attractive. Naturally, I'm going to stare, *bellezza mia*.'

He hadn't found her attractive enough to use her phone number, Holly reminded herself ruefully. 'No, don't say insincere stuff like that. All we really have to do here is be polite to each other,' Holly told him in the small, confined hall as he came to a halt beside her.

'I can manage much more than polite,' Vito declared, his long brown fingers settling down onto her slight shoulders and feeling the rigid tension that now gripped her small frame. She had the most luscious mouth he had ever seen on a woman, pink and soft and succulent. His jeans tightened at his groin, his physical reaction instantaneous.

At his touch, Holly turned rigid with discomfiture. 'I meant friendly rather than—'

'*Maledizione!* You want me to be friendly when I can hardly keep my hands off you?' Vito shot at her with raw incredulity. 'I don't think I can manage that.'

'But you have to. I wouldn't be comfortable with anything else,' Holly told him earnestly, convinced that only disaster would follow if she allowed any further intimacy to complicate an already tense relationship.

'*Have* to?' Vito queried, a flash of glittering challenge entering his searching gaze as he stared down at her. 'Have you got someone else in your life…another man?'

Holly dealt him a startled glance. 'No… Why are you asking that?'

Without warning, Vito moved forward, pinning her up against the wall behind her. 'Because if there was

I'd probably want to kill him!' he muttered in a raw undertone.

In wonderment, Holly looked up into his lean, darkly beautiful face and then her view blurred as he hauled her up to his level and opened her mouth with the crushing demand of his own. He tasted so good, all minty and fresh, and the strength in the arms holding her felt even better. Every hard, angular line of his long, lean physique was pressed against her as he braced her hips against the wall. The passion of that hungry kiss threatened to consume her and the anomaly between the cool face he showed the world and the uncontrolled hotness hidden beneath electrified her. The piercing ache she had almost forgotten tugged cruelly in her pelvis as his tongue tangled with hers. His mouth was sublime, the feel of his unyielding muscles, hard against her softer curves, incredible. Insane chemistry…insane behaviour, she translated, pulling back from him with shell-shocked abruptness because she knew with shamed horror that all she really wanted to do with him at that moment was drag him upstairs to her bed to rediscover the amazing pleasure he could give her.

'No, this is not what you're here for…' she muttered in curt reminder, her spine stiff as she turned her back on him to walk into the small sitting room. 'You're here to meet Angelo and that's all.'

'You make it sound so simple when it's anything but simple,' Vito countered with a roughened edge to his voice because she had pushed him away and he had had to resist a powerful urge to turn caveman and yank her back to him.

'If we both make the effort, we can keep this simple and polite,' Holly stated with rigorous resolve.

'I have something I need to explain to you first...'
But by that point, Vito could see over the top of Holly's
head and his attention zeroed in so quickly on the child
in the infant seat that his voice literally trailed away.

And for Vito it was as though the rest of the world
vanished. He focused in amazement on the baby who
bore a remarkable resemblance to a framed photograph
Vito's mother had of her son at a similar age. Huge
brown eyes from below a mop of black curls inspected
him with sparkling curiosity. A chubby fist waved in the
air and suddenly Vito froze, out of his comfort zone and
hating it. He had never gone weak at the knees for pup-
pies or babies, had put that lack of a softer side down to
his grandfather's rigid discipline. But now he was looking at his son and seeing a baby with his own features in
miniature and he finally realised that the very thought
of fatherhood unnerved him. His own father had been
a hopeless parent. How much worse would he do with
Angelo when he had no idea even where to start?

Holly paused beside the child seat to say awkwardly,
'So...er...obviously this is Angelo. He's a little bored at
weekends because during the week I look after a pair
of toddlers and it's a lot livelier here.'

Vito tried to stand a little less stiffly but in truth he
felt much as if someone had swung open the door of a
lion's cage and left him to take his chances. 'Why did
you call him Angelo?'

'Because you're Italian,' Holly pointed out, wondering why he was questioning the obvious. 'I looked up
Italian names.'

Vito forced himself closer to the baby. His hands
weren't quite steady as he undid the belt strapping An-

gelo into his seat. As Vito lifted the baby, Angelo gave his father an anxious, startled appraisal.

'You're used to children,' Holly assumed, rather taken aback by that deceptively confident first move.

'No. I don't think I've ever been this close to a child before. There are none in the family and most of my friends are still single as well,' Vito told her abstractedly, wondering what he was supposed to do with the little boy now that he was holding him.

'Thank you for having him,' Vito breathed in a driven undertone. 'You could have made a different decision but you didn't.'

Nothing about this first meeting was going in any direction that Holly had foreseen. And she was even less ready to hear her baby's father thank her for not opting for a termination. Her eyes prickled with sudden emotion.

'I wanted him from the first, never had any doubts there,' she admitted gruffly. 'He's the only family I have...apart from my friend Pixie.'

As Angelo squirmed and wriggled, Vito lifted him higher and swung him round in aeroplane mode.

The baby's eyes grew huge and he let out a frightened howl before breaking down into red-faced, gulping sobs.

'Let me take him,' Holly urged in dismay as Vito lowered the squalling baby. 'He's not used to the rough stuff. There are no men in his life, really, just Pixie and me...'

Vito settled Angelo back into Holly's arms with more than a suggestion of haste and relief. 'Sorry, I upset him.'

'He needs time to get used to you,' Holly explained. 'I'll put him on the floor to play with his toys.'

Vito was tempted to back off entirely but that struck him as cowardly and he held his ground to crouch down on the rug. Finally recalling that he had brought a gift, he removed it from his pocket and tipped it out of a box. 'It's only a little toy.'

Holly winced as she noted a piece of the toy break off and fall. It had detachable tiny parts and was totally unsuitable for a baby. 'You can't give that to him,' she told Vito apologetically. 'He puts everything in his mouth and he could choke on those tiny pieces.'

In haste, Vito removed the toy and its parts again and grimaced. 'I didn't think. I really don't know anything about babies.'

Holly pulled over Angelo's toy box and extracted a red plastic truck that was a favourite. 'He likes this... Coffee?' she asked.

'Black, no sugar,' Vito murmured flatly, recognising that getting to know his son and learning how to play with him appeared to be even more challenging than he had feared.

Holly made coffee, acknowledging that she was simply delighted that Vito had had enough interest to come and meet Angelo. She could see how awkward he felt with their child and knew that if she didn't make Vito feel more comfortable he might not want to make another visit. Not that he had prepared very well for this first visit, she thought ruefully, wondering what he had thought a baby would do with a miniature brick action figure festooned in even tinier weapons.

When she returned with the coffee, Angelo was sucking on his little red truck and refusing to share the toy with his father. Holly got down on her knees beside them and, with his mother on hand, her son relaxed his grip on the truck and handed it to Vito. For an instant he looked as though he had no idea what to do with the toy and then some childhood memory of his own must have prompted him because he ran the toy across the rug making *vroom-vroom* noises and Angelo gave a little-boy shout of appreciation.

A little of Vito's tension ebbed in receipt of that favourable response. It shook him to appreciate that he had actually craved that first welcoming smile from his son. He wanted the little boy to recognise him as his father, he wanted him to like him and love him, but it was intimidating to appreciate that he hadn't the faintest idea how to go about achieving those things.

Holly parted her lips to say, 'When you first came in you said there was something that you needed to explain to me…?'

Vito's lean, strong profile clenched and he sprang upright. 'Yes. That sex-party scandal that made headlines,' he framed with palpable distaste. 'That wasn't me, it was my father, Ciccio.'

As she too stood up, Holly's mouth dropped open in shock. 'Your…*father*?'

'I didn't deny my involvement because I was trying to protect my mother from the humiliation of having her husband's habits exposed so publicly,' Vito explained grimly.

Holly dropped down on the edge of the sofa behind her. 'Oh, my goodness.'

'My mother could confirm the truth if you require further proof that I wasn't involved. What did happen that night was that I received a phone call in the early hours of the morning telling me that my father had fallen ill and needed urgent medical attention,' Vito told her, his delivery curt.

'The person calling refused to identify herself, and that should've been my warning. My mother was in Paris and I had to take charge. I wondered why my father had taken ill at an apartment owned by the bank but the minute I walked into it I could see what I was dealing with, and that I had been contacted like a clean-up crew in the hope of keeping the wild party under the radar.'

Holly nodded slowly, not really knowing what to say.

'My father had had a heart attack in the company of hookers and drugs,' Vito volunteered grimly. 'I had him collected by a private ambulance from the rear entrance and, having instructed a trusted aide to dispose of all evidence of the party, I intended to join my father at a clinic. Unfortunately the press were waiting outside when I left and I was mobbed. One of the hookers then sold her story, choosing to name me rather than my father even though I had never met her in my life. She probably lied because there was more of a story in my downfall than in that of a middle-aged married man with a taste for sleaze.'

'So you took the blame for your parents' sake?' Holly whispered in wonderment.

'My *mother's* sake,' Vito emphasised drily. 'But my mother worked out the truth for herself and she is currently divorcing my father. She looked after him until he had regained his health and then told him that she wanted a separation.'

'And how do you feel about that? I mean, their divorce means that your sacrifice was in vain.'

'I'm relieved that they've split up. I don't like my

father very much…well, not at all, really,' Vito admitted, his wide sensual mouth twisting. 'He's a greedy, dishonest man and my mother will have a better life without him.'

Utterly amazed by that flood of unrestrained candour from a male as reserved as Vito, Holly continued to scrutinise him with inquisitive blue eyes. 'Why are you telling me all this now?'

'You're family now in all but name,' Vito told her wryly. 'And I couldn't possibly allow you to continue to believe that I am not a fit person to be around my son.'

Holly fully understood that motivation and muttered, 'I'm sorry I misjudged you. I was naive to believe everything I read on the internet about you. I told you before that I don't know who my father is,' Holly admitted, wrinkling her nose. 'My mother gave me several different stories and I challenged her when I was sixteen to tell me the truth but she still wouldn't answer me. I honestly don't think she knows either. In those days she was fairly promiscuous. I've had no contact with her since then.'

'You've never had a father…much like me. Ciccio took no interest in me when I was a child and when I was an adult he only approached me if he wanted something,' he revealed, settling down with striking grace of movement into an armchair. 'My grandfather was my father figure but he was seventy when I was born and he had a Victorian outlook on childcare and education. It was far from ideal.'

Holly was fascinated by what she was learning about Vito's background, although she really wasn't sure why he was choosing to tell her so much. 'I think very few people have an ideal childhood,' she said ruefully.

'But wouldn't it be wonderful to give Angelo that ideal?' Vito pressed, black velvet lashes lifting on glittering gold as he studied her.

Her heart raced and her mouth ran dry. Hurriedly she dropped her gaze from his, only for her attention to fall to the tight inner seam of his jeans stretched along a powerful muscular thigh. Guilty heat surged through her and she shifted uneasily. 'And how could we give Angelo an ideal childhood?' she asked abstractedly.

'By getting married and giving our son a conventional start in life,' Vito spelt out with measured assurance. 'I'm not only here to meet Angelo, Holly…I'm here to ask you to be my wife.'

Disbelief roared through Holly. She blinked rapidly, doubting the evidence of her ears. He was proposing? He was actually proposing marriage to her because she had had his child?

Holly loosed an uneasy laugh and Vito frowned, because that was hardly the response he had envisaged. 'I think your grandfather's Victorian outlook is showing, Vito. We don't need to get married to give Angelo a decent upbringing.'

'How else can I be a proper father when I live in a different country?' Vito demanded with harsh bite. 'I really don't want to be only an occasional visitor in my son's life or the home he visits for a few weeks in summer when he's off school. That is not enough for me.'

Holly watched Vito lean down to lift Angelo, who was tugging at his shoelaces. He closed his arms tentatively round Angelo's small restive body and settled him down on a lean thigh. There was something incredibly sexy about his newly learned assurance with their son and her cheeks coloured at that seemingly tasteless reflection, but the smouldering edge of Vito's sexuality seemed to be assailing her every thought. 'Well, I can see that it would be difficult for you and far from ideal, but marriage...well, that's a whole different ball game,' she told him regretfully. 'I want to marry a man who loves me, not a man who accidentally got me pregnant and wants to do what he feels is the right thing by me.'

'I can't change how we conceived Angelo but with a little vision you should be able to see that where we started isn't where we have to end up,' Vito responded smoothly. 'I may not love you but I'm insanely attracted to you. I'm also ready to settle down.'

'Yes, you were engaged, weren't you?' Holly slotted in rather unkindly.

'That's not relevant here,' Vito informed her drily. 'Stay focused on what really matters.'

'Angelo,' Holly replied, with hot cheeks, while her brain trooped off in wild, unproductive circles.

He was asking her to marry him... He was actually asking her to marry him! How was she supposed to react to that when she had been astonished by his proposal?

'You should also consider the reality that eventually Angelo will be very rich, and growing up outside *my* world isn't the best preparation for that day,' Vito pointed out. 'I want to be his father. A father who is there for him when he needs me. A benefit neither you nor I enjoyed.'

He was making very valid points but Holly felt harassed and intimidated rather than grateful for his honesty. 'But marriage?' she reasoned. 'That's such a huge decision.'

'And a decision only you can make. But there would be other benefits for you,' Vito told her quietly. 'You could set up as an interior designer and live your dream with me.'

'You're starting to sound like a trained negotiator,' Holly cut in.

'I am a trained negotiator,' Vito conceded. 'But I want to give our son the very best start in life he can have, with a genuine family.'

And that was the real moment that Holly veered from consternation and fell deep into his honeytrap. Those emotive words, 'a genuine family', spoke to her on the deepest possible level and filled her head with happy images. That was a goal that she, and surprisingly Vito in spite of his privileged background, both shared, and that touched her. As she studied her son sitting peacefully in his father's arms her heart melted. She had felt ashamed of the lack of caution that had led to her pregnancy. She had been mortified that she had failed her own life goals and could not give her son the family security and the opportunities he deserved. But if she married Vito she would be able to put all her regrets behind her and *give* Angelo two parents and a stable home with every advantage.

'Even people in love find it hard to make marriage work,' Holly reminded him, fighting to resist the tempting images flooding her imagination, and to be sensible and cautious.

'We're not in love. Our odds of success may well be better because we have less exalted expectations,' Vito contended silkily. 'And our arrangement need not be viewed as a permanent trap either. In a few years, should one or both of us be unhappy, we can divorce.

All I'm asking you to do at this moment in time, Holly...
is give marriage a chance.'

He made it sound so reasonable, so very reasonable.
He was inviting her to *try* being married to him and
see if they could make it work. It was a very realistic
approach, guaranteed to make her feel that by trying
she would have nothing to lose. And she looked back
at him in silence with her heart hammering while he
raked an impatient hand through his cropped black hair.

'I'll think it over.' Holly fibbed, because she had already thought it over and really there was no contest
between what Vito was offering Angelo and what she
could hope to offer her son as a lone parent.

'Be more decisive, *bellezza mia*,' Vito urged. 'If you
marry me I will do everything within my power to
make you happy.'

Holly had known true happiness only a few times
in her life. One of those moments had been waking at
dawn enfolded in Vito's arms. Another had been the
first time she had seen her infant son. But just being
with Vito also made her happy and that worried her,
implying as it did that she was craving something more
than a very practical marriage based on their son's
needs. Should she listen to that voice of reason and
warning now? Stay on the sidelines where it was safe
rather than risk dipping her toes into the much more
complex demands of a marriage?

But at the baseline of her responses there was no
denying that she wanted Vito Zaffari with a bone-deep,
almost frighteningly strong yearning. How could she
possibly walk away from that? How could she stand
back and watch him take up with other women, as he
would, and know that she had given him that freedom?

And the answer was that she couldn't face that, would sooner take a risk on a marriage that might not work than surrender any hope of a deeper relationship with him.

Holly breathed in slow and deep and lifted her head high. 'All right. We'll get married…and see how it goes…'

And Vito smiled, that heart-stopping smile that always froze her in her tracks, and nothing he said after that point registered with her because she was washed away by sheer excitement and hope for the future.

Vito registered the stars in her eyes with satisfaction. Having been driven by the need to secure the best possible arrangement for his son's benefit, he had expended little thought on the actual reality of becoming a married man or a father. He wanted Holly and he wanted his son: that was all that mattered. And Holly would soon learn to fit into his world, he thought airily.

CHAPTER SEVEN

'SMILE!' PIXIE TOLD HOLLY. 'You look totally stupendous!'

Holly smiled to order and gripped her hands together tightly on her lap. The past four weeks had passed in a whirlwind of unfamiliar activity and changes. Now it was her wedding day and hopefully she would finally have time to draw a breath and start to relax. Only not when it was a wedding about to be attended by a lot of rich, important people, she reasoned nervously.

'How are you feeling?' she asked her best friend and bridesmaid, ruefully surveying Pixie's legs, which were both encased in plaster casts.

Her housemate had returned from a visit to her brother badly battered and bruised from a fall down the stairs, which had also broken both her legs. The extent of her injuries had appalled Holly and, although the bruising had faded, she couldn't help feeling that there was more amiss with her friend than she was letting on because Pixie's usual chirpiness and zest for life seemed to have faded away as well. And although she had gently questioned Pixie on several occasions, she could not work out if it was her own imagination in overdrive or if indeed there *was* some secret concern that Pixie wasn't yet willing to share with her.

Predictably, Pixie rolled her eyes. 'I keep on telling you I'm fine. I'll get these casts off in a couple of weeks and I'll get back to work and it'll be as if this never happened.'

'Hopefully you'll be able to come out to visit us in Italy in a few weeks' time.'

'That's doubtful.'

'Er…if it's money—'

'No, I'm not taking money off you!' Pixie told her fiercely. 'You may be marrying Mr Rich but that's not going to change anything between us.'

'All right.' Holly subsided to scrutinise the opulent diamond engagement ring on her finger. Vito wasn't the least bit romantic, she conceded ruefully, because he had sent the ring to her by special delivery rather than presenting her with it. That had been such a disappointment to her. It would have meant so much to Holly if Vito had made the effort to personally give her the ring.

'Let's simply be a normal couple from here on in,' Vito had urged, and seemingly the ring signified that normality he wanted even if it had not entailed him changing his ways.

She had wanted to ask if it was the same ring Marzia, his previous fiancée, had worn but had sealed her lips shut in case that question was tactless. And staging a potentially difficult conversation with a male she had barely seen since she had agreed to marry him had struck her as unwise.

'Of course I'm very busy now. How else could I take time off for the wedding?' Vito had enquired piously on the phone when she'd tried to tactfully suggest that he make more effort to spend some time with her and Angelo.

Vito hadn't even been able to make time for Angelo, whom he had only seen once since their agreement. Of course, to be fair, he *had* suggested that they move into his London apartment *before* the wedding and she had been ready to agree until she had heard from Pixie's brother and had realised that there was no way she could leave her injured friend to cope alone in a house with stairs. She had had to put Pixie first but Vito had not understood that. In fact Vito had called it a silly excuse that was dividing him from his son. After the wedding she needed to explain to Vito just how much of a debt she owed Pixie for her friend's support during her pregnancy and after Angelo's birth, and she needed to explain that she loved Pixie as much as she would have loved a sister. Although, never having had a sibling of his own, he might not even understand that.

And there were an awful lot of things that Vito didn't understand, Holly reflected ruefully. He had been thoroughly irritated when she'd insisted on continuing her childminding until her charges' parents had had time to make other arrangements for their care, but Holly would not have dreamt of letting anyone down, and took her responsibilities just as seriously as he took his own.

Furthermore, in every other way Vito had contrived to take over Holly and her son's lives. He had made decisions on their behalf that he had neglected to discuss with Holly. Maybe he thought she was too stupid and ignorant to make the right decisions, she thought unhappily.

First he had landed her with an Italian nanny, who had had to board at a hotel nearby because there were only two bedrooms in the house Pixie and Holly rented. London-born Lorenza was a darling and wonderful with Angelo, and Holly had needed outside help to cope with shopping for a wedding dress and such things, but she still would have preferred to play an active role in the hiring of a carer for her son.

Secondly, he had landed Holly with a horrible, pretentious fashion stylist who had wanted Holly to choose the biggest, splashiest and most expensive wedding gown ever made. Only sheer stubbornness had ensured that Holly actually got to wear her own choice of dress on her special day. And it was a very plain dress because Holly was convinced that she was too small and curvy to risk wearing anything more elaborate. She stroked the delicate edge of a lace sleeve with satisfaction. At least she had got her dream dress even if she hadn't got any input into any other details because Vito had placed all the organisation into the hands of a wedding planner, whom he had instructed *not* to consult his future wife.

In truth, Vito was extremely bossy and almost painfully insensitive sometimes. He had left it to his social secretary to tell Holly that she had a day at a grooming parlour booked for a makeover. Holly had been mortified, wondering whether Vito thought her ordinary ungroomed self was a mess and not up to his standards. Pixie had told her not to be so prickly and had asked her if she thought there was something immoral about manicures and waxing. And no, of course she didn't think that, it was just that she had wanted Vito to want her as she was, not be left feeling that only a very polished version of her could now be deemed acceptable. After all, she didn't have the security of knowing her bridegroom loved her, flaws and all, and that made a big difference to a woman's confidence, she reasoned worriedly.

'Will you stop it? And don't ask me what you're to stop!' Pixie said bluntly. 'You're worrying yourself sick about marrying Vito and it's crazy. You love him—'

'I don't love him,' Holly contradicted instantly. 'I like him. I'm very attracted to him.'

'You look him up online just to drool over his photos. If it's not love, it's a monster crush. So you might as well be married to him,' Pixie contended. 'Vito's all you think about. In fact watching you scares the hell out of me. I don't think I could bear to love anyone the way you love him, but with a little luck in time he may well return your feelings.'

'Do you think so?'

'I don't see why not,' Pixie responded thoughtfully. 'Vito's the caring type even if he hasn't yet learned to share. Why shouldn't he fall in love with you?'

But it wasn't love she felt, Holly told herself urgently. It was liking, attraction, respect, nothing more, nothing less. Loving Vito without being loved back would simply make her unhappy and she refused to be unhappy. No, she was a very hands-on person and she was going to make the most of what she *did* have with Vito and Angelo, not make the mistake of pining for what she couldn't have. After all, she could plainly see Vito in all his very good-looking and sophisticated glory and she knew she was only getting to marry him because some crazy fate had deposited her as a damsel in distress on his doorstep one Christmas Eve night.

Her foster mother, Sylvia, pushed Pixie down the aisle in her wheelchair while Holly walked to the altar, striving not to be intimidated by the sheer size of the church and the overwhelming number of unfamiliar faces crammed into it. Vito stood beside a guy with black shoulder-length hair and startling green eyes whom she recognised from online photographs as his best friend, Apollo Metraxis. Holly only looked at the bronzed Greek long enough to establish that he was giving her a distinctly cold appraisal before her attention switched quite naturally to Vito, who, unromantic or otherwise, was at least managing to smile that breathtaking smile of his.

Her heart bounced around in her chest to leave her breathless and when he closed his hand over hers at the altar she was conscious only of him and the officiating priest. She listened with quiet satisfaction to the words of the wedding ceremony, grinned when Angelo let out a little baby shout from his place on Lorenza's lap in a front pew and stared down all of a glow at the wedding band Vito threaded smoothly onto her finger. It was her wedding day and she was determined to enjoy it.

When they signed the register, she was introduced to a smiling older woman clad in a lilac suit and hat with diamonds sparkling at her throat.

'I'm Vito's *mamma*, Concetta,' the attractive brunette told her warmly. 'I've met my grandson. He *is* beautiful.'

Unsurprisingly, Holly was charmed by such fond appreciation of her son and her anxiety about how Vito's mother might feel about his sudden marriage dwindled accordingly. Concetta, it seemed, was willing to give her a fighting chance at acceptance. Vito's friend Apollo, however, could barely hide his hostility towards her and she wondered at it. Didn't he realise that this marriage was what Vito had wanted? Did he think she had somehow forced his friend into proposing? Holly's chin came up and her big blue eyes fired with resolution because she was happy to have become Vito's wife and Angelo's mother and she had no intention of pretending otherwise.

After some photos taken at the church they moved on to the hotel where the reception was being held. 'There are so many guests,' she commented with nervous jerkiness when they climbed out of the limo, an easier exercise than it might have been because Holly's closely fitted gown did not have a train.

'My family has a lot of friends but some guests are business acquaintances,' Vito admitted. 'You shouldn't be apprehensive. Invariably wedding guests are well-wishers.'

Apollo's name was on her lips but she compressed it. She didn't think much of the Greek for deciding he disliked her, sight unseen. What happened to giving a person a fair chance? But she refused to allow Apollo's brooding presence to cast a shadow over her day. And although Apollo was supposed to be Vito's best man, and Pixie the chief and only bridesmaid, Apollo snubbed Pixie as well. Of course, he had brought a partner with him, a fabulously beautiful blonde underwear model with legs that could rival a giraffe's and little desire to melt into the background.

As was becoming popular, the speeches were staged before the meal was served. Holly's foster mother, Sylvia, had insisted on saying a few words and they were kind, warming words that Holly very much appreciated. Concetta Zaffari had chosen not to speak and Vito's father had not been invited to the wedding. When Apollo stood up, Holly stiffened and the most excruciating experience of her life commenced with his speech. In a very amusing way Apollo began to tell the tale of the billionaire banker trapped by the snow and the waitress who had broken down at the foot of the lane. Holly felt humiliated, knowing that everyone who had seen Angelo and worked out her son's age was now aware that he had been conceived from a one-night stand.

Vito gripped her hand so hard it almost hurt and hissed in her ear, 'I did not know he was planning to tell our story!'

Holly said nothing. She wasn't capable of saying anything, meeting Pixie's compassionate gaze across the circular table, recognising Concetta Zaffari's compassion on her behalf in her gentle appraisal. She could feel her face getting hotter and hotter and pictured herself resembling a giant blushing tomato and it was a mercy when Apollo had concluded his maliciously polite speech, which had left her pierced by a dozen poisonous darts of condemnation. He had outed her as a slut at the very least and a gold-digger at worst because he had made it sound the most impossible coincidence that her car had gone off the road at that convenient point. But worst of all, he had not uttered a single lie.

'What a bastard!' Pixie said roundly when she had contrived to follow Holly into the palatial cloakroom. 'Vito's furious! He asked me to come and see that you were all right.'

'I shouldn't be ashamed of being a waitress or a woman who fell pregnant after a one-night stand,' Holly muttered apologetically. 'But somehow sitting there in front of all those richly dressed, bejewelled people I felt like rubbish.'

Sylvia joined them at that point and put her arms

around Holly. 'That young man's a rather nasty piece of work,' she opined ruefully. 'That was a very inappropriate speech, in the circumstances. Holly...sticks and stones may break your bones but words can never hurt you.'

'Not true.' Holly sighed, breathing in deep. 'But don't worry about me. I can handle it—'

'But you shouldn't have to on your wedding day, as I told your bridegroom,' Pixie framed angrily.

'No, no, let it go,' Holly urged ruefully. 'I've got over it already. I was being oversensitive.'

Her foster mother departed and Pixie said several rather unrepeatable things about Apollo Metraxis before the two women began to make their way back to the function room. And then suddenly Pixie stopped her wheelchair and shot out a hand to yank at Holly's wrist to urge her into the alcove in the corridor. She held a finger to her lips in the universal silencing motion and Holly frowned, wondering what on earth her friend was playing at.

And then she heard it, Apollo's unforgettable posh British accent honed by years of public schooling. 'No, as you know, he wouldn't listen to me. *No* DNA test, *no* pre-nup...get this? He *trusts* her. No, he's not an idiot. It's my bet he's playing a deeper game with this sham marriage. Maybe planning to go for full custody of his son once he has them in Italy. Vito's no fool. He simply plays his cards close to his chest.'

Holly turned deathly pale because there was not the smallest doubt that Apollo was talking about her and Angelo and Vito. For a split second she honestly wished she hadn't eavesdropped and she could see by her friend's expression that Pixie was now regretting the impulse as well because of what they had overheard. But without a word she planted firm hands on the handles of the wheelchair and moved her friend out of the alcove and back towards the function room.

But Holly was shattered inside and her expressive face was wooden and, after one glance at her, Vito whirled her onto the dance floor and closed his arms round her. Rage with Apollo was still simmering inside Vito like a cauldron. Well aware of his friend's attitude towards his marriage, Vito blamed himself for still including him in the event. He had naively assumed that, after meeting Holly, Apollo would realise how outrageous his cynical outlook was when it came to her. But his misplaced trust in the Greek billionaire had resulted in his bride's hurt on what he very well knew she believed should be a happy day. Even worse, he was still recovering from the unprecedented surge of raw protective reaction he had experienced during that speech. Any individual who wounded Holly should be his enemy, certainly not a trusted confidant of many years' standing.

'I'm sorry, really sorry about Apollo's speech,' he told her in a driven undertone. 'If I'd had the slightest idea what he was planning to say—'

'You should've kept your mouth shut about how we met,' Holly told him in an unforgiving tone. 'If you hadn't opened your big mouth, he wouldn't have known—'

'Holly...I didn't know that we were going to end up together—'

'No, that came right out of left field with Angelo, didn't it?' Holly agreed in a saccharine-sweet tone he had never heard from her before. 'Just boy talk, was it? The brunette slapper I pulled at Christmas?'

Dark colour rimming his high cheekbones, Vito gazed down at her with dark eyes blazing like golden flames. 'Are you seriously saying that you didn't tell Pixie about us?'

Hoist by her own petard, Holly reddened and compressed her lips.

'Thought so,' Vito said with satisfaction and she wanted to slap him very hard indeed. 'We both spoke out of turn but you have the kinder and wiser friend.'

'Yes,' Holly conceded gruffly, tears suddenly shining in her eyes.

'I have spoken to Apollo. If it's any consolation I wanted to punch him for the first time in our long friendship. He's a hothead with a very low opinion of marriage in general. His father married six times,' Vito explained ruefully. 'I know that doesn't take away the sting but, speaking for myself, I don't care how many people know how I met my very lovely, very sexy wife and acquired an even cuter baby. You're a Zaffari now. A Zaffari always holds his or her head high.'

'Is that so?' Holly's heavy heart was steadily lightening because it meant a lot that he was perceptive enough to understand how she felt and that he had made his friend aware that he was angry about that speech.

'Yes, *gioia mia*. We Zaffaris take ourselves very seriously and if one is lucky enough to find a waitress like you in the snow he's grateful for it, not suspicious. Apollo and I have a friendship based very much on the fact that we are opposites in character. He distrusts every woman he meets. He's always looking for a hidden agenda. It must be exhausting,' he said wryly.

Holly rested her brow against his shoulder as they slow-danced and she let the mortification and the anger seep slowly out of her again. It was being with Vito that was important, being with Vito and Angelo and becoming a family that really mattered. And in her heart of hearts she could not credit that Vito was planning a sham marriage purely to try and deprive her of their son. That accusation was hopefully the suggestion of a troubled, misogynistic mind, she reasoned hopefully.

'This is *your* jet…like really? *Your own jet?*' Holly carolled incredulously a few hours later when she scanned the ultra-opulent leather interior of the private jet.

'I travel a great deal. It's convenient,' Vito parried, amused by her wide, shaken eyes.

'As long as sleeping with the cabin crew isn't included,' Holly whispered, her attention resting on the more than usually attractive team overseeing the boarding of Lorenza and Angelo and all the baby equipment that accompanied her son. In consternation Holly realised that she had accidentally spoken that thought out loud.

Predominantly, Vito was shocked by the concept of having sex with anyone who worked for him and then he looked at his bride's burning face and he started to laugh with rare enjoyment. 'No, that sort of entertainment is probably more Apollo than me. Although I did take advantage of *you*.'

'No, you didn't,' she told him before she hurried forward to grasp her son, having missed him during her enforced break from him throughout the day.

'Older, wiser, plied an innocent with wine…' Vito traded, condemning himself for his crime for her ears alone. 'But if I had the chance to go back I would *still* do it again.'

Encountering a lingering sidewise glance from black-fringed dark golden eyes, Holly felt heat lick through her pelvis as she took a seat and cuddled Angelo. For possibly the first time since she had conceived she looked back at that night in the cottage without guilt and regret. No, on that score Vito had hit a bullseye. Given the chance, in spite of the moments of heartache and stress along the way, she would also still have done the same thing again.

And if Vito could be that honest, why shouldn't she match him? Tell him about the phone call she had overheard Apollo making? She would pick her moment, she decided ruefully, and she would ask if he had ever thought of their marriage as a sham and if she had anything to worry about.

Angelo was asleep by the time they landed in Italy. Holly had freshened up, noting with disappointment that her outfit hadn't travelled very well. The fashion stylist had tried to persuade her to buy a whole host of clothes but with Vito already paying for the wedding and her gown she hadn't felt right about allowing him to pay for anything else before they were married. She had teamed an elegant navy-and-white skirt with a matching top but her get-up had creased horribly and looked as though she had worn it for a week rather than only a few hours. Straightening it as best she could, she wondered if Vito would even notice.

Holly was enchanted by the wonderful scenery that enfolded as the four-wheel drive moved deeper into the countryside. Charming low hills rolled across a landscape peacefully dotted with cypresses, serrated lines of fresh green vines and silvery olive groves. Medieval villages slumbered on hilltops while ancient bell towers soared into the cloudless blue sky. Occasionally she caught a glimpse of beautiful, weathered old farmhouses nestling among the greenery and the wild flowers and she wondered if Vito's home resembled them.

'There it is…the Castello Zaffari,' Vito announced with pride as the car began to climb a steep ribbon of road. Dead ahead Holly glimpsed a building so vast it covered the whole hilltop like a village while elaborate gardens decorated the slopes below it. She froze, convinced that that could not possibly be his home because it was a palace, not a mere dwelling. A giant domed portico denoted the front entrance where the car came to a halt.

'Is this it? Is this where you live?' Holly asked in a small voice, wondering crazily if she could hide in the car and refuse to emerge until he admitted that the palace wasn't really his and he had only been joking. It *had* to be a joke, she thought fearfully, because no ordinary woman could possibly learn to live in the midst of such medieval splendour.

Vito picked up on the edge in her voice and frowned at her. 'Yes. What's wrong?'

'Nothing,' she said hurriedly as she took Angelo to allow the nanny to climb out.

'Don't you like it?'

'Of course I like it,' Holly lied in a rush, utterly overpowered by the huge building as she accompanied Vito into a massive marble-floored hall studded with matching lines of columns. 'But you could've at least hinted that you lived like royalty.'

'I don't,' Vito incised in firm rebuttal. 'I live in a historic building that has belonged to my family for centuries. I live a very average, normal life here…'

Please tell me he didn't say that, Holly argued with herself as they rounded the gigantic centrepiece of a winding stone staircase and were faced with a long assembled row of what could only have been household staff all dressed up in uniform as though they had strayed off the set for *Downton Abbey. Average? Normal?* On what planet was Vito living?

Sick with the nervous unease of someone totally out of their comfort zone, Holly fixed a smile to her stiff face while Vito conducted introductions. There was a great deal of billing and cooing over Angelo and Vito's own former nanny, Serafina, surged forward to take the baby. Apart from her, Silvestro was the head honcho in the household and little giggly Natalia, it turned out, was Holly's English-speaking maid. With great difficulty Holly kept her face straight at the prospect of having a maid and watched while the two nannies carried Angelo off upstairs.

'Natalia will show you to our room,' Vito informed her at the foot of the stairs and then he paused, a frown etching between his level brows, his dark eyes semi-concealed by his ridiculous lashes as he murmured, 'I should have asked you—do you object to sharing a room?'

The planet he was on was definitely far, far from the moon, Holly thought crazily as she raised her brows. 'Where else would I sleep?'

'Obviously you could have your own room,' Vito told her valiantly.

And Holly almost burst out laughing because Vito was being his extraordinarily polite self and going against his own instincts. She could see it in the tension etched in his lean, darkly handsome face, hear it in the edge roughening his dark, deep drawl. He really, *really* didn't want her to choose a separate bedroom and she wondered why on earth he had made the offer. 'No...' Holly reached for his clenched hand. 'You're not getting rid of me that easily,' she teased.

Vito laughed and smiled almost simultaneously and all the tension vanished. *Silly, silly man*, she thought warmly as she followed Natalia up the stairs. Why had he even given her a choice? Separate bedrooms? Was that how husband and wife normally lived in such a gigantic house? How his parents and grandparents had lived? Well, from here on in Vito was going to have to learn how a normal, average couple lived, and having shared a bed with him once had only made her all the keener to repeat the experience, she acknowledged, her colour rising. But there was just no way of denying that the most unbearable hunger clenched her deep down inside when she looked at Vito.

Months had passed since that night in the cottage but she had learned a lot about herself after that first educational experience. Other men hadn't tempted her the way Vito had and she had always assumed that that'd meant she wasn't a very sensual person. Vito, however, had unleashed her newly discovered appetite for intimacy and taught her differently. He was definitely the right man for her. She could only hope that she would prove to be the right woman for him.

Natalia opened the doors of what had to be the most drop-dead ugly bedroom Holly had ever seen. It was truly hideous. Heavy dark drapes shut out most of the light and made the vast room gloomy. A material that looked and felt like dark red leather covered the walls and every other surface from the high, elaborately moulded and domed ceiling to the furniture, which was heavily gilded in gold. Holly swallowed hard. It looked as though it hadn't been decorated in at least a hundred years and it was very possible that the weird paper was antique like the furniture.

Well, Holly thought as her maid cast open the doors to show her around what appeared to be an entire suite of rooms for their use, she might be keen to share a bedroom with Vito but he might have to move the location of the shared bedroom to make her happy. Natalia beamed and showed her into a large room walled with closets, which she swept open to display the contents.

'Who does all this belong to?' Holly asked, recoiling while wondering if all the garment-bag-enclosed items of clothing had been left behind by Vito's former fiancée, Marzia.

'Is *your* gift…is *new*,' the brunette stressed while showing off a still-attached label to what appeared to be a hand-embroidered ballgown of such over-the-top glamour that it took Holly's breath away.

A gift that could only be from Vito. The gift of an entire wardrobe of clothes? Holly fingered through drawers packed with lingerie and nightwear in little decorative bags and stared at the racks of shoes and accessories Natalia was eager for her to see and appreciate. It was a mind-blowing collection and it was just way too much altogether for Holly, after the wedding, the massive palace Vito lived in and his revealing query about whether or not she was willing to share a bedroom with him. What on earth? What on earth kind of marriage was she in that he had told her so little about his life and yet bought her so much? Did he think flashing around his money made up for his failure to explain all the other stuff?

Catching a glimpse of her creased and tousled reflection in one of the many mirrors in the dressing room, Holly almost groaned. She didn't want to get tricked out in fancy clothes, she simply wanted comfort, and as Natalia opened Holly's single case on the now seemingly pitiful assortment of clothing that had been her lot pre-Vito, Holly bent down to scoop out her one extravagance: a shimmering maxi dress with an iridescent sheen that skimmed her every curve with a flattering fit. She was relieved to see that while the bedroom belonged to a bygone age, the en-suite bathroom, while palatial, was contemporary. Stepping into a wonderful walled rain-forest shower, she rinsed away the tired stickiness of travel and tried to let her anxieties float off down the drain with the soapy water.

A marriage was what you made of it and she had no intention of underestimating the challenge ahead. They had married for Angelo's benefit but their son could only enjoy a happy home life if his parents established a good relationship. Holly's childhood had been damaged by her mother's neglect and self-indulgence, Vito's by his father's indifference. He should've warned her about the giant historic house and the extravagant new wardrobe, but she could no more shout at him for being richer and more pedigreed than she had estimated than she could shout at him for his unvarnished generosity.

Dressed, her black hair tumbling freely round her shoulders, Holly explored the connecting rooms Natalia had briefly walked her through earlier. A door stood ajar on the balcony that led off the sitting room and she strolled out, watching the sun go down over the stunning landscape and the manicured gardens below and slowly veil them in peach, gold and terracotta splendour. Sounds in the room she had vacated alerted her to the arrival of a trolley, and the rattle of cutlery fired her appetite and drew her back indoors.

Vito was framed by a doorway at the far end of the room, his suit abandoned in favour of jeans and a white shirt open at his strong brown throat. Her tummy was awash with butterflies as she instinctively drew in a deep breath and savoured her view of him. He stood there, so tall and dark and devastatingly handsome, watching her with the assessing eyes of a hawk.

Vito finally tore his gaze from his bride's opulent curves, that were so wonderfully enhanced by the fine fabric of her dress, but the words he had been about to speak had vanished from his brain. Holly, he acknowledged simply, was an incredibly sexy woman. Innate sensuality threaded her every movement. It was there in her light gliding walk, the feminine sway of her hips, the swell of her breasts as she straightened her spine and angled her head back to expose her throat.

He had expected Apollo to recognise the sheer depth of Holly's natural appeal, but he couldn't be sorry that his friend's distrust had blinded him because when Vito had seen some of his guests look at his bride with lustful intent, it had annoyed the hell out of him. And that new possessive, jealously protective streak about what was *his* disturbed Vito, who was immensely suspicious of emotional promptings. He had always chosen women who brought out the rational side of his nature but Holly incited much more primal urges.

Vito's butler, Silvestro, moved forward to pour the

wine with a flourish and light the candles on the circular table. Holly tasted the wine with an appreciative sip.

'It's an award-winning Brunello my grandfather laid down years ago. This is a special occasion,' Vito pointed out as he dropped lithely down into his seat and shook out his napkin.

'I cut my teeth on wines that tasted like vinegar.' Holly sighed. 'I'm not much of a drinker.'

'Why would you be if it tasted that bad?' Vito asked with amusement.

'Why didn't you warn me that you lived in a vast house your family have owned for centuries?' Holly asked quietly.

'It didn't occur to me,' Vito admitted with a frown.

'This place was a shock…as was the new wardrobe.'

'You were supposed to shop for clothes at the same time as you chose your wedding dress but the stylist said you weren't interested. So I took care of it for you.'

'Thank you, I suppose…'

As Silvestro left the room, having drawn the trolley close to enable them to serve themselves, Holly embarked on the tiny delicate parcels on her plate. They were exquisitely displayed, and the oriental flavours tasted phenomenal. The courses that followed were even better. Holly had never eaten such fabulous food before.

'Who does the cooking here?' she asked.

'I have a very well-paid chef on staff. When I'm staying at one of my other properties he travels ahead of me.'

Bemused by the concept of a mobile personal chef, Holly blinked. 'You have *other* properties?'

'Here I have the apartment in Florence and a villa

on the shores of Lugano in Switzerland. Those were inherited. But I also own property in the countries I visit most frequently,' Vito admitted.

Holly was frowning. 'What's wrong with hotels?'

'I don't like them. I like quiet and privacy, particularly when I'm working,' Vito advanced smoothly. 'It's my sole extravagance.'

'When I called you a spoilt-rotten rich boy I wasn't far off the mark,' Holly dared.

'Had you ever met my grandfather you would never have awarded me that label. He was a rigid disciplinarian with a punitive approach. He thought my mother was too soft with me.' A rueful smile brought a gentler than usual curve to Vito's wide sensual lips. 'He was probably right.'

'Your grandfather sounds very judgemental. I don't think I would've liked him very much.'

'He was a dinosaur but a well-intentioned one. Since he passed away two years ago, however, I have instigated many changes.'

Holly dealt him a sidewise glance and whispered conspiratorially, 'Our bedroom is a complete horror.'

A flashing grin illuminated Vito's lean, dark features. 'Really?'

'Very dark and depressing.'

'I think I've only been in that room once in my life.' Her brow furrowed. 'You mean it wasn't yours?'

'No, it's simply the main bedroom in the house and Silvestro has been trying to move me in there ever since my grandfather departed,' Vito confided with amusement. 'But I always resist change and I need the allure of a wife there to entice me.'

Holly compressed her lips as she sipped her wine. 'I

have no allure,' she told him, wrinkling her snub nose in embarrassment.

Vito laughed, lounging back in his chair to study her with gleaming dark golden eyes. 'Being unaware of it doesn't mean you don't have it. In fact that very lack of awareness is incredibly appealing.'

'I should check on Angelo.'

'No, not tonight, *bella mia*,' Angelo intoned as he sprang upright to reach for her hands and raise her slowly from her seat. 'Tonight is ours. Angelo has two nannies and an entire household devoted to his needs. After all, he is the first child in the Zaffari family for a generation, and as such more precious than diamonds to our staff.'

Her throat tightened as he looked down at her with glittering golden eyes fringed by ridiculously long lashes. Suddenly she couldn't breathe or move. 'Er… what are we standing here for?'

'I want to see this horror of a bedroom,' Vito said thickly and then he lowered his head and sealed his mouth to hers with hungry, driving urgency.

Like a flamethrower on a bale of hay his passion ignited hers with instantaneous effect. Her arms closed round him, her small hands roving up over his strong, muscular back to cling to his shoulders. His tongue slid moistly between her lips and an erotic thrill engulfed her in dizzy anticipation. Her nipples prickled into tingling tightness while damp heat surged between her legs. She pressed her thighs together, struggling to get a grip on herself but still wanting him so much it almost hurt…

CHAPTER EIGHT

HAULING HOLLY UP into his arms, Vito carried her into the bedroom and settled her on the foot of the bed to remove her shoes.

'I didn't appreciate how dark it was in here,' Vito admitted as he switched on the bedside lamps. 'Or how hideous. My grandfather liked grand and theatrical.' He sighed.

Holly scrambled back against the headboard and studied him with starry eyes. He stood half in shadow, half in light, and the hard, sculpted planes and hollows of his lean, strong face were beautiful. She marvelled at the fate that had brought two such different people together and rejoiced in it too. Liking, respect, attraction, she listed with resolution inside her head, buttoning down the stronger feelings battling to emerge, denying them.

'Did your parents occupy separate bedrooms?' she asked curiously.

'It was always the norm in this household. I didn't want it for us.' Vito came down on the bed beside her. 'If you only knew how much I've longed for this moment. I wanted you with me in London *before* the wedding.'

'But it couldn't be done. I had responsibilities I couldn't turn my back on.' Holly sighed.

'I could've made arrangements to free you of those duties.'

'Not when they're dependent on friendship, loyalty, and consideration for other people,' Holly disagreed gently, lifting a hand to follow the course of his jutting lower lip and note the stubborn angle of his strong jawline. 'You can't rearrange the world only to suit you.'

'*Sì*…yes, I can,' Vito declared without shame.

'But that's *so* selfish—'

'I will not apologise for being selfish when it comes to your needs and Angelo's.' Vito marvelled at her inability to appreciate that he would always place their needs over the needs of others. What was wrong with that? It was true that it took a certain amount of ruthlessness and arrogance, but he had fought hard in life for every single achievement and saw nothing wrong with an approach that maximised the good things for his family and minimised the bad. The way he saw it, if you made enough effort happiness could be balanced as smoothly as a profit-and-loss column.

With his strong white teeth he nipped playfully at the reproving fingertip rapping his chin.

Holly startled and then giggled and sighed. 'What am I going to do with you?'

'Anything you want… I'm up for *anything*.' Vito savoured her, his dark golden eyes holding hers with explicit need for a heartbeat. He pushed her back against the pillows and then his mouth claimed hers with hungry, delicious force.

Heat unfurled in her pelvis. Her heart raced and the tension went out of her only to be replaced by a new kind of tension that shimmied through her bloodstream like an aphrodisiac and made her heart race. Her breath came in quick, shallow gasps between kisses, each leading into the next until he rolled back and, having established that there was no helpful zip, he gathered the hem of her dress in his hands and tugged it up over her body and over her head to pitch it aside.

'That's better,' he growled, pausing to admire the picture she made in her pretty bridal lace lingerie.

'Except you're still wearing far too many clothes,' Holly objected, embarking on his shirt buttons.

Vito yanked off his shirt without ceremony, kicked off his shoes, peeled off his socks, only to halt there, his long, lean frame trembling while Holly's hands roamed over the hills and valleys of his hard, muscular abdomen. Her reverent fingers took a detour to follow the furrow of dark hair vanishing below the waistband of his jeans.

'I missed you,' she said truthfully. 'I missed *this*…'

Unfreezing, lean dark features rigid with control, he unsnapped his jeans and vaulted off the bed to take them off. 'It was the best night of my life, *bellezza mia.*'

And yet he still hadn't made any mention of seeing her again that night or the following morning. That still stung and Holly said nothing. Had he really not seen her note? Could she believe that?

'That note I left at the cottage for you—' she began breathlessly.

'I didn't see it.'

'Would you have phoned if you'd had my number?' she prompted in a reckless rush.

'I don't know,' Vito responded quietly. 'Certainly I would've been tempted, but on another level I distrust anything that tempts me.'

His honesty cut through her. Even if he had found the

note, he wouldn't have phoned her, she decided painfully. He would have written off their night of passion as a once-in-a-lifetime experience and left it behind. That hurt, but there was nothing she could do about it. She wanted to know who else had since shared his bed but it wasn't a question to be asked on their wedding night even though her heart cried out for reassurance. It would be an unfair question when he had not owed her loyalty. Of course there had been other women in the months they had been apart. That was yet another pain she had to bear.

'I've never wanted a woman the way I want you,' Vito told her thickly.

He flung a handful of condoms down by the bed and stripped naked without inhibition while she watched.

Pink washed Holly's face because he was fully aroused and ready.

'I couldn't get enough of you that night and that unnerved me,' he framed abruptly. 'You were a very unexpected discovery.'

He reached for her again, deftly skimming off her bra and panties, twisting his hips away when she tried to touch him. 'No… If you touch me, you'll wreck me. I'm on a hair trigger after months of abstinence,' he growled, lean brown hands roving over the full curves of her breasts, lingering over her pink pointed nipples to tug and tease until little sounds she couldn't silence broke from between her lips.

Vito flung back the sheet and settled her beneath him to pay serious attention to her swollen mouth and the glorious swell of her breasts.

'Months of abstinence?' Holly encouraged helplessly, her breath tripping in her throat as he sucked on a protruding bud while long, skilled fingers stroked her thigh.

'I'm not an easy lay,' he told her. 'I'm very, very fussy.'

'Nothing wrong with that,' Holly framed in ragged reassurance, all the feeling in her body seemingly centred between her thighs where she was scarily desperate for him to touch her.

And then he did and she gasped and her eyes closed and the fire at the heart of her grew hotter still, hips shifting up and from side to side, the drumbeat of need awakened and throbbing and thrumming through every skin cell. Vito shifted down the bed and parted her thighs. He knew exactly what he was doing. She had discovered that the night Angelo was conceived.

He teased her with the tip of his tongue, slow and then quicker until she could no longer stay silent and whimpers and gasps were wrenched from her. A long sure finger stroked through her wet folds and she quivered, every nerve ending jumping to readiness as the excitement crept higher.

At the height of her climax she cried out his name, lost in the convulsive spasms of erotic pleasure. She was so lost in that pleasure that she struggled to remember what day it was and even where she was. Her lashes flickered when she heard him tear open a condom. As he returned to her she wrapped both arms round him possessively, her body temporarily sated.

He pushed her back and drove into her with a guttural groan of satisfaction. 'Like wet satin,' he bit out appreciatively.

Hunger sizzled through her as his bold shaft stretched her and sank deep. Suddenly she was sensually awake again, her body primed as he angled his lean hips to ensure that she received the maximum enjoyment. His hunger for her was unhidden, his strokes were hard and fast, tormentingly strong. The ache low in her body pinged and climbed in intensity. She wanted, oh, *how* she wanted, craved, needed and longed for that maddening pulse of yearning to be answered, overwhelmed. And then her spine was arching and her body jerking and the waves of hot, drenching pleasure were like a shooting star flaming through her and setting her on fire with the wondrous release from her own body.

'Sexiest, most amazing woman ever…and *mine*,' Vito husked in her ear, his weight heavy on her as he rolled over and pulled her down on top of him. 'That's the most important fact. You're mine, *gioia mia.*'

'Are you mine too?' Holly whispered dizzily.

'*Sì*…'

'Is sex always this good?'

'Not even half the time. We have our own unique variety of fireworks.'

Holly rested her cheek on a damp bronzed shoulder, her body replete. He smelled so good she drank him in like a drug. She liked being his. She liked that possessive note she heard edging his dark drawl because it made her feel less like Angelo's mother and more like Vito's wife, valued, needed and wanted on her own account. Long fingers traced the path of her spine as he shifted position.

'I have an impossibly fast recovery time with you,' Vito husked, sliding her back onto the sheet on her front, lingering on the soft full curves of her behind.

He reached for another condom. Holly didn't even lift her head. She was still in that place somewhere between total satiation and awareness, shifting obediently as he eased a pillow below her hips, raising her, rear-ranging her to his satisfaction. And then she felt him rigid and full at her entrance where she was now tender and swollen. He drove in hard and she came suddenly fully awake, eyes wide, throat catching on a breath, heart hotwired back into pounding. He buried himself deep and it felt so good she moaned.

'I like the little sounds you make.' He ground into her with power and energy and a spontaneous combustion of heat surged at the apex of her body.

Excitement crowned with her every cry and snatched breath. She couldn't breathe against the onslaught of raw, surging excitement. With every savage thrust he owned her in a way she had never thought to be owned and she gave herself up to the rise of the hot, pulsing pleasure. The excitement crested with white-hot energy and the sweet waves of deep, quivering pleasure consumed her. Winded, she slumped back down into the pillows.

'Shower time,' Vito told her, lifting her out of bed. 'You're not allowed to go to sleep yet.'

'You and your son have a lot in common.'

'We're both very attached to you?' Vito urged her into the shower.

'You don't sleep at night,' she contradicted. 'Although I have to admit that you're more fun than he is in the middle of the night. Angelo gets grouchy when he's teething.'

'I won't get grouchy with you in my bed,' Vito assured her, leaning back against the tiled wall, lean, bronzed and muscular, a study in male perfection.

Holly was like an energy drink, releasing his tension, refreshing him, leaving him feeling amazingly relaxed. Vito had never done relaxed and wasn't quite sure how to handle it. It was a great deal easier simply to concentrate on working off that surplus energy in bed.

Even with the honeyed ache of sex and satiation Holly wanted to put her hands all over him and explore him with the freedom she had restrained on their first night together. She was so comfortable with him, so indescribably comfortable it almost spooked her. 'I can sleep standing up,' she warned him, resting her damp head down on a strong brown shoulder.

'I have to work tomorrow, *bellezza mia*. Make the most of *now*,' Vito murmured huskily, gathering her close.

Her eyes opened very wide on the tiled wall. He had to work the day after their wedding? Was there some crisis on?

'No. I just like to work,' Vito confided lazily, as if there were nothing the slightest bit strange about his desire to act as though the day after their wedding were just like any other day.

'Are you taking *any* time off?' It was a loaded question but she tried to make it sound casual and unconcerned and then held her breath.

'I'll be home every night...you can bet on that,' Vito growled, nipping at the sensitive flesh below her ear until she shivered helplessly against him and his big hands rose to cup and massage her breasts. 'I'll be keeping you very much occupied.'

Sex, she thought dully. Nothing wrong with his enthusiasm in that department but was that really all he was interested in, all he had ever been interested in? Or simply all she had to offer? Her teeth gritted. What did she have to offer in the intellect category? No, she

was never going to be his equal there. Were they going
to be one of those couples who never interacted except
when their child was around? Would she chatter on re-
lentlessly about Angelo and only ever really get Vito's
attention in bed? It sounded a sad and desperate role to
her but what was she going to do about it? She couldn't
make him want more or force him to see her in a different light, could she?

A sham marriage? That overheard phone call returned to haunt her. How hard could it be for Vito to
fake being genuinely married when all he intended to
do was have sex with her? A chill trickled through her
tummy and made her tense. Suddenly fears that she had
earlier dismissed were becoming a source of genuine
concern. Why had she so easily believed that Apollo
was talking nonsense about Vito's intentions? Apollo
Metraxis had known Vito since childhood. Apollo probably knew Vito a great deal better than she did and if
he suspected that Vito had only married her to gain
custody of his son, shouldn't she be sincerely scared?

When she wakened it was still dark, with only the
faintest glimmer of light showing behind the curtains.
She was deliciously comfortable. Vito had both arms
wrapped round her and she was snuggled up to him,
secure in the warmth and the wonderfully familiar
scent of his skin. He was stroking her hip bone and
she stretched in a helpless little movement.

'I want you, *tesoro mia*.'

Her eyes flew wide as he shifted against her back,
letting her feel the hard swell of him. *'Again?'*

His sensual mouth pressed into the sensitive skin of
her throat. 'Don't move. I'll do all the work.'

And he did, repositioning her, gently rousing her

from her drowsiness and then sinking into her with exquisite precision. She heard herself gasp and then moan and the sweet swell of pleasure surged up and overpowered all her anxious thoughts. Excitement took hold and she trembled with need as his smooth thrusts rocked her sensitised body. She couldn't fight her responses or the uncontrollable wave of ecstatic sensation that swept her to an explosive climax.

'What a wonderful way to wake up,' Vito groaned into her tumbled hair. 'I never dreamt that having a wife could be so much fun. Are you joining me for breakfast?'

Behind her hair, Holly rolled her eyes. She was married to one of those horrid people who came alive around dawn and acted as though it were late morning. Either she stayed in bed and saw very little of him or she changed herself to fit. She lay listening to the shower running and watched him emerge swathed in a towel, the long, lean length of his unspeakably beautiful body mostly exposed. Her mouth ran dry as he disappeared into the dressing room and opened another door. Closet doors were rammed back, drawers opened and closed. She scrambled out of bed and ran for the shower before she could be tempted to backtrack and fall back asleep. Dabbing on minimal make-up, she brushed her hair and extracted some of her new clothes to wear because a pair of jeans and a washed-out cotton top didn't seem quite sufficient for the grandeur of the Castello Zaffari.

Clad in beautifully tailored chinos and a filmy blouse in autumn shades, she slotted her feet into canvas shoes and went out to join Vito. He looked as he had the day she had confronted him at the Zaffari Bank: cool, sophisticated, remote, very much the banker. And at the same time he contrived to look amazing whether he was slotting cufflinks into his cuffs or brushing his cropped black hair.

'Who wears cufflinks these days?' Holly prompted.

Vito shrugged. 'We all use them at the bank.'

'Not at the cutting edge of fashion, then,' she mocked, although his dark suit was incredibly well tailored to lovingly shape wide shoulders, a broad chest, narrow hips and long, powerful legs. Just looking at him, she wanted to touch him.

'Breakfast,' he reminded her, heading for the door.

The *castello* was silent until they reached the ground floor where vague signs of industry could be heard somewhere in the distance. Silvestro entered the hall and looked taken aback to see them. He burst into Italian and Vito responded with quiet amusement.

'Why does everybody think I should be staying home today?' he quipped, leading the way into a sunlit dining room.

'Maybe…because you should be?' Holly dared. 'Just married and all that…'

Silvestro fussed round the table making unnecessary adjustments while Vito translated all the many options Holly could choose for breakfast. As the older man sped off Vito lifted one of the financial newspapers piled at his end of the table and began to read it and Holly wondered whether she should have stayed in bed. She wanted to go and see if Angelo was awake but she didn't want to leave Vito lest he leave for the bank while she was gone.

She had already decided to confront Vito about that phone call she had overheard Apollo making but she had intended to pick and choose the right moment, which might well have been while they were still wrapped round each other in bed. But something about the way Vito lifted that newspaper after dragging her downstairs awakened her temper.

'I overheard Apollo talking on the phone to someone at our reception yesterday.'

Vito lowered the newspaper and frowned at her. 'Overheard?' he questioned.

Below the onslaught of his dark glittering gaze, Holly went pink. 'Well, eavesdropped…I suppose.'

'Are you in the habit of listening in on other people's phone calls?'

'That's not really relevant here,' Holly fudged in desperation, feeling like a child being called to account for misbehaviour. 'Apollo was so obviously talking about us…about our marriage. He was saying that you hadn't had a DNA test with Angelo and that there had been no pre-nup—'

'You're trying to shock me with facts?'

Holly scrambled out of her seat and squared her small shoulders. 'Apollo was sneering about his belief that you trust me.'

'Obviously I won't be trusting you in the vicinity of confidential phone calls,' Vito pronounced, deadpan.

Somehow the confrontation was not proceeding in any expected direction and Holly was stung into anger. 'Apollo thinks our marriage is a sham!'

Vito elevated an ebony brow. 'I think the only two people who can comment on that probability are the two of us.'

'Apollo seemed to believe that you had only married me to get me to move to Italy. He thinks you're planning to go to court and try to claim full custody of our son.'

'I'm not sure whether to be more offended by my friend's low take on my morals or by my wife's,' Vito imparted very softly, marvelling that she could have placed credence in such an unrealistic plot, which smacked very much of Apollo's sensational outlook on life. 'Do you think I would do that to you and Angelo?'

'That's not the point,' Holly protested.

'It is exactly the point,' Vito incised with ruthless bite. 'Why else are you challenging me with this nonsense?'

As Silvestro reappeared with a tray Holly sank back down into her seat. She was angry and mortified at the same time but clung to the comforting fact that Vito had called her concerns 'nonsense'. While food was being laid on the table, Holly studied her pale pink nails and suspected that one day she might possibly throw a coffee pot at Vito for his sarcastic cool.

'To clarify matters,' Vito mused as Silvestro retreated, 'Apollo was most probably talking to a mutual friend called Jeremy, who happens to be a lawyer trained in family law. Although it is ridiculously unnecessary, Apollo tries to protect me from the gold-diggers of this world. If it is any consolation he was no keener on Marzia. He would never marry without a pre-nuptial agreement in place. I deemed it unnecessary because I would not marry a woman I couldn't trust. You're being naive and insecure.'

Holly bridled at that blunt speech. 'I don't see how.'

With precise movements that set her teeth on edge, Vito poured a cup of black coffee. 'I would not deprive my son of his mother. I was sent to boarding school abroad at the age of seven, Holly. I was incredibly homesick and unhappy. Do you honestly think I would subject Angelo to anything similar?'

Holly studied her cup of tea with wooden resolve. Her face was so hot she could feel her ears heating up in concert. No, she could not see him planning to do anything that would damage their son. Boarding school abroad at the tender age of seven? That was brutal, she thought helplessly.

'I *love* my son. I will try hard never to hurt him and I know how much he needs his mother,' Vito framed with measured cool. 'I am also an honourable man. I am not deceitful in personal relationships. I married you in good faith. If eavesdropping on Apollo can rouse your suspicions to this level, what are our prospects for the future? Trust has to work both ways to be effective.'

Holly swallowed hard. Vito was annoyed with her for doubting him and for paying heed to a stupid phone call she shouldn't have been listening to in the first place. She wasn't sure she could blame him for that. On the other hand his determination to head to the bank the day after their wedding was hardly likely to boost her confidence in his attitude towards either her or their marriage.

How much did Vito value her? Just how unimportant was she in his desire for a marriage that would not interfere in his inflexible daily schedule? To thrive, all relationships needed compromise, commitment and the luxury of time spent together. Didn't he appreciate that? And if he didn't, was she clever enough to teach him that she could offer him something more worthwhile than sex? That was a tall order.

Vito rose from his chair and studied her in brooding silence. 'By the way, we're dining out this evening with friends.'

Holly looked up in surprise. 'What friends?'

'Apollo and his girlfriend and Jeremy Morris and his wife. They're currently staying on Apollo's yacht with him.'

The prospect of spending an evening in Apollo Metraxis's radius appealed about as much to Holly as a public whipping. She frowned, studying Vito with incredulous eyes. 'Knowing how I feel about Apollo, why would you arrange something like that?'

Vito compressed his stubborn mouth. 'He's a close friend. He made a mistake. You need to get over it.'

Temper threw colour into Holly's cheeks. 'Do I, indeed?'

Vito gazed expectantly back at her. 'I want it all smoothed over and forgotten...'

'Right, so that's me got my orders, then.' Holly lifted her chin.

'It's not an order, Holly, it's advice. I'm not dropping a lifelong friend because you don't like him.'

'And isn't there some excuse for that dislike?'

'Apollo didn't tell any lies about how we met. Remember that,' Vito retorted with succinct bite.

A painful flush illuminated Holly's face.

'Why shouldn't we have a night out?' Vito fired at her in exasperation. 'I thought you would enjoy getting dressed up and socialising—most women do.'

'That's not my world,' Holly breathed in taut objection.

'It is *now*,' Vito pointed out without hesitation, his impatience unconcealed. 'You need to make an effort to fit in. Why do you think I bought you all those clothes? I want you to have the expensive trappings and to *enjoy* having them.'

As Vito strode out Holly held her breath, feeling a

little like someone trying to fight off a panic attack. He had voiced truths she didn't really want to face. This was his world and, in marrying him, she had become part of that world. He saw no reason why his life shouldn't continue the way it always had and he was making no allowances for Holly's insecurities. No, it was her job to swallow her ire with Apollo and be nice. Well, that certainly put her in her place, didn't it? Vito's long-standing friendship with the Greek billionaire meant more to him than his wife's loss of face at her own wedding. Just as work still meant more to him than settling into marriage and fatherhood. Vito, she recognised painfully, was highly resistant to change of any kind...

CHAPTER NINE

AFTER LUNCH THE same day, Holly lifted Angelo out of the high chair in the dining room and walked outside to settle the baby on a rug already spread across the grass. Her son beamed as she arranged several toys within his reach, enjoying the change of scene.

'Tea,' Silvestro pronounced with decision, having followed her, and he sped off again. Holly made no comment, having already learned that Silvestro liked to foresee needs and fulfil them before anyone could make a request and, truthfully, she did fancy a cup of tea.

She cuddled Angelo and studied the bird's-eye view of the gardens spread out below in an embroidered carpet of multi-hued greens with occasional splashes of colourful spring flowers. Daily life at the Castello Zaffari promised to be pretty much idyllic, she reflected ruefully, feeling ashamed of her negative thoughts earlier in the day when Vito had left her to go to work.

Here she was on a permanent holiday in a virtual palace where she ate fabulous food and was waited on hand and foot. She had beautiful clothes, an incredibly handsome, sexy husband and a very cute baby. What was she complaining about? For the first time ever since Angelo's birth she also had free time to spend with her son. As for the dinner outing? That was a minor hiccup and, having examined her new wardrobe, she had decided to follow the 'little black dress rule' rather than risk being over-or underdressed for the occasion.

A woman in a sunhat with a basket over her arm walked up a gravelled path towards her. Holly tensed, recognising her mother-in-law, Concetta Zaffari.

'Are you on your own?' the small brunette asked. 'I thought I had seen Vito's car drive past earlier but I assumed I was mistaken.'

'No, you weren't mistaken. He's at the bank,' Holly confirmed, as the older woman settled down beside her to make immediate overtures to Angelo.

'Today? My son went into work *today*?' his mother exclaimed in dismay.

Holly gave a rueful nod.

'He should be here with you,' Concetta told her, surprising her.

The rattle of china and the sound of footsteps approaching prompted Holly to scramble upright again. She handed Angelo to Concetta, who was extending her arms hopefully and chattering in Italian baby talk. The two women sat down by the wrought iron table in the shade while Silvestro poured the tea. He had magically contrived to anticipate the arrival of Vito's mother because he had brought an extra cup and a plate of tiny English biscuits.

'A honeymoon isn't negotiable. It should be a given,' Concetta pronounced without hesitation.

'If Vito wants to work, well, then he wants to work,' Holly parried, tactfully non-committal.

'You and this darling little boy are Vito's family

and you must ensure that my son puts you first,' Vito's mother countered. 'That is very important.'

Holly breathed in deep. 'Vito loves to work. I don't feel I have the right to ask him to change something so basic about himself.'

'Priorities have to change once you're married and a parent. As for having the right...' The older woman sipped her tea thoughtfully. 'I will be open with you. I saw your distress after Apollo made that unsuitable speech at the wedding yesterday.'

Holly winced. 'I was more embarrassed than dis-tressed...I think.'

'But why should you be embarrassed by this gor-geous little boy?' Concetta demanded. 'Let me tell you something... When I married Vito's father, Cic-cio, thirty-odd years ago, I was already pregnant...'

Holly's blue eyes widened in surprise at that frank admission.

Concetta compressed her lips. 'My father would never have allowed me to marry a man like Ciccio in any other circumstances. He knew that Ciccio was a fortune hunter but I was too naive to see the obvious. I was eighteen and in love for the first time. Ciccio was in his thirties.'

'That's a big age gap,' Holly remarked carefully.

'I was an heiress. Ciccio targeted me like a duck on a shooting range,' the brunette declared with a wry twist of her lips, 'and I paid a steep price for being young and silly. He was unfaithful from the outset but I closed my eyes to it because while my father was alive divorce seemed out of the question. Only when Ciccio dragged our son's reputation down into the dirt with his own did I finally see the light.'

'The scandal in the newspapers?' Holly slotted in with a frown, fascinated by the elegant brunette's candour.

'I could not forgive Ciccio for saving himself at Vito's expense.'

'Vito wanted to protect you.'

'That hurt,' Concetta confided tautly. 'It hurt me even more to see Vito falsely accused and slandered but it also let me see that he was an adult able to handle the breakdown of his parents' marriage. Now I'm making my middle-aged fresh start.'

'It's never too late,' Holly said warmly, noticing how Angelo's sparkling dark eyes matched his father's and his grandmother's.

Concetta confided that she regularly took the flowers from the garden at the *castello* as arranging them was her hobby. Holly admitted that she had never arranged a flower in her life and urged the older woman to keep on helping herself. Vito's mother promised to continue doing the flowers for the house and the two women parted on comfortable, friendly terms.

Holly spent what remained of the day doing her hair and her nails and refusing to think about the evening ahead. Thinking about it wasn't going to change anything. Apollo was Vito's friend and he thought highly of him, she reminded herself. Unfortunately it didn't ease the sting of the reality that her husband seemed to rate Apollo more highly than he rated his wife.

Vito collected her in a limo. He wore a sleek dinner jacket. 'I used my apartment to change,' he admitted, smiling as she climbed into the car. 'You look very elegant.'

But as soon as Holly arrived at the restaurant and saw the other two women she realised she had got it wrong in the frock department because she had played it too safe. Apollo's girlfriend, Jenna, wore a taupe silk dress that plunged at both back and front and was slit to the thigh, while Jeremy's wife, Celia, wore a short fitted scarlet dress that showed off her very shapely legs. Holly immediately felt frumpy and dumpy in her unexciting outfit, wishing that at the very least she had chosen to wear something that displayed a bit of cleavage.

While the men talked, Celia shot inquiries at Holly and it was no surprise to discover that the highly educated and inquisitive redhead was a criminal lawyer. Having her background and educational deficiencies winkled out and exposed made Holly feel very uncomfortable but her attempts to block Celia's questions were unsuccessful and she was forced to half turn away and chat to Jenna to escape the interrogation. Jenna, however, talked only about spa days and exclusive resorts.

'You've never been on a ski slope?' she remarked in loud disbelief.

'I'll teach Holly to ski,' Vito sliced in, smooth as glass.

Holly paled because the idea of racing down a snowy hill at breakneck speed made her feel more scared than exhilarated. As the entire conversation round the table turned to ski resorts and talk of everyone's 'best ever runs', she was excluded by her unfamiliarity with the sport. Jenna's chatter about hot yoga classes and meditation were matched by Celia's talk about the benefits of an organic, *natural* diet, ensuring that Holly felt more and more out of her depth. She was also bored stiff.

'How do you feel about yachting?' Apollo asked smoothly across the table, his green eyes hard and mocking. 'Do you get seasick?'

'I've never been on a yacht, so I wouldn't know. I'm fine on a fishing boat or a ferry, though,' she added with sudden amusement at the amount of sheer privilege inherent in such a conversational topic.

'Who took you fishing?' Vito asked her abruptly.

'Someone way before your time,' Holly murmured, unwilling to admit in such exclusive company that it had been a rowing-boat experience with a teenaged boyfriend.

'Way to go, Holly! Keep him wondering.' Celia laughed appreciatively.

Her mobile phone vibrated in her bag and she pulled it out. 'Excuse me. I have to take this,' she said apologetically, and rose from the table to walk out to the foyer.

It was Lorenza phoning to tell her that Angelo had finally settled after a restless evening. Aware that her son was teething, Holly had asked the nanny to keep her posted. On the way back to the table she called into the cloakroom. She was in a cubicle when she heard Jenna and Celia come in.

'What on earth does a guy like Vito see in a woman like her?' Jenna was demanding thinly. 'She's like a little brown sparrow beside him.'

Angry resentment hurtled through Holly and in the strangest way it set her free to be herself.

'Jeremy thinks Vito must have had a pre-nup written up by another lawyer,' Celia commented. 'There's no way Vito hasn't safeguarded himself.'

Emerging, Holly washed her hands and glanced at the aghast pair of women frozen by the sinks. 'At least I've got a wedding ring on my finger,' she pointed out to Jenna. 'You have to be at least number one hundred in Apollo's long line of companions.'

'We had no idea you were in here,' Celia began sharply, defensively.

'Ah, Celia,' Holly pronounced gently, flicking the tall redhead a calm appraisal in turn. 'I can assure you that there is no pre-nup. My husband *trusts* me.'

And with that ringing assurance, Holly turned on her heel, head held high, and walked back out to the table. And she might resemble a little brown sparrow, she thought with spirit, but she was married to a guy who found little brown sparrows the ultimate in sex appeal. Amused by the level of her own annoyance, Holly returned to her seat and in a break in the conversation addressed Apollo. 'So where's the best place for me to learn to ski?' she asked playfully.

Vito dealt her a bemused look and watched her begin to smile at Apollo's very detailed response because Apollo took his sports very seriously.

A deep sense of calm had settled over Holly. She was still furious with Vito for subjecting her to such an evening with very little warning but, having stood up for herself and spoken up in her own defence, she felt much more comfortable. After all, she could be herself anywhere and in any company. The only person able to make her feel out of her depth was herself and she was determined not to let those insecurities control her reactions again. So, she was more accustomed to stacking shelves in a shop and occasional trips to the cinema but she could do spa days and skiing and yachting trips if she wanted to. It was Vito's world but that wedding ring on her finger confirmed that now it was her world as well and she needed to remember that.

She would have to adapt. But Vito had to learn to adapt too, she reflected grimly. He had told her over the breakfast table that she had to trust him, but so far he had done little to earn that trust. And so far, Holly had been the one to make all the changes. She had given up her home, her country, her friends, and her entire life to come to Italy and make a family with Vito. True, it was a gilded life but that didn't lessen the sacrifices she had made on her son's behalf. When was Vito planning to become a family man, who put his wife and his child first?

'You've been very quiet,' Vito remarked as Holly started up the stairs.

'I want to check on Angelo.'

'There is no need.'

'There is every need. I'm his mother,' Holly declared shortly. 'It's immaterial how efficient or kind your staff are, Vito. At the end of the day they are only employees and none of them will ever love Angelo the way I do. Don't ever try to come between me and my son!'

In silence, Holly went up to the nursery, tiptoeing across the floor to gaze down at the slumbering shape of her little boy lying snug in his cot. Smiling, she left the nursery again.

'I wouldn't try to come between you,' Vito swore.

Holly ignored him and went down to their bedroom, kicking off her shoes before stalking into the bathroom.

'Holly...' Vito breathed warningly from the doorway.

'I'm not speaking to you. You have a choice,' Holly cautioned him thinly. 'Either we have silence or we have it out. *Choose.*'

Vito groaned. 'That's not much of a choice.'

'It's the only one you're going to get and probably more than you deserve.' Holly dabbed impatiently at her eyes with a cotton pad and eye-make-up remover.

'Have it out, I suppose,' Vito pronounced very drily.

Holly tilted her chin. 'You had no business forcing me out to that dinner tonight because I wasn't ready for it. I was uncomfortable, of course I was. Two days ago I was living in an ordinary world with ordinary jobs and meeting ordinary people and now I'm in this *weird* new environment,' she framed between compressed lips. 'And I know everyone seems to think I'm in clover and it *is* wonderful not to have to worry about money any more, but it's strange and it's going to take me time to get used to it. You haven't given me any time. You expect *me* to make all the changes...'

Vito had paled. 'You're making valid points. I'm not a patient man.'

'And you don't always live up to your promises either. You said you'd do everything within your power to make me happy,' Holly reminded him doggedly. 'Then you go back to work within a day of the wedding even though you have a son you barely know and a wife you don't know much better. If you want me to trust you, you have to show me that you value me and Angelo, that we're not just new possessions to be slotted into your busy life and expected not to make any waves. You have to give us your time, Vito, take us places, show us around our new home.'

Holly was challenging him and he hadn't expected that from her. She had thrown his words about trust back at him. And she was also telling him that he was already failing dismally in the successful husband stakes. He had married her one day and walked away the next, acting as though a wedding ring were more than sufficient proof of his commitment.

And had Holly been Marzia it *would* have been sufficient. Marzia had wanted that ring and his lifestyle. She would have thrown a party to show off the *castello* and she would have invited all the most important socially connected people to act as her admiring audience. She would have spent half the day at a beauty salon and the other half shopping for couture garments designed to impress. Vito had lost count of the number of times he had returned to the town house he had once shared with Marzia only to discover that they were hosting a dinner when he was longing for a quiet evening. Marzia had been easily bored and had needed others to keep her entertained. Holly, in comparison, asked for and expected very little. In fact she was asking for something she shouldn't have had to ask for, he acknowledged with a grim look in his dark, unusually thoughtful gaze.

Family came first...*always*. Even his workaholic grandfather had never put the bank before his family. What had he been thinking of when he'd left Holly and Angelo to amuse themselves? They needed him and he hadn't spared them a thought.

'And tonight?' Vito prompted.

'It was bearable. I heard Celia and Jenna bitching about me but I stood up for myself and I couldn't care less about their opinions. But I would've been more equipped to enjoy myself and relax if I'd had more time to prepare.'

'I screwed up,' Vito acknowledged broodingly.

'Yes,' Holly agreed, sliding into bed while he still hovered. 'And sometimes I'll screw up. That's life.'

'I'm not used to screwing up,' Vito told her.

'Then you'll try harder not to make the same mistakes again,' Holly riposted sleepily.

* * *

Holly slept in the following morning. She woke with a start, showered and pulled on jeans to pelt upstairs and spend some time with Angelo. In surprise she stilled in the doorway of the nursery bathroom when she saw Vito kneeling down by the side of the bath and engaged in dive-bombing plastic boats for Angelo's amusement. She had simply assumed that Vito had gone into the bank as usual but it was clear that at some stage, even though he had dressed for work, he had changed his mind. His jacket and tie were hooked on the radiator, his shirtsleeves rolled up.

'Vito...'

Raking damp, tousled black hair off his brow, Vito turned his head and flashed her a heart-stopping grin. 'Angelo emptied his cereal bowl over his head at breakfast and I decided I should stay home.'

Holly moved forward. 'I can see that...'

'I'm very set in my ways but I believe I can adapt,' he told her, laughing as Angelo smacked the water with a tiny fist and splashed both of them.

'He'll grow up so fast your head will spin. You won't ever get this time back with him.' She sighed. 'I didn't want you to miss out and then live to regret it.'

'You spoke up and that was the right thing to do. I respect your honesty. Parenting is a whole new ball game and I still have to get my head around it,' Vito confided, snatching down a towel and spreading it on the floor before lifting Angelo's squirming little body out of the bath and laying him down.

'How to get yourself soaked!' Holly groaned.

'I'm already drenched to the skin,' Vito riposted with quiet pride. 'Angelo and I have had a lot of fun.'

The nursery was empty and Holly rustled around gathering the necessities. 'What have you done with the nanny posse?' she asked curiously.

'I told them to take a few hours off. Being so new to this I didn't want an audience.'

Holly dried Angelo and deftly dressed him. Vito unbuttoned his wet shirt, the parted edges revealing a bronzed sliver of muscular torso. Together they walked downstairs.

'Do you have any photographs of when you were pregnant?' Vito asked, startling her into turning wide blue eyes onto his lean, dark face.

'I don't think so...I wasn't feeling very photogenic at the time. Why?'

'I'm sorry I missed all that. Something else I can't get back,' Vito conceded gravely. 'I really would have liked to have seen you when you were carrying our child.'

Regret assailed her, for she would have loved to have had his support during those dark days of worry and exhaustion. She had struggled to stay employed and earning for as long as possible so as not to be a burden on Pixie.

'As for that challenge you offered me,' Vito mused, walking back to their bedroom to change. 'Draw up a list of places you would like to go.'

'No lists. I'm phobic about lists,' she told him truthfully. 'Let's be relaxed about what we do and where we go. No itineraries laid out in stone. Are you taking time off?'

'Of course. But I'll catch up with my email in the evenings,' he warned her. 'I can't completely switch off.'

'That's OK,' she hastened to tell him. 'But you may be bored.'

'Not a chance, *gioia mia*,' Vito riposted as he cast off his wet shirt. 'You and Angelo will keep me fully occupied from dawn to dusk and beyond.'

'And beyond' was very much in Holly's mind as she studied his muscular brown torso, a tiny burst of heat pulsing between her thighs. It was the desire she never really lost around Vito. Her colour heightened. She was so pleased, so relieved that he had listened to her, but there was a fear deep down inside her that she would not have enough to offer to satisfy him outside working hours.

'When was the last time you saw your mother?' Vito asked lazily as they lay in bed six weeks later.

Holly stretched somnolent limbs still heavy with pleasure and rolled her head round to face him, bright blue eyes troubled. 'I was sixteen. It wasn't the nicest experience.'

'I can deal with not nice,' Vito volunteered, closing an arm round her slight shoulders to draw her comfortingly close.

Holly felt gloriously relaxed and shockingly happy. With every day that passed she was increasingly convinced that Vito was the man of her dreams. He was everything she had ever wanted, everything she had ever dreamt of. But even better, he had proved that he was capable of change.

Six weeks ago, she had reminded Vito that he had to learn how to be part of a family instead of an independent operator seeing life only from a work-orientated point of view. He had started out wanting to make up lists and tick off boxes as if that were the only route to success. He had a maddening desire to know in advance exactly what he would be doing every hour of every day and had only slowly learned to take each day as it came.

Holly had spent several days creating a mood board of her ideas on how to redecorate their hideous bedroom. While she was doing that, Vito had learned how to entertain Angelo. Settling on a colour palate of soothing grey enlivened with spicy tangerine accents, Holly had ordered the required products and utilised a local company to do the actual work. Throughout the entire process, Vito had shown depressingly little curiosity, merely agreeing that it was many years since the *castello* had been decorated and that, as his mother had never had any interest in revitalising the interior, he was sure there was plenty of scope for Holly to express her talents.

Leaving the work team to handle the decorating project, Holly and Vito had taken their son to stay on the shores of Lake Lugano. Vito's family had bought a Swiss villa because, like Zurich and Geneva, Lugano was a major financial centre. Over the generations the Zaffari bankers had found the shores of the lake a convenient business location to stash the family while they worked.

At the villa they had thrown open the shutters on the magnificent lake views and enjoyed long lazy meals on the sun-dappled *loggia*. By day they had explored the water in a private boat, stopping off to ramble around the picturesque little villages on the rugged shoreline. Some evenings they had sat on the lake terrace drinking garnet-coloured Brunello di Montalcino wine while they watched the boats sailing by with twinkling lights. Other nights they had strolled round the cobbled lanes in Lugano to pick a quiet restaurant for dinner, but none had yet lived up to the perfection on a plate offered by Vito's personal chef.

They had visited the Zoo al Maglio, where Angelo had been enchanted by the antics of the monkeys and had struggled fiercely to copy them. They had caught the funicular railway to the top of Monte San Salvatore to enjoy the alpine scenery and on the way back they had stopped off at a chocolate factory, where a peckish Holly had eaten her weight in chocolate and had sworn never to eat it again while Vito teased her about how much he adored her curves.

There had been shopping trips as well, to the designer boutiques on the Via Nassa, where Holly had become bored because her new wardrobe was so expansive she saw no reason to add to it. She had much preferred the bustling liveliness of the farmers' market in the Piazza Riforma, from which she had returned home carrying armfuls of the flowers she couldn't resist. Discovering that arranging them was more of an art than a matter of simply stuffing them in a big vase, she had resolved to ask her mother-in-law for some tips.

'Your mother...' Vito reminded her. 'Are you going to sleep?'

'No. It's only two o'clock in the afternoon.' But in truth she was already smothering a yawn because their post-lunch nap had turned into a sex-fest. 'Mum...' she reminded herself. 'It was the last time I ever lived with her. I thought she wanted me back because I was no longer a child who needed looking after twenty-four-seven. I thought she finally wanted to get to know her daughter. But I got it all wrong—'

'How...?' Vito asked, long fingers inscribing a soothing pattern on her hip bone.

'Mum was living with a guy who owned a little supermarket. She asked me to help out in the shop...' Holly's voice trailed away ruefully. 'It was a crucial school year with exams and I didn't want to miss classes but she insisted she couldn't cope and I fell for it—'

'And...?' Vito prompted when she fell silent again.

'It turned out that she only wanted me working in the shop to save *her* having to do it and they weren't even paying me minimum wage. I was just cheap labour to please her boyfriend and give her a break.' Holly sighed. 'I missed so much school that social services took me back into care. Of course I failed half my exams as well. I haven't seen her since. I realised that she was never going to be the mother I wanted her to be and I had to accept that. She wasn't the maternal type—'

'And yet you're so different with Angelo.'

'And if you compare your relationship with your father, aren't you different with Angelo too? We both want to give our son what we didn't have ourselves,' Holly murmured, rejoicing in the heat and strength of his long, lean length next to hers. 'Why didn't you invite your father to our wedding?'

'I thought it would be too awkward for my mother and our guests, particularly when Ciccio is fighting for a bigger divorce settlement because he stands to lose a lot of things that he's always taken for granted.'

'Concetta seems quite happy...well, for someone going through a divorce, that is,' Holly qualified ruefully.

'With my father gone she has a lot less stress in her life and for the first time she has her independence without the restriction of either a father or a husband. She loves her new home and the freedom she has there.'

'It's a new life for her,' Holly mused drowsily, thinking that her own new life was still in the honeymoon
period and wouldn't really officially start until they returned to the *castello* the following day and embarked
on a more normal routine.

'I didn't realise that marrying you would be a new
beginning for me as well,' Vito admitted thoughtfully,
acknowledging that he had not fully thought through
the ramifications of marrying and becoming a parent.
He had plunged into matrimony, dimly expecting life
to go on as it always had only to learn that change was
inevitable.

'Do you have regrets?' she whispered fearfully. 'Do
you sometimes wish you were still single and unencum-
bered? I suppose you must.'

'I have no regrets when I'm in bed with you...not a
single one.' Vito gazed down at her with dancing dark
golden eyes alive with wolfish amusement. '*Sì*, I knew
you'd be annoyed by that point but, *Dio mio*...at least
I'm honest!'

And as his eyes laughed down at her, her heart
swelled inside her and she knew, just *knew* in her very
soul that she loved Vito. She loved him the way she
had tried not to love him. She had tried so hard to protect herself from feeling more for Vito than he felt for
her because that was the hard lesson she had learned in
loving her unresponsive mother. You couldn't *make* a
person care for you; you couldn't force those feelings.

In any case, it had crossed her mind more than once
that Vito's emotions might be quite unavailable in the
love category. Holly had met Vito on the rebound,
shortly after his fiancée had ditched him. That Christmas theirs had been a classic rebound attraction. Was

Vito still in love with Marzia? Had he tried to return to the beautiful blonde during the fourteen months he and Holly had been apart? Had he mourned the loss of Marzia once he'd decided that he had to marry Holly for his son's sake? And how, when he never ever so much as mentioned the woman, could Holly possibly ask him to tell her honestly how he currently felt about Marzia?

She couldn't ask because she didn't think she could bear to live with the wrong answer.

CHAPTER TEN

TWO WEEKS LATER, Holly shuffled the messy pile of financial publications that Vito always left in his wake and lifted the other, more gossipy newspapers out to peruse. She flicked through the pages, thrilled when she was able to translate the occasional word of Italian.

Her knowledge of the language was slowly growing. She could manage simple interactions with their staff and greetings. Hopefully once she started proper Italian lessons with a local teacher later in the week her grasp of Italian would grow in leaps and bounds. After all, both her son and her husband would speak the language and she was determined not to be the odd one out. Vito's desire that their son should grow up bilingual was more likely to be successful if she learned Italian as well.

Abandoning the papers, she selected a magazine, flipping through glossy photographs of Italian celebrities she mostly didn't recognise until one picture in particular stopped her dead in her tracks. It was a photo of Marzia wearing the most fabulous sparkling ballgown with Vito by her side. She frowned and stared down at it with such intensity that she literally saw spots appear in front of her eyes. She struggled to translate the blurb beneath the picture. It appeared to be recent and it had been taken at some party. The previous week, Vito had spent two nights at his Florence apartment because he had said he was working late. Well, the first time he had been working late, the second time he had actually said that he had to attend a very boring dinner, which invariably would drag on into the early hours...

For dinner, read dinner *dance*, she reflected unhappily. Her entire attention was welded to the photo. Vito and Marzia had been captured at what appeared to be a formal dance with their arms in the air as if their hands had just parted from a clasp. Both of them were smiling. And my goodness, didn't Marzia look ravishing? Not a blonde hair out of place. Holly's fingers crept up to finger through her own tumbled mane. She studied Marzia's perfectly made-up face and thought about her own careless beauty routine, which often consisted of little more than eyeliner, blush and lip gloss. Looking at that gorgeous dress, she glanced down at her own casual silky tee and skirt and low-heeled sandals. She was dressed very nicely indeed in expensive garments but there wasn't even a hint of glamour or sequinned sparkle in her appearance.

Maybe it had only been one dance that Marzia and Vito had shared. And of course they had been photographed for such a potentially awkward moment between former partners was always of interest to others. And they were smiling and happy together. Why not? Her heart had shrunk into a tight, threatened lump inside her chest and her tummy felt as though it were filled with concrete. Vito had spent a couple of years with Marzia. They knew each other well and why should they be enemies? There was no reason why they shouldn't dance together and treat each other like old friends, was there?

Vito hadn't broken any rules. He hadn't told her any lies. All right, he hadn't mentioned the dancing or seeing Marzia, but then he never mentioned his ex, a reality that had made it very difficult for Holly to tackle the subject. Wasn't Vito entitled to his privacy in relation to past relationships? In any case he was not the kind of man who would comfortably open up about previous lovers. Her eyes stung with tears because trying to be reasonable and take a sensible overview was such a challenge for her at that moment.

At the heart of her reaction, Holly registered, was Marzia's sheer glamour and her own sense of inadequacy. Holly didn't do glamour, had never even tried. The closest she had ever got to glamour was a Santa outfit. But what if that kind of gloss, *Marzia's* gloss, was what Vito really liked and admired?

Obviously she had to confront him about the photo and there would probably be a perfectly reasonable explanation about why he had said nothing...

'I knew you would make a fuss,' Vito would be able to point out quite rightly.

She was a jealous cow and he probably sensed that. Although she had never been competitive with other women, having a rival that beautiful and sophisticated could only be hurtful and intimidating. She loved Vito so much and was painfully aware that he did not love her. In addition, she was always guiltily conscious that she had won her wedding ring purely by default. Vito had married her because she was the mother of his son.

Mother of his son, Holly repeated inwardly. Not a very sexy label, certainly not very glamorous. But it didn't have to be that way, she reasoned ruefully. She could walk that extra mile, she could make the effort and dress up too. But she needed the excuse of an occasion, didn't she? Well, at least to begin with... On her passage across the hall, she spoke to Silvestro and told him that she would like a special romantic meal to be served for dinner.

Silvestro positively glowed with approval and she went upstairs to go through her new wardrobe and select the fanciest dress she owned. In the oddest way she would have liked to put on a Santa outfit for Vito again but it wouldn't work out of season. She would tackle Vito the moment he came home. She wouldn't give him time to regroup and come up with evasions or excuses. What she wanted most of all was honesty. He needed to tell her how he truly felt about Marzia and they would proceed from that point.

Did he still have feelings for the beautiful blonde? How would she cope if he admitted that? Well, she would have to cope. Her life, Vito's and Angelo's were inextricably bound to the stability of their marriage. Would he want a separation? A divorce? Her brain was making giant leaps into disaster zones and she told herself off for the catastrophic effect that photo had had on her imagination and her confidence. Since when had she chosen to lie down and die rather than fight?

From the dressing room she extracted the hand-embroidered full-length dress, which glittered with sparkling beads below the lights. It definitely belonged in the glamour category.

Vito knew something strange was afoot the instant he walked into the hall of the *castello* and Silvestro gave

him a huge smile. Silvestro had the face of a sad sheep-
dog and was not prone to smiling.

'The *signora* is on the way downstairs...' he was
informed.

Vito blinked and then he saw Holly as he had only
seen her on their wedding day, and quite naturally he
stared. She drifted down the staircase in a fantastic
dress that seemed to float airily round her hourglass
curves. It was the sort of gown a woman wore to a ball
and Vito suffered a stark instant of very male panic.
Why was she all dressed up? What had he forgotten?
Were they supposed to be going out somewhere? What
special date had slipped past him unnoticed?

Silvestro spread wide the dining-room door and Vito
saw the table set in a pool of candlelight and flowers
and thought...what the hell? He spun back as Holly
drew level with him, her blue eyes bright but her small
face oddly tight and expressionless. A pang ran through
Vito's long, lean frame because he was accustomed to
his wife greeting him at the end of the day as though
he had been absent for a week...and in truth he thoroughly enjoyed the wholehearted affection she showered on both him and his son.

'You look magnificent, *bellezza mia*,' Vito declared,
while frantically wondering what occasion he had overlooked and how he could possibly cover up that reality rather than hurt Holly's feelings by admitting his
ignorance.

She was so vulnerable sometimes. He saw that sen-
sitivity in her and marvelled that she retained it even
after all the disappointments life had faced her with.
His primary role was to protect Holly from hurt and
disillusionment. He didn't want her to lose her inno-

cence. He didn't want her to turn cynical or bitter. But most of all he never ever wanted to be the man who disillusioned her.

'Glad you like the dress,' Holly said a tad woodenly. 'Shall we sit down?'

'I'm no match for your elegance without a shower and a change of clothes,' Vito pointed out with a slight line dividing his black brows into the beginnings of a frown because her odd behaviour was frustrating him.

'Please sit down. We'll have a drink,' Holly suggested, because she had laid that photo of Marzia and him at his place at the table and she was keen for him to see it before she lost her nerve at confronting him in what was starting to feel a little like a badly planned head-on collision.

Maybe she should have been less confrontational and given him warning. Only not if the price of that was Vito coming up with a polite story that went nowhere near the actual truth. She didn't believe he would lie to her but he wouldn't want to upset her and he would pick and choose words to persuade her in a devious way that her concerns were nonsensical.

Vito was on the edge of arguing until he glimpsed the photo, and its appearance was so unexpected that it stupefied him. He stared down at the photo of himself dancing with Marzia in wonderment while Silvestro poured his wine. Why were they apparently celebrating this inappropriate photograph with rose petals scattered across the table and the finest wine? His frown of incomprehension deepened.

'What is this?' he demanded with an abruptness that startled Holly as he swept up the photo.

Consternation gripped Holly because he didn't sound

puzzled, he sounded downright angry. 'I wanted to ask you to explain that picture,' she muttered warily.

'So you set me up with some sort of a romantic dinner and tell me I can't have a shower? And sit me down with a photo of my ex?' Vito exclaimed incredulously. 'This is more than a little weird, Holly!'

Legs turning wobbly as she encountered scorching dark golden eyes of enquiry, Holly dropped reluctantly down into her chair. 'I'm sorry. I just wanted to get it over with and I wanted you to say exactly what's on your mind.'

'Weird!' Vito repeated with an emphatic lack of inhibition, crumpling the photo into a ball of crushed paper and firing it into the fire burning merrily across the room. 'Where did you get that photograph from and when did you see it?'

Holly sketched out the details, her heart beating very fast. She hadn't expected to feel guilty but now she did because taking Vito by surprise had only annoyed him.

'Today?' Vito stressed in astonishment. 'But that photo is at least three years old!'

'Three years old…' Holly's voice trailed off as she studied him in disbelief.

'It was taken at our engagement party. Why on earth would it be printed again now?' he questioned.

Holly scrambled out of her seat and pelted off to find the magazine she had cut the photo from. Reappearing, she planted it into Vito's outstretched hand while Silvestro struggled to set out the first course of the meal.

'Per l'amor di Dio…' Vito groaned. 'You need to learn to read Italian!'

'It's not going to happen overnight,' she grumbled.

'That photo was quite cleverly utilised to symbolise

the fact that I have now cut my ties to the Ravello Investment Bank,' Vito framed in flat explanation. 'Note the way our hands are pictured apart...'

'What does the Ravello Bank have to do with anything? What ties?'

'Marzia is a Ravello,' Vito informed her drily. 'When we got engaged I agreed to act as an investment adviser to the Ravello Bank. When Marzia ditched me her father begged me to retain the position as Ravello was going through a crisis and my resignation would have created talk and blighted their prospects even more.'

Holly blinked. She had become very pale. 'I had no idea you had any business links to Marzia and her family.'

'As of yesterday I *don't*. I resigned the position and they have hired the man I recommended to take my place. Once you and I were married it no longer felt appropriate for Marzia's family and mine to retain that business link,' Vito pointed out wryly.

Holly had been blindsided by an element of Vito's former relationship with Marzia that she could not have known about. A business connection, *not* a personal one. 'You know, I assumed that that was a recent picture of you with Marzia,' Holly confided. 'I thought that dinner you mentioned last week must have been a dinner dance.'

'Had it been I would have taken you with me or bowed out early to get home to you. As it was I was landed with a group of visiting government representatives, whose company I found as exciting as watching paint dry,' Vito told her drily and pushed back his chair. 'May I have my shower now?'

'No, we can't just abandon dinner!' Holly breathed

in dismay. 'Not when Francisco has gone to so much trouble to make us a memorable meal.'

'So, you've been down to the kitchen and have finally met our chef?' Vito gathered in some amusement.

'Yes, he's a real charmer, isn't he?'

'I'm sure he can reheat the food,' Vito pronounced impatiently.

'But we haven't finished talking yet,' Holly protested, all her expectations thrown by Vito's eminently down-to-earth explanation of that photo and its meaning.

'Why are you dressed as though you're about to attend a costume ball?' Vito shot at her.

Holly went red. 'I wanted to show you that if I made the effort I could polish up and look all glam like Marzia.'

Vito groaned out loud. 'You look amazing but I don't want you to look all glam like Marzia.'

'But you bought me all those fancy clothes…'

'Only to cover every possible occasion. And when would you have bothered going shopping?' Vito enquired drily. 'You hate shopping for clothes.'

Holly compressed her lips. 'You don't like me glammed up? Or you don't want me copying Marzia?'

'Both,' Vito told her levelly as he signalled Silvestro and rose from his chair again. 'I like you just to be yourself. You're never fake. I *hate* fake. But why did you think I would be out dancing any place with Marzia?'

'What are you doing?' Holly gasped as he scooped her bodily out of her seat.

'I'm going for my after-work shower and you're either coming in with me, which would sacrifice all the effort you have gone to, or you're waiting in bed for me,' Vito informed her cheerfully.

'I thought you still cared for Marzia,' Holly finally confessed on the way up the stairs. 'I thought you might still love her.'

Vito grunted with effort as he reached the landing. 'I can carry you upstairs but I can't talk while I'm doing it,' he confided. 'I never loved Marzia.'

'But you got engaged to her... You *lived* with her!'

'Yes, and what an eye-opening experience that was!' Vito admitted, thrusting wide the door of their bedroom. 'I asked her to marry me in the first place because she was everything my grandfather told me I should look for in a wife. I wasn't in love with her and when we lived together I discovered that we had nothing in common. I don't want to dance the night away as if I'm still in my twenties but Marzia does. She has to have other people around all the time. She likes to shop every day and will avoid any activity that wrecks her hair... up to and including a walk on a windy day and sex.'

'Oh...' Open-mouthed and taken aback by that information, Holly fell very still as Vito ran down the zip on her dress.

'I was relieved when she ditched me. Not very gallant but it's the truth. We weren't suited.'

'Was my ring...? I've always wanted to ask,' Holly interrupted, extending her ring finger. 'Was it Marzia's before you gave it to me?'

An ebony brow shot up. 'Are you joking? Marzia didn't return her engagement ring and even if she had I hope I would've had more class than to ask you to wear it.'

'You *never* loved her?' Holly was challenged to credit that fact because it ran contrary to everything she had assumed about his engagement.

'When I met Marzia, I had never been in love in my life,' Vito admitted ruefully. 'I got burned young watching my mother trying to persuade my father to love her. I spent my twenties waiting to fall in love, convinced someone special would eventually appear. But it didn't happen and I was convinced it never would. I decided I was probably too practical to fall in love. That's why I got engaged to Marzia the week after my thirtieth birthday. At the time she looked like the best bet I had. Similar banking family and background.'

'My word…that sounds almost…almost callous,' Holly murmured in shock. 'Like choosing the best offer at the supermarket.'

'If it's any consolation I'm pretty sure Marzia settled for me because I'm extremely wealthy.'

Vito yanked loose his tie and shed his jacket. Holly's dress slid down her shoulders and for an instant she stopped its downward progress and then she let it go and shimmied out of it. In many ways she was still in shock from Vito's honesty. He had never fallen in love? Not even with the gorgeous Marzia, who by all accounts had irritated him in spite of her pedigreed background and family. She swallowed hard, trying not to wonder how much she irritated him.

'You're definitely not joining me in the shower,' Vito breathed in a roughened undertone as he took in the coffee-coloured silk lingerie she sported below the dress that had tumbled round her feet. 'You can't deprive me of the fun of taking those off.'

His shirt fell on the floor and she lifted it and the trousers that were abandoned just as untidily to drape them on a chair along with her dress. Sharing a bedroom with a male as organised as Vito had made her clean up her bad habits. Vito had paused to rifle through his jacket and he strode back to her to stuff a jewellery case unceremoniously into her hand. 'I saw it online, thought you'd like it.'

'Oh…' Holly flipped open the case on a diamond-studded bracelet with a delicate little Christmas tree charm attached. 'Oh, that's very pretty.'

'It's very *you*, isn't it?' Vito remarked smugly.

'Why didn't you give it to me downstairs over dinner?' Holly exclaimed, struggling to attach it to her wrist until he stepped forward to clasp it for her.

'I forgot about it. You swanning down to greet me dressed like Marie Antoinette put it right out of my mind.'

'And then you just virtually threw it at me,' Holly lamented. 'There's a more personal way of giving a gift.'

'You mean romantic.' Vito sighed as he strode into the en-suite bathroom, still characteristically set on having his shower. 'Shouldn't the thought *behind* the gift count more?'

Holly thought about that and then walked to the bathroom doorway to sigh. 'You're right. I'm sorry. It's a cute, thoughtful present and I love it. Thank you.'

'My thank you was your face. It lit up like a child's when you saw the Christmas tree,' Vito confided with amusement before he turned the water on.

Holly kicked off her shoes, stared down appreciatively at the bracelet encircling her wrist and lay down on the bed. He had never loved Marzia. Marzia was wiped from Holly's standard stock of worries for ever. Marzia was the past—a past Vito neither missed nor wanted to revisit. That, she decided, was a very encouraging discovery.

All of a sudden hiding her love, being so painfully careful not to let those words escape in moments of joy, seemed almost mean and dishonest. Vito loved Angelo so freely. She witnessed that every day. Her husband hadn't even had to try to love his son and Angelo loved his father back. Perhaps in time Vito could come to love her too, she reflected hopefully. When he had told her that he much preferred her to just be herself around him without the fancy clothes or any airs her heart had taken wings. He liked her as she was. Wasn't that wonderful?

Vito strode out of the en suite, still towelling dry his hair. 'We'll have a very special Christmas this year. For the first time I'll happily celebrate the season. That's the effect you and Angelo have had on my Scrooge-like outlook.'

'I'm grateful because I will always love Christmas.'

'Because that's how we met,' Vito reasoned. 'And I've never forgotten how appealing you looked dressing that little tree at the cottage.'

'Is that so? And yet you made me fight for the opportunity,' Holly reminded him.

'You gave me a fresh look at the world and it's never been the same since,' Vito intoned very seriously as he settled down on the bed beside her and closed her into his arms.

'Meaning?'

'Remember I said I went through my twenties waiting for someone special to appear?'

Holly nodded and rubbed her cheek against a damp bronzed shoulder.

'And then she came along when I was thirty-one years old and, unfortunately, incredibly wary and set in my ways.'

Her brow furrowed because she thought she had missed a line somewhere. '*Who* came along?'

'You did,' Vito pointed out gently. 'And I wasn't waiting or looking for love any more, and my practical engagement had gone belly-up. So, when you appeared and you made me feel strange I didn't recognise that it was special. The sex was incredible but I was blind to the fact that everything else was incredible too.'

'I made you feel…*strange*?' Holly exclaimed in dismay.

'Confused, unsure of myself. I behaved differently with you, I *felt* more with you…and it troubled me. So, like an idiot, I walked away from what I didn't understand,' he completed.

'I wish you'd found my note,' Holly lamented.

'When you walked out first, I told myself that was for the best, that we could never work in the real world. But we *do* work,' Vito told her with quiet satisfaction. 'We work like a dream on every level and I have never been as happy as I am now…'

Holly was thinking about what he had said and a spark of excitement lit inside her.

'If you and Angelo hadn't found me again, where would I be now? The heart and soul of my world was the Zaffari Bank but the bank wasn't enough to satisfy me.'

'Are you trying to tell me that you fell for me that night?' Holly whispered shakily.

'Well, if you have to ask, obviously I'm not doing a very good job of the telling.' Vito groaned. 'What you made me feel unnerved me. I wouldn't even let myself try to trace you because I was too proud. If you didn't want me I wasn't going to chase after you. I tried very hard to forget that night. I even tried to sleep with other women.'

'And how did that go?' Holly broke in to demand.

'It didn't. I made excuses to myself that I was stressed, overtired. I had endless fantasies about you.'

'Me...the temptress,' Holly framed blissfully. 'Who would ever have thought it?'

'You're the love of my life...the *only* love I have ever had,' Vito husked, clamping her to his long, powerful length with strong arms. 'And I fell hard. I fell *so* hard I can't imagine ever living without you and our son. You have brought passion and fun into my daily life and I never had either before.'

'I love you too,' Holly muttered almost shyly.

Vito smiled down at her with burnished golden eyes and her heart skipped a beat. He kissed her with hot, hungry fervour and she ran out of breath. He lifted his tousled dark head and murmured, 'I have one special request. Would you consider having another child?'

'Another?' Holly gasped in astonishment.

'Not immediately,' Vito hastened to assure her. 'I want to share your next pregnancy, *be* there when my child is born, and experience everything I missed out on with our son. If you employ an assistant, even if you get pregnant I don't see why you shouldn't still be able to concentrate on your interior design plan.'

Holly smiled at that prospect. Her very successful bedroom project had quickly spread to include other major rooms at the *castello*. She had had the adjoining reception room done in toning colours before moving on to attack the scarlet Victorian dining room. At present she was well aware that the *castello* was large enough to offer her the chance to utilise her talents and gain proper experience before she considered moving on to tackle outside projects.

'I'll think about another baby,' she told him thoughtfully. 'I would prefer Angelo not to be an only child.'

Vito stared down at her as she gazed up at him with starry eyes. *He loves me, he loves me, he* loves *me,* she was thinking on a happy high. She ran an appreciative hand up over a long, muscular, hair-roughened thigh and sensible conversation ceased around that point. Vito told her he loved her. Holly told him she loved him too. No sooner had they exchanged those sentiments than they both succumbed to an overwhelming desire to dispel the tension with the passion they shared.

Long after, Vito lay studying Holly as she slept, marvelling at how happy he felt. He wondered if he could persuade her into another sexy Santa outfit at Christmas and wondered if it would be a little pushy to buy one for her. Pushiness came so naturally to him that he soon convinced himself that his laid-back bride would simply laugh.

He curved an arm round her slight body.

'Love you...' Holly mumbled automatically.

Vito smiled. 'Love you. You're my happy-ever-after, *amata mia.*'

EPILOGUE

VITO STRODE THROUGH the door and was immediately engulfed in the flying energy of his son, who flung himself at his knees in a classic tackle. Angelo started chattering in a hail of words, only a handful of which were in distinguishable Italian and occasional ones were in English. *Mamma* figured a lot. *Nonna*, as he called his grandmother Concetta, figured too. If Angelo was to be believed, he, his mother and his grandmother had spent the afternoon feeding a dinosaur. A very small dinosaur was waved in Vito's general direction and comprehension set in as he crouched down to dutifully admire the toy.

A giant Christmas tree adorned the hall. It was festooned with ornaments and lights. There were no gifts heaped below the branches because Angelo loved to rip off wrapping paper. Silvestro had been heard to tell a tenant that the Zaffaris were having 'an English Christmas', and Vito's chef, Francisco, had been feeding them turkey for weeks as he fine-tuned his recipes to provide them with an English banquet on Christmas Day. In respect of the Italian traditions, Angelo would receive *la calza*—a stocking full of sweets. The red-suited Babbo Natale would obviously visit on Christmas Eve, but the kind-hearted Italian witch La Befana, who searched for the Christ child in all the houses, would visit at Epiphany with more gifts.

Vito breathed in deep as he saw a small figure clad in white-fur-trimmed scarlet appear at the top of the stairs. 'You're not wearing your hat,' he complained.

Holly stopped midway and jammed it on over her mane of hair and made a face at him. 'Satisfied now?'

Vito angled a lazy, sexy smile at her. 'Don't I have to wait until bedtime for that?'

'Maybe I'll suggest an early night.' Holly remained anchored two steps up so that she was almost level with him.

Vito took the invitation, leaning down to claim that lush pink mouth that he still fantasised about and curving his hands to the swell of her hips to lift her up into his arms. Her hands locked round his neck with satisfying possessiveness and held him fast. He could feel the slight bump of the baby she was carrying against his stomach and he smiled as he lifted his head again.

'I love you,' he groaned.

'Love you madly.' Holly felt ridiculously intoxicated and happy. One kiss from Vito could do that, two were irresistible, and three would only end with her dragging him up the stairs. Evidently falling pregnant sooner than they had expected had done nothing to cool her husband's desire for her and that truly did make her feel as alluring as some legendary temptress. That was very welcome to a woman who was five months pregnant and subject to all the usual aches and complaints of her condition.

Her redecoration schemes at the *castello* had led to an approach from an exclusive interiors magazine, which had taken a whole host of photos. The glossy photo spread and the accompanying article had ensured that within days of the magazine going on sale, Holly was inundated with exciting offers of design work.

This, however, was their first family Christmas and she was revelling in every detail because Vito had really thrown himself into the spirit of the holidays and she didn't think it was solely because he had become a father. She reckoned he had put his sour childhood memories of Christmas behind him. His mother, recently divorced, was joining their festivities and hugely excited about the second grandchild on the way.

'Please tell me turkey isn't on the menu again tonight,' Vito murmured.

'No, we're having steak. I told Francisco I fancied steak,' she admitted.

'When are our guests arriving?' Vito prompted.

'Well, they were supposed to be here for dinner but Apollo's social secretary rang to say they would be late. Why does he need a social secretary?'

'He's always got hundreds of invitations and he's never at home.' Vito paused. 'I appreciate you being willing to give him another chance.'

Holly gave him a soothing smile that concealed her tension. It was past time to forgive and forget—she knew that. After all, Apollo was Vito's closest friend, but Holly had only seen him twice since their wedding. And when she had made the mistake of voicing her opinion on what he considered to be his private business it had been awkward as hell. But she was madly curious to see who he was bringing with him as a guest. Another leggy underwear model? Or his *wife*?

That, Holly supposed, would be another story...

* * * * *

COMING SOON!

We really hope you enjoyed reading this book.
If you're looking for more romance
be sure to head to the shops when
new books are available on

Thursday 16th
January

To see which titles are coming soon, please visit
millsandboon.co.uk/nextmonth

MILLS & BOON

LET'S TALK

Romance

For exclusive extracts, competitions
and special offers, find us online:

🅕 MillsandBoon

𝕏 @MillsandBoon

📷 @MillsandBoonUK

♪ @MillsandBoonUK

Get in touch on 01413 063 232

MILLS & BOON
MODERN
Power and Passion

Prepare to be swept off your feet by sophisticated, sexy and seductive heroes, in some of the world's most glamorous and romantic locations, where power and passion collide.

Eight Modern stories published every month, find them all at:

millsandboon.co.uk

MILLS & BOON

THE HEART OF ROMANCE

A ROMANCE FOR EVERY READER

MODERN

Prepare to be swept off your feet by sophisticated, sexy and seductive heroes, in some of the world's most glamourous and romantic locations, where power and passion collide.

HISTORICAL

Escape with historical heroes from time gone by. Whether your passion is for wicked Regency Rakes, muscled Vikings or rugged Highlanders, awaken the romance of the past.

MEDICAL

Set your pulse racing with dedicated, delectable doctors in the high-pressure world of medicine, where emotions run high and passion, comfort and love are the best medicine.

True Love

Celebrate true love with tender stories of heartfelt romance, from the rush of falling in love to the joy a new baby can bring, and a focus on the emotional heart of a relationship.

HEROES

The excitement of a gripping thriller, with intense romance at its heart. Resourceful, true-to-life women and strong, fearless men face danger and desire - a killer combination!

From showing up to glowing up, these characters are on the path to leading their best lives and finding romance along the way – with plenty of sizzling spice!

To see which titles are coming soon, please visit

millsandboon.co.uk/nextmonth

GET YOUR ROMANCE FIX!

Get the latest romance news,
exclusive author interviews, story
extracts and much more!

blog.millsandboon.co.uk